Evening Gray
Morning Red

Also by Rick Spilman

Hell Around the Horn

The Shantyman

Bloody Rain

Evening Gray Morning Red

Copyright © Rick Spilman 2017
Published by Old Salt Press, LLC
ISBN: 978-1-943404-19-3

EVENING GRAY MORNING RED

A Novel by

RICK SPILMAN

To Karen,
for all her love, support
and, perhaps, most of all, her patience

ACKNOWLEDGMENTS

Thanks to the authors Joan Druett, Alaric Bond, Linda Collison, V.E. Ulett and Antoine Vanner for their valuable comments and guidance. Thanks also for the insight and support of the members of my critique group - Bruce Woods, Ken Kraus, Kelly O'Donnell, Shelly Nolden, Jael McHenry, and Stephanie Feuer. I would also like to thank the readers and contributors to the Old Salt Blog (oldsaltblog.com) for their continued encouragement and support.

TABLE OF CONTENTS

BOOK ONE — EVENING GRAY

BOOK TWO — MORNING RED

BOOK ONE

EVENING GRAY

The Pharisees also with the Sadducees came, and tempting desired him that he would shew them a sign from heaven. He answered and said unto them, When it is evening, ye say, It will be fair weather: for the sky is red. And in the morning, It will be foul weather to day: for the sky is red and lowring. O ye hypocrites, ye can discern the face of the sky; but can ye not discern the signs of the times?

Matthew 16: 1-3

CHAPTER ONE

May 29, 1768

In the darkness, the brig *Mary Ellen* danced to the rhythm of the following sea. Braced against the stern rail, Thomas Larkin couldn't see the swells but could hear their soft hiss as they boiled beneath the transom and he could feel the deck rise and fall in the muscles of his legs. The only light was the lume of the compass binnacle, casting the helmsman as a pale silhouette, pushing the tiller to leeward and then hauling back to windward as the small ship surged down the face of the wave before wallowing in the trough and beginning again the long climb to the crest.

Thom was sixteen, tall and lanky with a shock of sandy hair tied back in a queue. The mist carried on the unseasonably cold sou'westerly burned against his face. He wore a large woolen coat that had belonged to the captain, the collar pulled tight about his neck. On his frame, the sodden coat made him look a bit like a scarecrow standing watch in the bitter dark.

A shadow approached along the windward rail. John Stevens, the acting mate, bounded up the three steps to the quarterdeck and strode over to the hourglass. Stevens was almost twice Thom's age, and half again his size, with an unfashionable beard that was rumored to hide an ugly saber scar from his days as a privateer.

When the last grains of sand fell in the glass, he turned and said, "Eight bells, Capt'n. Permission to change the watch?"

Captain. Thom didn't feel like a captain. He was no more a proper captain than John Stevens was a proper mate. But there was nothing to be done about either.

Thom pulled himself up as straight as he could, took a deep breath and hoped his voice wouldn't waiver.

"Mr. Stevens. Call all hands, if you please. I believe it is time we point her jib boom for home."

Johnny grasped the bell rope and gave a dozen sharp yanks as he bellowed, "All hands. All hands. Braces and bowlines."

Muttered grumbles from the men on watch, ready to go below, blended with the tattoo of bare feet on the wet deck as the off-watch scrambled to the leeward pin rails. Johnny dropped down to the main deck to stand by the weather braces.

Thom turned to the helmsman. "Mr. Jenkins, the course is west by nor'west."

"West by nor'west, aye," the helmsman echoed, as he pushed the tiller slowly to leeward. The ship rounded up closer to the wind and the sails began to luff, flapping like so many canvas flags.

Johnny yelled, "Haul away" as he eased the weather braces. The yards swung slowly, closer to the wind until, in turn, the sound of luffing sails was replaced by the soft rush of water along the larboard rail.

Once the lines were coiled down, Johnny returned to the quarterdeck.

"I believe that she is anxious to get home," Thom said, followed immediately by the thought that he dare not say out loud, 'if only I can find our way.'

"Trail the log once she settles down."

"Aye, Captain," Johnny replied.

"Captain, indeed," Thom thought as he went below.

❖❖❖

Thom turned up the glowing oil lamp, took off the damp coat and began to shake uncontrollably. His shirt and breeches were soaked through and whatever warmth that remained beneath the coat left him the moment he took it off. Stiff from the cold, he felt barely in command of his limbs, much less of the ship. He stomped his feet and held his hands up to the lamp's glowing globe until slowly the shaking stopped.

The cabin was small with just room for a bunk and a table, where a chart lay open with a course marked in his own hand. The faint marks on the paper would bring them safely to port or leave them broken on the reefs and shoals of the Massachusetts coast.

When Captain Evens died of fever, Thom was the only one aboard who knew how to navigate. Lacking anyone else, the crew had chosen him as their captain. Now, Thom wondered about the wisdom of their choice.

He had never felt so alone. In his bunk in the fo'c's'le, wedged into the bow among the sea chests and dirty bodies of the rest of the crew, he had felt tired, cold, hungry, angry or homesick, but never alone. Now in the captain's cabin, Thom felt a desperate and frightening solitude.

He glanced again at the chart and thought of his grandfather – his teacher, confidant, and one true friend. His grandfather had fought with his father over the proper education of a young man, declaring, "Any grandson of mine will know how to navigate through more than a Latin primer." In the end, a local parson was hired to teach Thom Latin and Greek, while his grandfather taught him navigation.

"You'll have a more need for a sextant than for 'amo, amas, amat,' or whatever all that may be," the old man had told him with a wink. He opened a walnut case that held the magical instrument that could pull the stars from the sky and fix them on a chart. His grandfather's sextant shone like gold in the lamplight and, at first, Thom was afraid to even to pick it up.

He would learn that there was no magic to navigation, except perhaps in the minds of the crew. Any schoolboy who could read and cipher could do as well, taking the numbers from the sextant and copying figures from the Almanac's tables. Now, it seemed just a carnival trick and Thom felt himself no more than an apprentice trickster.

The only thing he needed to make the trick work was the sky, but the heavens had conspired against him. The past days rain and fog had robbed him of both the sun and stars. He had been lucky to the catch the sun at noon two days before through a break in the clouds – a single sight, perilously little for setting a course toward the rocky Massachusetts coast.

He ran his fingers across the chart, outlining the islands and shoals that fringed Boston harbor like angry sentinels. An error of a few miles in his reckoning would see the *Mary Ellen* reduced to splintered timbers and a hold full of cargo awash in the sea. Hogsheads of molasses splitting on the rocks and all the crates of fine fabric, ceramics and paper sodden in the surf, along with the bodies of the crew in the roiling waters. Not an image to hold in his thoughts, but he had difficulty shaking it.

❖❖❖

A knock at the door was Stevens with the log. "Five and a quarter knots, sir. Like a filly heading for the barn."

Thom smiled. He took the dividers and walked off the distance on the chart from his fix to the entrance of Boston harbor. "Tomorrow evening, if the wind holds."

"Ah, wind'll hold, Capt'n. If anything, it'll build."

"May it be so. Call me at the change of watch."

"Aye, Capt'n," Johnny replied and disappeared on deck.

Thom turned the lamp down to a low glow, took off his wet shirt and breeches and stretched out under a scratchy wool blanket. Staring into the darkness, he felt like a twelve-year-old again, sailing as cabin boy on his first voyage to the West Indies. Only four years ago, it felt like a lifetime, yet the feelings were all the same -- boundless fear, tinged with anticipation and the certain knowledge that whatever happened, nothing would ever be the same.

Thom went on deck an hour before dawn. Patchy fog had replaced the mist, making the horizon a shifting circle, opening for a time, hopefully, as if the weather might, at last, clear, and then shrinking around them again like a slowly tightening noose. There were no stars in the morning sky, no chance to confirm their position. With nothing else to be done, he stared out at gray-white blankness of the fog. Wherever fate might bring, they continued to sail closer to salvation or destruction.

Thom had always dreamed of commanding a ship. Now, he understood that a dream realized could be a fearsome thing. His father owned a small shipyard and Thom had been set to work as soon as he could carry tools and run errands. He watched the boats and ships grow from keel to frames to planking and rigging, until they slid down the ways and sailed off, disappearing beyond the horizon. He always wanted to sail with them, to escape the shipyard, and find adventure on his own.

Thom was his father's second son and so would have to make his own way in the world or stay forever a shipwright in the family's employ. When his grandfather found him a berth on an Indies bound ship, Thom was overjoyed to escape to sea. And now that his dreams had become unexpectedly real, he understood, like King Midas, that the prettiest dreams could be the most deadly.

❖ ❖ ❖

Thom smiled to see the cook emerge from the fo'c's'le walking aft, crab-like, swinging a steaming pewter pot bound up in a sennit braid.

"Brought ya' some tea, Capt'n."

"You're a blessing, Mr. Staples," Thom replied, as the cook poured the dark, steaming liquid into a ceramic mug that he took off his belt. Thom took the cup in both hands, savoring the warmth.

"And how fare we all this morning, Capt'n?" the cook asked, peering up intently.

"We fare very well indeed, sir. This fine breeze'll bring us home right smartly."

"Tis a joy to hear, a joy indeed. You finding our way in this foul and fitful weather, an' all."

Thom couldn't tell whether the last was a statement or a question. Whatever he told the cook would be soon passed to the entire crew. The cook always knew more aboard ship than anyone else, often including the captain.

"Let's just hope it turns a touch dryer," Thom said.

"That I'll pray for, to be sure." The cook stomped one foot. "Hate this cursed cold 'n damp. This knee's a torment when the fog's in. God damn the Frenchie that shot me." He shook his head. "Nothin' be done but warm it by the galley fire." He looked back at Thom. "Be wantin' breakfast, would ya, sir? Got some good burgoo and biscuit hot."

"That'll serve me well, Mr. Staples."

❖ ❖ ❖

The cook knuckled his brow and hobbled back toward the galley, swinging his steaming pot like a censer.

Just before the main hatch, the cook walked by Johnny at the pump and mumbled, "Mornin' John." Johnny Stevens only nodded back, busy counting pump strokes as two sailors, Asa Jackson and George Morton, bent over the double pump handle, one rising up as the other pushed down, each stroke sending a gush of green water swirling across the deck to the leeward scuppers. Asa looked up at Johnny and opened his mouth as if to speak, but Johnny scowled at him, not wanting to lose count.

When the pump finally only gurgled and spat, Johnny stopped counting and said aloud, "Sixty-four." He pulled his notebook from his pocket and scratched in the figure. "Fifty-one strokes, yesterday. Still true and tight." Johnny snapped the notebook shut and turned to walk aft.

Asa looked over at Johnny and murmured, "Think the boy'll get us home? Does he ken the latitude and such, or we be better off wit' him back a'fore the mast?" The two sailors looked at Johnny expectantly.

Johnny glanced up at Thom, pacing the quarter-deck. The heavy coat made him look thin and small, and the face that had always seemed to be just about to smile was tense, his jaw clenched. For an instant, Johnny wondered himself whether they had made the right choice, then pushed it from his mind. Who better he thought? Better'n me, to be sure.

Johnny turned and fixed Asa with his stare. "Bible says, 'And behold, there arose a great tempest in the sea, insomuch that the ship was covered in the waves. And the Lord saith unto them, 'Why are ye fearful, Oh, ye of little faith?'"

Johnny paused for a moment, holding the sailor with his gaze, then spoke softly in a tone tinged with anger. "So listen here, Asa Jackson, you chose him as captain, 'long with rest of the crew and I'll warrant ya Captain Larkin'll get us home. I hear anybody say otherwise, I just may toss 'em overboard and let 'em swim to Boston." His voice rose again. "Now get back to work, ya' lazy bastards, and make a joyful noise while you're at it, or I'll sic the mate on ya." Asa grumbled to himself and walked forward, though George Morton looked confused. "Thought you were mate now?"

"An' you just keep thinking that way, Mr. Morton." A smile curled at the corners of Johnny's mouth. Another verse came to mind, from Paul, "And when neither sun nor stars for many days appeared, and no small tempest lay on us, all hope that we should be saved was then taken away." Johnny snorted to himself. No need to start thinking like Asa Jackson. Besides the church rector had always predicted that he would come to a bad end. As the saying went, a man meant for hanging wouldn't ever likely drown.

When he reached the quarter-deck he walked over to Thom, "Sixty-four strokes, sir. Bit more'n yesterday but still tight."

"Thank you, Mr. Stevens," Thom replied. Johnny withdrew to the leeward rail, leaving Thom alone to windward, standing watch in the place reserved for the captain.

❖ ❖ ❖

Throughout the morning, the wind freshened and they shortened sail. Squalls lashed at the *Mary Ellen* with blinding rain and wailing wind. Between the squalls, drifting walls of fog swallowed them, then spat them out again like Jonah's whale, leaving them pressed between the same slate-gray sea and sky.

 Thom stayed on deck, unwilling to go below except to update their position at each change of watch. They were getting close now. If he'd underestimated the current or made a mistake in his figures, they were just close enough to fetch ashore before they even knew they were within soundings.

If he brought the *Mary Ellen* in safely, he might sail on the next voyage as <u>mate</u>, instead of as merely an able seaman. And if he didn't, there was a good chance that all aboard, including himself, would be dead by next day's noon. Oddly, the worst part of that seemed to be that it would prove his father right, that perhaps he should have stayed put, swinging an adze in the shipyard. Somehow, it was better to risk the rocks than to be stuck ashore as little more than the family man-servant.

Thom was not alone in his darker thoughts. The tension on board was as tangible as the wind humming softly through the windward stays. One by one, the crew drifted on deck, off-watch and on. The older sailors stood or sat, looking out into the fog with a certain gruff resignation while the younger seamen looked back at Thom intently as he paced the small quarterdeck, with questioning looks for which Thom had no answer.

Their course was set and only the wind, current and perhaps the hand of Providence would send them safely into harbor or to their death on the rocks. Whatever questions the crew might have, that was the only answer.

In the afternoon, the wind eased and they shook out the t'gallants. Patches of blue appeared between the banks of clouds. The horizon, close in and menacing for days, began a measured retreat. Thom had allowed himself to relax a little, when suddenly a sailor on deck cried out, "Breakers! To larboard! I hear breakers to larboard!"

Everyone rushed to the larboard rail, each staring frantically out into the whiteness, each murmuring thoughts to his fellows. Thom's heart raced as he stared into the shifting walls of fog.

"Silence, fore and aft!" Thom bellowed, as loudly as he could manage. They all grew quiet and listened but heard only the sound of the breeze and the soft creaking of the rigging in the low swells.

In a few minutes, John Stevens snorted. "Fog's making you batty, Ezra."

The sailor looked sheepish. "Swore I heard breakers. On all that's holy, swear I did."

"Better to shout out and be wrong, Ezra, than to keep your counsel when you may have heard true," Thom called down from the quarterdeck. "More than enough rocks and shoals in these waters to bear keeping out a weather eye and ear."

The sailor shrugged and sat back down on the hatch.

Then, a few minutes later, the fog shifted and there, well off on the larboard side, was a sinuous line of boiling white, roughly parallel to their course, waves breaking on a ledge. Thom stared at the breakers. His heart raced, the sound of this heart beating in his ears drowned out the sound of the menacing surf.

Thom shouted "Helm down! Bring us a point to starboard."

"A point starboard, aye," echoed the helmsman. The sails began to luff.

The crew scrambled to the leeward braces and hauled as Johnny eased the windward, then moved to the jib and staysail. Soon the sails were trimmed and the line of breaking waves grew more distant until another wall of fog obscured them all together.

Thom called out, "Ezra, my compliments on your fine hearing."

"Thank you," Ezra replied, as those around him agreed, laughing.

Sam Joseph, a sailor even older than Johnny, returned to his previous seat on the hatch grating and muttered darkly, "Hobomock nearly got us. Indians say an evil spirit lives out here in the rocks. Maybe that's who we heard, Hobomock, calling us'n to his lair."

Johnny growled. "Another word about evil spirits, Sam, and I'll feed you to Hobomock myself. You Ipswich men never had no sense." Sam Joseph scowled, got up, and stomped off to the fo'c's'le.

Thom shook his head. Hobomock, indeed. The fog was closing in again. He stepped to the rail and listened intently, holding his breath, trying to ignore the noises of the ship, and straining to hear anything else out in the fog. Thom stood for a moment but now could hear nothing but the wind and the creaking of the rigging as she rolled along.

He went to the cabin to look at the chart. It appeared that they had been set to the west, closer to Cohasset Rocks. But was that the ledge they saw? It had to be. And if he was wrong, he would learn soon enough. He plotted a new course and went on deck to give it to the helmsman.

❖❖❖

Four bells into the afternoon watch, the lookout cried, "Deck. Sail to larboard" and everyone on deck rushed to the rail. Thom clambered up the ratlines to the cross trees alongside the lookout. He glanced down at the deck and saw a dozen upturned faces looking up at him expectantly from far below. For an instant, he felt dizzy and gripped the shrouds with both hands.

"Still hull down, 'bout two points for'ad the beam," the lookout said as he handed Thom the glass. Once his vision cleared, he saw a small cutter with only her mast and sails above the horizon. A long narrow pendant fluttered from her masthead. Thom steadied the glass, not wanting to let wishing obscure his vision. They were on a crossing course. Slowly, ever so slowly, the distant sail grew in the spyglass and Thom knew that he wouldn't be disappointed. The sail was the pilot boat. He had brought them home.

The tension, a weight he had carried without quite realizing it, flowed from his shoulders. He felt like laughing, crying, dancing and singing all at once. Instead, he smiled, a broad face stretching grin that seemed entirely beyond his control.

He slapped the lookout on the back, handed him the glass, and grabbed the backstay. With a yelp, he dropped to the deck, sliding down the stay as fast as gravity would take him, tightening his grip only at the last moment to slow his descent. He landed on the deadeye and jumped to the quarterdeck with a satisfying thump, his hands smarting from the friction.

With everyone on deck gaping at him, he immediately felt foolish and then realized that now he didn't care. He squared his shoulders in his oversized coat and turned to Johnny Stevens, who was standing at the rail.

"Mr. Mate, from the pennant at her masthead, she appears to be the Boston harbor pilot." Johnny let out a cheer, followed by cheers from the other sailors.

Thom laughed freely. He shouted along with the rest, hallooing to the wind, sea and sky. Finally, he stopped and shouted to the still boisterous crew, "Enough of that. Let's sail to meet her right smartly, like proper seamen. Not a bunch of screaming old women." He was greeted with laughter as the crew took their stations.

He called for the cook. "Mr. Staples, at change of watch, be so kind as to serve a double tot of rum to all hands. I doubt the owners would mind and I think we have all earned it."

"That I will, sir," replied Staples, who hobbled off with a more sprightly gait than Thom had seen since the beginning of the voyage.

Thom turned to Johnny. "Mr. Stevens, shorten sail to meet the pilot boat if you please."

Stevens smiled, "Aye aye, Capt'n." He began giving orders to the sailors standing nearby. Thom stayed on the quarterdeck, watching the pilot boat's sail, visible now from the deck. The quartermaster steered to meet her, as the topmen struck the t'gallants and the rest of the crew trimmed the sails as they changed course. Thom watched the yards turn, the oiled spars gleaming golden in the broken beams of sunlight. She wasn't anything fancy, but the *Mary Ellen* was a lovely old gal, soon to be home.

❖❖❖

When the pilot boat was close aboard, Thom hove the *Mary Ellen* to. With her main topsail backed and her fore topsail drawing, she sat nearly motionless in the light chop. A boat cast off the pilot sloop and pulled alongside. Thom met the pilot at the rail. "Welcome aboard, Sir," he said shaking the pilot's hand.

The pilot looked confused. "This Captain Evers's ship?"

"Yes, sir. Captain Evers is dead, sir. Took fever ten days out of Statia." Thom replied.

"Condolences, sir. And the Mate?" the pilot asked. Thom looked at Johnny Stevens who was now standing just to his side. "Mr. Stevens is the acting Mate."

Stevens took a step forward and said, "Bes' you deal with Capt'n Larkin here. He's the best damn navigator you ever saw."

Thom shook his head. "I'm the best navigator on board. Shipped as seaman, but helped with navigating when the Mate was put ashore in Guadeloupe. Convulsions." Behind him, Stevens raised his hand as if drinking from a bottle. "When the captain passed, I was the only one aboard who could chart a course."

The pilot stared at him. "My compliments. Remarkable, sir."

"Ain't it, though," Johnny Stevens replied, slapping Thom on the back hard enough to all but knock him over.

❖❖❖

In the last light of day, the brig *Mary Ellen* anchored off Castle William to await the morning tide. The mist carried the sweet shore breeze and Thom thought he heard the church bells of Boston.

"Set the anchor light, if you please, Mr. Jenkins."

"Aye, sir," Jenkins replied, bustling off below for the lantern.

A few minutes later, the dull thud of a cannon fired hourly from Boston Light to guide voyagers in the fog, echoed about them, a resounding coda to the voyage. Thom set to work below updating the log book. On deck, the *Mary Ellen*'s fog bell rang out softly in the fading light.

CHAPTER TWO

The next morning the *Mary Ellen* raised anchor and ghosted toward Long Wharf on a zephyr breeze and a rising tide with only her topsails set. Thom paced the quarterdeck as Boston grew from the haze, first the masts of ships, then shadows of steeples, and finally the low shapes of warehouses lining the wharves. John Stevens, standing in the waist, looked back at him and Thom immediately wondered if his anxiety was showing.

As they neared the last bend in the channel, Thom walked over to the harbor pilot. He felt ridiculously young and green standing next to the silver haired mariner, who began to speak as soon as Thom joined him. "Tide'll set you onto the dock," he said, still looking straight ahead at the approaching wharf. "Less than a knot, though. Put her in between the coaster and the smack." The pilot turned his head and glanced at Thom as if to ask, "Have ye any questions?" Lacking a response, he turned and walked off toward the stern. Thom followed him back toward the quarterdeck.

Long Wharf, jutting a half-mile out into the harbor, was lined with warehouses and shops on the eastern side. Longshoreman swarmed the length of the wharf, unloading coasters and deep-sea ships while teamsters drove teams pulling carts to and from the warehouses. Apprentices in their leather aprons followed the riggers, joiners, and chandlers to the shops and lofts along the dock. Along with those working, an equal number of idlers stood by, looking for any employment to be had. Thom could just hear the clatter of horses' hooves on cobblestones and the creak of block and tackle. The sound of voices was a low indecipherable drone beneath the rattle of rigging and wagons.

Thom felt a sudden panic, now not sure what to do. There was a sloop tied up at the near end of the wharf and a fishing smack a bit further down. There looked to be enough room between them, but if he didn't check her speed at the right moment, they might run down the smack. The image of sinking both the *Mary Ellen* and the fishing boat flashed before him. It was not how he wished to end the voyage.

Thom realized that Johnny Stevens was standing at his elbow. "Might wish to ease the helm, sir."

"Ease your helm, Mr. Jenkins," Thom said with all the force and confidence that he could muster. "Thank you, Mr. Mate," Thom said softly, turning his head toward Johnny. Johnny nodded, still looking straight ahead.

As the quartermaster eased the tiller over, the *Mary Ellen* approached the wharf at a shallow angle, aiming for the space between the coaster and the smack. Thom watched as her bowsprit pointed toward the gaping door of a warehouse. They were getting awfully close.

"Shall we back the topsail, sir?" Johnny asked softly.

"Good time as any," Thom replied. He took a breath and shouted, "Back your main-topsail."

The sail fluttered as the crew hauled on the braces, then filled again on the opposite side with a crack. Thom knew the next order. "Larboard your helm," he said to the quartermaster who pushed the tiller across the deck. The *Mary Ellen* stopped moving forward with a gentle shudder and slipped directly sideways against the dock. "Ease your braces and strike the topsails," Thom shouted.

Bow and stern, line handlers threw their heaving lines, followed by the hawsers. Longshoreman began manhandling the shore gangway in place.

"Nicely done, Capt'n. Nicely done," Johnny said.

Thom laughed and bowed his head slightly. "Thank you for your timely counsel, Mr. Stevens. Was a bit concerned that we might sink the dock."

Johnny smiled broadly and nodded. "Been a pleasure sailing with you, Capt'n."

Thom laughed. "Wasn't Captain long and I'm not anymore. I'll thankee now to call me Thom." He held out his hand. "And thanks once more for all your help."

Johnny looked startled. "Tis I should be thanking you. Squall and fog, you got us home." He gave Thom's hand a vigorous shake.

"Anyone could have done it."

"No else one aboard who was breathing, if my memory serves."

Thom shrugged and looked off toward the wharf. "Don't know Boston. Could you recommend decent lodging?"

"Mrs. Hawthorne's on Ship Street. Not too fancy but quiet and clean enough."

"Good, and will you join me for dinner this evening?"

Johnny beamed. "A pleasure. The Crow and Crown after Vespers? Do you know it?"

"That I do. Until then."

Johnny glanced aloft and shouted. "Give that topsail a harbor furl, you useless blaggards, and be quick about it. No business looking slatternly now."

Thom turned and walked toward the cabin. He reached the companionway door just ahead of a short man who appeared to be the first one up the gangway. The man wore a periwig with a tattered queue, a linen vest, and breeches, and had gold rimmed glasses perched perilously on a rather sharp nose. In one hand he carried a large leather satchel.

"Do I have the pleasure of addressing Thomas Larkin?" he asked, with an expression that did not entirely convey pleasure.

"Yes, sir," Thom replied. "And might you be the ship's agent?"

"Indeed I am. Zebulon Flanders, ship's agent, port purser, aide to Mr. Nimroy, at your service, sir. May we speak below?"

In the confines of the cabin, Flanders sat down. "When the pilot boat brought in news of a boy seaman sailing in as captain, well, I must say, you caused quite a stir. A fine piece of navigating, or so I am told. The owners, Mr. Nimroy and Mr. Brown, are most pleased with your service."

Thom wasn't sure what to say and apparently didn't need to say anything as Flanders began again. "Mr. Nimroy dispatched me here to relieve you of the burden of dealing with matters of cargo declarations, customs, and duties, that sort of thing. In these times, a certain delicacy may be required."

Other than keeping the log up to date and worrying about bringing the ship to port, Thom hadn't given a care to customs.

"I am most pleased," Thom replied. He reached into a drawer under the small writing desk and handed Flanders a leather-bound ledger. "Here is the Owner's Manifest and Accounts." He pulled out another ledger from the second drawer. "And here is the Cocket, the Certified Cargo Declaration. I would be pleased if you handled customs and port duties. I do not claim to fathom such matters."

Flanders raised one eyebrow behind his glasses. The boy seaman Captain understood enough about the honorable practice of evading customs duties to keep the two manifests separate. He slipped the Owner's Manifest into an inner pocket of his leather bag.

"You mentioned a 'certain delicacy'? Have matters so changed?"

The agent sighed. "The new Commissioners of Customs, scarcely here a year, have wholly disrupted the old harmony of commerce between the merchants and the Crown. Not only do they seek to squeeze out the last pence, but have taken to violating the King's law as well.

"Scarce a fortnight ago, a customs tide waiter, one Owen Richards, was observing the discharge of Mr. Hancock's brigantine, *Lydia*, which was well enough within his right as long as he remained on deck. When he believed himself unseen, he slipped below to ferret out undeclared cargo or engage in some other nefarious act." Flanders smirked. "Well, the crew returned somewhat earlier than the scoundrel had hoped and the bosun found him cowering in steerage. I'm told that he received a bit of rough handling, though no more than he deserved. The Customs Commission then had the temerity to charge Mr. Hancock with the carriage of undeclared goods. Mr. Hancock, in response, has charged the Commission with felonious trespass. I have no doubt that Mr. Hancock will prevail."

"Then I am doubly pleased for your services, sir," Thom said. "I surely lack Captain Evers' experience in such matters. 'Tis indeed a sorrow that he didn't live to see the end of the voyage. Prices were good and he traded well."

"Yes, I have no doubt that he did. Mr. Nimroy will be pleased, to be sure. Well then, the cash box should be arriving shortly and we will begin the payoff."

Flanders pulled out a pocket-watch from his vest, snapped it open, looked at the time, snapped it shut and returned it to his pocket. He stood up, picked up his bag and left the cabin.

As if summoned by the snapping of the purser's watch, two large men came aboard carrying a strongbox. They set up on a bench just aft of the main mast as Thom retrieved the Articles from the cabin.

Each man signed off the ship, signing or making his mark on the Articles next to where he had signed on four months before. The crew lined up, dressed in their finest going-ashore clothes, festooned with ribbon and braid, chattering to one another, anticipating their first night ashore.

Flanders counted out each man's wages according to his rating, deducting for advances, allotments, and purchases from the slop chest. Thom stood behind Flanders, his last duty before he too became just another seaman looking for a berth. The sailors smiled, knuckled their brows or tugged their caps or forelocks as they were handed their wages. Each then hoisted his sea bag on his shoulder and headed for the gangway, bound on a new voyage to the delights of the taverns and women ashore.

As an officer, if only in name, Johnny Stevens was last in line. "Mr. Stevens, you signed aboard as bosun and served as mate following Captain Evers' death. From the log, you sailed ninety-two days as bosun and twenty-three days as mate and you'll be paid accordingly. Does this meet with your approval?" Flanders looked up.

"Right by me," Johnny replied watching carefully as Flanders counted out the coins. "Thank you, sir," Johnny said to Flanders. "Till this evenin' then, Thomas."

Flanders turned toward Thom. "Mr. Larkin, I have been directed by Mr. Nimroy to pay you all wages owed and a bounty for your service after Captain Ever's death. " He smiled as a questioning look spread across Thom's face. He began counting out the wage then he looked up as if distracted. "Oh, yes, I also have a message from Mr. Nimroy." He put the coins on the top of the chest, pulled from his bag a piece of paper sealed with wax, and handed it to Thom.

Flanders resumed counting and Thom stood watching him, holding the note in his hand. Paid a bounty or no, old habit wouldn't allow him to look away while the purser was counting out his wages. As he watched, a smile spread wide across his face. Flanders handed Thom the coins, more gold than silver shining amidst the stack. Thom held in his hand more than he had earned in several years sailing as a seaman. He fumbled for his purse, put the stack in and stowed it in an inner pocket of his waistcoat, which he imagined now hung lopsided from the weight of his new wealth.

Flanders looked at him and then at Nimroy's note which Thom still clutched in one hand. "Oh, yes." Thom broke the wax seal and read the note.

*On behalf of myself and my partner in this venture, Mr.
John Brown of Providence, I wish to thank you for your
exemplary enterprise and skill on the Mary Ellen on her late
voyage. If it should prove convenient, please wait upon myself
and Mr. Brown at my counting house on North Street this
afternoon so that we may have the pleasure of meeting with you
personally.*

> *Your obedient servant,*
> *James Nimroy*

"Any message that I may relay to my employer, Mr. Larkin?"
Flanders asked, with a trace of impatience in his voice.

"Oh, yes, of course, Thom replied. "Please tell Mr. Nimroy
that I would be most pleased to attend him and Mr. Brown this
afternoon."

"Very well then," Flanders replied. He nodded his head
toward his two assistants who lifted the strongbox, then the three
marched off to the gangway, leaving Thom alone, still grinning
foolishly. Flanders paused only to speak to the long shore gang
boss waiting for him on the dock before proceeding down Long
Wharf.

Thom looked about at the old *Mary Ellen* one last time, his
entire world for these months past and now only a small ship
alongside the wharf in the mighty harbor. His work finished, he
hoisted his sea chest to his shoulder, strode across the deck and
down the gangway, past the gang of waiting longshoremen
anxious to begin their labors.

❖❖❖

As he walked along Long Wharf, the granite dock seemed to
heave and sway beneath his feet, his sea-legs not yet acclimated
to the shore. The weight of the coins heavy in his waistcoat
seemed to throw him further off balance.

There was nothing like the joy of ending a voyage. The bad
food, rigid discipline, brutal weather all replaced by the pleasures

and freedom of the shore. And now he strode the dock not just as any other sailor but as the boy captain who brought the ship in through fog and mist. Not so grand a claim to fame, but perhaps enough for a shipwright's second son.

The morning mist had cleared and the harbor spread before him, crowded with craft of all sizes and shapes -- coasters, fishermen, brigs, shallops, ships, and barks. One of Hancock's sloops, the *Liberty* was tied alongside Clark Wharf, across the roadstead. In the distance, the HMS *Romney*, a fifty-gun man-of-war, glowered over the merchantmen.

During the last war, a warship would have been a rare but welcome sight. The coast was too often abandoned to the marauding French, the colonies' harbors not warranting the attention of the Admiralty. The war had been over for these eight years and now the man-of-war was as welcome as the French had been, a needless reminder of the hard times that followed the war, of Grenville, the Stamp, Sugar, and Townsend Acts, and all the other insults from the Crown. England sought to pay off her war debts on the backs of her colonies, disrupt their trade, and enforce laws long winked at and ignored. A warship in the harbor might bring obedience but never loyalty.

This was something neither the Crown nor Thom's father understood. Philip Larkin expected obedience when he bade Thom turn his back to the sea and work in the family shipyard. He also forbade him from consorting with the local Sons of Liberty, whom the old man considered nothing less than treasonous rabble. Thom's grandfather was a leader of that rabble, much to his father's dismay. Philip Larkin said that as long as his son lived in his house, he would obey his father's wishes. That was when Thom packed a bag and left for sea. As the second son, it was Thom's charge, after all, to make his own way.

He reached the end of the wharf and descended into the winding streets of the town. Boston was a maze of low frame and brick buildings -- houses and stores packed tightly together, each leaning upon the other for mutual support. The streets were crowded with merchants wearing wigs of various sizes and styles, their slaves and apprentices tagging close behind. Sailors from dozens of ships strutted in their best shore clothes, ribbons braided in their hair and waistcoats, coins jingling in their purses, while whores tempted them from the open windows of taverns and boarding houses. Carriage wheels rang and horses hooves clattered on cobblestones, competing with the cries of the fishmongers. Thom looked over a lobsterman's bright blue cart filled with a moving mass of lobsters. "Get your lobs. Get 'em here. Fresh this very mornin'. Get your lobs," he yelled as he wheeled his way down the bustling street.

The air swirled with a maelstrom of smells -- of tar and drying cod, coffee, tobacco, and horse manure, rum, chamber pots, cooking and low tide. Thom was always surprised by the stench of the waterfront when first off a ship. The fo'c's'le, after all, smelled worse than any seven cities, but the clear air on deck was never more than a few steps away. In a city, there was no escape from the odor and the sky was just a space between the buildings, rising two and even three stories high, smudged by the smoke of a hundred chimneys.

Thom would have liked to dive into the first tavern he passed but he remembered his grandfather's three rules for coming ashore. Never fall in love with the first lovely you see, nor get drunk at the first tavern, and always, always keep your purse tight in your fist. And Thom had an appointment to keep that afternoon. Arriving drunk might not enhance his reputation.

Strangely, his future meeting with the owners of the *Mary Ellen* concerned him. He was no longer the carefree sailor discharged from his duties free to enjoy the pleasures of the port. He now needed to account for his actions and perhaps justify the bounty which hung heavy in his purse. Would they find him presumptuous for taking command? Then again, there was no one else who could. He returned to them their ship and its crew and they had rewarded him for his service so they could hardly be displeased by his actions. Unless for some reason they were.

The street was crowded and Thom was repeatedly bumped and jostled. He kept reaching for his waistcoat to check that his purse was still under hatches, several times coming perilously close to dropping his sea chest in the maneuver, grimly reminding himself that there were often as many shoals, reefs, and sharks ashore as there were at sea.

❖❖❖

A short walk down King Street led Thom to Dock Square and Faneuil Hall. He put down his sea chest for a moment to rest his shoulder and to admire the city. The square and the hall that was its centerpiece were simple yet stately. The hall was as grand as any of the ornate and haughty buildings left by the Dutch burghers that his grandfather had shown him in New York. Faneuil Hall had burned down six years before, as had half of Boston, and had been rebuilt finer than the original. This was the new Boston, Boston as it thought of itself and would like to be thought of, ever changing, rising from the ashes of the past, bold and optimistic, a temple to commerce, to liberty, to the colony, perhaps even to America herself. Thom stood for a moment in the hubbub of the square looking up at Peter Faneuil's creation. Carriages and carts passed before him and the highest and lowest of Boston hurried by on the sidewalk behind, before Thom too hoisted his sea chest, turned and made his way on toward Ship Street.

❖❖❖

"So you're Captain Larkin are ye?" The plump woman peered at him from the doorway. "Mr. Stevens asked me to save a room for ye."

"I'm glad you did, ma'am, but Johnny's jesting with you. I'm just a seaman."

Mrs. Hawthorne looked disappointed, perhaps figuring that she couldn't charge a seaman as much for a room as she could a captain. "Well, come in whatever ye are. I've got a nice room in front."

Thom followed her up the narrow stairs, which listed slightly to starboard, to a simple room with a small window.

"Mind your head now," Mrs. Hawthorne said as she showed him in. The ceiling was low with exposed beams and he had to duck to avoid hitting them. The room reminded him of the cabin of a ship.

"Should suit my needs just fine." He paid her for a week and settled in, organizing his gear almost as if he was on board ship. He took out his grandfather's Bible, rigging knife and needle and thread from his sea chest. He careful slit open the Bible's cover stitching and set to work. When he was finished, he put the re-sewn Bible back in the chest and stowed it under the bed. He didn't realize how tired he was until he stretched out and fell asleep. He slept till early afternoon, waking with a start. He dressed hurriedly and made his way to North Street.

❖❖❖

There were few street numbers in Boston, so the street names changed every few blocks to aid or confuse the traveler. Thom walked down Middle Street till it became North Street and was pleased to see the sign, "*J. Nimroy and Company, Merchant*" hanging from a cast iron brace above a heavy oak door.

He knocked on the door and was admitted by Zebulon Flanders. "Oh yes, Mr. Larkin, do come in. Mr. Nimroy will be with you presently."

Thom sat down on a bench near the door and waited, nervously. Two clerks stood at their desks tallying accounts, the scratching of their quill pens against the paper the only sound in the room, save the occasional "harrumph" from Flanders, at his desk, reviewing the ledgers. The light of the afternoon sun played across the room through three small windows in the far wall.

In a few minutes, the door to the inner office opened and a beautiful girl with long dark hair walked out in a swirl of dark green silk. She looked straight at Thom, in a manner that at first seemed dismissive and then as merely direct. Her large dark eyes flashed and seemed to smile, just as surely as the subtle rising curve of her lips. She had glanced at him for only an instant, yet he felt caught full aback as if by a sudden shift of wind. He rose and smiled back at her, self consciously, mindful of his grandfather's advice -- never to believe in the beauty of women until ashore at least a week, for until then one's judgment was rarely sound. Still, he suspected that a week's passing would do little to change his opinion.

"Are you the young captain of whom I have heard so much?" she asked.

He bowed. He was almost afraid to speak. "Ma'am, ahh, Thomas Larkin, at your service, ma'am."

A deep voice behind her said, "Thomas Larkin. I see you've already met my daughter, Angela. She's fully fifteen, yet not nearly as demure as a young lady should be, I fear. She's spent more time with merchants and ship's captains than is proper for a gentlewoman."

Thom looked up and saw two men, one tall, the other shorter and more rotund. The tall stout man, who had been speaking, walked toward him, his hand outstretched. "John Brown of the Providence Plantations, at your service." He turned slightly. "And may I have the honor of naming our host in this fair city, Mr. James Nimroy."

Nimroy nodded and turned toward Flanders. "Zeb, call the carriage for Miss Brown. She shall be calling upon her aunt."

John Brown smiled. "My dear sister fell ill and asked Angela to come ease her suffering, which fit well with my travel plans. She made a miraculous recovery as soon as Angela arrived, so Angela is either a gifted nurse or my beloved sister suffers more of loneliness than the ague."

Nimroy turned back toward Thom. "Come in, Mr. Larkin. We have much to speak of." Thom glanced at Angela and thought he caught a coy smile and tilt of her head as she left with Flanders, though he wasn't sure. The flash of her dark eyes alone may have fired his imagination.

Thom was led into the office and sat down. He didn't know exactly what he had expected, but these men surprised him. Neither wore a wig or powdered his hair and while their dress was quite fine, silk stocking and waistcoats, neither wore lace at throat or cuff. Perhaps in the presence of a mere seaman, they surrendered the pretense of the gentry.

Nimroy settled into a chair behind a large table and Brown sat to one side. Accounts and ledgers were stacked high on the far corner. James Nimroy was fair and round, in a manner bespeaking prosperity. John Brown, in contrast, was darker with an angular face and eyes that could sparkle or penetrate, as he saw fit. Brown looked at Thom with a smile in his gaze.

"We were saddened to hear of Captain Ever's death but were most gratified that you stepped forward to bear the burden of navigation."

"Well, I didn't have much choice if I wished to get home, sir." That immediately seemed to Thom to have been the wrong thing to say, yet in response, Nimroy chuckled and Brown smiled. "And, ah, I do appreciate, gentlemen, the generosity that you have shown me. Your kindness..."

John Brown leaned forward in his chair. "No more need be said. The safe arrival of the *Mary Ellen* promises good fortune for our venture, so we are pleased to share some portion of that bounty."

"You know, young man, I met your grandfather, quite a few years ago, when I was not much older than yourself. My family had a small interest in a privateer which he most ably captained. Gave the French grief and ourselves and the other owners great joy." Brown smiled and looked toward Nimroy who smiled back. "I hope he fares well."

"I regret, sirs, that he took ill last winter and passed on."

"You have our heartfelt condolences. He was a skilled captain and a brave man."

"That he was," Thom replied.

"And how fares the rest of your family?" Nimroy asked.

"Well, thank you. My father is a shipwright, has a yard in Cold Spring Harbor, Long Island. My mother and older brother attend him."

"It must be difficult being away from your family so long," Nimroy suggested.

"I do miss my mother. My father and I are not close. He would rather that I had not gone to sea, though whenever I was at home, we quarreled. And I am his second son, so my prospects are best elsewhere. I also share my grandfather's views, which my father considers too radical. He is not an admirer of Whigs."

Brown laughed. "Prefers his wigs powdered does he? Well, he may just be right. Trouble makers the lot of us." Nimroy's brow furrowed as if to question the propriety of such candor. Mr. Nimroy spoke up.

"As we have said, we are most pleased with your service, Mr. Larkin. The *Mary Ellen* is due for a thorough refit, so I am unable to offer you employment on her for a period of time." He paused.

John Brown filled the silence. "I may have a position to offer you, however. I'm fitting out a vessel for the Indies later this year and I could use a good chief mate, particularly one who can navigate. Would this be of interest?"

Thom sat up straighter in the chair. "Most assuredly so, sir. Thank you, sir."

"Good, she'll sail in early September. Please attend me at my office in Providence."

"Yes, sir, thank you, sir. That is most kind, sir." Thom hesitated a moment. He wondered if he would be overstepping to ask for more. "Mr. Brown, sir. Please excuse my impertinence, sir, but on the *Mary Ellen*, the bosun, John Stevens, a Rhode Islander as well, was of great assistance to me and .."

"Tell Mr. Stevens to call as well. We'll surely find him a berth."

"Thank you, sir. Thank you again."

When Flanders showed him out, Thom walked down North Street, turned at Mill Creek and walked back toward the docks, hard pressed to resist the temptation to skip. Storms and fog, fear and stress, all seemed far away. He slapped his coat, heard the soft clink of silver and gold in his purse, and once more laughed out loud.

He remembered his grandfather telling him that fortune shifted like a northwesterly wind, the first gusts hot and dry off the land, then turning cool, clear and fine, and when you caught it you could press on with full sail and make distance for as long as the northwesterly blew. You had to wring every last mile from that blessed breeze before the wind turned again. Thom felt fortune's wind behind him as he walked off toward the boarding house, the rays of the summer afternoon sun casting long shadows on the narrow streets.

It was dark when Thom left the boarding house and made his way off the street down a narrow alley to the Crow and Crown. Save for the glow from a few shuttered windows on the lane, the light shining from the doorway was the only illumination. A large wooden crow held a gilt crown in his talons above the door. Beneath the smoky light of tallow lanterns, the inn was crowded with sailors at a bar along the front wall and at tables packed into the rectangular room. Laughter and shouts occasionally rose above the din of sailors drinking, playing whist and cribbage, and telling tales to their fellows and to the serving girls. To the left, a fire smoldered in a large hearth with a black pot hanging from a hook over the flames. The aroma of stew mixed with the smell of tallow, tobacco, sweat, and ale.

Johnny Stevens sat in the back, distinguished by his full black beard that gave him the look of a buccaneer ashore for plunder, with a large bowl of porter before him on a table, now less than half full. "Thomas," he cried out over the clamor of the other sailors and waved an arm. Thom waved back.

"Good evening to you, fine sir" Johnny said, as Thom sat down on the bench across the table from him. "Mary dear, bring another mug and your pitcher over here for my illustrious young friend."

In a minute the serving girl worked her way to their table, plunked a clay mug down in front of Thom and poured porter from her pitcher into their bowl. "Watch yerself with this one here," she said pointing to Johnny. "Looks like trouble to me."

"The sort of trouble ya dream about, m'darling."

"Well, we do all have nightmares, time to time," she laughed. "Now will ya be eatin', young man?"

"A bowl of whatever's on the fire'll be fine, thankee."

Thom raised his mug, "To fair winds and liberty, Mr. Stevens."

Johnny raised his mug. "To our share of each."

Thom drank deeply, savoring the bitter warmth. As he put down his mug, Mary slid a bowl of stew towards him from down the table, followed by a wooden spoon. He caught the bowl just before it landed in his lap.

"Did I hear your friend here call you Larkin?" Mary asked, one hand on her hip. "Any relation to Captain Malcolm? He's a brother-in-law named Larkin."

Thom shook his head. "I've no relations in these parts, though please wish the good Captain well if you should see him."

She laughed. "I'll do it, though Malcolm's got enough well wishers on the docks, 'cept for the sheriff and his informers."

Johnny laughed. "Captain Malcolm sounds like a relation of mine, if not young Thomas'. An' how did Captain Malcolm become so popular?"

"Oh, 'ain't you heard? Must'a just arrived." Mary put down her pitcher and leaned closer to Thom and Johnny, presenting to Thom a most pleasant view of her cleavage, which rather increased his interest in her story.

"Well, now, seems that Customs men showed up at Captain Malcolm's door with a writ of resistance."

"Believe that's writ of assistance," Thom suggested.

"Ah, whatever it may be, it's a piece of paper that claims to take all and any Englishman's rights to hearth and home. Anyway, Captain Malcolm treats them most courteously and lets them look about as they wish. His house and storehouse are just at the end of the block there at King's Street. He lets 'em look anywhere save one room in his cellar," she said with a sly smile. "Says that store room is rented out to one Captain McKay and only McKay has the key to the lock. They say to break the lock and Malcolm says he'll be damned if he does. Lock's not his to break.

"They went off and tried to find McKay but couldn't, so they come back to Malcolm's with Sheriff Greenleaf and demands that the lock be broken. Captain Malcolm bades 'em go to the devil and that they aren't welcome in his house and bars the door for proof. Now the sheriff, ..."

"Damn it all, Mary. Men with empty tankards and here you are yammering the night away."

Mary looked over at a round man of middling height, with a blue apron about his waist. "No harm in being sociable, Jacob Abrams. Telling 'em about Captain Malcolm and the writ, but if drink is more important than Christian civility, I'll leave you to answer for it" and bustled off to the other end of the room where several sailors were calling for rum.

The innkeeper bowed before Thom and Johnny. "No disrespect intended, gentlemen, though tis hard enough to run an establishment with a wench who'd rather gab than serve. "

"No offense taken, sir," Thom replied, "though I would be grateful for the end of the tale. What happened to Malcolm after the customs men returned with the sheriff?"

The innkeeper laughed. "Ah, the good Captain Malcolm, so that's what she was going on about. Well now, the question might be, what happened to the sheriff?

"When Malcolm wouldn't let them in, they found that a crowd was formin' behind 'em. A right civil bunch, though wantin' to make sure that justice was done if ye catch my meanin'. Now Sheriff Greenleaf asks all to assist him, as is his right and power, and to a man, the crowd agrees, provided that the customs men swear an oath to name the informer that gave up Malcolm.

"Well now, the customs man refuses and so crowd refuses the Sheriff and that's the way it stands for several hours until school lets out and a few score of young boys add their number to the festivities.

"It's near enough to dark when the sheriff and customs give up and Malcolm comes out of his house and leads a parade to this very door, where he buys every man jack of 'em a round of ale. A fine man, that Captain Malcolm."

A call broke through the din of voices and the innkeeper turned and yelled, "Be there presently." He turned back to the table, "An' a good evenin' to ye gents."

As he watched the innkeeper's back working his way across the room, Johnny said, "Easy enough to see why the innkeeper favors Captain Malcolm."

Thom smiled. "For all the Customs Commission pays its informers, 'tis a small enough price that Malcolm paid for the ale." Thom took a deep swig of his own.

"Enough of the days' troubles, I bring joyous news, Johnny. A new ship and a berth for each of us, if you care to join me."

Johnny looked surprised, though pleased. "Tis grand news, indeed. What have ye found?"

"A ship fitting out for the Indies in Providence. Sailing early September. Owned by a Mr. John Brown, half owner of the cargo on the *Mary Ellen*."

"Damn it, man, you can be my business agent anytime." Johnny laughed. "Takes a New Yorker calling in Boston to find a Newport man a berth on a Providence ship. God bless ye."

"Sometimes fair fortune smiles, Johnny, sometimes she smiles." Thom filled his mug from the bowl and drank again.

"That's right. You're from Newport aren't ye? Why can't a Newport man ship out of Providence."

"Ach. All nonsense. First fifty years, Rhode Islanders fought agin' the other colonies. Last fifty, we fight each other when we aren't fightin' the French or the Spanish. Newport folk generally support Nicholas Ward and his faction, you see, and Providence folk support Stephen Hopkins and they sort'a take turns getting elected governor. My family's always supported Hopkins, more the fool for it. Supporting Hopkins, I couldn't find a ship in Newport, and as a Newporter had no hope in Providence, so I ship out'a Boston. Foolishness, all of it. First, you keep us off the rocks, Thomas, and now you find us a ship. Drink up."

"Well then, to our next ship," Thom said raising his glass.

"Our next ship," Johnny echoed.

"You know, I am grateful for your help this morning Johnny. I probably would have sailed right through a storehouse."

Johnny laughed. "You would have done fine with or without me. Nothin' to ship handlin' once ya get the feel. Now navigatin', that's something else again. That's as close to witchcraft as ever I saw. Just amazing."

"Not so hard," Thom replied. "I'll teach you navigation if you teach me your ship handling."

"I'll get the better deal there. I'll take you up on that offer, I will."

They drank for several hours, Johnny telling sea stories and Thom mostly listening. Johnny had sailed on a privateer against the French.

"Privateersman's booty is like sand in a youngster's hand. Just pours out into the ocean. Like the bible says, 'thou shalt bestow that money for whatsoever thy soul lusteth after, for wine, or for strong drink and thou shalt eat and thou shalt rejoice,' leastwise till your purse runs empty.' A light purse is indeed a heavy curse indeed."

At the far door, through the smoke and the noise, a tall Naval officer in a fine blue coat with a saber at his belt stepped in, with three Marines close behind. In a loud voice he began, "In the name of His Majesty King George the Third, I summon all able ..."

From the other side of the room, someone yelled, "Press Gang." The redcoats stepped around the officer and rushed the room, followed by four more just behind. The first two were knocked down by a bench, swung like a claymore by a huge sailor near the door. Another crumpled as a well-aimed tankard exploded on his forehead. The other soldiers swung clubs and toppled sailors who stood to fight. "Bloody sons of whores." "To the devil wit ye." Howls of rage and pain filled the small room. An equal number of sailors seemed to be attacking and fleeing in a tumble of bodies flailing and shouting amidst overturned tables and spilled ale.

Johnny jumped up, grabbing Thom's arm. "Quick, out the back!" They dashed toward the back door, scrambling over benches and tables. Johnny hauled on the wooden handle but was knocked aside as the door burst open. Four Marines brandishing belaying pins rushed in, the first striking Thom on the side of the head with a blow that sent him reeling.

Johnny leaped back to his feet, only to be pinioned from behind. The grip on his arms weakened as that Marine had a mug broken across the back of his head and Johnny squirmed free. He looked for Thom and saw only the butt of a Marine musket coming at him. His vision exploded in blue sparks and blackness.

CHAPTER THREE

Johnny woke in a pool of blood, his head pounding. He had been knocked under a table, where apparently the press gangsters had missed him. Slowly he pushed an overturned bench out of his way and rolled out from under. Mary, the serving girl, was sweeping and gave a start, "Oh. Didn't see you over there. Lay still now."

Around him were shattered tables and benches scattered across the floor, which was deep in broken crockery. A single lamp and the dull glow of the fireplace cast long shadows across the room.

Mary leaned the broom against a broken table, walked over to the bar and fetched a pitcher. She handed him a cup. The water felt cool and quenched the burning in his throat. She poured some water onto a rag that she pulled from her apron. "Here, wipe your face. Make you feel a bit more like yourself."

He pressed the rag gently against his forehead. Gingerly he touched the gash in the side of his face, which now felt like a flaming iron. He grimaced and Mary smiled at him. "Once you're on your feet, I'll get you some rum. That'll make you forget your pains."

"Thankee," Johnny replied, not quite managing a smile. Mary went back to sweeping.

A sailor half hidden in the shadows leaned against the counter. "Gave 'em a good fight anyway, the bastards. We's not at war. No call for a press gang. Rotten blaggards, all of 'em."

Johnny struggled to his feet. "Did ye see? Did they take a boy, tall, sandy haired?"

The sailor shook his head. "Hard to say. Too many cudgels and tables flying to see much of anything."

Johnny wobbled to the bar and took the rum that Mary had set out. It both cleared his head and made it hurt more. After a moment, he made his way to the door. Down the lane, on Water Street, he saw of a flood of men carrying torches. The Royal Navy would press no more men this night. But where was the press gang now? And where was Thom?

Johnny stumbled down the narrow lane and joined the stream of men flowing toward the wharves. He wasn't quite sure where they were going but followed along regardless. His head ached and his sight was blurred, the lights from the torches seeming to dance like whirling fireflies just beyond his vision. Cries of "Town born -- turn out!" filled the night, rising above the angry drone of voices and the sound of hobnails on cobblestones. Some shouted, "Press gang's out!" while, others called "Burn the boats!" the last bringing bitter memories of another night three years before

The "better sort" in their comfortable parlors might call the press gang "regrettable", or perhaps a "necessary evil" in the maintenance of the navy. Johnny knew what the press meant from the cobblestones of the docks. The press gangsters robbed a man of all he had. His liberty, his family, his life itself were all forfeit when the gang's net was cast upon the streets. Neither sailor nor landsman was safe and all the fine words about the "rights of an Englishman" blew like dust before a gale.

A press gang had swept up Johnny's favorite cousin, Andrew Simmons, in Newport one night in '65. With a hundred or so other Newporters, they rushed to burn the boats so the gang couldn't return to HMS *Maidstone*, anchored in the harbor. The press gang slipped by them, stole other boats and returned to the ship that carried away Andrew and a half dozen other Newport men. Two years later Andrew died of fever in the Indies. Johnny had never forgiven the Crown for Andrew's death and carried a very personal hatred for press gangs and impressment.

After failing to save Andrew, Johnny felt bound to do whatever it took to rescue Thom. On the *Mary Ellen*, there had been moments where Johnny wondered whether they would make it in or if they would end up dead on the rocks. But Thom brought them into port safely, and now Johnny swore to do the same for Thom. He owed him as much.

As more men joined from the taverns, alleys, and lanes, the stream became a river and then a torrent. In the moving mass, Johnny grew dizzy and slipped, only to be lifted to his feet by strong unseen hands around him. A stranger, Johnny was now part of their legion, a brother to be supported and protected.

He knew these men, not by name, but by situation, for he had been one of them and might yet be again. Some carried torches or cudgels, but most were bare handed, roughly dressed in homespun and flax. They were sailors between ships, itinerant laborers, craftsmen without shops, bakers without ovens, shipwrights without timber. They fought in the last war and knew the hard times that followed. Ships laid up by taxes. Shops shut down in the slump. Landless, lacking title or connections, they were feared by the gentry, who tried to ignore them altogether, yet more than half of Boston could be counted in their number.

The crowd reached the naval landing and flowed along the shore. The *Romney*'s longboats were gone and only the *Romney* herself, at anchor in the darkness, her deck alight with lanterns, was evidence of the press gang's raid. Men were dispatched to find a boat and a delegation was chosen to petition the ship. From where Johnny stood at the edge of the crowd, the delegates appeared to be merchants of a middling sort, a cut above the mob, but not so far removed. A boat was found and the delegation rowed out to the *Romney*. The mob hushed as the boat, now just a shadow on the dark water, hailed the ship. Their tone was civil and proper. The Marine at the gangway called the Captain who shouted, "Get away, you scoundrels. Pull away or be fired upon."

The crowd couldn't quite hear all of what was being said, but read the meaning from the tone. A cry went up as the boat pulled back toward the landing. One of the leaders of the mob began to speak. Johnny could only make out part of it. " ... thieves in the night, they trample the freedom of all Englishmen, sheathing their swords not in a scabbard, but in the bowels of their kinsmen." The mob roared its agreement. "O' Babylon, we shall escape thy chains. We shall break thy bonds as ..." The speaker warmed to his task only to be drowned out by the enthusiasm of his audience. Johnny felt dizzy again and slipped to one knee. A voice behind him muttered, "Amen, brother."

The speaker wound down, the mob shouted "God Save the King" and dispersed, leaving a small guard to give alarm should the press gang return. Johnny slipped from his knee to the ground. A tall sailor with a torch looked down at him. The torchlight shone on the black bruise across Johnny's face and the blood on his shirt. "By the Lord, man, you're hurt."

Johnny looked up through a haze at the large man bending over him. "Press gang took Thomas. Fought 'em, but ..."

The sailor hoisted Johnny up. "Where should we take you, friend?"

Johnny mumbled, "Hawthorne's, Ship Street," before passing out.

❖❖❖

Johnny woke with Mrs. Hawthorne sitting at his bedside. Sunlight streamed in through the window. "Brought ye some broth. Had me a fright that ye might not make it when they brought ye in." She held a steaming spoon to his lips and he sipped the salty liquid.

"And what of your friend, Mr. Larkin ? 'e never came back."

"Taken, I fear. Taken..." Johnny closed his eyes for a moment. His head pounded like cannon fire and thinking of Thomas made it worse. "We'll get him back," he stated as if an established fact.

"I'll get him back," he said, quietly, not sure how, yet no less certain.

"Terrible times these," Mrs. Hawthorne replied, offering Johnny another spoonful.

In an hour, Johnny had cleaned himself up, putting on his best shore clothes and shoes. He looked at himself in the small mirror over the basin. His face could frighten children and horses. His left eye was swollen almost closed and his forehead was purple and black. A deep gash ran down his left cheek. Nothing else to be done, Johnny thought.

He made his way across Boston. It was late afternoon and the mob was out. Small groups formed up on street corners and marched off toward the wharves. Johnny walked past them toward James Nimroy's counting house, trying to order his thoughts and prepare what he needed to say.

He knocked on the heavy door and got no answer. He knocked again. A voice from behind the door called out, "Who is it?"

"Johnny Stevens, sir." He shouted to be heard through the oak. "Mate from the *Mary Ellen*, sir. I must see Mr. Nimroy. Thomas Larkin's been taken by the press. Have to get 'im back, sir."

The door opened and a voice said, "Come in." It was Flanders, his arms full of ledgers. He looked at Johnny and gasped. "You look like the devil," offering Johnny a chair.

"True enough, sir. Mr. Nimroy here?"

"He is not. We've more troubles this day than the press gang, bad as that may be. We have been informed that Customs intends to seize the sloop *Liberty* this evening. Ship and all her cargo. They claim that Mr. Hancock failed to declare a full cargo of Madeira, damn Charley Townsend's eyes. Mr. Nimroy is seeing to his affairs. When I see him I'll tell him of poor Mr. Larkin, see what can be done."

"They've no right to take 'im, sir. We've got to get 'im back."

"They've the power, which may matter more than the right. I'll ask Mr. Nimroy for his help. He has an excellent lawyer and some influence. Yet, if even Mr. Hancock's ships are forfeit, I despair at what a lesser merchant may do. Now, if you will excuse me, I too must away." He followed Johnny out the door and locked it behind them.

"Thank you, sir," Johnny said to the small man's back as the agent hurried off down the street clutching his ledgers.

Not knowing where else to go Johnny walked back toward the docks, the streets slipping into the long shadows of early evening. Clumps of men gathered a few blocks away. Each group had a leader of sorts, chosen on the spot. When they were ready, they marched off, in a ragged formation. Johnny trailed behind one group, which merged with a second, then a third. On the quayside, the mob swelled to hundreds.

The sloop *Liberty* was tied up alongside Clark's Wharf. In the distance loomed HMS *Romney*. The Customs men stood along on the dock, or paced about, surveying the growing mob. Their wigs, waistcoats, and silk stockings set them apart from the crowd in flax and homespun. These were the new customs agents, not a year off the ship from London. The old officers grew wealthy looking the other way when merchants brought in cargoes forbidden by the Navigation Acts. These new agents had sworn to enforce the Acts with a firm resolution. Now, looking out at the swelling mob, they appeared decidedly worried. The chief customs officer, Joseph Harrison, alone glared imperiously at the mob, as if the power of his stare could make the rabble hold its distance.

Not far from Harrison, a short way across the quay, the mob leaders gathered and talked. Johnny recognized Ebenezer Mackintosh, the cobbler who led the attack on Governor Hutchinson's house in the Stamp Act riots. Crispus Atticus was with him, the towering black sailor standing head and shoulders above the rest. After a time, the leaders broke up and returned to the mob, which seemed almost an army, with its own officers and foot soldiers, and a rough sort of discipline, suitable for the street, if not for standing in ranks.

The mob had rioted against the press gangs in the last war and had tasted victory only a few years later, driving the stamp-men from the colonies, finally defeating the Stamp Act. Now they'd fight both the press gangs and the customs house.

The word spread through the crowd in a rumbling murmur. "Taking the ship. Sailors be ready." Johnny worked his way forward, but heard cursing that coursed through the crowd like a wave, starting nearest the water and rolling toward him.

In a moment he saw the reason, as signal flags fluttered from the *Liberty*. Long boats crowded with Marines had pulled away from the *Romney* and soon the Marines were clambering over the decks of John Hancock's sloop. A drummer beat a steady tattoo as the Marines spread out along the rail, muskets at the ready, their redcoat's glowing angrily in the twilight, bayonets flashing in the last rays of the sun. As the crowd jeered, the sloop was cast off and towed out by the *Romney*'s boats then tied up, literally under the guns of the man-of war.

Harrison and his men smiled at each other, glancing over at the small sloop, seeming even smaller against the side of the *Romney*. Suddenly, Harrison looked about and realized that he had failed to provide for his own escape. The look of satisfaction turned to terror and he spun and ran down the quay, followed closely by the rest of the customs officers.

The mob exploded again in curses and screams. The order of a few minutes before vanished. Leaderless, now only rage held sway as men picked up ballast stones piled along the quayside and ran after the fleeing men, the mob's anger as dark as the night just settling over the streets.

Johnny ran with them, screaming in his own personal fury, picking up a piece of dunnage from the ground for a club. His anger grew like a thundering broadside, and he screamed at the press gang, the customs men, at all the powdered gentry who presumed to lord over him, who demanded his coin and his homage, who dared to kidnap Thom to man a King's ship. Now they would receive what they were truly due, would reap what they had for so long sown.

Ahead, he saw Joseph Harrison dragged down and pummeled on the street. Another customs collector ran away screaming, holding a broken sword, his clothes ripped from his back. A third, not so lucky, wailed as he was dragged down the street by his hair. The doors of the customs warehouse were broken open and casks of fine Madeira wine seized from the *Liberty* were hauled out into the street and broken open to the howls of the crowd.

Behind him at the dock Johnny heard a cry, "The boat! It's Harrison's!" The crowd turned and ran back to the custom collector's yacht. The boat was almost thirty feet long, but a hundred strong hands now dragged it up over the granite wharf. Johnny lent a hand, hauling it up to where others could help carry. Like an almond on the backs of ants, the fine craft moved a full mile down the winding streets to the Commons, floating on a sea of angry men. In the darkness of the early evening, they dropped the boat on the grass of the Commons below Beacon Hill, in front of John Hancock's fine house, high on the crest above.

Soon the yacht was smoldering, then burning freely, surrounding by cheering and hooting men, silhouettes against the dancing flames. A cask of Madeira was dragged onto the Commons and someone handed Johnny a tankard. He drank deeply and laughed as the fat customs collector's boat burned, sending red sparks spinning skyward.

It had gone too far. A tall man in homespun, looking old and weary in the firelight, made his way through the crowd. He shouted, "Enough. Enough," raising a trembling hand. A few men looked toward the solitary figure. "To your tents, O Israel. To your tents," the lone man bellowed.

Johnny turned to a fellow drinker and asked, "Who might he be?"

The man looked startled. "Must not be from around here, if you don't know Sam Adams."

The other men around Johnny turned and looked at each other, then dropped their tankards and clubs and began to go home.

Johnny returned to Mrs. Hawthorne's after midnight, tired, drunk and guilty that he had forgotten Thomas during the melee. Not that there was anything more he could have done. He was increasingly concerned that nothing could be done at all.

❖ ❖ ❖

The next morning dawned clear and bright and Johnny knew, sure as the sunlight, there was nothing that he could do to rescue Thom from ashore. He looked in his mirror at his full black beard and took out his straight razor and sharpening strop. When he was satisfied with the edge he poured water into the bowl on the nightstand and lathered his face. Where he was bound, all were clean-shaven. Taking one last look in the mirror at his beard, now covered in suds, he began to shave. Behind the beard was a face he hadn't seen in years with an ugly gash running from his lower left jaw almost to his ear, a gift from a Frenchman's cutlass in the last war. He laughed at himself. His new bruises and wounds blended in with the old scar.

He fetched Thomas' sea chest and packed most of its contents into his own. He packed his shore clothes away and put on his seaman's jacket and breaches, carefully pulling a cap down over his battered forehead. When he came down the stair, Mrs. Hawthorne started, "Oh, scarcely recognized ye clean shaven an' all."

"Not a pretty sight, to be sure," Johnny replied. He paid Mrs. Hawthorne to store whatever he couldn't pack and walked down toward the wharf.

For a moment, he stood on the dock and looked out at the *Romney*, her gun ports open, her gun barrels pointing at the town. Johnny leaned against his sea chest and almost smiled. He knew that he was crazy, perhaps struck mad by the blow to the head, but he didn't care. He felt like a privateersman again, sure that luck was with him regardless of the odds, perhaps because of the odds. Success always had its greatest chance when the adversary was the most assured that it was impossible. Johnny laughed to himself. If Thom was to escape the *Romney*, he might just need a privateer's luck.

Johnny paid a chandler's water clerk to row him out to the *Romney*. She towered over them as they rowed closer, black from the waterline to the gundeck and ochre to the quarterdeck, which was a deep royal blue. Up close the barrels jutting out from the gun ports, didn't seem so threatening, their muzzles plugged with wooden tampions.

"Ahoy, the *Romney*," Johnny bellowed. From the gangway, the Marine guard looked at him suspiciously and called the midshipman. The young midshipman looked warily at Johnny bobbing in the small boat. "And what might you want?" he called down.

"Like to volunteer, sir. An experienced seaman, I am, sir." Johnny replied.

"Haven't had too many volunteers of late,"

Johnny pulled off his cap and pointed to the bruise on his forehead. "Had a bit of a disagreement with a young lady's father. Thought it might be a good time to do my patriotic duty, sir, perhaps leavin' town, if you get my meaning."

The midshipman laughed. "Come aboard then. You'll sign articles this very day."

Johnny grasped the boarding ropes and climbed the battens on the hull, pulling his sea chest up after him and disappeared onto the deck.

CHAPTER FOUR

A t first, Thom was only aware of the pain, far behind his eyes, that grew slowly, spreading until it encircled his head like a band of flaming iron. He reached back and felt a sticky mat of dried blood and sweat in his hair and the jab, as sharp as a sword's point when he touched a spot near the base of his skull. All about him was blackness and for a moment he wondered whether he was indeed blind. He didn't need his eyes to know where he lay. The murmur of waves against planking, soothing and distant, was a bitter contrast to the smell - the familiar, fetid, almost overpowering stench of dry rot, moldering stores and accumulated filth, that told Thom he was somewhere in the hold of a ship.

He turned his head slightly, the pain rising with each minute of arc, and saw a pale light glowing through the grating of a single hatchway. The light filtered down through other gratings from the decks above, indirectly, obliquely, losing strength at each level, until the summer sunlight was no stronger than the glow of a distant candle. Thom's eyes adjusted slowly and he saw other men in the narrow compartment, six or seven on each side, each sitting with his back to the bulkhead and legs outstretched, the boots of the men facing starboard almost touching the boots of the men facing to larboard.

The deck above was low, made lower by the deck beams. Thom guessed they were in the hold beneath the orlop deck, thrown into an empty storeroom like so many barrels of salt beef. There was no room to stand, even if they could, which they could not. The shackle on Thom's left ankle grated as he shifted his leg.

Sitting there backs upright and legs out straight, reminded him of hammatack knees, the crooked roots and branches of trees so valued by shipwrights, forming natural brackets to bind together the decks and frames of ships. It seemed now that the Royal Navy was built with men rather than oak and ironwood.

The thought brought a jumble of memories, of the *Mary Ellen*, of Nimroy and Brown, of gold and silver, of porter and laughing with Johnny Stevens and a comely serving girl - pleasant memories all, thoroughly mixed with anger and rage, of the press gang bursting into the room crammed with sailors, of fighting back with a tankard and his fists before everything ended with an explosion of blackness. His good fortune and fine prospects had vanished like the snuffing of a candle. A fury rose within, making his head hurt all the more and for a moment he tried not to think, closing his eyes till the wave of pain passed, then opening them again to see more of his prison.

A few of the men were unconscious or asleep while the others stared out blankly into the near dark. Their clothes looked more like rags than clothing in the gloom. Gray shadows scurried about and as one jumped on the leg of the man directly across from Thom, he gave it a sharp kick. The rat landed on Thom's legs with a yelp and scampered off faster than Thom could react.

"Sorry, friend. Didn't mean to send him your way. Hate 'em buggers."

Another voice some distance away picked up the conversation. "Not so bad. Sailed once on a brig. Stores so rotten, we ate the rats first. Called 'em Purser's pigeons, we did, and were happy for 'em. Right tasty if cooked proper and you're hungry enough."

A third voice replied, "Miller's men. White as ghosts from eating through the flour. Hard to find a steward can cook 'em. Got to be cleaned just right and loaded up with spice."

From somewhere deep inside himself, Thom heard a voice, insistent, rising up and echoing within his skull. "They've got no right." At first Thom wasn't sure whether the voice was just in his head or whether he was speaking. The talk of rodents stopped, replaced by silence and then muted murmurs of agreement which echoed in the storeroom.

Another voice spoke in the darkness. "Right or no, they got us. Sailors ain't got rights. Never had, nev'r will.

"They've got no right," Thom repeated in an even tone.

"Bes' keep your feelings to yourself, son. Ask for your rights and you'll find yourself tied to a grating with a cat opening your back."

"They've got no right," Thom repeated, this time at little more than a whisper, a promise to himself, something between an oath and a prayer.

❖ ❖ ❖

The midshipman looked at Johnny quizzically. Johnny looked back with not quite a smile, drew himself up and touched his cap in an informal salute. "Jonathan Alexander Saunders, at your service, sir." No reason to give his proper name, if he planned on leaving as soon as the opportunity arose.

The midshipman looked no more than fifteen, yet wore a proper uniform, a frilled white shirt, short blue jacket, black tricorn hat, white breeches, and stockings, despite the midday heat. He had acquired an officers bearing, looking at Johnny as if he was a prize steer arriving unexpectedly a week before the start of the county fair. "Midshipman Paulings", he said with a curt nod as he turned on his heel. "Follow me, then."

Johnny hoisted his sea chest onto his shoulder and followed the midshipman to the break of the quarterdeck. A group of gentlemen and ladies was clustered at the starboard rail in the shade of a canvas tarp rigged over the deck. They talked among themselves and to a tall blond officer, hovering at the periphery of the group. They all seemed to be looking out at a ship anchored close astern, a small black hulled sloop that Johnny recognized as the *Liberty*. As the midshipman climbed the quarterdeck ladder he took off his hat and stuck it under his arm. Johnny looking up from the waist, followed his example and took off his cap as well. The officer glanced over at the midshipman, appeared annoyed at the being disturbed and walked over to the rail. The gold anchor buttons shone on his fine blue coat. He looked down at Johnny standing in the waist.

"And what do we have here, Mr. Paulings?"

"A volunteer, sir. Signing him on, sir, " the midshipman replied gesturing down toward Johnny.

"My, my. Volunteers been as scarce as virtuous women in this port. By all means. Locate the purser and sign the good man on." The officer, who spoke with a soft Scottish burr, gave an imperious smirk then turned and strolled back to the party on the stern as Midshipman Paulins returned to John on the main deck.

"And who might that be, sir?" Johnny asked.

"The guests are Customs Officers and their families. Ruffians ashore chased them away. And that was Lieutenant Dudingston. A fine officer from a wealthy family." The midshipman colored slightly as if embarrassed by saying so much to a stranger and a seaman to boot. Johnny smiled to himself, recognizing now one or two of the gentlemen from the melee of the previous evening, and glancing out again at the sloop, the misbegotten *Liberty*.

"Heard there was some trouble in town. Good to see that the Navy's protectin' the King's officers," Johnny commented with a half smile. The midshipman didn't deign to reply.

"Wait here. I'll see if the purser is available." The young officer turned on his heels and disappeared into the deckhouse.

While he waited, Johnny glanced about the deck of His Majesty's ship *Romney*, both pleased and troubled. The deck was immaculate like no merchant ship would or could ever be, everything either painted, polished or scrubbed. The teak deck almost glowed a pale white, while the bulwark and cap rails were painted the deepest of royal blue. The brass watch bell, rail caps and fittings shone like gold in the sun. The shrouds and stays glistened black with Stockholm tar and each of the halyards and sheets was coiled and belayed immaculately on the pin rails. The masts rose a clear white against the sky and the oiled spars glowed golden, mirroring the brass brightwork on deck. Were the ship not full size, she would have looked like a model for an Admiral's son, an extravagant toy, labored over for months by a skilled craftsman.

The *Romney* was small for a ship of the line, only 50 guns, a fourth rater, no match for a 74, or even a 64 and too slow to keep up with a frigate. Her Captain probably believed that a trim ship, ship shape and polished, just might get him a promotion to a far better ship, in somewhere other than a backwater port.

The deck was as crowded as a town square on market day. On the bow, a dozen sailors worked on their hands and knees recaulking the fo'c's'le deck, driving oakum between the deck planks with mallets, followed by sailors with hot tar, sealing the seams, careful not to stain the teak planks. A gang of sailors worked on the starboard side serving and parceling a mooring line. Above him, Johnny could make out the silhouettes of sailors, tarring shrouds and stays, and rigging chafing gear on the standing rigging, looking like so many apes high in a jungle canopy.

Johnny looked around chagrined, realizing that the *Romney* would be a hard ship from which to escape, wondering whether he had made a horrible mistake. He hadn't expected deserting to be too difficult, but now he wasn't so sure. The bulwarks were five feet high with spare spars stored fore and aft between the quarterdeck and the fo'c's'le. The ship's cutter was stowed lashed to the spars. Along the bulwark walkway, boarding nets were rigged, meant to keep boarders off, now intended to keep the crew aboard. At the head of the ship Johnny could see the red jacket of a Marine standing guard, just as there had been one at the gangway and no doubt on the stern as well. The only view of the world that he had left was through the row of gunports, themselves almost fully filled by the barrels of the 12 pounders.

Johnny felt both foolish and trapped. Too late to change course now, he thought. Absentmindedly, he ran his hand over his chin, stroking the beard that he had forgotten he had shaved off that very morning. His fingers brushed across the scar on his jaw from a Frenchman's cutlass, earned when he attacked the quarterdeck of a French Navy brig without looking to be sure that his shipmates followed his lead. He'd always charged when more prudent men would run. Perhaps he had charged full speed into trouble again.

Midshman Paulins reappeared a few minutes later. "Leave your sea chest on deck and follow me." Johnny followed him to the purser's office.

❖❖❖

The purser, a shuffling crab of a man, snorted when he opened the muster book. Johnny paused for a moment, trying to decide whether Saunders was spelled "Saunders" or "Sonders" and decided he liked the former. He reached for the quill and signed his new name with a flourish on the ship's articles, next to the "X's" of most of the other crew. The midshipman brought him back out on deck and yelled for the bosun. "Mr. Lasco, take Mr. Saunders here and show him his mess, if you please."

The bosun motioned with a round and balding head that Johnny should follow. "Say you're a seaman. Well, this 'aint no merchantman, never carry more 'an topsails. You're on a man-of-war now."

Bosun Lasco was short and walked with an almost simian roll. Burly, despite his size, he was clearly not one to be challenged. In his belt was a length of square sennett braided with stout rope, finished off with a star knot, making a flexible and sturdy club, stained brown either by dirt or blood. Lasco turned his head slightly and looked up at Johnny as they walked.

"How'd you get that scar?"

"Gift from a Frenchman, just before I blow'd him to hell," Johnny replied. "Sailed a privateer in the last war."

"Ever sail Navy?"

"No, but I can serve a gun with the best of 'em."

"Well, we'll see about that."

The bosun led Johnny down the ladder to the gun deck. The order and discipline of the upper deck ended at the ladder. The deck, bulwarks, and overhead were painted blood red so as not to alarm the crew when their blood was spattered about in a sea action. Now, it reminded Johnny of either a Surinam whorehouse or a cattle pen, or perhaps a bit of each.

The deck was crowded with sailors relaxing as best they could, the off watch sitting on sea chests between the carriages of the four and twenty-pound guns and wherever there was space on deck, enjoying the faint breeze from the open gun ports. Some slept, but most talked, carved or mended clothing in their few free hours. In the center of the deck, between the main and fore mast, the sail maker and his assistant worked mending a staysail, robbing the seaman of what little space there was.

The crew was a ragged bunch, with a goodly share, by all appearances, of the Lord Mayor's men - drunks and roustabouts donated by the Lord Mayor of London to clear his jails and city streets of troublemakers. Johnny guessed that most of the rest were pressed men long resigned to their fate. A few of the number may even have been young volunteers, their heads turned by grand stories of adventure and gold, only to regret their folly within a day of signing on.

Scattered among the sailors like flowers in flotsam were the "ladies" of the port, sitting on the deck among the crew, talking, drinking, often as not with sewing spread across their laps. One dark eyed lass mending a pair of torn breeches gave a low whistle and smiled as Johnny and the bosun passed only to be backhanded by the sailor sitting next to her. "Got no call," she began, stopping when she saw the look in her sailor's eyes. She shrugged and got back to her needle and thread.

The bosun stopped between two guns near midship. "Mess where you like. Stow your gear and get your hammock." A weathered sailor stood up and walked over. "Smithers here'll show you the ropes."

Smithers was about Johnny's age with hair just beginning to gray. "From that bruise on ye head, looks like the press gang found ye."

"Young lady's father. And her brothers besides. Thought it best if I shipped out."

Smithers hooted. "Lord in heaven, a volunteer. Either crazy or stupid. Know that to be true, cause I volunteered myself, four years back." He smiled, his face a maze of weathered wrinkles. "I called it huntin' and the gamekeeper called it poachin'."

Johnny looked around. He hadn't seen Thom on board and was beginning to worry. "Luck there is still room for a volunteer. I hear the press gang's been out. "

"Number that took French-leave 'n scalliwagged ashore, there's no worry there," Smithers replied.

"How many pressed men they get this time?"

"Dozen or so, hear tell. Got in quite a scrap on shore, I hear. Would have gotten more otherwise."

"Where are the pressed men, do you reckon?"

Smithers laughed. "Lower hold, most like. You Yanks got a lot a fight in ya, so they is giv'n 'em a few days to cool down."

Part of Johnny still hoped that Thom had escaped the press and was hiding somewhere ashore. Deserting wouldn't be easy and he would be just as happy to try it alone.

He opened his sea chest, took off his jacket and shoved it in. Smithers stood not far behind him looking into the chest. "Got enough gear for two men there," he commented with a laugh.

Truer than you know, Johnny thought. "A pack rat. Never stay long enough one place to leave anything behind." He closed the chest and locked it.

Johnny found a place to sit, to pass the time and watch and listen. He was now a member of the starboard watch, but he didn't know which division. He heard four clangs from the ship's bell over the sound of scrubbing from the deck above. It was the afternoon watch and in two hours he would turn to with the rest of the starboard watch as the larboard watch filed below to take their ease.

Johnny turned toward Smithers who sat leaning against a gun carriage. "So, ship's had a lot of runners, have you?"

Smithers laughed. "Let us all have shore leave when we first got here and half the crew fell in love and didn't come back. Offered bounties to the shore folk for turning in sailors who run, but didn't do no good. Way it was if it kept up, I thought I'd find myself alone on this barky. Got her sealed up tight now. Nets on deck, guards fore an' aft. Even got a boat load of Marines rowin' about all day and night to stop swimmers. Tighter than a virgin's legs. I hadn't planned on running m'self, o' course."

"Course not. Me, I'm more worried 'bout what's ashore than what's on this ship."

"She's not a bad ship. Tough sometimes, everything Bristol fashion, but do your duty and you'll be all right." Smithers looked around. "Gotten crowded here, last few days. Lieutenants gave up their cabins for the Customsmen. They shifted to the master and mates cabins, who threw out the midshipman, who shifted the bosun and his mates onto the gun deck, where they're crowding in on us. Everything'll back to normal when Customs moves back out to Castle Island in a few days, or so I hear tell."

Johnny smirked. When he helped burn Harrison's boat he hadn't expected to be sharing quarters with him on a man-of-war.

At eight bells, Johnny, Smithers and the rest of the starboard watch paraded, over one hundred sailors pouring onto the deck. Lieutenant Dudingston walked over to Johnny, followed by Bosun Lasco, with Midshipman Paulings taking up the rear.

Johnny snapped to a rough attention when the officer approached. "So here is our killer of Frenchmen. More likely a barroom brawl. Now, what shall we do with you, Mr. Saunders?"

"Always sailed topman, sir."

It appeared that the lieutenant hadn't expected an answer to his question, but wasn't wholly displeased with the response.

"Topman, indeed. Not too old for that sort of thing? Think you can still move fast enough?"

"Yes, sir."

"Then topman it is." Lieutenant Dudingston looked toward the bosun, who said, "Mainmast." The lieutenant nodded his agreement and moved down the line.

Bosun Lasco lagged behind. Standing close to Johnny he said, under his breath, "You bloody well better fly up that rigging like a bird wit' his tail feathers a'fire, or you'll deal wit' me."

Johnny smiled down at him. "Yes, sir. Like a bird, sir." He only hoped he chosen the right division. If he and Thom were on different watches and different divisions they might see each other only in passing, just another two of the three hundred or so souls crowded onto the *Romney*.

Of the five divisions, he figured that the pressed men would not be assigned to the foredeck, which was usually saved for the oldsters, the more experienced if less agile sailors. The topmen were the elite, clambering over the rigging, setting and reefing the sails. Most of the pressed men were likely to be made waisters, hauling on halyards and sheets in the waist of the ship, between the quarterdeck and the fo'c's'le. Thom, as a sailor and a young one at that, would more likely be made a topman, but a waister was still possible. Didn't seem likely that a pressed man would be made either afterguard or idler. So topman, it had to be, or so Johnny hoped.

He had no more time to think about it as he was handed a bucket of tar and a brush and told to attend to the main top futtock shrouds.

"Aye, aye, sir," Johnny replied and scampered up the mainmast, careful not spill a drop of the hot tar and spent the rest of the watch retarring shrouds that already had altogether too much tar on them and enjoying the view of Boston harbor. The shore seemed tantalizingly close, yet as he watched he saw that Smithers was right. A longboat full of Marines rowed slowly by, going nowhere, just watching the ship. He looked aft at the

Liberty, a fine trim little ship, probably to be auctioned off by the Admiralty court unless Hancock's lawyers found a means to return it to their master.

He went back to tarring, half-heartedly, more concerned with not dripping tar than protecting the already encrusted shrouds. The problem with a warship sitting at anchor, with a full crew, sufficient to fight all guns and maneuver under sail, was that there was nothing to do except paint, tar and drill. No wonder so many had run off.

At the end of the watch, he hurried below, hot and thirsty. Smithers and two others he hadn't met were all waiting expectantly. The mess cook carried over the pot of bully beef and hard tack to the table set up between the guns. As he put it down the purser rang the bell and a fifer took up "Nancy Dawson." Soon the entire deck was singing and the messman hurried back for the tub of grog dispensed from the purser's barrel. An evening's half-pint of rum cut with two pints of water was handed out and each man drank quickly.

Johnny felt better about the world. When he tapped his hard tack a division of weevils escaped, scurrying in all directions across the table. The bully beef had a green tinge and challenged his teeth to chew through. It didn't matter. He would get off this ship and if Thom was on board he'd take him along. It might take patience and watching but they would get ashore to freedom.

❖❖❖

The other pressed men talked softly among themselves, saying less and less with time. One man named Michael Skinner, at the far end of the hold, wept freely at first and now sobbed to himself. He was a weaver out celebrating when the press gang grabbed him. "I never drank. Never spent my money on porter, but I had a new son, my first, my only son. Seemed worth raising a toast for. Named him Robert. Now I may never see him or Mary again." He broke into tears, repeating the names of his wife and son. Other voices in the hold tried to cheer him up. "Ach, you'll get back to 'em. Have a fine sea voyage, you will." "Things 'll turn out, always do." Their words were hopeful yet their tone betrayed the truth. After that there were long periods of silence, save the sound of Michael's misery, and when someone spoke it was at little more than a whisper.

If his mind wasn't playing tricks on him, Thom thought that they had been in chains for two days when the grating was lifted and a short man jumped down, growling that they had better behave themselves, as he began unlocking their leg irons. They each crawled out, except for one man too weak to jump up to the hatchway, who Thom and one of his fellows helped lift to the deck above.

They staggered onto the orlop deck and so up the ladders to the main deck, the sunlight blinding after the darkness of the hold. Officers in blue awaited them, accompanied by the faded scarlet of the Marines at attention, muskets at the ready. The small man swung a short rope club at one of the pressed men and shouted, "Toe the line there." The line shifted, each man lining the toes of his shoes with the same seam running along the deck. Thom felt dizzy and confused, his legs shaky from inactivity. The short man, who Thom assumed was the bosun, yelled, "Take off your shirts, you stinkin' bastards. An' hurry up or I'll rip 'em off ya."

The men, in a ragged line, struggled to comply, pulling off their shirt or smocks, unsteadily, as if their arms weren't fully under their command. A bent man in a dirty black coat and a cane, slowly walked the length of the line, looking each man up and down, poking occasionally with the head of his cane, mumbling a question here and there. When the man stood before him, Thom saw the permanent flush of the bent man's complexion, the thousands of tiny capillaries in his face blooming like furze on a snow field. Thom could smell stale rum, suggesting either a village drunk or ship's doctor, depending on the setting.

He barely glanced at Thom, then passed to the next man in the row, seeming to spend less time with each as if he wanted to escape the summer sun. At the end of the row, the doctor walked aft and said, "All fit for duty, Captain. Bit of cleaning up, they'll be fine."

"Thank you, Dr. Matthews." Thom turned his head and saw the Captain, a rotund man in a fine blue coat with brass buttons, a white waistcoat, breeches, and stockings. Next to him stood a tall blond officer. "Mr. Fleming," the Captain called, "the shillings."

Purser Fleming, a small squinting sort, didn't seem any fonder of sunlight than Doctor Matthews. He carried a purse on his belt and a large ledger under one arm. "Give me your hand," he demanded of the first man in line. He reached into the purse and pressed a shilling into the outstretched palm, then moved down the line pressing a shilling into each man's hand, pausing at the end of the line to count heads and record the amount in his ledger book.

Thom looked down at the shilling in his hand and wanted to throw it back at the purser, to scream, "No" at the top of his lungs and dive for the ship's rail, imagining that he would move faster than the Marine guards. Instead, he closed his eyes and murmured a silent curse. The shilling had been pressed in his hand. He was now officially a pressed man as if the blow to his head from a Navy cudgel days before weren't enough.

"I am Captain Corners." The Captain roared in a voice meant to carry over the thunder of guns in a sea fight and now to intimidate the new "recruits" lined up before him. "You've taken the King's shilling and are now members of the crew of His Majesty's Ship *Romney.* Do your duty to your king and to the ship and you'll be rewarded with fair treatment. Fail to do your duty and you'll face the consequences. Mr. Dudingston, the muster book if you please."

Lieutenant Dudingston walked with the bosun, recording each man's name and home, noting any tattoos or other distinguishing marks. The bosun measured each man's head and chest which the lieutenant also took down.

"Name," the Lieutenant demanded.

"Excuse me, sir. There's been a mistake. I'm not eighteen yet, sir and I'm the mate from the Brig *Mary Ellen*. Sailed in as captain after the master died. I can't be pressed as a seaman, sir."

Dudingston looked up. "You appear to be eighteen to me. Sailed Captain, you say?" He raised an eyebrow. "You damn colonials don't know your place. I don't care if you're the Queen mum, you're crew now. Name?"

"But, sir."

In what seemed to be a single move, the bosun pulled his from his belt and struck Thom in the temple with a blinding blow, sending him crumpling to the deck.

"Get to your feet, you worthless piece of scum," the bosun hissed, leaning over as Thom struggled to get up. "Talk back once more to the Lieutenant and you'll get far worse than a love tap to your noggin."

"Name," the lieutenant demanded.

"Thomas La.." He stopped himself. "Lewis, sir. Thomas Lewis of Boston, sir." The bosun measured his chest and then yanked the cord tight around Thom's battered head, causing him to wince.

The lieutenant was ready to move on to the next man but paused for a moment. He glanced back to at Thom and said almost casually, "You know, Mister Lewis, I really don't like Americans. Dr. Johnson said you are a race of convicts, and ought to be thankful for anything short of hanging. He was right, you know. You should keep that in mind."

The Purser's assistant followed behind, dropping a bundle of clothes at each man's feet and demanding a signature or mark on his ledger. Thom's head still spun as he signed for the gear, seeing grimly that he'd been charged three guineas for clothing worth a quarter the amount. He felt the weight of the King's bloody shilling, still in his hand and once again fought the urge to use it as a weapon, to throw it hard enough to split the skull of the Purser's Mate. But there was nothing to be done. Standing there under the guns of the Marines, the sun boiling his brain, it was all Thom could do to keep from swooning.

❖❖❖

Johnny had a bad night. The regulation distance between hammocks was 14 inches, which wasn't so bad at sea when one watch was always on deck, but with port watches all the sailors got a night's sleep crammed hanging in their hammocks. They were packed together like hanging beef in an icehouse. Next to Johnny, a sailor he didn't know and who Johnny damned to hell under his breath several times during the night, snored loudly and rolled about in his hammock, jostling Johnny with a knee or an elbow at every turn. And if that wasn't enough, one of the Boston "wives" a few hammocks away decided to play pinch and tickle with her fancy man just as Johnny was drifting off to sleep again. The sailors weren't allowed to go ashore but married men could invite their "wives" aboard and dozens of willing women, usually the same ones who came aboard the last Royal Navy ship to call the port, boarded just before dusk to visit their beloved husbands and protectors. Johnny had been at sea three months before signing on the *Romney* and the sound of a woman's laughter wasn't conducive to restful sleep.

At four AM the bosun and his mates blew their shrill whistles on the gun deck. "Starboard Watch Ahoy. Sleepers rouse out there. Out or down. Show a leg. Out or down," they yelled. The bosun's mates had their knives out and they cut the lashings of the hammocks of the men slow to wake, dumping them on the deck. The women in the hammocks were left alone, provided they stuck one leg out of the hammock to show their gender. Johnny rolled out of his hammock. He'd slept fully dressed and landed on his feet. He unhooked his hammock and scrambled off with the rest of the watch to begin the morning holystoning the decks and polishing the brass in the pale light before the dawn. At eight they broke for a breakfast of burgoo, a coarse almost inedible oatmeal, and Scotch coffee, burnt bread boiled in water, sweetened with a little sugar. He dozed most of the off watch.

At the start of the afternoon watch, Bosun Lasco called the Mainmast topmen together. "Now that you have a strapping volunteer to help you, let's see how well you dance. You have fifteen minutes to strike the t'gallant yard and rig it on deck. Take longer you lose the evening's grog." He pulled out his watch. "Go."

The mast captain, a tall Yorkshireman named Andrews, gave Johnny a withering look before they all scrambled up the ratlines. At the main top, he yelled, "You, Saunders, cast off the sheets, bunts, bowlines and clews. Make 'em fast to the cross-tree, and mind the bloody halyard," as the other topmen rigged the jack block around the t'gallant mast. "Work faster, you useless bastard," the mast captain barked, though Johnny had just cast off the last buntline. "Now all heave." Johnny helped guide the heavy yard as it swung out, seemingly ready to fall into space and down to the deck, one hundred and forty feet below, but the other topmen hauled to lower it slowly, stopping to secure the halyard for the longest part of the trip down. One man careened down a backstay to ease the mast onto the deck, careful not to gouge the sanded teak.

Johnny and the rest followed him and lined up before the bosun, who clicked his watch shut. "Close enough. Now rig it back. An' all the running gear better be set right and proper."

At the end of the watch, Johnny was exhausted. His shirt was soaked in sweat and clung to his skin. He knew that he had passed. Andrews, the mast captain, had nodded his way after they had rerigged the spar, the other topmen were beginning to call him by name. The bosun seemed truly disappointed when they set-up the t'gallant yard almost as quickly as they had struck it down just minutes before.

He drank a gill of water at the scuttle, swallowing quickly, not looking at the bitter greenish swill from the cask, and sat down determined to take his ease. He heard murmuring and saw a bedraggled clump of men, herded like so many Guernseys, flowing down the ladder to the gun deck.

Johnny looked for Thom and was shocked by what he saw. It wasn't that Thom seemed in bad shape for being locked in the hold for a few days. It was more the look in his eyes, a wild dazed look of rage, a deep glow like a slow match ready to set off a keg of powder. Johnny was glad now that he had volunteered. His job would be more than just getting himself and Thom off the ship, it would be keeping them alive while they were on board, keeping the glowing spark from reaching the charge until they needed it, as surely they would.

Thom didn't see him as he sent to a mess forward. Johnny got up and called to the bosun as he turned to leave. "Scuse me, sir. One of the pressed men, sir. Thom, an old shipmate of mine. Fine young lad, sir, but something of a temper. Might be able to help him settle in, so to speak. There is room at my mess, sir."

"All right, Saunders." Lasco smiled. "Your responsibility now. Any trouble with the young whore's son and you both get the lash." He stepped closer. "Don't trust you, Saunders. Never trusted volunteers." He laughed. "Course never trusted pressed men either." He turned and climbed the ladder to the main deck.

Thom sat slumped on deck forward. When he looked up and saw Johnny, he closed his eyes and held his head.

"Saddens me sorely to see you, Johnny. I thought you'd escaped. Damn them all."

"Keep your voice down, for God's sake", Johnny said in a hush. "Come on with me now." With a strong hand he lifted Thom to his feet and walked him back midships. "Got to learn to keep your feelings to yourself," he said at not more than a whisper. "Three hundred men, boys and whores on this ship and I swear there's a thousand ears. Anything said for'ad makes its way aft quicker than you'd know."

"Good to see you anyway, Johnny. When did they get you?" Thom asked keeping his voice low.

Johnny smirked. "Never got me. I volunteered."

Thom's eyes widened and his face grew ashen. "Have you gone entirely mad?"

"You aren't the first to suggest it. No, you promised to teach me to navigate and I'm not about to let you run out on your promise." He lowered his voice. "We are getting off this ship, Thom. It'll take time, patience and luck, but we're getting off. That I'll promise you."

CHAPTER FIVE

After twenty years at sea, Johnny could call a change in the weather without looking at the storm glass, could sense whether the wind would clock or veer and judge the set of the current by the look of the wake. A ship had its own rhythms, just like the sea, usually as simple and predictable as pork on Sunday, beef on Saturday, and grog when the beer ran out.

Yet within a week aboard the *Romney*, Johnny felt himself a fool. He had been so certain when he came aboard that that he could watch out for Thom and find a way for them to escape. How difficult could it be to slip away from a ship at anchor so close to Boston town? Yet, the *Romney* was different, a strange and dangerous ship. She seemed less a man-of-war than a teeming prison hulk, her inmates crowded together, restrained within her wooden walls by an odd blend of discipline and debauchery.

Even with stores boats and launches plying back and forth from the ship to the docks, with the docks tantalizingly close, the ship was sealed up tighter than miser's purse. Marine guards were posted fore and aft, and at midships, for good measure. A watch boat was constantly rowed around the ship in case anyone made it past the marines on deck. By all accounts, too many sailors had taken French leave and forgotten their way back. Now the officers took all measures to see that no more followed their example.

Still, there had to be a way to escape. It might take watching and patience to find their way off the barky, but Johnny swore to himself that they would.

In the meantime, he worried about his young friend. Johnny had given Thom the key to his sea chest and he knew that the young man felt better with his own gear, a tenuous connection to his past, but a connection none the less. He watched as Thom pulled his grandfather's Bible from the chest, ran his hand gently over the cover and smiled to himself.

Thom fit in well enough with the crew, but he didn't jump quite as fast as he should when the bosun yelled, and the look in his eyes remained defiant even when scrambling to do his duty. He was one of the best sailors among the pressed men. Young and agile, he swung through the rigging like an acrobat with only the most experienced topmen even trying to keep up. Yet, it was clear that he didn't fully understand the new world in which he found himself.

One day when the watch bell rang, and the din of the crew coming off watch blended with the crew going on deck, Johnny pulled Thom aside and said, "I can't do this alone."

"What in hell are you doing?" Thom snapped, "Always 'yes, sir', 'right away, sir', you sound like the damn bosun's toady."

"Listen to me now, Thomas. You're in the claws of a bear and you never, ever, fight the bear's claws. Give these bastards the slimmest reason and they'll make your life hell, flog the flesh off your back. Leave you a cripple, if they leave you breathing at all." He saw resistance flare in Thom's eyes, followed slowly by recognition. "You better start playing the jolly tar and happy blue jacket if you want to get off this ship. Put on a fine show of just how happy you are to sail in the King's Navy.

"And that's just to start. We need to keep our eyes open. You and I are gonna watch everything that goes on on this God-forsaken barge. Every boat that calls, everything delivered, everything taken away, every change of watch. We'll find a way off, but you have to stay out of trouble till we do."

Thom smirked and nodded his head, defiant but understanding, or so Johnny hoped.

"Do you know what they do to a pressed man who'se caught trying to run? A thousand lashes round the fleet," Johnny said fixing Thom with his gaze.

"That's a death sentence."

"It's meant to be. Lashed to a frame in a longboat, they row from ship to ship, slowly beating the bastard to death. A slower and uglier death you'll never find. So, we'll just be careful and bide our time."

Thom shrugged and walked over to the number 8 gun and slumped down in the spot where he had laid an informal claim. Johnny followed and sat beside him. For a time, neither spoke, then Thom glanced over at Johnny and half smiled.

"Carpe diem quam minimum credula postero," Thom said. Johnny only stared back at him.

"From Horace. 'Reap today's harvest, trust not tomorrow.'"

John shook his head. "You've got it wrong there. The Bible says, 'Tribulation worketh patience; and patience, experience and experience, hope.' Care not for today but trust in tomorrow. Time will show us the path."

Thom looked off. He made out the shores of Boston through the narrow space of the far gunport not blocked by the gun. The shore, teeming and alive like some great animal, might as well be a thousand leagues distant. He sighed, "Perchance you may be right. Still, let them beware the fury of a patient man."

Johnny looked over at his young friend. "Quotin' Horace, is it? And what is a scholar doin' aboard a man-a-war? Mighty fancy for a jack tar. "

Thom laughed, laughed for the first time in as long as he could recall. "That last bit was Dryden, not Horace. But no, no scholar here, my friend. Pretense may serve, lacking all else. You quote the Bible and I spout Latin doggerel and the English poets. What is a false scholar but a fool? All I've ever learned worth knowing, I learned on a ship or on the wharf. And look where I have ended up."

"But you've some proper education, anyhow. Mind, may prove more valuable than you now give it credit."

Thom turned, leaning against the gun carriage. "I doubt my father would think so. Years ago, he hired Mr. Webly, a minister who taught 'young gentlemen.' The minister came on my grandfather's recommendation. That was the year Great Awakening passed through Long Island and many a minister of the church found himself turned out by the zealots, or so my father would have called them. He thought that our Mr. Webly was one of their number and that by hiring him he was supporting traditional piety. My father's a great supporter of tradition.

"We began our studies every morning by singing the hundred and seventh psalm,

Oh give ye thanks unto the Lord,
Because that good is he,
Because his loving kindness lasts,
To perpetuity.

"For the first few months, my father would attend us as class began and would hear the singing of the psalm and feel content in his choice of instructor. He didn't realize until much later that my grandfather had recommended Mr. Webly because of his deistical beliefs. His parish turned him out for heresy, not tradition. He was particularly fond of the third verse of the psalm:

Then they did to Jehovah cry
when they were in distress;
Who did them set at liberty
Out of their anguishes.

"He said it spoke to us of our liberation from the Stuarts and of the Glorious Revolution itself. I do believe that he had more faith in the hand of man than in Jehovah. So in my schooling, I read Locke, Rousseau and Voltaire and several other gentlemen for whom my father has a particular antipathy.

"But, my father caught on. It wasn't so long before the Reverend Mr. Wembly was seeking other employment and I was back wielding an adz in the shipyard. So I am no scholar. I've memorized some Latin but am wholly innocent of Greek."

Johnny shook his head. "Wish I coulda' learned more. The only book I was ever instructed in was the Bible. Aunt Sarah said it was everything worth knowing, but I have my doubts."

"That's blasphemy, John."

"Aye, and not the first time neither."

❖❖❖

From then on, Thom spent his free time learning the ways of the Royal Navy ship, which was so very different from that of a merchantman. The lieutenants gave the orders, enforced by the petty tyranny of the midshipmen, supported by the rougher order of the bosun and his mates, with the Marines' muskets and bayonets as final guarantor of harmony.

On the gundeck, the sailors off-watch held sway, dividing the cramped spaces between their messes, entertaining the fair whores of Boston, who had been allowed aboard after swearing to be "wives" of sailors. They all remained as drunk as duty would permit on the ship's grog rations and the Boston kill-devil rum smuggled from ashore by their sweethearts. Thom kept close to Johnny and tried to blend in, an easy enough undertaking.

The officers were content to keep the ship's people busy. In addition to the daily labor, on his knees scrubbing the decks white with holystones every morning, and all the tending to the rigging that was the topman's inevitable lot, Thom settled into the ship's daily routines.

Tuesday was gunnery practice, when the great guns were cast loose from their lashings and rattled back and forth in mock earnest, play acting a battle at sea - a grand dumb show. They couldn't fire powder, of course, anchored with Boston town so close alongside. There were problems enough ashore without the town radicals claiming that they were under attack from naval guns. Still, from the looks of it, Thom doubted that the *Romney* often practiced live firing.

The allotment for powder was tightly controlled and a good captain spent his own coin to provide practice powder, but Thom quickly concluded that Captain Corners was not such a captain. The service of the guns was the only reason for three hundred souls to be crowded aboard the ship, yet even to Thom's untrained eye, they seemed poor servants indeed. He hoped that he and Johnny got away before the *Romney* ever had cause to fight her guns because Tuesday practices told him that they would be blown to bits by any ship whose crew understood gunnery.

It wasn't wholly time wasted. Johnny had learned of guns and gunnery on a privateer and taught Thom what he could. Smithers, Wilkins and the others in their gun crew quickly began to pay close attention to Johnny's instructions until their gun seemed to move with its own grace and they waited for an instant for the command to feign firing while the other guns caught up. Midshipman Paulings, nominally in command of the battery, drifted down toward their gun to listen as Johnny called out the commands in hushed tones.

Wednesday was musketry practice where the ship's company were issued guns from the ship's armory and again play acted at firing, against the day when the ship's force might need to support the Marines in an assault ashore. Thom held the heavy sea-service musket in his hands, both wishing that he had ball and shot and grateful that he did not. It would be sorely tempting to blow a hole in one of the ship's officers.

On Thursdays, the hammocks were hauled up, aired and the gun deck was scrubbed with vinegar, holystoned, flogged and sanded. Nevertheless, the deck still smelled foul even after their careful attention.

The other days, except half of Sunday when the deck was rigged for church, were endless rounds of scrubbing and painting. The Sunday sermon by the ship's chaplain was easy enough to ignore, but dozing off was rewarded by a hard colting from the bosun's rope end. Johnny bought a blue jacket and ship's bonnet from the slop chest and saw to it that Thom did the same, as the Captain expected his crew to dress in "good and proper attire" for Sunday services. At the end of the service they stood for inspection, all in blue jackets and white duck trousers, ship's caps with velvet ribbons marked HMS *Romney* fluttering in the breeze.

At the end of services, Captain Corners and his officers in dress uniforms and powdered wigs, inspected the ship, looking for any flaw, be it tarnish on the brasswork, a halyard frayed or not coiled properly or a crewman's trousers not quite spotless. Any infraction was rewarded the next day when the grating was rigged for punishment and some poor soul had the life nearly beat from him by the bosun's cat, usually for something that wasn't his fault.

Captain Corners was a pompous buffoon, an opinion Thom suspected most of the crew shared with him, but none would dare breath. First Lieutenant William Dudingston, following close behind the captain, was a dangerous bastard. A Scotsman, he was handsome in a nondescript sort of way, with cold blue eyes and blond hair. Still in his middle twenties, with a father in Parliament and with extensive lands, he had connections with the Admiralty, or so Thom pieced together from whispers on the gun deck. Much of what was properly Captain Corner's duties, he deferred to his first lieutenant and young Dudingston latched hold of the power as if it were his birthright. If arrogance were ability, Dudingston would have been a superb captain, a role he clearly relished.

Thom had barely seen the ship's Master, Joshuah Finney, who looked drunk those few times that he had made an appearance. His responsibilities and authority, save perhaps supervision of the spirit locker, also seemed to have been taken over by Dudingston.

The other three lieutenants, bringing up the rear of the inspection, weren't so bad, Thom decided. They even went easy on the pressed men, assuming them all to be landsmen.

Second Lieutenant Harold Lester, a tall and lanky officer, was easy going, more likely to smile than scowl, not troubled by Captain Corner's haughtiness or Lieutenant Dudingston's sarcasm. Following behind him was Third Lieutenant Marcus Adams, a small man and a nervous sort, the object of much of Lester's mirth. Adams always walked frenetically as if someone was in pursuit. During the inspection, he slowed to Lester's pace yet, still glanced about furtively. Fourth Lieutenant Samuel Perkins, a master's mate promoted to lieutenant in the last war, still seemed unable to believe his good fortune and had no ambition for loftier rank. His uniform didn't fit him properly and a shock of red hair stuck out at an odd angle from beneath his hat. He followed casually and was more familiar with the crew than an officer should be, which earned the disdain of both the crew and his fellow officers.

❖ ❖ ❖

When he could, Thom took it upon himself to help the some of the other pressed men, particularly Michael Skinner, the forlorn weaver, who was hopeless at everything except scrubbing the deck. Bosun Lasco gleefully colted Skinner for offenses real and imagined, leaving him bloodied and barely standing, and Thom went out of his way to help Skinner clean up, telling him softly how the halyards should be coiled, how the sheets were led in the waist, giving him what little instruction that he could in ways of the sea that to the confused weaver were as foreign as if Thom had been speaking in Persian.

The small kindness was noted by the first lieutenant and attracted the bosun's wrath. Dudingston had taken a dislike to Thom, who didn't lower his eyes as the first lieutenant passed but rather fixed his gaze as if confronting an equal. The bosun took

Dudingston's dislike as a signal to harass Thom, to try to wear
him down, to see what it would take to break him. At change of
watch, Lasco would come up behind Thom and strike him behind
the ear with his hemp starter, then scream as Thom staggered,
"Move faster you lazy bastard or I'll have you on the grating this
forenoon."

The bosun also saved tasks normally left for the ship's boys to
Thom. "Lewis, the manger needs a cleaning and bes' make it
spotless if you don't want me to move your mess up wit' the
hogs." Thom would pause for a moment then take a bucket
forward to the manger where the two remaining ship's pigs were
kept, now more as pets than provisions, and begin swabbing out
the manure and rotting slops.

The treatment was picked up by the bosun's mates and the
midshipmen, but sharp looks from the mast captain, Patrick
Andrews, cooled the midshipmen's ardor, preferring not to cross
the old sailor.

Patrick Andrews was a weathered sailor, looking older than
his thirty-eight years. He had sailed Royal Navy since he was
twelve, a street urchin snatched from the gutters. He held no real
title and drew the same seaman's wages as the rest, yet he was the
"captain of the main top" and not one to be crossed. "You'll mess
with us from now on," he announced to Thom and Johnny one
afternoon. "I'll speak with the bosun. You're topmen. No business
messing with waisters. Besides, you've got a white mouse next to
ye," he said looking over toward Zebulon Smithers.

Johnny looked over and immediately felt the fool. Smithers, a
white mouse, a narker, the bosun's ears – an informer? He was
only glad that he and Thom had been careful when talking.

Johnny and Thom moved their gear forward to where other
topmen messed. The choice of messmates was almost the only
choice a sailor could make on a man of war and it felt good to be
with the other topmen, who thought of themselves as the princes
of the gundeck and scorned the waisters and the afterguard.

The shift in their mess eased the harassment by the bosun's mates but not the bosun. Bosun Lasco was undeterred by Andrews and seemed to enjoy trying to push Thom beyond the edge.

"Driving me crazy, Johnny. I can obey orders, but damn, the bosun never lets up riding me. Came close to talking back to him this morning. Hell, I came close to swinging at him."

"That's just what he wants you to do."

❖❖❖

The worst time of the day was evening muster when the drums would roll and the fifes would play and the whole ship's company would assemble for inspection. Thom wasn't sure whether the evening grog ration made it better or worse, whether the rum eased the pain or made him more homesick. The fifes always played "Heart of Oak" and Midshipman Paulings would sing the words in his clear reedy soprano voice as Lieutenant Dudingston looked on smiling.

> *Come cheer up me lads, tis to glory we steer,*
> *to add something new to this wonderful year.*
> *To honor we call you, not press you like slaves,*
> *for who are so free as the sons of the waves.*
> *Heart of Oak are our ships, jolly tars are our* men ...."

Some of the crew sang along softly, even some of the pressed men would join in and sing "to honor we call you, not press you like slaves," as if the words themselves had no meaning, entirely caught up in anticipation of the grog, the roll of drums and the infectious tune squealed out by the fifes.

Thom wanted to scream, to shout out at how meaningless the vaunted "rights of Englishmen" were if a sailor could be snatched from the street with no more rights than a stray cat. Instead, all he could do was stare straight ahead and try not to let his face show his feelings as Dudingston and the rest paraded by, looking him up and down like a horse at auction.

Eventually, even Thom came to smile as the rum tub was rolled out and the purser mixed the soothing drink in accordance with the doggerel – one of sour, two of sweet, three of strong, four of weak –as he ladled the lime juice, sugar, black rum and water into the tub. The grog always made things better for a time but the glow didn't last.

There were times, late at night when Thom would wake and somehow mercifully have forgotten where he was. When he felt the press of other hammocks against his and he again remembered his situation, tears would come to his eyes. In the cocoon of his hammock, the only privacy to be found on the cursed ship, he let himself cry softly until sleep again took him away.

In the gray morning, he tried to keep up his spirits, but he found it hard to avoid slipping back into the blackest funk. Still, he wouldn't give up. They would escape in time. Whether this was true, he wasn't sure, but he would repeat it to himself until it was.

And like Johnny, he watched. He watched the guards on deck, the officers, the warrant and the petty officers. He watched as the lieutenants inspected the women coming aboard, checking each woman for smuggled liquor, making sure she wasn't stealing anything going ashore.

Lieutenant Adams was a stickler for propriety. He made each woman swear that she was the properly married wife of her chosen sailor, even so far as refusing those permission to go aboard who forgot their beloved's name. "He's kinda tall, like, with sorta sandy hair. You know the one," earned the unfortunate "wife" a row back to shore.

Lieutenant Perkins allowed only the prettiest aboard without a shilling slipped into his pocket and would not bother to examine melons or bales of laundry with spirits hidden inside, provided that another coin found his palm.

Thom watched the gig in its regular trips carrying the Captain to dine ashore and to visit other Navy ships calling the harbor and the bum-boats coming alongside trying to sell jewelry and soap to the crew. He kept an eye on the purser and the cooks and provisioning boats.

For several days Thom stopped trying to think. His mind was filled with schemes yet for these weeks all had come to naught. He was sitting by an open gunport on the gun deck when the marine sentinel boat pulled alongside. He heard voices.

"A long time since breakfast, in'it?"

"And what you complaining 'bout? You weren't rowing like no bleeding galley slave, now were ye?"

Out of the corner of his eye Thom saw the wash boat with Aunt Molly hauling on her oars. Aunt Molly was a rather rotund woman who rowed out every few days to pick up and deliver officer's laundry. Rather than hire a water clerk to row her out like the other women aboard, she rowed her own skiff.

"Will you bloody lobsters get your bloody boat away from the damned gangway?" she bawled. "What's a fine lady to do, if'in' I can't get aboard cause your fat arses are in the way?"

The marines laughed. "Sorry Auntie, just coming in for a bite of lunch. Don't have anything against lunch now do you?"

"Don't have nothing against nothing. Just move the bloody boat, ye bloody bastards."

The marines laughed, scampered up the battens and paid out the line letting their launch drift back to make room for Aunt Molly.

Thom sat up and quickly walked over to the ladder and began the climb to the weather deck. He got there just as Molly was heaving herself on board and pulling up a great bale of clean laundry behind her.

"Here, help an old lady," Molly said as she dropped the first bundle into the arms of Midshipman Morris, who stumbled and seemed to disappear under it.

Lt. Perkins was standing close by, chuckling when a second bundle swung his way. "You can help too. No need standing by while a lady struggles now."

Together the midshipman and lieutenant stumbled into the main cabin prodded by Aunt Molly, much to the delight of all on deck.

Thom smiled like all the rest, but for an entirely different reason. Time to consult his Bible, then have a chat if he could manage it with Aunt Molly before she departed.

❖❖❖

"I've found it, John. The way out." Thom spoke softly.

"Really?" Johnny bent closer.

"All arranged. Next Tuesday."

"Aunt Molly brought the officer's laundry today. Caused quite a stir on deck. Did you see?"

"Can't say that I did but I've seen her before. Knows how to throw her weight around, and she has a good bit to throw. But what's that have to do with anything?"

"Next Tuesday she's coming back and just like today she is going to arrive just as the Marine's launch is tied up for lunch." Thom paused.

"Go on."

"When she creates enough confusion you and I are going to take her boat and cut the painter on the launch. If we are fast enough we'll be a shore before they notice a thing. It has all been arranged."

Johnny suppressed a smile. "Might just work. How did you get Aunt Molly to play along?"

"Aunt Molly is a righteous woman, and fond of shiny coins," Thom replied with a wry grin.

The next week moved slowly. When Tuesday finally arrived Thom tried to stay calm. The rest of his gear in Johnny's sea chest would be forfeit but he stuck his grandfather's bible in his belt.

Just before lunch, he watched as the marine guard boat pulled toward the *Romney* and smiled as he saw Aunt Molly rowing out as if on queue.

Suddenly Thom heard the drums beating to quarters and squeal of the fifes. He stood, dumbstruck as men rushed around him. He saw Aunt Molly's skiff bump along side only to hear the lieutenant shout, "Cast off, away with ye. Come back tomorrow." The lieutenant pointed off toward the horizon.

Thom looked up. A small fleet of warships and transports was standing into the harbor. The occupation of Boston had begun.

CHAPTER SIX

The drums beat General Quarters and the crew ran for their stations. Thom and Johnny fell in with the rest scampering up the ratlines to their places in the main top. On the foredeck a spring line was rigged to the anchor rode and led aft. "Heave her round boys," the bosun shouted, and the waisters hauled in long straight pulls, turning the ship till she was beam on to the town. "Belay," the bosun called. The drum beat again and the waist crew ran for their places on the gun deck.

Seven ships moved down channel in a stately procession. The *Asia*, a two deck 74-gun ship of the line led, followed by four transports. The 74 gun *Prescott* and the frigate *Scarborough* of 28 guns brought up the rear.

The *Asia*, *Scarborough* and the *Prescott* anchored north of the *Romney* and warped themselves around in siege formation, so that in an hour all of Boston was under the guns of the Royal Navy. The transports, anchored behind, began discharging their troops in longboats and barges. Regiments of crimson with white sashes and black tri-corned hats began forming up at the landing and marched off into town. As Johnny and Thom watched from the yards, more boats and more soldiers continued to land, a flooding tide of red uniforms, flashing silver and bronze.

The sound of fifes and singing wafted over the water. From one of the transports, boatloads of tall men in yellow trimmed coats and high bearskin hats were pulled toward the docks -- Grenadiers. They sang boldly as they formed up on the dock.

Some talk of Alexander,
and some of Hercules
Of Hector and Lysander,
and such great names as these.
But of all the world's great heroes,
there's none that can compare
With a tow, row, row, row, row, row,
to the British Grenadier.

The Empire's finest, they formed lines, four abreast and marched off beneath a flourish of banners and the beat of drums. Behind them came the Light Infantry with blue and buff sashes, trained in American forests in the last war, vanquishing the French and their Indian allies. Now the cannon had turned around. They sang a song that Thom had not heard before:

"Yankee Doodle went to town a-riding on a pony
stuck a feather in his cap and called it macaroni."

The watch was over before they were told to stand down. For four hours they watched the flood of a thousand or more troops come ashore. That night fireworks erupted from Castle Island as Tory revelers sang Yankee Doodle boisterously into the night.

"Mind the music and the step
and with the girls be handy."

"The bastards are laughing at us," Thom thought.

The provisions boat returned the next day, loaded with stores, and carried away the empty casks. The water barrels were hoisted into the longboats and rowed up the River Charles to sweet water to be refilled. Stores, spars and equipment were brought aboard and secured in what seemed an endless progression. Joshua

Finney, ship's Master, regained his sobriety and attended to his duty supervising the storing of the holds and supplies.

Thom watched for Aunt Molly's return. There might still be a chance. She had taken his coin, but it was clear that that was an investment lost. She did not reappear among the flotilla of boats and barges that worked between the ships and the landing.

There might be another opportunity in another boat and Thom kept a weather eye but was always so busy, along with the rest of the crew, that he never saw another chance to get clean away.

The gun deck was abuzz with rumors of sailing for England, Halifax or the West Indies. Everything had to be done double quick now. The lieutenants, midshipmen and the bosun drove the crew with a new urgency. Lieutenant Lester's normally sunny disposition, if anything, brightened. "To sea, the only place for ships or sailors. Spread your sails and shake off the dry rot."

Lieutenant Adams seemed merely harried as he stormed about. "Not a moment to be lost. Move your lazy ass, move it there." Lieutenant Perkins seemed chagrined by the prospect of going back to sea, losing his petty income from the ladies at the gangway.

For some reason, First Lieutenant Dudingston spent much of the time ashore, leaving in full uniform in the mornings and returning in the afternoon looking grim and weary.

The gun deck was emptied, the women sent ashore, causing greater sorrow, it seemed, to the sailors than their beloved. The whole deck was scrubbed and loose gear stowed below. While the stench of the deck seemed unchanged, all was now well ordered. For the summer months the guns had been rolled out with their barrels protruding from the ports, in part to look suitably belligerent and in part for space and ventilation. Now they were snugged down for sea, the tackles hauled tight and the gunports caulked shut.

The *Romney* and the rest of the fleet were warped out to anchor off Castle Island and Thom's hopes shrank as the distance across the harbor grew. Instead of staring out at Boston as he had for months, he now tried not to look at *Asia*'s batteries or the continuous boats of soldiers and marines shuttling back and forth from Castle Island to shore.

For a time, nothing more happened, save a change in the weather. October arrived wet and cold, as unpleasant in its own right as an invading army, with its drum rolls of thunder and dreary cadence of rain. Beneath it all, Boston was quiet. The militia paraded listlessly on the Commons but nothing was heard from the interior. No great army of farmers had risen up to expel the new arrivals. The rebels melted away before the might of the British military.

For two weeks the *Romney* sat at anchor with the rest of the fleet glowering at Boston town beneath a gray canopy of clouds. Then, on a Tuesday morning, boats began returning from the landing, carrying not troops but the family, baggage, and effects of Governor Bernard. Now that Boston was freed from the grip of ruffians and the Customs agents, their families and Tory friends released from hostage on Castle Island, Francis Bernard was going home.

After days of loading the Governor's baggage, the Marines stood at attention at the break of the poop, while Captain Corner, the lieutenants, midshipmen and warrant officers stood in their best uniforms on the quarterdeck as the bosun piped Royal Governor Bernard, his family, and retinue on board to the sound of the ship's fifes and drums. Francis Bernard was returning to England after a stop at St. Kitts to see to his estates there, or so said the scuttlebutt on the gun deck.

On the morning tide, one month to the day after the start of the occupation, all hands were piped out to raise the anchor. HMS *Romney* stood out of the harbor on a southwesterly breeze. Thom and Johnny scrambled up the ratlines with the rest of the topmen to set sail. Thom moved mechanically, trying to think only of the tasks at hand - laying out on the yard, casting off the gaskets once the bunts and clews were eased. Only when the t'gallants filled did he allow himself to glance back at Boston, slowly slipping away in the distance.

❖❖❖

Johnny was next to Thom and looked over at him. He was surprised and slightly pleased to see no obvious anger or even sorrow in his young friend's face. Only a slight tightness in his jaw gave away a tension not normally to be seen.

Johnny felt his own anger and frustration well up. He'd been a fool to think that he could slip off with Thom and be back in a Boston tavern in a week's time. Four months later, with nothing but hard work, bad food and no prospect for escape, he too watched Boston slip below the horizon as they stood out into the broad Atlantic. The October sky was leaden and the wind cold as they climbed down from the cross-trees back to the main deck on the ship from which there was now no escape.

CHAPTER SEVEN

The weather and wind stayed fair but Lieutenant Dudingston was grim and angry, snapping at the master's mates and midshipman. Whatever caused his discomfort affected Lieutenant Lester as well. His good cheer, which had only grown with the preparations for sea, now seemed to vanish and while in any other man his spirits might have appeared merely somber, in Harold Lester they seemed almost funereal.

"What's with the officers?" Johnny asked of Andrews at the noonday meal. The old sailor laughed and said in a conspiratorial tone, "The captain's clerk says that Lieutenant Dudingston expected a commission on one of the revenue schooners fitting out in Marblehead. Was to 'ave his own command and a share of all the contraband seized. Sounds like his orders never came through. Hear tell that aft ain't a pleasant place to be right about now, what with all the officers losing their berths to the Guv'nor and his brood and no promotions on the way. If Dudingston left, all the other lieutenants might move up a peg. Ain't nobody's happy now."

Only a day out from Boston Light, at evening muster, just after supper, the drums beat to quarters. All hands ran to their stations for inspection. As the lieutenants and midshipman inspected the men and the guns, Master at Arms, Ned Lucas, trailed behind. As he passed Michael Skinner, the weaver smiled. Lucas hadn't seen anything but sorrow on Skinner's face since the man had been dragged aboard. He wondered where Skinner had gotten the extra ration of rum, perhaps bought or traded from a shipmate.

"You drunk, Skinner?"

"No, sir," he replied, still smiling, then with a slight roll of the ship, toppled over insensible. Crew fore and aft broke into laughter, stilled suddenly as Lieutenant Dudingston roared, "Enough. I'll show you how drunkards fare on this ship." He paused and looked about in the silence. In a voice softer but no less threatening, he said, "You're lazy and you're soft. I'll make a King's crew out of you if I have to flog every worthless whore's son of you." He motioned to Lucas, "Get that bastard below. Lock him in irons."

The next day at the end of the forenoon watch, the bosun piped all hands to witness punishment. Captain Corner stood to windward on the quarterdeck in dress uniform with Lieutenant Dudingston by his side. Dudingston's face was an imperious mask. Behind him the other lieutenants stood, their faces expressionless. The marines fell in at attention on the poop with their muskets and side arms in a wall of scarlet and white. The midshipman and the warrant officers gathered under the break of the poop while the rest of the crew clustered forward on the lee side of the ship along the booms, the boats, and the rail.

Captain Corner glanced about then ordered, "Rig the gratings."

The carpenter and his mate dragged two gratings from the main hatch and laid the first flat on the deck. They lashed the second upright to the ship's bulwark then the carpenter turned, said, "Gratings rigged, sir" and retired with his men. The Master at Arms brought Skinner on deck, half dragging him as he stumbled, and deposited him, standing unsteadily, before the Captain.

"Mr. Skinner, you have transgressed the Articles of War by wanton drunkenness on duty. Do you have anything to say?"

Michael Skinner raised his head and began to open his mouth, but read the stern look from the Captain, dropped his head and shook it.

"Strip." Skinner didn't react for a moment so a bosun's mate stepped up behind him and ripped his shirt from his back. Seeing the man's confusion, a small smile curled at the corner of Dudingston's mouth.

"Seize him up," the Captain ordered.

Two bosun's mates grabbed Skinner by each arm and dragged him against the upright grating. They lashed his arms with spun yard, cinching the cords tight against his pale skin. "Seized up, sir."

Captain Corner swept off his tricornered hat and pulled his copy of the Articles of War from his coat. In one smooth movement, the rest of the other officers doffed their hats as a show of respect to the Articles. Captain Corner droned on reading Article Two forbidding profane oaths, execration, drunkenness, uncleanliness and other scandalous actions "in derogation of God's honor, and corruption of good manners." Bosun Lasco stepped up as the Articles were being read and drew the red handled cat from a red baize bag.

Captain Corner finished ready and looked up. "Three dozen, Mr. Lasco."

A murmur passed through the ship's crew to which Dudingston barked, "Silence."

"Do your duty, Mr. Lasco." The bosun stepped forward and with the full sweep of his arm and the force of his upper body swung the cat, cutting diagonally across Skinner's back. Skinner screamed, the air driven from his lungs by the force of the blow, the knotted tails of the cat ripping the skin from his back. Lasco drew the cat between his fingers to wipe off the blood and then struck again. By the sixth blow, Skinner's entire back was bloodied and he wailed in agony, his cries rising and falling with each strike. At twelve lashes blood stained his breeches and his back was a horrid mass of deep cuts with strips of free hanging flesh. At two dozen lashes, Bosun Lasco stopped and his mate Stanford Neven, stepped up to relieve him and laid into Skinner's back with an ugly glee. When it was over, Skinner was cut down and Thom, Johnny and a messmate carried him below deck to the surgeon. They laid Skinner down gently. He was not quite conscious, moaning incoherently. Dr. Matthews, who was almost as drunk as Skinner had been when clapped in irons, looked down at the miserable wretch before him and said, "Ah, he'll be fine in a day or two."

That evening at supper, Andrews said, "Well, they nearly skinned Mr. Skinner."

"Three dozen, the bastards," Thom replied, his voice trailing off at the last word. Johnny looked over with a glance that said, "Watch yourself."

Andrews snorted. "Articles says a captain can only give a dozen lashes. Anybody in the Navy knows that well enough. Sending us a message, they are. They'll give as many lashes as they want. Do with us all as they please."

"Bastards," Thom said, so softly that word formed on his lips but made no sound.

The next morning the grating was rigged again, for a mess cook who spilled a pot of burgoo and earned a dozen lashes for his trouble. When it was over, the Captain spoke. "This ship was in port far too long. Your performance is sloppy and slothful. Starting today that will change. I have directed my officers to drill you to a suitable state of smartness. Anyone who does not do his duty will answer to me and the Articles of War." He nodded his head toward the still rigged grating.

That afternoon the off watch was called on deck and all hands practiced tacking the ship. Sailing Master Finney stood on the quarterdeck as the waisters and topmen stood at their posts. The midshipman, bosun and his mate were spread across the deck, keeping a sharp eye on the crew. Dudingston stood on the poop watching everyone. Thom and Johnny took their stations at the main braces.

"Shake out the running gear," Finney yelled and the waisters cast free the carefully coiled ends of the braces and the sheets. "Ready about," Finney shouted, then spoke a few words to the helmsman who turned the wheel a few spokes down, letting the ship bear off the wind to pick up speed. Finney waited a minute then roared "Raise tacks and sheets," then a moment later, "Helm's alee." The helmsman spun the wheel up and the ship slowly began to swing into the wind.

Forward, a midshipman yelled "Loose the head sheets," and three sailors cast off the lines controlling the jibs, spilling the wind, filling the air with the frantic flapping of canvas, while aft, the spanker was hauled flat. From bow to stern, the sails began to shiver, flapping wildly in the wind as the ship continued to round up.

In the flood of orders Thom paid attention only to his task. When Finney bellowed, "Mainsail haul," he and Johnny and a half dozen others hauled on the main braces, hand over hand, pulling the yard around. The mainsail backed, filling with a crack, helping to swing the bow through the eye of the wind. Bosun's mates ran along the length of the men hauling or paying out the braces, shouting and swinging their canes and rope ends at any sailor not hauling fast or hard enough.

"Jibs home to weather." The command was relayed forward by a dozen voices and the fo'c's'le crew sheeted the jib sails home, trying to catch the wind and pull the bow around. For a moment the sails began to draw and but then the wind shifted, the jibs fluttered then backed and began to pull the bow the other way. "Loose the headsails, damn it!" Finney shouted in frustration as he saw what was happening. They had stopped swinging into the wind and now agonizingly slowly fell off again. They would fail the tack.

The inevitable voice behind him carried half the length of the ship, and it was clear that it rankled the sailing master.

"You'll have to do better than that, Mr. Finney."

All he could do was answer, "Yes sir, Lieutenant," to Dudingston's supercilious tone and walk forward shouting orders to get the *Romney* ready to try again.

The next tack succeeded as did the next and the one after that, Mr. Finney apparently wanting to erase the memory of the first failed attempt.

"Topmen, to stations." Thom, Johnny and the other topmen scrambled up the ratlines. "Furl the t'gallants, ease sheets, up bunts and clews." At the t'gallant yard, Thom ran along the footropes, with Johnny and the others lagging only a bit behind. The yard swung beneath them and the sail began to draw up like his mother's curtains. The topmen grabbed for the dancing sailcloth, pulling up the remainder with both hands, bending over the yard bracing themselves on the footropes.

"Move, you lazy bastards," Lasco called from the deck. "I've seen slugs move faster than you useless lubbers. Move." Thom could just hear him above the noise of the wind and the flapping canvas. He could see forward that they were well ahead of the topmen on the foremast. He fought with the sail beneath him and grabbed for the gasket to tie it into a manageable bundle. He glanced down the yard and saw that the others were finished as well, so he caught his breath then followed in the race to get to the deck first.

When Thom dropped gasping on the deck, he heard the shout, "Set royals and t'gallants" and he scrambled skyward again as the bosun shouted insults. Off on the horizon, high cumulus clouds scudded by, far to the west.

After setting the sails, Finney gave the order to wear ship and the *Romney* spun about practicing changing course by letting the stern cross the wind.

By the end of the watch, the crew trooped below to the gun deck for supper, exhausted and sore. They chewed the biscuit and salt junk listlessly and some didn't even sing along with the fifer as the grog was issued.

The next day the gratings were rigged again. There were a dozen lashes for the fo'c's'leman who didn't cast off the jib sheet fast enough during the first failed tack. "That was a wind shift. Wasn't his fault," Thom whispered to Johnny. "Doesn't have to be his fault to get the blame. Keep your mouth shut," Johnny hissed back.

Another dozen lashes were given to a foretopman who tangled a topsail buntline tackle. Thom stood silently with the rest of the crew. The young topman took the flogging with little more than a few quiet grunts and pulled his shirt over his bloody back with a defiant grimace.

The afternoon was a repeat of the day before, tacking, setting and striking sail, of threats and the bosun's rope end, and more names taken for punishment at the next forenoon. The crew was growing more skilled, faster at their duties, but their weariness was showing. The grumbling on the gun deck grew and fights between sailors increased as nerves frayed and animosities rubbed raw.

Patrick Andrews kept the main topmen together. "They won't keep this up much longer. I seen it before. The officers'll tire out just as you're getting used to the drill. You'll see."

In contrast to the days, the night watches were almost restful. The watch standing lieutenants had recovered their spirits and cared only for keeping the ship sailing smoothly, making good distance in the steady wind beneath a canopy of stars. There was no easing of discipline. No one dared sleep on watch even when there was nothing to do, save watch the sails and sky. The mood at night was different in small ways, from the tune that Lieutenant Lester hummed to himself as he paced the quarterdeck or the stories Lieutenant Perkins quietly told the quartermaster, low, but still loud enough to carry to the mainmast.

The waisters on night watch sat or stood where they could on the upper deck, silent shadows in the darkness unless needed for trimming the sails. The topmen took to the rigging, settling in the mast tops, making padded chairs and loungers for themselves on the bagged studding sails. Thom and Johnny sat and talked among themselves, with Patrick Andrews and a few others who had become close friends.

There are no secrets at sea. Sitting talking with Johnny and Patrick, Thom knew almost as much about each of them as he knew of himself, and if there was any part of him that he had not revealed to the others, not shown in word or action, he was unaware of it.

Patrick was a few years older than Johnny and said little at first, but soon his stories of Yorkshire and of all the ports he had seen in his life at sea came pouring out. A life at sea was his only life. He had no other expectations and fewer hopes. He had survived the past twenty years and just might make twenty more. He smiled at Thom's rashness, his stubborn independence, the last of which he saw in Johnny as well. "You damned colonials ain't nothing but trouble. Stiff necked and sassy, never knowin' your place," he said with a chuckle and a flash in his eyes that was both mocking and admiring. He knew without anything being said that Thom would run one day and that Johnny would go with him and he seemed to watch out for them both because one topman always looked out for another.

With the first hours of dawn, on four hours of sleep or seven depending on the night and the cycle of watches, the crew set about scrubbing the ship in relative peace until breakfast and the punishments of the morning watch. Despite Andrews assurances, the new pattern on the ship went unbroken day after day, the gratings rigged in the forenoon, floggings for the slightest offense, transgressions previously overlooked or laughed at, each man in the ship's crew a grim observer of a fate he might expect any day. The blood was washed off the deck before dinner and the afternoon was endless drill, shepherded over by Lieutenant Dudingston.

On Tuesday, one of the foremast topmen that Thom knew only as Old George fell from the t'gallant yard. He was a young man, called Old George to distinguish him from another older foremast topman of the same name. Dudingston said the foremast men were moving too slowly and promised a flogging to the last man off the yard. Old George, the youngest and most nimble of the fore mast crew, was always the first up the mast and took the place of honor at the outer end of the yardarm, which meant he was usually the last man down. As he scrambled from his post, he missed a handhold, slipped and tumbled the forty feet to the deck, a bloody mass of broken arms and legs. As his fellow topmen and waisters rushed to him Lieutenant Dudingston roared, "Get back to your posts, you useless bastards. I don't care who falls off the yard, get that t'gallant furled, you hopeless curs." The crowd around the sailor parted as Old George lay on deck, groaning. Dudingston pointed to two waisters. "Get him below and be quick about it." Old George's screams as he was carried below echoed across the ship and the crew listened to his agony for the next three days as he lay dying on a pallet on the orlop deck.

❖ ❖ ❖

The next day Michael Skinner returned to duty, his back still a constant torment, but fit to scrub decks and haul on a sheet. Thom went to see him at the next day's supper and found him hunched over the mess table, his eyes dull and sunken. "I'm all right," he said. "All right," nodding to himself. Sidney Thompson, another pressed man, said, "He'll be fine," somewhat tentatively but clear enough to tell Thom that his mess mates would watch out for him. Thom only hoped that his spirit would heal as fast as his lacerated back.

The next forenoon as they were called on deck, the topmen falling in behind the waisters, streaming up the ladder to the upper deck, Bosun Lasco sidled up next to Skinner. "Bout time you got back to duty, you lazy bastard."

Skinner just nodded and said, "Yes, sir."

As the crew reached the deck they ran to their stations. Skinner was a step behind and Lasco swung his club at Skinner's back. Skinner screamed and black blood stained his shirt. "Move faster, you lazy son of a whore. Run, you useless worm."

Thom was just behind Skinner and Lasco. He was tired. Old George's groans had denied him sleep and suddenly he couldn't take it any longer. It was one thing to bear cruelty, to bow and bend and scramble, but quite another to watch it, to stand by and do nothing.

"No," he shouted at Lasco. "Stop, you bloody dog." He started to raise his hand to strike but someone grabbed his wrist. Thom looked down and saw Patrick Andrews' hand holding his arm in an iron grasp. Everything stopped. The deck was silent.

Lasco spun on his heals. To starboard, Thom heard the contemptuous tone of the first lieutenant. "What did you say, Mr. Lewis?"

Thom stood there, his anger still boiling, yet understanding what it could mean. "Nothing, sir."

"It appeared to me that you wished to strike the bosun. Could that be?"

"No, sir," Thom replied.

Lieutenant Dudingston, who stood off to weather, smirked. "You and all like you shall learn discipline, and I do not care whether or not you survive the instruction."

Lasco only smiled, turned and walked off. At the end of the watch, the master of arms took Thom below deck and clasped him in irons.

He stood before Captain Corner and Lieutenant Dudingston the next day as the captain read Article Twenty two of the Articles of War pertaining to arguing or talking back to officers. "Do have anything to say for yourself, Mr. Lewis?"

"No, sir."

"Strip."

Thom pulled off his smock and threw it on the deck.

"Seize him up." Thom felt two sets of hands push him against the grating and tie his arms tightly.

"Two dozen Mr. Lasco. Do your duty."

The first blow was a knife slicing at his back between his shoulder blades. It shot like a lightning bolt in all directions, from his toes and fingernails to the top of his head. Every nerve in his body screamed in pain. He gasped, the wind knocked from his lungs, and for an instant felt like he was drowning in fire, his body burning, his lungs unable to catch a breath. The spasm passed, but the pain lingered, a reminder of the next blow, which seemed to take an eternity to arrive, and yet then came far too soon.

With the next lash, the pain in his lungs seemed greater than the pain in his back, as if all his internal organs were bursting from the impact of the cat. More blows fell, seeming to come in syncopated waves, flattening his lungs just as he tried to breathe. His gasps became quick and desperate and collapsed into sobs. The cat made a vicious hiss, announcing its approach, and rang like the shot of a cannon when it hit. He lost count of the number of blows, lost track of everything except the agony. He had descended into the inferno, where there was no time or space and the only constant was boundless suffering. He tasted blood in his mouth and realized that he had bitten his tongue or his lips and tried to spit out the blood fearing that he would choke as he struggled for each breath.

Then there was silence. The song of the cat had stopped and what seemed a long way away, he heard the captain's voice say, "Cut him down." He felt the cool blades of knives against his arms slicing the spun yarn. He tried to stand. He wanted to walk away proudly, defiant, but his legs weren't under his command and he slipped down the grating like a marionette with severed strings.

He felt strong hands and heard Johnny's voice. "It'll be all right, Thomas. We'll get you below." Thom struggled to regain his legs, leaning on Johnny as they shuffled across the deck. Below deck Dr. Matthews sponged his back with brine, which felt like a second flogging. Johnny stood nearby, gasping along with Thom at the surgeon's ministrations. Thom's back looked like roasted meat burned almost black before a scorching fire.

"You'll get better, Thomas. Might take awhile, but it'll get better."

Johnny heard what may have been a laugh beneath the quiet whimpers as the doctor sponged his back. "As long as it doesn't get too much worse, I'll manage," Thom replied at not more than a whisper.

Johnny smiled. No more than the flesh had been torn, a good sign.

Thom came back on duty two days later. He was welcomed back to the mess as an old friend. He thanked Johnny for the food that he brought to him and for standing by him. "I didn't do a thing," Johnny replied.

Thom looked at him seriously and said, "I know what you've, done, Johnny and it's a debt I'm not sure I can ever repay."

Johnny laughed. "If it's a debt, I doubt it'll ever be called. I don't mind just earning interest."

Later, Thom went over to Patrick Andrews. "I owe you my life, I know that. I would have struck the bosun and if I struck him I could have killed him."

"Ach, the lash knocked all the sense out of ya," Andrews replied with a laugh.

❖ ❖ ❖

On watch, Thom scrambled with the rest of the topmen, though his back tormented him. He tried to think of nothing but the sail to be furled or set, the ratlines to be climbed, showing nothing of his discomfort except the short gasps as pain jabbed at him like a sword point, and the blood that stained his shirts as his partially healed wounds opened.

Luck was with him nevertheless. As Patrick Andrews had predicted, the daily drills came to an end and the starboard watch was surprised to find itself left alone on the gun deck during the afternoon watch. The press of the hammock on his back caused him pain, even when he tried to sleep on his stomach. When he did at last drift off to sleep, the confines of the hammock made him dream of being tied to the grating and he would awake with a start, reigniting the fires on his back.

Each day Thom felt a little better, and each day they logged more distance south, closer to the islands of the Indies that Thom now held in his mind like a talisman. Things would change in the Indies. Things would change.

One day he swore to himself that he would kill Dudingston. It was a simple and silent oath, a cold certainty that he carried with him. One day, accounts would be settled. One day, all would be repaid.

CHAPTER EIGHT

The south-westerlies faded slowly, the *Romney* plodding along to weather in ever-lighter air. Each day grew hotter and all eyes aboard searched the horizon looking for anything that might suggest a change in the wind. With the warmer weather, Governor Bernard and his family made their first extended appearances on deck. Lieutenant Dudingston hovered close by on the quarterdeck, not above toadying when the opportunity arose.

On the morning of the sixteenth day out of Boston, the ship sat becalmed, rolling gently on a glassy ocean. With the first rays of the sun, a hint of the northeast trades stirred the light canvas of the royals. By noon, the breeze had strengthened and the *Romney* set off on a broad reach, the wind just aft her beam, sailing south toward the islands beyond the ever shifting circle of the horizon.

At the masthead, in free air high above the deck, safe from unwanted ears, Thom said to Johnny, "Don't worry, we'll run in the Indies, make our way home from there."

"Hope so," Johnny replied.

"Oh, we will. If I didn't believe that with all my heart I would have already killed the son of a whore Dudingston and probably his dog, Lasco, for good measure." Thom watched a bank of high clouds on the southern horizon. "We made better distance on the bowline than I expected. I'd say we've a few more days southing before we turn for the islands. That bastard Bernard must have wanted to leave Boston awfully bad to sail to the Indies in the storm season. Too late in the year to worry, I guess. Probably miss the big blows, anyway."

Thom turned back toward Johnny. "It's funny, I heard the ship talking last night when everything was quiet, the water against the hull, dancing, rattlin', chuckling along. Felt good to be sailing again, even if this barky isn't my choice of berths." He laughed. "We'll get off in the islands, Johnny, mark my words."

Johnny wasn't sure what to say. All of his advice to Thom thus far had brought them no closer to freedom. Perhaps it was time to listen to his young friend.

Three days later, after the Sailing Master took his noon sight, Bosun Lasco blew his whistle and the drums beat "All Hands". The waisters hauled the braces about and the helm was brought up, setting the *Romney* on a due westerly course. From the maintop, Thom commented to Johnny, "Now we'll see what sort of navigator Master Finney is."

The lookouts were doubled, and the topmen who weren't sent to the masthead as lookouts, spent the watch staring ahead anyway. A navigator could measure his latitude by sighting the sun or stars with his sextant, but could only estimate his longitude. They were at St. Christopher's latitude, but their longitude was the Sailing Master's best guess, a mix of dead reckoning, experience, and hunch, allowing for leeway, the set of the current crossing the Gulf Stream, and the accuracy of the helmsman's course over almost two thousand miles.

Thom would have liked to look over the Master's shoulder, check his sights and calculations, but in even thinking the thought, he knew that he was forgetting himself. No mere sailor had the right to know where he was or where he was going, at least not according to those lodging aft of the main mast, and for that, almost as much as the stripes, red and ugly, on his back, he hated them.

He never knew that hate could be so large, so overpowering and that carrying it could be such a burden. He watched the sky just above the horizon for clouds that would mark St. Kitts.

Somehow they would escape in the islands. In the islands, he repeated to himself.

Two days later they hove to at dusk, still not close enough to see the island, but too close to risk running ashore in the darkness. The next day in the second watch, the lookout cried, "Land, ahoy. Land two points to starboard." Master Finney broke into a self-congratulatory smile and the off-watch crowded at the fo'c's'le rail to catch a glimpse of St. Kitts, till Bosun Lasco chased them off back to the gun deck.

By late afternoon the *Romney* sailed down the channel between St. Kitts and Nevis and rounded up into Frigate Bay, standing on far enough to fire a seven-gun salute to the fortress on Brimstone Hill. The thirty-two pounders from the fortress echoed their salute, the deep throated rumble of the cannon reverberating across the bay.

❖ ❖ ❖

The *Romney* jibbed back and anchored off Basseterre, the island's capital. After the empty expanse of the sea, St. Kitts seemed unnaturally green and lush, the smell of sugar cane sweet and heady, carried down the slopes on the northeasterly trades. Even in many-steepled Boston, the ship's masthead had been the tallest point. Now Mount Misery soared above them, making the man-of-war seem small and insignificant against the sweep of the cane fields climbing the lower slopes of the volcanic peak. Tucked amidst the palm lined shores, Basseterre was a miniature, glowing white against the green tableau, a delicate mix of British and French architecture reflecting the alternating ownership of the island.

Governor Bernard demanded to be put ashore as soon as the anchor was down, as anxious to leave the ship as he had been to depart Boston. Once the ship was secure, Bernard and his family were piped over the side with all the ceremony the ship could muster and departed in the ship's long boats, soon disappearing against the shadow of the shore. A detachment of servants was left behind to see to the luggage.

The gundeck hummed with the preparations of sailors getting ready to go ashore. Their best clothes were retrieved and freshened up. Mess mates took turns retying each other's queues, the more stylish dipping their plaited hair in tar. Only after most were as scrubbed and as finely dressed as they could be, did the word come done that there would be no liberty. A low murmur of angry and disgruntled voices spread the length of the ship as the men began to take off and refold their going-ashore clothes. Only when the long boats returned full of young slave women did the mood change. There weren't enough to go around, though sharing wasn't frowned on.

The women were distributed on the gun deck like so many servings of ship's biscuit or grog. Johnny looked around and didn't see Thom so he climbed the ladder to the main deck and then the fo'c's'le where he found Thom staring off to the north toward Brimstone Hill.

"That's an ugly fortress if ever I saw one," Johnny commented.

Thom glanced over his shoulder, distracted. "S'pose it is. Wasn't the fortress I was looking at. Trying to remember the chart, the distances. She's just over there beyond the point. Twenty miles? Thirty miles? Can't be any further. I just don't remember."

"What's over there?"

Thom looked at Johnny with a half smile and said at little more than a whisper, "St. Eustatius, Statia. We get to Statia and we're free." He turned back toward St. Kitts. "If we run to Basseterre, the locals will turn us in for the bounty and if we hide out in the jungle, more'n likely die of yellow jack or some other fever than ever see home again. But Statia is different.

"You can see it from Brimstone on a clear day. I know, I've seen Brimstone from Statia." He strained to see it in his mind. The Golden Rock, a tiny island, transshipment port for goods from all over the world, no tariffs charged, no tariffs paid. Call it free trade or smuggling, it didn't matter, the Dutch understood these things. And the Crown held no sway in a Dutch colony.

"You've heard? No liberty."

"I heard. We'll have to find another way to get to Statia."

Johnny left Thom at the rail staring out at St. Kitts, dreaming of their freedom, as he went below to find comfort of another sort.

CHAPTER NINE

Three days later the morning dawned an ordinary shade of gray, but the trade winds had stopped blowing and the *Romney* wandered at her anchor, no longer sitting to the wind, but now a captive of the slow swirling currents of the bay. The air was calm and a heavy haze hung over the southern horizon. An oily swell rolled in, wrapped around the island, deflecting off Brimstone Point and gently rocked the ship. The sea gulls flew low to the water, flapping their wings frantically, as if an unseen hand held them down.

"It's gonna blow," Thom said.

"I know," Johnny replied. "Ever seen a real West Indies storm?" Thom shook his head. "Neither have I. I hear a hurricane's the most magnificent storm God ever made. Less'en it kills you, of course."

The parade of boats continued. Francis Bernard's baggage wasn't fully unloaded before he began to entertain the Captain and ship's officers. Even the warrant officers were included in what seemed abundant gratitude for carrying him away from the troubles of Boston.

The shortage of officers slowed the unloading. The longboats continued to pull away with trunks and chests retrieved from the hold, and the jolly boat and the cutter continued to ply back and forth with the lieutenants, midshipmen and master's mates in their finest uniforms bound for the Basseterre landing, carrying back the same officers somewhat worse for the consumption of the Governor's reportedly excellent wine.

Even the best of the Governor's Madeira didn't wholly obscure the change in the weather for Sailing Master Finney, who sat alone in the stern of the cutter cursing at the boat's crew to row faster as they cut through the swell on their way back to the *Romney*.

He climbed aboard, ignoring all formalities at the gangway and went into the quarterdeck cabin, appearing a moment later shouting for the lieutenant on watch.

"You blind, man?" he bellowed, when Lieutenant Adams appeared. Finney's voice carrying the length of the ship. Libations ashore had eased his sense of propriety and he bawled at the officer as if he was a scullery maid.

"Quick, send the midshipman to call back the captain and the others. Better yet, do it yourself. You're useless to me here."

Adams' face reddened. Finney had no business addressing a commissioned officer with such a lack of respect. The lieutenant drew himself up as if ready to put the warrant officer in his place, but whether it was the prospect of a storm darkening the horizon, or the immediacy of the storm from the sailing master, his resolve faded and kept his mouth clenched.

The lieutenant wrote a note to the captain. "Please give my respects to the captain and give him this message," he said handing the folded page to the midshipman. "And move lively, if you please." The midshipman disappeared down the ladder into the waiting boat.

Before he left, Master Finney was already shouting to the deck. "All hands. Topmen strike the royal and t'gallant yards and masts, fore, main, and mizzen. And jump to it. There's a great wind comin' and I'll have those spars on deck afore she blows."

Johnny, Thom and the rest of the topmen scrambled to the ratlines and the race was on. Each mast, always trying to outperform the others in settling and shortening sail, now had an almost identical task and the foremast men were determined to beat the main men in striking the royals and t'gallants. The mizzenmast topmen had smaller rigging to strike but scrambled as if the small mizzen t'gallant mast was as large the main mast itself.

As the spars and yards were being lowered onto the deck, with the main topmen well ahead, boats began returning from ashore. The deck, which had been comparatively calm while the battle raged in the rigging, burst into activity. The remaining trunks and chests were hauled out of the hold, rather roughly, or so it appeared to a servant of Mr. Bernard, who came back to the ship to watch the discharge. He implored caution, speaking loudly of delicate porcelain dishes in the crates, while the bosun's mates yelled louder about the approaching blow.

Captain Corner, who had just returned with Lieutenant Dudingston, interrupted Master Finney's shouting of orders. Thom couldn't hear what was being said but the meaning was clear enough. The Captain was questioning Finney's authority to rerig the ship and generally set things in an uproar, while Master Finney gestured toward the horizon, showing less deference than Captain Corner expected. As the sky off toward the south grew darker, the Captain's concern shifted from Master Finney to the impending storm and he went below, leaving Finney free to bellow as seemed appropriate. The issue of authority resolved, Lieutenant Dudingston charged about the deck, followed by the junior lieutenants and the midshipmen, making their own contribution to the bedlam.

With the yards and t'gallant masts stowed spanning the waist, Thom, Johnny and the other topmen set to doubling the shrouds and rigging preventers as the waisters worked to stow the guns for sea and seal the gunports, generally getting in the way of the seamen trying to unload the last of the Bernard party's baggage. The ship's boats began to ferry the remaining trunks ashore as loose gear was secured all over the ship.

Aloft and alow the crew scrambled as if clearing for action, but for this battle, neither powder nor shot would be called for. The younger men muttered among themselves, questioning whether such a fuss was warranted, only to be hushed by the older men who had survived the great winds of the West Indies. The work continued with all hands through the second dog watch, then slowed as the officers looked about for what was left to be done and saw little.

All heads turned toward shore from whence Governor Bernard and his family should have been returning, and though there was activity, the Governor's family was not to be seen. The ship's boats returned, filled again with the Governor's baggage, trunks bound for England, replacing those bound for his plantation. Midshipman Paulings was sent back with the empty boats to request that all haste be made in repairing to the ship. Paulings returned an hour later in boats again loaded to their gunnels. He reported below to the Captain. Presently, First Lieutenant Dudingston was sent ashore to lend his authority and the Captains' urgent request for alacrity. If Governor Bernard and his families final destination was indeed England, a measure of alacrity would be required.

As darkness fell, so did the rain, sweeping in a torrent as dark as the night itself. Deck seams that had opened in the tropic heat, funneled water into the gun deck, onto the men in their hammocks. Only those farthest forward under the fo'c's'le head and those aft under the quarterdeck stayed dry. Sometime after midnight the wind began to blow, first from the west but then veering south turning Frigate Bay from a secure anchorage to leeward of St. Kitts to an exposed roadstead off a lee shore. A short chop built slowly to a full swell and *Romney* began to pitch and yaw at her anchor, slowly at first but with ever greater urgency.

At dawn, the rain continued and the wind built, howling furiously through the rigging. As they got up to go on watch, Johnny saw Thom take something out of his seabag, stick it in his shirt and cinch his belt tightly to hold it. "What you got there?" Johnny asked.

"My Grandfather's bible," Thom replied with a grin.

"Never knew you to be a religious sort."

Thom shrugged. "Not particularly, but never hurts to be ready." He lowered his voice. "That might be the wind of freedom blowing out there. Our chance. Be ready." Thom turned and headed up the ladder into the storm, leaving Johnny standing for a moment, looking at his friend's back, fearing that he may have become unhinged. Listening to the mad wailing of the wind might set anyone off.

Johnny climbed the ladder and ran for the cover of the upper deck walkway with Thom and several other sailors, finding what refuge they could from the driving rain. Captain Corner paced the quarterdeck looking off toward Basseterre demanding, shouting over the wind, apparently demanding that Midshipman Paulings tell him where Bernard and Dudingston could be? Why they were taking so long? The young midshipman seemed to cower equally before his questions and the weather.

"Think he'll sail afore the Governor comes back?" Johnny wondered as Thom and a few others huddled beneath the upper deck walkway.

"Doubt he'd dare. Lacks the nerve." Thom laughed under the howl of the wind.

A squad of marines, looking unhappily soaked, formed on the upper deck and climbed down heavily into a bobbing longboat pulled alongside.

Johnny laughed as well. "Looks like he's sending the Gov'nor some help in leaving the island."

The longboat blew down quickly to the beach at Basseterre and disappeared into the white line of breaking surf. One of the sailors lost his bet when the boat reappeared on the beach, hauled ashore by the Marines. "Was sure they would'a broached," he said disappointed.

Three hours later, two longboats put off through the surf and slowly worked out against the wind and building sea. The *Romney* was pitching wildly at anchor now and Master Finney kept taking bearings off both ends of the island to make sure that they weren't dragging. When the longboats made it back, they bounced madly against the hull and a sling was lowered to haul Governor Bernard aboard, who looked angry, miserable and thoroughly drenched. Dudingston and the rest scampered up the battens on the hull. One Marine fell off and had to be fished into the longboat before he sank or blew back to Basseterre.

The wind in the rigging had risen to a steady roar, varying only in pitch, rising several octaves in the gusts from a bellowing bass to a sopranic scream. Master Finney shouted against the wind from the quarterdeck, then seeing that he wasn't being heard, bolted forward, shouting at each of the mast captains who then shouted the word to the topmen. The waisters formed up around the double drums of the capstan, one miserable lot on the weather deck and an only slightly less sodden group the deck below. The main topmen scrambled up the windward ratlines, holding the shrouds tightly against the wind and the dancing of the ship. As the waisters stamped around the capstan drums, hauling the ship forward painfully slowly toward her anchor, the topmen stood by. A midshipman on the fo'c's'le shouted, "Up and down," though no one could hear him. He pointed up and down with his arm. Finney saw the signal and motioned to the afterguard to set the mizzen spanker to hold the ship's bow into the wind. Then he signaled to set the topsail. The topsail alone would let them claw off the lee shore.

Once the gaskets were cast off and the bunts and clews eased, the sail backed with a tremendous crack that nearly shook Thom and the other topmen off the spar, breaking the anchor free of its grasp of the bottom, but also pushing the ship backwards toward the beach. Finney ran forward, bellowing at the men hauling on the weather braces. Slowly the topsail swung around and filled and the ship began to move forward, inching to windward, seven points off the wind.

Thom and Johnny grasped the spar tightly and jammed their feet into the foot ropes with all the force they could muster. Thom watched forward as Brimstone Point loomed off the bow. "Think we'll clear?" he shouted at Johnny.

Johnny yelled back. "A close thing." Thom couldn't hear him but understood and agreed. If the ship didn't gather weigh and sail close enough to the wind, she wouldn't clear the northern end of the island and would have to tack, though in the confused seas and wind she might not be able to swing her bow through the eye of the wind. She could wear, letting her stern cross the wind, but that took more room and might well be blown down on the lee shore.

Slowly the topmen worked their way down the mast, clutching the shrouds desperately, choosing each step with care. They huddled behind the break of the fo'c's'le deck, alternatively watching ahead and hiding from the waves breaking on the deck, rolling back toward them in solid walls.

Thom climbed the fo'c's'le ladder, stopping to hold on as green water washed over him. At the top of the ladder he wrapped both arms around a stanchion, braced his feet and hung on. The ship was lifted as the wind shifted a half point south. It appeared that she would clear Brimstone on one tack. Thom tried to estimate the bearing off the bow and guess at the ship's speed, with little luck as the *Romney* pitched wildly in the confused sea. The wind was tearing the tops off the waves and the air was white with spray and foam. Thom kept rubbing his face against his arm to try to clear his eyes of water.

Johnny crawled up the ladder to the fo'c's'le and shouted to Thom. "You all right?" The ship pitched and a wave broke over the bow, lifting Johnny off his feet. He flailed for the ladder and caught hold just before the wave carried him aft or overboard.

He crawled back to Thom and grabbed on to the stanchion. "I'm fine," Thom yelled back. "Hold on, Johnny. We're not leaving yet." Thom laughed wildly or at least Johnny thought that he was laughing. It was hard to tell in the wind and spray, which no longer felt like water but like something solid - sand, grit or

ice, like each and none of these, trying to tear the skin off his face
and hands.

Johnny looked aft. The mast captain was gesturing and the
other topmen were moving aft to the main mast. Johnny rapped
Thom on the back and pointed and they both crawled from the
fo'c's'le, down the ladder to the deck. They followed the other
topmen up the ratlines to the reef the topsail. The wind was
building and the sail was in danger of exploding into so many
canvas shreds.

Once again the topmen clambered aloft, pressed flat against
the windward ratlines by the force of the blow. They worked their
way onto the topsail yard as the sheets were eased and the
buntlines bowsed tight. As they grabbed at the heavy canvas, the
sail flapped and fought them with a hell-borne fury. Thom
gripped the yard with all his strength and clawed at the wild
canvas. They fought the sail for what seemed like hours, but
succeeded at last in tying in the reef points, leaving a smaller
double reefed topsail, still stretched tight and hard as iron,
continuing to roll the ship along in the wailing gun-metal
madness of the storm.

When they had finished reefing the sail, the topmen hung on,
too tired to fight the wind on their way down the mast. Thom
lifted his head, looked over his shoulder, and saw that the time
had come. All his muscles ached, he shivered, drenched and bone
chilled in the wind, but none of that mattered.

Through the spray he saw a group of waisters and marines on
the quarterdeck struggling with the ship's boats, left trailing
astern in the haste to get underway. One longboat was already
lashed to the spars across the waist. Its stern looked stoved in.
The other longboat's bow was raised up on a tackle off a staysail
boom and six men fought to haul the stern aboard. The cutter
appeared to be missing, possibly swamped and carried away,
though the jolly boat still danced at the end of its painter, trailing
well aft, bobbing up then dropping down, disappearing entirely to
rise up again, shearing across the top of the wave.

Thom stared off to the north but saw only clouds and spray. It didn't matter. He knew it was there. It had to be there.

"Johnny," he yelled. "Time to go." Johnny looked over at him not quite believing.

"We're takin' the jolly boat. Statia's dead downwind."

"What?" Johnny screamed back.

"Statia's downwind. Takin' the jolly boat." When Johnny didn't reply, Thom screamed, "Going alone if I have to."

In the roar of the wind and the pelting spray, there was a sort of solitude, an isolation of hearing only the thunderous blasts of the storm, of not seeing far beyond the circle of the ship. Johnny looked at his friend and laughed. Laughing felt good, freeing the muscles of his face from the wind driven grimace, ease coursing through muscles crying from exertion.

Thom might be crazy, but craziness had its own magic, and there were worse things than being crazy. He had been crazy for following Thom onboard the *Romney*, vainly sure that escape would be easy. Should he follow Thom now in a cockleshell boat in a West Indies blow? He'd trusted his life to the youngster on the *Mary Ellen*, though then there had been no other choice. Johnny opened his mouth and howled wildly. He was crazy himself but it felt good.

He and Thom were the last ones make the climb, so they were the closest to the mast. Thom worked his way slowly the few feet back down the yard, and Johnny followed. When he reached the ratlines, Thom reached out and grabbed the main shroud with both arms and dropped freely to the deck. A line from an old forebiter came to Johnny's mind. A man who's meant for hanging never will be drowned. He only hoped that the old song was right as he grabbed the shroud and dropped toward the deck as well.

He stumbled across the main deck, keeping low, following Thom's shape in the spray. He ran the length of the quarterdeck just behind Thom and saw that the second longboat was on deck and the jolly boat was being hauled in. Thom ran to the rail, barely noticed by the sailors and marines hauling on the painter.

Johnny came up beside him, gasping. "You ready?" Thom yelled. He looked down at the jolly boat, a quarter full of water, fighting those hauling on the line.

"Let's go," Johnny shouted back.

Thom leapt over the rail and dove for the painter, sliding down the wet hemp rope to the bow of the boat. A wave almost knocked him free but he held on, sliding down along the gunnel, swinging a leg up over the side. The boat rolled, almost swamping, water pouring over Thom, then righted itself, lifting Thom up, letting him pull himself aboard.

He lay for a second across the thwart, then forced himself up, looking for Johnny. The jolly boat crashed against the dark side of the *Romney*, another wave breaking over him, and above he heard shouting. For a moment he couldn't find Johnny, then was relieved to see him grasping the transom with both hands, struggling to climb in. Thom pulled out his sheath knife and crawled to the bow. He sawed on the painter and when the line parted, the jolly boat sheared off and the *Romney* raced ahead. Thom crawled back and helped haul Johnny aboard.

Thom bailed with both hands as Johnny unlashed the oars and secured them in the tholes. Johnny swung the stern of the small boat dead on to the seas and fought with the oars to keep from broaching as the stern lifted and the whole boat was thrown down the face of a foaming wave. The *Romney* was a dark smudge on the gray background, growing ever smaller. There was no separation now between sea and sky, no gradation between light and dark, only raging water surging at them from all directions in countless shades of silver, gray and black.

"Which way is Statia?" Johnny yelled to Thom, over his shoulder in the bow of the bow. He didn't have to yell quite as loud now with no rigging for the wind to wail through. In the troughs, the wind didn't blow at all for a moment, then blasted them full force on the crests.

"You're on course. Straight downwind, more or less." The stern rose and Johnny shoved his right oar and pulled on the left to straighten the boat on the wave.

"More of less? What's next land if we miss Statia?" A wave, appearing from nowhere, broke over the side of the jolly boat.

"St. Bart's, then Africa." Thom laughed, bailing furiously. "Don't worry. We'll find Statia. Tell me when you need a rest."

"Just you find the island," Johnny yelled back, pausing a moment as the boat rose on the crest of a wave. He held the oars straight out, letting the wind and spray carry them, blowing against the oars, the boat, and his chest until they slipped back into the trough again and he had to fight to keep from being rolled sideways. On the crests he turned his head to the side, trying to avoid the blinding spray, shifting the oars by the feel of the boat as much as by what he could see. He wasn't rowing so much as fighting to keep from capsizing, letting the wind carry them where it may, and trusting in Thom's skill or luck.

Time was reduced to each wave, each small battle to stay upright and Johnny wasn't sure how long it was before Thom yelled, "Larboard side. Breakers." Johnny turned, looking over his left shoulder and saw a sinuous line of white, well off to larboard disappearing into the gray-black sea. Statia. They were missing the island and would be carried off to sea if they didn't change course.

"Give me an oar," Thom yelled reaching for the oar with both hands. Johnny fought for a moment, his grip resolute and unyielding, until he realized what Thom was doing. Thom wrested the oar free and set it in the thole next to the forward thwart. Together they hauled, each pulling on a single oar with all the force they could muster toward the distant line of the surf. They crabbed sideways, swinging the stern around toward the rolling walls of water trying to swamp them, then pulling desperately to larboard on the back of the waves, not looking where they were going, knowing that they could do no better against the running sea. The waves seemed to be growing steeper but Thom might have imagined it. All he knew was the wail of the wind, the bite of the spray, and the screaming ache of his arms and back.

Thom didn't see the wave that lifted the jolly boat in one smooth motion and tossed it like any other bit of surf borne flotsam. For an instant, everything was sideways and twisted, and Thom looked down on Johnny and the entire length of the boat, risen up from the wave, falling sideways into the boiling water, until the world seemed to collapse on him, driving him deep into the swirling tumult. As he fell he held his breath, just like he had done as a boy, diving for pebbles off the dock of his father's shipyard in Cold Spring Harbor. It was an odd and pleasant memory interrupted by a sharp blow to his shoulder. He spun underwater, feeling the gunnel of the boat, then dove deeper, swimming to get free. His lungs bursting, he finally rocketed to the surface, gasping, only to be knocked by another breaking wave. He fought his way up again, turning his back to the waves and saw or thought he saw the dark line of the shore ahead, still a long way off, but there, a direction to swim toward.

He struggled to keep to the surface, rip currents and the weight of the waves conspiring to drown him, but kept on, yielding to the strength of the surf when it broke against him, but also using it, letting it carry him shoreward. He caught glimpses of the beach and swam harder down the back of the waves until he felt sand swirling in the water, filling his mouth with grit, and the water ceased to be water, but an angry foam, too thin to swim in and too thick to breathe. He sank beneath the mass of water, wind, and sand, hitting the bottom hard, tumbling, rolling, being dragged along, shoreward, then back out toward deep water. He fought to stand but was knocked down. He got up again, at times in a crouch, at times a crawl, and struggled against the breakers, the surf, and the sand. He was swept back again and in a final angry rush he rose and charged toward the dark line of trees now visible above the beach. He was knocked aside, then struggled back, plodding, clawing, crawling until only the wind wailed and the surf at his back, cursed at him. He crumpled on the sand, sore and bleeding, shivering uncontrollably from the cold, and fell asleep, exhausted, still fighting the storm in his dreams.

Johnny simultaneously felt and heard the wave sweeping up off their quarter and knew even before it struck that this was the wave that he couldn't fight. The boat rolled and rose, lifted as if by a vast hand, sliding down the wild slope of the wave. Then the wind caught the exposed stern and threw the boat end over end like a leaf on a summer breeze. Johnny dropped the oar, grasped the gunnel tightly and braced one leg against the thwart. He wasn't a strong swimmer and now he wasn't sure where the sky ended and the sea began. The jolly boat had carried them this far and he would ride it a bit further.

When they hit the water, he was almost thrown free, save his hold on the gunnel. When he pulled himself back, he climbed on the bottom of the boat, hanging on to the keel, riding the back like some sort of deranged turtle through the maelstrom. They were swept sideways, rolling crazily, Johnny's legs trailing like seaweed, swept back and forth as he dug his fingers into the oak. When the boat seemed ready to roll upright and shake him off, he used all his strength to swing his body and pull it back. Finally, with no strength left, the boat rolled and his hands dragged across the planks, grabbing desperately at the gunnel. His hands slipped, finally holding on to the transom, his arms straight out with enough energy only to lift his head, gasping to stay above the water. Suddenly, the boat lurched and he was thrown hard against the stern. The sea seemed to tumble around him, roaring at him as he crawled across the broken boat, up toward the beach.

❖❖❖

Thom awoke to silence, his cheek cool against the sand. For a moment he heard nothing, then faintly, the sound of birds, the harsh cry of a gull ringing sweetly in his ears. He rolled over and saw a sky, blue and vibrant with scudding clouds more white than gray.

"Bout time you woke up." Thom spun to see Johnny sitting with his back against a palm tree. "Saw you were alive so thought best let ya sleep."

Thom laughed. His chest hurt and his shoulder cried as he tried to sit up. His shirt was torn and blood soaked, most of the skin of his chest abraded and bleeding. He felt around behind him was relieved to find his grandfather's bible, no longer cinched in his belt, but caught in the back of his shirt.

"I thought that if we ran in the storm, they'd be as likely to mark us dead as deserted. Hadn't planned on coming so close to being both."

It was Johnny's turn to laugh and he raised his head to the sky and bellowed as if Thom was gifted with a ferocious wit. He continued to howl till the laughter passed and he wiped his eyes. "I must say Thomas that when you said we'd run in the islands, I thought you meant leaving closer to shore."

Thom smiled. "Doesn't always work the way we planned, does it?" Thom surveyed his condition, moving his arms and legs tentatively. Nothing seemed broken, though he was sore everywhere there was to be sore, and including many places whose acquaintance he made now for the first time. He stood up warily.

"How you doing, Johnny?"

"Not so bad. Got a twisted ankle. A little hard to walk, but I'm all right. You?"

"Sore's all." He rotated his right shoulder, grimacing. "Shoulder hurts, but still in the socket, I think." He looked down the beach. In the distance Orangestad's Lower Town was a dark shadow against the arc of the sand. Thom looked back at Johnny. "Welcome to Statia."

And then for reasons he didn't fully understand, Thom began again to laugh, freely and out of control. The laughing hurt his chest and his shoulder but it didn't matter. It was as if he needed to catch up after all the days and months without laughter, without joy. He lay back on the sand and could see a bit of clearing, hints of blue in the maelstrom of clouds.

CHAPTER TEN

In a small stone building behind a warehouse, Andrew McIver worked at his desk tallying accounts. There had been considerable water damage but otherwise the storm had struck them only a glancing blow. His linen shirt was open at the neck with the sleeves pushed up past the elbows. His waistcoat hung unbuttoned from his shoulders. He was a short man with flaming red hair and a deeply freckled face that made him appear younger than his years.

"Good morning to you, sir."

McIver put down his quill pen and looked up at the silhouette standing in his doorway, outlined by the morning sun. The figure stepped through the threshold and McIver's expression shifted to irritation, and not a little astonishment. Thom looked down at his bloody shirt, torn pants and bare feet, then over at Johnny, who had followed him in, and looked no better than himself, and chuckled.

"May I be of service to you, ... gentlemen?"

"I pray sir, that you'll excuse our appearance. We've had a somewhat difficult ... passage. We met quite briefly, sir, last April. Was with Captain Evers of the *Mary Ellen*. I am Thomas Larkin and .."

"On my word." McIver sat back in his chair and a broad smile spread across his face. "By all the angels in heaven." McIver jumped up and strode around his desk to grasp Thom's hand. "I can hardly believe it, sir. I recall you very well indeed. Mr. John Brown had written to me of your deliverance of the *Mary Ellen* and of your subsequent capture by the press gang. Dreadful, dreadful business." McIver continued shaking Thom's hand vigorously, until he gave it one more resolute shake and stepped back.

"Your arrival is a most gratifying surprise, all the more so for arriving on the back of a hurricane, " McIver said still smiling. "Ah, should I assume that you have recently departed the Royal Navy ship on which you were held?"

"We borrowed one of the King's jolly boats. Which accounts for our somewhat disheveled aspect. " Thom replied.

McIver raised an eyebrow and smiled. "Well, we need speak no more of such things. And your companion?"

Thom turned toward Johnny. "May I have the honor of introducing Mr. John Stevens, ex-mate of the *Mary Ellen* and a particular friend."

"Well, a warm welcome to you both. Please do have a seat, gentlemen. Take your ease." McIver sat down behind his desk, then glanced about as if not quite sure what to do next. He stood again. "If you will wait here, I will make arrangements on your behalf. I'll arrange a carriage. It isn't a long walk to my house in the Upper Town, but I'll wager that you wouldn't mind riding." Thom and Johnny sat on the rough bench by the door as McIver bustled out.

For a few moments Thom and Johnny sat quietly in the small office, their backs leaning against the cool stone wall. "It seems all a dream. A nightmare, perhaps. I just pray to God that I've fully awake."

"Ah, it's over," Johnny replied staring out into space. "Just need to catch a ship home, if we can find a berth."

Thom reached back into his torn shirt and pulled out his grandfather's Bible. The pages were swollen with salt but the leather cover was intact.

"Won't be doin' too much reading of that," Johnny commented.

Thom flipped the book over in his hand and said, "Guess not."

Johnny thought for a moment and said, "'The Lord on high is mightier than the noise of many waters, yea even than the mighty waves of the sea.' Looks to me that the sea won this time."

Thom smiled, reached for his knife but found the sheath empty. He reached across McIver's desk and grabbed a letter opener. He slipped the slender blade between the stitching on the cover of the Bible, cutting and pulling the thread. When he was three-quarters the way around he pulled the leather cover back. Even in the pale light of the office, the shine of gold was dazzling. Circles cut into the thin boxwood core held ten gold pistoles.

"Passage money," Thom said with a smirk. "Wages from the *Mary Ellen*. I think we're due a trip as passengers."

"You continue to amaze me, young Thomas," said Johnny shaking his head.

"First time he shipped out, someone stole my grandfather's clothes and gear, everything save his Bible. From then on, he always hid his money in the cover. Gave it to me once he came ashore. Told me that it had always been lucky for him."

Johnny grinned. "O you who dwell by many waters, Abundant in treasures..."

Thom quickly replaced the letter opener and pulled the leather cover back over the Bible at the sound of hooves outside the door. McIver appeared at the doorway. "This way, if you please, gentlemen."

Thom and Johnny climbed into a small carriage, the two fitting tightly in the coach. McIver pulled the side curtains closed. "Better no one sees you just yet. T'is a small island and one never knows where King George has eyes." He turned to the black coachman. "I'll meet you at the house, Philip. Tell Anders to see that these gentlemen are made comfortable."

With a start, they were off, clattering over worn cobblestones up the narrow lane, pressed between the counting houses and warehouses of the Lower Town. Thom felt the carriage lurch in a turn and the press of gravity against the seat as they began the steep ascent to Orangestad's Upper Town. He closed his eyes, lost in the sound of the wheels on the lane and the gentle rocking of the carriage climbing the hill.

"Well, you gentlemen look far better than when last I saw you." McIvers smiled at them from across the parlor. Johnny felt a touch silly in the silk waist coat and breeches, but the linen shirt was soft against his skin and the scent of lilacs still floated around him, a sweet and gentle reminder of the glorious soaking in the tin tub with a house slave scrubbing his back, from which he had emerged only with the greatest regret. The fine clothes were a luxury, even if he felt that he was flying false colors. The fresh water bath, however, now that was a true and marvelous indulgence.

Andrew McIver's parlor was, like the house itself, deeper than it was wide, well furnished with arm chairs of elm with velvet cushions. Johnny sat up straight, then let himself sag back. Thom, who only hours before was as disagreeable a mass of jetsam as Johnny himself had been, now looked to be a merchant's son, or the heir of a lesser lord, in his short coat with a scarlet ribbon tied about his pigtail. He didn't seem to share Johnny's unease at their new surroundings and attire, which caused Johnny a moment's envy.

"I have some rather good Madeira if you gentlemen would care to partake. It is just late enough in the day so as not to be unseemly."

"Wine would be most welcome, sir," Johnny piped up. Thom agreed without quite the same eagerness. McIver opened a cabinet and brought out a decanter and crystal glasses. The wine, if neither the crockery nor the settling, reminded Johnny of Hancock's fine Madeira, passed out by the tankard full as the mob howled around Hutchinson's burning yacht. Only five months before, it seemed part of another age.

"I've taken the liberty of entering your names on the logs of a trading vessel, the *Dorthea*, which arrived a few days before the storm. Mr. Larkin, I hope you don't mind if you become, at least for your stay here with us, a Mr. Tobias Taylor, a merchant's agent from Boston, and Mr. Stevens, you are his compatriot, Mr. Robert Tucker. You gentlemen are making inquiries related to the transshipment of naval stores."

Johnny laughed out loud while Thom smiled. "We would be pleased to be whomsoever you choose, sir," Thom replied. "And we are sincerely grateful for the hospitality that you have shown us."

"Ach, nonsense, tis my great pleasure to do so. My only regret is that now that you have suitable identities against an unlikely inquiry by Crown agents, I will be prevented from telling the true story of two guests who arrived by jolly boat in a hurricane." McIver smiled and drained his wine in one long swallow. "Well, if you will excuse me, gentlemen. Still damage from the storm to be accounted for." He made a shallow bow and swept from the room.

Johnny laughed to himself. "Doesn't look like that one slows down much. Always thought the islands induced idleness. His accent sounds half Scots 'nd half-Dutch. Wonder how long he's been in Statia."

Thom smiled weakly, seemingly distracted. He rose and walked to the window. Sunlight shifted on the street, caught between the stone and frame houses. "I could use some air. Care to join me, Johnny?"

They strolled down the main street of Orangestadt, hemmed in on each side by houses which looked wholly Dutch save for the incongruous colors - pale blues, yellows and pinks, harmonizing with the darker blue of the sky and the high clouds, fluffy white with only hints of gray. Johnny had been in Statia three or four times and had never seen the street so deserted.

The houses to their right blocked a view of the sea, while to their left the cane fields, a deep sea of shifting green, rose over the roofs beneath the weathered volcanic crest of the island, dark against a luminous sky. Smoke rose from sections of the fields, obscuring the orange flames burning away the chaff before the sugar cane could be harvested, disappearing into the sky in pale tendrils against the blue.

The island had two volcanic peaks that a shipmate had once described as looking as welcoming as a woman's breasts. Johnny never saw the resemblance. His friend must have been at sea for too long if the craggy peak to the north and the Quill, the larger peak at the southern end of the island, covered entirely in forest, reminded him of the fairer gender.

Halfway down the street, they passed a synagogue. "Makes me feel like home," Johnny said. "You know I haven't seen Newport most of two years. It'll feel good to get back."

Thom stepped back and looked at the building, rough stone with a stained glass window high above the wide doors. "I've never seen one myself. A Jew's church. You're no Jew, are you Johnny? Always assumed you were preacher's son from the way you spout verse."

"No Jew and no preacher's son, neither. My aunt taught me to read from the Bible. She said that it was the only book worth reading. Can't say I wholly agree with her." He smiled. "She was Baptist and my Uncle was Quaker. Rest of my family were Congregationalist. And there was a synagogue down the street. No wonder I turned out so wayward, so many contradictory creeds claiming to be the one true path. So, I decided to more or less ignore them all."

As they reached the end of the street, the road turned back and ran down the steep hill to Lower Town. Above and behind them, the cannon of Fort Orange loomed over the harbor, the gun barrels black against the dusty gray of the stone fortress. Before them, the arc of the horizon unfolded.

A day before, it had only been the gray oblivion of the storm. Now the air was clear, the sea a deep and dazzling blue, and the only sign of foul weather was a distant fleet of clouds scudding off to the north, and the rolling swells, lonely reminders of a once mighty wind. The swells deflected around Saba, a tiny island, little more than a rocky pinnacle overgrown with cedar, twenty miles north and east. They then rolled in toward Statia, sweeping across the anchorage and bursting against the stone docks in a white foam, mixed with the myriad colors of the rainbow.

"Don't expect to ever see that sight again," Johnny said looking down at the empty anchorage. "Busiest port in the Indies and nary a ship, boat nor cockleshell." He shook his head. "Not that I blame 'em. Not much of an anchorage, much less a harbor in any sort of blow."

Thom had been staring off at the horizon and now looked down at the shallow indentation in the lee of the island that was the only place for ships to anchor. Between the passing swells, he could see the sandy bottom, glowing blue through the waves.

"Can't say you're too talkative this afternoon," Johnny commented, looking over at his silent friend.

Thom shrugged. "Nothing really to say." He looked up. "Tis a beautiful day, but I still seem caught in those clouds," he said nodding toward the north. "Didn't expect to feel this way. I thought that when we finally escaped, a great weight would be lifted. Seems to be with me still. " He paused. "I held in my anger for so long, that now there's no place for it to go. Part of me's still on that ship, ready to knock down Lasco and spit in Dudingston's eye. Or maybe cut his throat."

Johnny rested his hand lightly on Thom's shoulder. "Pretty thing to dream of, but they're a hundred miles over the horizon, and happy we should be to see 'em gone. Go easy on yourself. The anger'll pass. You've been near 'nough to hell and your spirit just needs some time to recover from the scorching."

Thom smiled. "Time. Time, it'll take I'm sure." He stood silent for a while looking out at the sky. "You know what I feel like Johnny? Ever seen a ship that has come through a blow - battered, sails torn, but seemingly sound? But her masts are sprung, even though the cracks haven't worked their way through, and her frames are twisted, caulking ready to let go. The first summer squall that blows up will send her rigging over the side, open up every seam and dispatch her straight to the bottom.

That's the way I feel right now. And sinking doesn't seem the worst thing."

"Just give yourself time," Johnny said, hoping he was right. "Proverbs says, 'A time to heal, a time to break down and a time to build up.' This is your time to heal and build up again, that's all." They turned and walked back to McIver's house, passing only a few words between them, Johnny whistling a chantey to himself to fill the silence.

When they went in to supper that evening Thom was quiet, responding to casual conversation, while offering none of his own. McIvers, Thom and Johnny sat in a dining room with two large mirrors that reflected the light from the candles. Johnny looked over at his friend wondering whether his mood would pass or whether he had been scarred so deeply that the pain would fester like a cancer.

His worries about Thom were swept away by the magnificent smell of the food, more intoxicating than McIver's Madeira. Johnny sliced and tasted the fresh lamb tentatively as if it might vanish back into his imagination with rougher handling. After months of salt beef, better suited for tanning than eating, the lamb, tender and delicately seasoned with spices that Johnny couldn't quite place, was nothing less than ambrosia. The boiled potatoes were thin skinned and looked to be straight from the garden, as were the greens, pungent and vital. Johnny forced himself to eat slowly, to resist the desires of gluttony and savor the extraordinary repast.

Later that evening, after more of McIver's Madeira, he settled snug into a wondrous feather bed, only to wake several times, ready to jump from his hammock. He glanced around at the strangeness of a room and the bed, realizing that he could sleep for the entire night, free of the tyranny of a four hour watch. The bed still shifted beneath him as he slept, his body, unaccustomed to the stillness of the shore, adding motion where there was none. Several times he woke to Thom's low cries, murmurs in angry dreams. He looked over at his friend, tossing in the bed across the room, and could only hope that the days would be more tranquil than his nights.

❖ ❖ ❖

Slowly, ships returned to Statia. Every morning Johnny walked down to the docks to stand watch as lookout. At times, Thom would walk with him though more often than not he kept himself to McIver's house, in the library reading, or just sitting alone.

The first day a small sloop ghosted in, her topmast carried away and her crew manning the pumps. The next day a barque and ship arrived, followed by a brig and two schooners. Within a week, the anchorage was crowded with over a hundred ships, with more arriving each day, dropping their anchors farther out in the roadstead. The sound of wagons and the babble of languages returned, echoing between the cobblestones and the warehouses. Ships loaded and discharged alongside the wharves and into boats at anchor as long boats and skiffs crisscrossed between the anchorage and the docks.

Johnny walked the length of Lower Town every morning, watching and learning the rhythm of the port. Sailors and burghers jostled between the wagons and carts, the first on their way to the taverns, the second, to their ledgers. Slave longshoremen labored at the docks, singing work songs in Dutch as they hauled on the derrick hoists or rolled drums of molasses up ramps to ship's sally ports. Sailors and captains of all stripes did their best to understand each other in pidgin English, French, or Dutch, or most often a mix of each.

The bustle of the docks reminded him of Newport or Boston, or half a dozen other places and he enjoyed being an observer with nothing whatever to do. He liked being Robert Tucker in his fine new clothes, with the handful of coins Thom had given him, jangling in his pocket. He'd been a sailor all his life and as he watched the strutting merchants leaving their counting houses to check on cargoes at the waterfront, he was free to strut a bit himself.

His only regret was that he could share few of a sailor's pleasures, gazing for a moment wistfully at one of the several taverns tucked away between the warehouses. A sailor's beer was no equal to McIver's fine wines, so the sacrifice was none too great. He did slip away the third evening of his stay to visit a particularly comely maid who had caught his eye, lingering in a doorway, but he didn't tarry and felt that he had not compromised his position.

Johnny soon learned that he was not the only participant in the little charade. Conversations would suddenly stop on his approach or switch from English to Dutch. While Johnny had no great facility with languages, he could tell that they were talking about him. More than once he heard a snippet of a tale being told of two sailors who sailed through a hurricane in a jolly boat.

If anything his stature in Lower Town seemed to rise as the word spread, a secret now commonly held. Merchants would greet him, "Morgen, Mr. Taylor," with a grin and a nod. "Good morning to you, sir," Johnny would reply, "Looks like another fine day," and continue his stroll down the strand.

❖ ❖ ❖

After a bit more than a week, Thom knew that he couldn't spend all his time sitting in the shadows of the parlor, sinking ever deeper into the shadows of his memory. For a time, McIver's excellent library had been a partial reprieve from his anger and hurt, allowing him to get lost in the chronicles of ages past. He was pleased that his host was no greater scholar than himself and that his books were in Dutch or English rather than Latin or Greek - popular translations of Cicero, Plutarch, the Grecian tragedies, and Thucydides.

Even the diversions of the mind weren't enough. Tales of the Peloponnesian wars with descriptions of the great fleet battles, Athenian versus Corinthian galleys, brought him back to the

Romney. In his thoughts, he would rage against Dudingston and Captain Corner, weep for himself and poor Michael Skinner as if his mind had a will of its own, unwilling to part from that accursed ship and the scoundrels that put him there.

One morning, seeing no bottom to the chasm into which he was surely sliding, Thom escaped the parlor, seeking out the cook for the makings of a midday meal. He set off an hour after Johnny departed on his rounds of the harbor, with a slice of beef, some bread and fruit wrapped in a napkin, and a bottle of water swinging in the pocket of his breeches. He left McIver's front door and turned away from the docks, walking the road that ran toward the sugar fields and the volcanic peaks beyond.

The morning was clear and bright. The pace of the island, which seemed almost deserted on their arrival, was now both impressive and more than a little frightening. Carriages, horses and mules clogged the narrow streets. The sidewalks and alleys bustled with servants, slaves and seamen, striding purposefully in their finest gear or humblest rags, sharing almost the same space without notice or recognition. Thom blended in, just another traveler in the throng.

McIver had mentioned at a previous supper that fifteen thousand souls occupied the tiny island, a figure too large for Thom to believe, even if their host did not seem one to exaggerate. If so, Orangestadt, for there appeared to be no other space on the island to support habitation, was more populous than Boston itself. The proposition seemed preposterous when dining but now seemed almost possible as he made his way, walking against the tide of the traffic.

Soon the jumbled commerce on the lane thinned and the rows of fine houses on either side grew more modest until they were no more than sheds of wood bleached gray by the sun. At the end of the road lay an ocean of cane fields and in the distance an army of black men swung machetes amidst the green swells. Thom turned down the road running along the edge of the fields, the cane now shoulder high, forming a wall to his left, the road rising gradually as the peak of the long dormant volcano that McIver called the Quill came again into view.

After a mile this road too came to an end in a stand of soaring palm trees and hardwoods, dense bushes and low ferns. Thom stood in the shade and listened to the sounds of birds high in the canopy and breathed the dark sweet smell of the forest.

From the road's end, a foot path wound off into the woods and for a moment, Thom hesitated to step into the shadows, to surrender himself to the tangled jungle. After standing for what seemed a great while, he started off, following the path wherever it would lead.

A few paces later, he stopped again to let his eyes adjust to the pale green light that filtered through the foliage. He expected an overgrown maze but was surprised to see his way open, the ferns and bushes growing low in the limited light. He strode on at a steady pace, the path, now clear, then indistinct, leading him steadily upward.

He walked for several hours. It was difficult to tell exactly how long, as he had no watch and he couldn't see the sun through the high and tangled branches. The grade was easy at first, rising gradually, then progressively steeper, until finally Thom had to stop regularly to catch his breath before going on. His shirt clung to his skin, soaked with sweat, and his feet began to slip in the dark soil, the climb too steep for his shoes.

His way became was less clear, the path, or at least what he took to be a path, was vague, a slight depression, a subtle change in the color of the soil, mixed with rotting leaves. If he was not imagining the trail, what trail there was, was little used. He wondered if he was lost, if he could find his way back through the dim green nether world.

Tired now, he laughed to himself. It occurred to him that getting lost would do his reputation as a navigator no good. Nor would disappearing forever in a jungle on the back of a volcano.

He kept on, for there seemed no other choice. Then, suddenly, he saw light. He hurried on and stepped into the brilliant midday sun at the edge of the forest. The rocky crest of the Quill was but a hundred yards before him. The climb was steep and barren, the black volcanic rock hot on his feet, but he scampered up, his weariness left behind in the shadows, the trade winds cooling as they blew through his sweat soaked shirt.

At the crest, he gave a cheer, a shout like that of a lookout spying a landfall after a month at sea. He peered out over the rim of the volcano and saw another forest, a rich and lush green garden cradled in the bowl of the crater, nurtured by the rain carried on the relentless wind. Around him, the greater bowl of the horizon cradled the sea on which the island itself floated, a rocky speck in the boundless blue.

The crater's rim was broken and worn but Thom found a comfortable place to enjoy his lunch, with a flat rock for a chair and another adjacent for a table. The rocks were warm from the sun, and now, in the wind, their warmth was a comfort.

Thom ate, then simply sat, realizing that for the first time in months he was truly alone, by himself, at the top of the world. His legs and feet were sore, but that was all that troubled him. The crowded gun deck of the *Romney* was another place where once he had lived, and but now it couldn't reach him, there high above the sea. He knew that he hadn't escaped it fully, that at sea level the old specters might return as before, but the knowledge that he had escaped them, if but once, could just be enough, the certain promise that he could escape them again.

In the silence of the wind, thoughts of home flooded back to him. They were scattered images, for he wasn't fully sure where home was anymore. There were memories of New York with his grandfather and of his father's house in Cold Spring Harbor. He remembered his one happy day in Boston and the girl in the green satin dress in Nimroy's counting house, who he saw for but a moment and yet whose dark eyes seemed so to flash when she glanced his way.

He basked in the sun like a harbor seal and reveled in the cool trade winds that carried away the heat. Finally, he knew it was time to go, time to get back, back down the volcano to McIver's house. And back to New England to start his life again. Just as the horizon spread out before him, so too lay his future, indistinct perhaps, just beyond the razor line of the horizon, but there waiting for him. It was time to seek it once more.

The way down the volcano was easier and faster than the climb, as much due the certainty of his course as the descent. Thom made his way back to McIver's in the late afternoon and was greeted by Johnny just arriving from the harbor.

"And where have you been, good sir?" He paused and looked Thom over. "Hardly presentable, I dare say, in those soiled clothes."

Thom laughed. "Scaled a volcano, I did."

Johnny raised an eyebrow. "First a hurricane, now a volcano. You're surely bound for trouble, young man."

❖❖❖

Johnny continued to visit McIver's office twice daily, and now, often as not, Thom tagged along. Johnny had settled well into playing the part of the traveling merchant, always asking the agent of news of any ship sailing for New England, always being assured that passage would be arranged on the first northbound ship. McIver took Johnny's persistent inquiries with a good humor which waned only slightly as the days passed. He was grateful enough that Johnny had kept to his part as a trader and had not resorted to frequenting the sailor's taverns of the Lower Town.

"As soon as a suitable ship completes loading and is scheduled for sailing, I will be the first to apprise you," McIver would say with a slow and patient smile.

Then one the evening three weeks after Thom and Johnny's arrival, when he met the two in his parlor and beamed, "We have a ship for you, gentlemen. The *Black Swan* sails within a week for Newport, your original home I believe, Mr. Stevens." His exuberant smile faded slightly as Johnny looked up and said, "*Black Swan*, you say," then paused as if to consider whether to accept the offer.

"You know the ship? Is she not suitable?" McIver asked, somewhat taken aback.

"Indeed, I know the ship, a snow rigged brigantine of three hundred tons," Johnny replied, then smiled. "She will serve us just fine, thank you, sir."

McIver, still a bit flustered, mumbled, "Well, very well then," and left the parlor.

Thom looked over at Johnny. "What do you know of the ship?"

"Not much. Know the owner better'n the ship. Alexander Mullins. Not the most savory sort. Got a sense of humor, I'll give 'em that. The *Black Swan*, she's a black bird and a black birder. In the Guineaman trade. But she'll get us home. She's loading molasses. Sold all her slaves in Monserrat. Captain's not much, but the ship's all right, what I hear tell."

Thom laughed. "So, it seems that you knew when the *Swan* was sailing well before our host got wind of it."

Johnny returned his smile, pleased with himself and delighted that Thom was smiling freely again. He opened the parlor cabinet. "Don't think Andrew would mind if we have a touch of his excellent Madeira, do you?"

❖❖❖

Four days later McIver's carriage deposited Thom and Johnny at the landing, each with a small sea chest packed with new clothes and with the clothes they had worn on their arrival, cleaned and restitched.

Andrew McIver arrived a few moments later. He pulled a small purse from his waist coat and handed it to Thom. "The remainder of the money you left in my care, after the cost of the passage and incidental expenses." He pulled a folded piece of paper from his coat pocket. "And here is a complete accounting of the sums," he said handing it to Thom with a flourish. "One other thing, would you gentlemen be so kind to carry this correspondence to Newport and see that it makes its way to Nicholas Brown and Company in Providence?"

"It would be our great pleasure, sir," Thom replied, extending his hand. "And may I say how grateful we are for all your hospitality."

"Twas my pleasure." McIver smiled and shook first Thom's hand then Johnny's. "Well, I wish you a speedy voyage home. A fair breeze and a gentle sea. If you'll excuse me, I'll take my leave."

When he was gone, Thom glanced at the figures on the accounting.

Johnny looked over. "So, did he charge us for room and board?"

Thom smiled. "A Scotsman on a Dutch Island employed by the sharpest traders in Rhode Island. Of course he charged us, and for the clothes, as well. Would concern me if he had failed to do so."

"Lucky there was anything left over."

"Ah, he treated us fairly and looked out well for our interests."

"Can't ask for more," Johnny agreed. He turned and looked toward the anchorage. The *Black Swan* was anchored close ashore and Johnny bellowed, "Hallo, the *Swan*." In a few minutes, a longboat pulled away from the ship and headed toward the landing.

"Mr. Taylor 'nd Mr. Tucker," the coxswain called from the longboat as it pulled alongside. "Aye," Johnny replied, hoisting his sea chest and stepping easily from the stone wharf into the bobbing boat. Thom followed with a half smile taking the seat facing Johnny. As the seamen pulled to the oars, Thom leaned forward and whispered, "I've forgotten. Am I Tucker or Taylor?"

Johnny laughed and whispered back, "Tucker."

BOOK TWO

MORNING RED

"The Revolution was effected before the War commenced. The Revolution was in the minds and hearts of the people; ...This ...was the real American Revolution."

John Adams

CHAPTER ONE

The *Black Swan* was a small ship whose high stern and quarterdeck made her appear even shorter than she was. Her flat transom had large windows and a rounded top, like the dormer on a Dutchman's house in Orangstadt. The two masts rising from the break of the quarterdeck and forward of the hatch only added to the illusion. Her hull was black, streaked with gray where the scuppers drained and she rode low in the water, loaded to capacity with molasses.

"Not much to look at, is she?" Johnny murmured softly.

"As long as she gets us home, she'll serve well enough," Thom replied.

The two sailors at the longboat's oars rowed with a measured rhythm, keeping a wary eye on their passengers in the stern. In his fancy clothes, Thom felt like a chicken impersonating a peacock and he looked back dumbly at the two seamen bending over the oars.

When they pulled close aboard the *Swan*, the longboat bumped clumsily along the side and was greeted by a voice on deck. "Watch your helm, God damn it." The coxswain looked up at the unseen speaker with a scowl and motioned to Thom and Johnny. "After you, gents."

Thom followed Johnny up the boarding ropes and found himself standing in front of a dark man of medium build wearing a fine blue coat and white breeches, topped with a bicorne hat. His attire contrasted with the otherwise squalid deck and its similarity to that of the Royal Navy gave Thom a momentary start.

"Welcome to the *Black Swan*, gentlemen. Samuel Martin, Chief Mate, at your service. Steward'll help you with your gear." He made a quarter turn and bellowed, "Phillips, on the double."

In a moment, a rotund man beneath a cocked hat appeared from the below. He tipped his hat, grabbed Thom's and Johnny's sea chests and started aft, then stopped when he realized that he wasn't being followed.

"Might we pay our respects to the captain?" Thom asked the mate.

Samuel Martin smiled. "Bit under the weather. Be all right a'fore we sail. Pay your respects then." Martin looked again toward Johnny, his brows furrowed for a moment, tilting his head slightly. Thom glanced toward Johnny, who smiled beneficently.

Thom looked about the deck of the little ship. Her main hatch was still open, barrels visible in the dark hold. Halyards and sheets lay jumbled on the deck planking, which itself looked none too clean. Suddenly, Thom felt uneasy, due either to the general disorder around him or something else that he couldn't name.

The steward cleared his throat and Thom and Johnny turned to follow. "Mind ya heads, now," Phillips said, as he led them below to a cabin in steerage, an eight by six cubicle with two bunks. One small port gave the only light and neither Johnny nor Thom could stand upright beneath the deck beams.

"Anything you want, give a call, gents," Phillips mumbled as he took his leave.

❖❖❖

Johnny stretched out on a bunk. "Fairly comfortable. Has the stench of a slaver."

The smell - that was what was bothering him. It brought Thom back to the hold of the *Romney*, of sitting in shackles like a bondsman. The odor of the *Black Swan*'s previous cargo, lost souls sold ashore to work the plantations of the sugar islands, had worked its way down between the ballast stones and would stay with the ship until she rotted or was torn apart on a reef.

Johnny stared off into space. "Ever sailed a blackbirder?" He glanced back at Thom who shook his head, "No." "I did once. Only once. An ugly business."

Thom glanced over at Johnny. "The mate gave you a knowing look. Crossed his way before?"

"He's met me, but doubt he can place it. I had the beard then. He's an arrogant bastard, not half as good as he thinks he is. Still, no worse than some. Watch him. Tried to cheat an uncle of mine once. Keep your coins in your pocket, and don't leave your purse in the cabin if you want to keep it till Newport."

Johnny seemed content to remain in his bunk as Thom repaired on deck for fresh air and to watch the last of the preparations for sea. He was not altogether pleased with what he saw, yet was not so unhappy as to warrant a complaint.

The mate and crew went about their tasks barely glancing at their passenger, leading Thom to believe that the story of their arrival on Statia had not drifted across the harbor to the *Swan*. Save the mate's first quizzical look at Johnny, the parts they played appeared to satisfy all concerned. Thom straightened his waistcoat and looked back at Statia, both saddened and pleased to be leaving the crowded island.

The *Black Swan* sailed that afternoon. Captain Middleton ascended to the quarterdeck only after the anchor was hove short. He stood unsteadily at the windward rail, the immediate effects of alcohol and the longer-term consequence of overeating, much in evidence. The crew lay fore and aft as the mate shouted commands, the crew in the waist hauling halyards, sheets, and braces as topmen scampered up the ratlines to cast off the gaskets.

The dirty canvas sails fluttered, then filled in the breeze and the wake began to whisper, then hum, as the brigantine gained speed, showing her larboard quarter to Statia. Thom savored the feel of the deck beneath his feet, the ship heeling ever so slightly in the fair and rising wind. Johnny came on deck and walked over to Thom on the leeward rail. "Good to be underway," Thom said.

Johnny nodded his agreement with a smile. "It'll be good to get home again. Has been quite a trip."

As Statia slipped astern and the mate shouted orders to harden up on the wind, Thom and Johnny climbed the ladder to the quarterdeck to stand at the leeward rail. Captain Middleton stepped over to them. "Gentlemen, pleased to have you aboard." Thom then Johnny made their introductions and were invited to share the captain's table that evening before Middleton resumed his post to windward.

If Thom or Johnny had hoped that the captain's corpulence suggested a fondness for savory provisions, they were disappointed. The steward served steaming salt pork and suet pudding that Captain Middleton attacked with vigor. Martin also ate with enthusiasm, if not the speed of his superior officer. Johnny thought wistfully of McIver's tender lamb as he sawed through the slab of meat glistening on his plate and silently cursed his hosts for choosing not to buy fresh stores ashore. Thom gave Johnny a wry smile as he ate methodically, not wishing to linger over the meal.

Captain Middleton had regained most of his sobriety now that they were underway and drank the coarse red wine from his decanter in moderation. "Well, gentlemen, I hope your trading here has been worthwhile. Ourselves, we did right well this trip. Loaded a hundred an' sixty-two Africans, boys, and women on the Guinea coast and delivered a hundred and thirty, almost anyway." He glanced over at Martin who piped up, "Near enough hundred and thirty, sir. Hundred and twenty-eight, all sold at good prices."

Middleton smiled. "And I don't think we could load a thimbleful more of Statia's fine molasses in her hold, try as we might." He took a deep drink from his glass. "As perfect a trade as God in his heaven could devise. So very like the chain of creation itself. Our molasses be distilled to rum, to trade for slaves, to trade for more molasses, to make more rum, for more slaves, each trade bein' more profitable than the last." His face bore a look of an almost complete contentment.

"I'm familiar with the trade, sir," Thom commented.

"Oh, have you and your partner plied the Gulf of Guinea?"

"No, sir. Can't say that we have."

"And may I ask, gentlemen, what trade are you in?"

Thom glanced at Johnny who replied, "We've been talking 'bout a new venture in Statia. Not at liberty to say much more."

"Yes," Thom joined in. "Regrettably, very preliminary and confidential, but offering much promise."

Captain Middleton snorted and the conversation shifted to the recent movement in sugar prices, but as Thom knew nothing of the subject, his contribution was mostly nods and non-committal asides. He hoped that Johnny might have picked up some specific knowledge on his rounds at Statia, but judging from his near silence, Thom guessed that Johnny knew as little as he.

Middleton and Martin appeared to view the quiescence of their passengers as a further unwillingness to discuss their business venture. This deprived them of a principal topic of conversation during the voyage, which on a ship as small as the *Black Swan* bordered on rudeness. Throughout the meal, Martin kept staring at Johnny as if puzzled, trying to place him. Thom decided that they might be better taking their supper in the cabin in the future. They could always feign seasickness if need be.

❖❖❖

Back in the cabin, Thom and Johnny took to their bunks. Johnny began speaking as if continuing an interrupted conversation.

"A perfect trade, the good capt'n called it. Perfect hell, if you ask me. The sole and solitary slaving trip I was on was near enough to perdition as I care to travel."

"*Romney* was close enough to a slaver for me," Thom commented.

"Compared to a slaver, the damned Royal Navy be a pleasure cruise," Johnny replied.

"The trip south was fine, the winds light in the middle passage but enough to move us along. But once in the bight of Benin, I truly caught a glimpse of the depths of the devil. The chiefs who sell the slaves will only keep a few together at a time, to stop the captives from rising up in rebellion. So getting a full cargo's a wearisome slow business.

"While the captain's ashore parlaying with the Africans, we just sat at anchor, rolling in the swells, bakin' in that infernal heat. To keep busy the bosun had us painting, and scraping and soogeying, mending anything that shows a bit of wear. 'Fore long there's nothing left to do but watch the carpenter buildin' the slave decks, not enough room to ship livestock, but that's all the room that the poor bastards were given.

"Daytime, the heat got so bad the tar melted from the deck seams and we took turns hauling buckets of salt water to douse each other trying to keep cool, or else we lay under awnings to keep out of the demon sun. When it was still, the heat could drive a man mad and when the wind blew, the harmattan, they called it, carried sand, fine and dry, an' would fill our ears and eyes and every mouthful of food.

"An' when the sun finally went down, the miskitties and gnats swarmed off the stinkin' green shore like the devil's own legions.

"Sounds grim," Thom said.

"Aye, an' that was just the start. We sat there for more'n three months and every day and every night a savage, near enough to a giant and close to blue as black, wearing nothing but rags and carrying a spear, stood watch on the beach, making sure that we didn't come ashore, as if ashore's where we so 'specially wanted to go. The insects never seemed to bother him neither, just standing there watching us, never sayin' a word."

Johnny hooked one toe to the heel of his other boot and kicked it off. "Course the bugs weren't the worst of it by a long shot. The miasma from shore would drift across at night and wasn't a month before the first fever came aboard. Before we had more'n a handful of blacks, the sailors began to die. T'was but good fortune I wasn't among 'em.

"The mate kept track of the tribes we were loading, mixin' 'em up so they didn't speak the same lingo, so they couldn't plan an escape. We loaded Mandigos, flat nosed bastards, and Ashantis, them with the high cheek bones and straight features. Even picked up a few Fulas with round heads and skins the color of apricots.

"We finally got a full load of 'em and every day we all stood an extra watch just making sure they didn't try to take the ship while we were still close enough to the shore that they stood a chance of gettin' home. The wail they set up once we were well away at sea was like the keening at a grave, knowing they would never see their kin again.

"Course, soon enough, they started dying, from fever or sorrow - times hard to tell which. We lost more'n a third of the slaves and an equal share of the crew 'fore we fetched the Indies again.

"T'was as ugly a business as I've ever seen or fear to see again. Never sign on a slaver. Started me thinkin' like my Quaker relations."

Johnny kicked off his other boot, turned on his side and slipped into sleep. Thom stared at the deck beams above him for what seemed like most of the night until sleep finally embraced him.

❖❖❖

For Thom, the nights and days that followed were strange and unsettling. The *Romney* returned in his dreams, lured by the roll of the ship and the stench below decks. Thom dreamed he was shackled in the hold. Dudingston's laugh, cold and indifferent, echoed around him. When he did wake, often in the small hours of the morning, it took time to realize where he was. In the quiet darkness, with only the hull softly groaning to the swell, Thom could swear he heard the clank of shackles, still bolted to the *Black Swan*'s frames in the hold, shifting as the ship rolled and was reminded that there were indeed worse nightmares than the *Romney*.

The enforced idleness of the days was vexing as well. While there was an indolent pleasure in watching others set and trim sails, lacking anything thing else to occupy him, the joy of it soon faded. The Captain had no library aboard and having chatted further with the man, Thom doubted that he had the need of one ashore either. He regretted now not offering to buy the additional copy of Plutarch's Lives that he found on McIver's bookshelf.

Still, the weather was fair and the *Black Swan*, close hauled on the trades, made good distance. Thom did his own calculations as to when they would make the turn north on the south-westerlies, glancing when he could at the mate's chart, careful not to show too much interest or too much knowledge.

❖ ❖ ❖

During the afternoon watch, Thom liked to climb to the maintop to sit and watch the horizon. The topmen, at first were concerned that he would fall, then quickly saw that Thom had been aloft before and returned to the deck or up to the t'gallant yard to allow the passenger his privacy. As often as not, Johnny joined him, the top perfectly sized for two to sit and talk.

"You know, Johnny, my father calls your fair colony Rogue's Island. Said it was laden with sharp dealers, pirates, whores, heretics, and thieves. "

Johnny laughed. "Not true, sir. Not true at all." He smiled. "There are in fact very few pirates. An' most of them were hired by His Majesty's Customs and moved on to Boston or New

London." Johnny glanced over toward Thom. "You spent much time in fair Rhode Island and the Providence Plantations?"

Thom shook his head. "Passed through, s'bout it."

Johnny cocked his head. "Stay a spell this time. Think you'll like it. A contrary, scrappy sort of place, some say. Every creed, race, and persuasion - all mixed up. No one able to gain a whip-hand. And no better place for a man to be whatsoever he chooses."

He paused for a moment, looking out at the high clouds. "An' it's awfully pretty. If you're around come spring I'll take you up to my cousin's farm. He's got apples and pears in his orchard an' his fields are chock full of pheasants and quail. You hunt much?"

Thom smiled. "Only a little. Never had the time. In my father's shipyard, if it was a day fair enough for hunting it was fair enough to be swinging an adz."

"Then I'll take you hunting. Last war I did pretty well with a rifle from the foretop pickin' off Frenchmen. When the captain asked how I shot so well, I told him that I just imagined that the French officer was a pheasant, ready for the spit."

"Imagine the roast pheasant tasted better than the Frenchman," Thom suggested.

Johnny laughed. "I hear tell that Frenchies can be right tasty, but they are woefully hard to clean."

The ship below them was quiet, save the sound of the wind and the creak of the rigging. Thom watched Martin walk forward to the ship's bell. He grabbed the bell rope and struck the bell eight times. As the crew scrambled for their stations, there was a cry from the lookout on the foremast crosstrees.

"Sail," he bellowed. "On the starboard bow. Looks to be a man-of-war." Thom and Johnny both turned and strained to see the ship, still hull down on the horizon. The ship would likely be either French or British. If they were on a crossing course, Thom prayed that it was French.

"From the cut of her t'gan'sails, I guess she's Royal Navy. Not a French cut," Johnny commented.

Thom snorted. "More's the pity. Rather not face another press gang just yet."

Johnny glanced at Thom, "Impressment's not legal in the Indies. That's the law."

Thom shrugged. "I know. Just like the law says they can't press a man younger than eighteen. Didn't stop them from grabbing me in Boston. All I got for reminding them of my age was a colting from the bosun. That Royal Navy Captain might not be so fastidious about the geography."

"True enough," Johnny replied. He squinted at the distant ship. "Her sails look awfully new. White and clean, like they were fresh from the sail maker. At least we know that she's not the *Romney*."

"I guess that is something. *Romney*'s top hamper is old and tired, to be sure."

The man-of-war stood towards them for another hour, rising slowly on the horizon until her black and ocher hull was just visible. Then she turned away on an opposite course, sailing sou'west to their north east. Thom breathed easier, though he watched the ship until it disappeared in the failing light of dusk.

❖❖❖

Once they turned north with the southwesterly breeze, lighter than the trades but still steady, pushing them along on their larboard quarter, the weather began to change. The perpetual springtime of the Caribbean winter began slipping away and Thom and Johnny were grateful again to McIver as they pulled out woolens from the sea chests that he had provided.

Thom spent less time at the main top and more on the fo'c'sle, still warm enough on a broad reach. As they crossed the Gulf Stream he reveled in the antics of the dolphins playing tag in the bow wave, gracefully, effortlessly darting ahead then falling back. Two, then three, or four, their backs glistening gray and blue, their beaks leaving their own bow waves of dancing diamonds as they chased along, perfectly free, without care, in the boundless glory of the moment, skimming along on the limitless vault of the sea.

Once the Chesapeake Capes drew abeam, unseen far below the horizon to larboard, the weather turned bitter and Thom spent most of his hours below deck. When he did venture on deck, the wind tore through him and seemed to rob him of his strength. He cursed his own idleness and returned below. Johnny carved a cribbage board from a scrap of timber he bought from the ship's carpenter and successfully beat Thom game after game. Those few games he won, Thom suspected, were merely inducements granted by his wily opponent to hold his interest and keep him playing.

After a fortnight at sea, the lookout sighted Monhegan Bluffs on Block Island, shining gold and green against a hazy blue dawn. All hands turned to, anxious to make the first glimpse of home.

Thom had difficulty rising that morning. The cold of the season seemed to seep through the very planks of the ship. His bones ached and he shivered as he climbed from the berth, as anxious as any to see land again. Bundled in his coat he stepped beside Johnny on the quarterdeck.

Thom glanced over toward the mate. "Well, can't fault his navigation." He shuddered. "Damn it's cold," and pulled his jacket tighter around him.

"No, he did all right this time," Johnny replied. He looked over toward Thom who was shaking visibly now and his forehead was bathed in sweat. "Damn it man, you've got fever. Let's get you below." He threw his arm around Thom's shoulder and helped him to the cabin, covering him with both blankets.

"Not just the weather." Thom said with a weak smile.

"We'll get you to shore soon enough and you'll be just fine. You rest easy now." Thom appeared to be drifting off to sleep so Johnny left the cabin to find the captain.

The waiting was the worst part. They were close, but not yet alongside. After a thousand miles of empty ocean, Montauk Point was slowly pulling abeam and the whole of Block Island emerged from the haze. Johnny strained to see Point Judith as if looking harder could pull it closer. He had served on ships where landsmen passengers demanded to be put ashore as soon as the lookout sighted land, still a day out of port. He had always thought them fools yet now he could, at least, sympathize with their sense of urgency. The *Black Swan* continued to make good speed, perhaps four knots, but was slowed by currents sweeping out from the Race on the ebb tide. Johnny went below again to roust out the steward. Thom could use some broth, perhaps with a tout of rum.

Thom was sweating copiously and shivering from the cold when Johnny went in to check on him. Johnny covered the blankets with Thom's coat and called the steward again to see about the broth. When it finally arrived he succeeded in getting Thom to drink only a few swallows. Johnny swore to himself, cursing all the angels of heaven. He had seen too many shipmates die of fever. They had come too far for it to end like this. Thom was young and strong and he prayed that that would be enough.

It was midday before Block Island fell astern and the bearing on Point Judith began to widen. By early afternoon, Johnny could just make out Beavertail Light, a stone tower on the end of Conanicut Island, marking the entrance to the East Passage.

Shadows lengthened quickly in the light of the winter afternoon. The day was fair except when the wind gusted, sending an icy blast through his coat. Johnny looked for the mate, finding him on deck speaking to the bosun. When he finished Johnny took him aside.

"Shall we fetch Newport tonight?"

"Not likely wit' the darkness and the ebb against us, " Martin replied with almost a sneer.

"So, you'll anchor in Hull Cove?"

The mate raised an eyebrow as if to ask what Johnny knew of Hull Cove. His gaze narrowed slightly, as he said, "Good chance we will. Might do some unloading in the cove tomorrow. Not get to Newport till the following day, maybe later."

Johnny understood what he meant. They would discharge as much molasses as possible to avoid the duty before arriving in Newport, a reasonable practice. Only he and Thom weren't waiting. "I'll need to borrow your longboat once you anchor. My associate, Mr. Tucker, has fever. I want him ashore to a doctor tonight."

"You want my longboat? You'll get ashore when I want you ashore and not one minute before and the same goes for your friend, fever or no." Martin smiled a mirthless grin until Johnny took one step closer and took hold of his shirt.

Johnny was three inches taller than Martin and more heavily built. He fixed Martin's gaze with a glare of iron and pulled him closer by his collar. His voice was low. "You send me and my friend ashore tonight in your longboat and by dawn tomorrow, you can have a half dozen boats unloading your goddamn molasses.

"Or, sure as the sun sets o'r Point Judith, I'll throw your worthless hide overboard and we'll take the longboat to fish you out. Now, maybe we'll find you in the darkness and maybe we won't, but I will be in Newport tonight with Mr. Tucker, one way or the other. "

"Take your hand off me, you bastard," Martin growled.

Johnny's grip tightened. Martin could feel himself being lifted and his shirt beginning to tear. "Maybe I should toss you over the side right now just for the practice." Johnny's other hand grabbed the mate's belt and Martin felt his feet begin to leave the deck. Johnny glanced over Martin's shoulder to see if the bosun would come to the mate's aid. If the bosun came at him, he would keep Martin between them and knock down them both down at once. The bosun and several of the crew were just standing by, looking away, hearing all that was said, not interested in lending a hand. Giving the bastard all the loyalty he deserves, Johnny thought.

Martin's face was beginning to turn purple as his collar cut into his throat. "You'll have your longboat, you son of a bitch, now take your hands off me."

Martin's heels returned to the deck with a thud when Johnny released his grasp. "Until tonight then, sir," Johnny said with a half smile, turned and went below. From the corner of his eye, he saw the bosun trying to suppress a grin as Martin stomped off scowling to the quarterdeck.

❖❖❖

The sun, wrapped in fire swept clouds, sank quickly behind the dark shore of Point Judith. The sky bled from blue to purple to black, the stars shining dimly compared to the stronger beacon on Beavertail Point. The lighthouse was an old friend greeting Johnny on yet another passage home, a cold white light on a colder still winter's night.

The *Black Swan* ghosted in close ashore, avoiding the worst of the ebb tide trying to push it back out to sea. As they passed the lighthouse, the light cast long shadows through the rigging, illuminating the deck unnaturally, and the crew looked away so as not to be struck night-blind. Johnny went below to get their gear together. Thom was still sleeping, breathing heavily and Johnny decided not to wake him. He carried the two sea chests up on deck as the bow of the *Black Swan* rounded up into Hull Cove.

The bunts and clews were hauled, halyards were let fly, and all hands scrambled to furl the sails and to ready the ground tackle. Johnny could hear more than see what was going on. He felt the ship swing around, her bow into the wind, and heard the anchor splash down, the rode running out as the ship fell back.

He waited for her anchor to be set and for the commotion on deck to subside before he sought out the bosun. "Believe the mate has been kind enough to lend us the longboat to get my friend ashore this evening."

The bosun smiled and nodded. "See to it presently, sir."

❖❖❖

Thom was stretched out in the bottom of the longboat, covered with blankets, neither sleeping nor quite awake, shivering from fever, as four seamen hauled on the oars. Johnny sat in the stern with a shielded lantern. The wind was gusting bitterly now and flurries of snow cut at their faces. They followed the shadow of the island, rowing just far enough off the bank to keep their oars in the water, staying in the eddies that swirled off the shore, hiding them from the force of the ebb. At Bull Point they turned to cross the East Passage, crabbing their way across the channel, pointing the bow higher than their course as the tide tried to carry them back downstream. A short, steep chop slapped the hull, throwing an icy spray at the oarsmen, a light mist hitting Thom, carrying aft to burn on Johnny's cheeks. Finally, on the far side, they slipped beneath the shadow of Fort Point and into the sheltered waters of Breton Cove.

The longboat wove through the crowded anchorage, past myriad moored boats and ships, black and looming shapes in the darkness, as Johnny directed the oarsmen toward Long Wharf. Once alongside, he heaved the sea chests onto the dock, lifted Thom carefully from the bilge of the boat and with one arm around his waist and the other on his shoulder, carried his friend up onto the wharf.

"Wait a while," the coxswain called as he climbed on to the dock, followed by a sailor. "Johnson here'll help you with your gear."

CHAPTER TWO

A block from the wharf, Johnny stood before a shuttered chandlery. He held Thom with one arm beneath his shoulders. "Uncle Isaiah! Rouse yourself, Uncle!" Johnny bellowed. He stood there shouting for a time before the shutters on a second-floor window swung open and a familiar face beneath a stocking cap peered from the darkness.

"Who in bloody 'ell is makin' such a racket?" His eyes narrowed and his brow knit. "Johnny? Well, I'll be damned." His scowl softened. "When did ye get back? What ship?"

"Just arrived, Uncle. I've a friend with fever. Want to get him by a fire."

The shutter swung shut and in a moment the front door opened and Johnny helped Thom across the threshold. Once inside, Isaiah led Johnny and Thom through the dark chandlery and up the narrow stairs to a small parlor. A fire, banked for the night, glowed dully in the hearth and a gray-haired woman stood in the doorway of one of the two rooms off the parlor. Johnny nodded to her with a smile. "Evening, Aunt Liz'beth. Sorry to make such a ruckus and so late."

"Ach, good to see you, John, anytime. Set yourself down while I make up a bed for you and your friend. Isaiah, give the fire a stir." The old woman shuffled off into the other room as Johnny helped Thom down onto a bench, leaning against the wall opposite the fire. Thom opened his eyes slightly and looked over to Johnny. "You'll be fine, Thom," Johnny said, putting his hand on his friend's shoulder. Thom closed his eyes again and said softly, "Feels like my head is split wide open." He raised both hands to his face.

In a few minutes, Johnny helped him into the other room, hardly larger than their cabin on the *Swan*, where his Aunt had made up two beds. Isaiah pulled on a pair of pants and threw a coat on over his nightshirt. He stuck his head in the door. "Be back with the doctor soon as I can." Thom tossed fitfully on the narrow bed as Johnny sat next to him on a bench.

Johnny fell asleep sitting up and woke with a start as Isaiah and a man he didn't know came into the room. "Make way for the doctor, John." There wasn't room for all of them, so John and Isaiah stood by the door as the doctor examined Thom. The doctor looked drunk or just sleepy and Johnny hoped for the latter. Thom's eyes were half open yet it appeared unseeing.

In a few minutes, the doctor shuffled from the room. "Ship's fever, no doubt, caused by the miasma in the recesses of the vessel. Too soon to tell if it should manifest as putrid or bilious or even yellow fever. Keep him comfortable as best you can and I'll call back in a few days unless he takes a turn for the worse."

❖❖❖

The next morning Johnny took the bundle of letters given to him by McIver bound for John Brown in Providence. He wrote a note to Mr. Brown forwarding the bundle, apologizing for not calling in person, mentioning Thom's fever. He wrapped and sealed it along with the other correspondence and sent it off with the morning express rider to Providence. He paid the rider, as he had the doctor, with coins from Thom's purse, feeling a bit like a thief, but seeing no immediate alternative.

In the evening, two days later, a rider arrived at Uncle Isaiah's door, a tall dark haired man in his early twenties holding a small bag in one hand. "John Mawney, at your service, sir. I am here representing Mr. John Brown."

"You 'is messenger?" Isaiah asked, not quite sure what to make of the man before him, well-dressed, if muddy from the road.

"No, sir. I am most assuredly not." Then the young man paused a moment and said with half a smile, "Well, perhaps in this instance, I am, at least in part. Mr. Brown wished to express his concern over Mr. Larkin's condition and he asked me to call and observe him myself. I am a physician."

"A touch young to be a doctor aren't ye?"

"Graduated two years ago, medicine and physics, fourth in my class, sir," he replied with just a hint of irritation. "Now may I see Mr. Larkin?"

Isaiah stepped aside and motioned up the stairs.

Mawney found Thom lying on his cot in a deep stupor with Johnny sitting beside him wiping his head with a cool cloth. Mawney introduced himself and began examining Thom.

"Doctor the other night said it was likely ship fever," Johnny volunteered.

"Where'd you say he sailed from?"

"The Indies, Statia," Johnny replied. "On the *Black Swan*."

The doctor checked Thom's pulse and looked at his arms and legs. "Not too likely that it is yellow jack. The miasma, the bad shore air, would have affected him sooner. *Swan*'s a slaver, isn't she. All sorts of different fevers on the Guinea coast. Still, I agree with your doctor's diagnosis. Probably, ship fever - typhus. Did he complain of anything else?"

"Said he had a headache. Doctor gave him some laudanum."

Mawney nodded. "Headache's fairly typical of typhus. His humors are dangerously out of balance. I'll bleed him to reduce the strain on his nerve fluids and give him another draught of laudanum to ease the pains in his head. See this rash around his hands, also a clear indication of typhus. Be best to burn his clothes in case the effluvium may have lingered. Don't want it to spread."

When he was finished he handed Johnny a small bloody basin and several stained towels. "Please look after these, if you will. Why don't we speak in the parlor? Less likely to disturb Mr. Larkin."

Johnny stepped backward from the room and waited as Mawney packed his small bag.

"Well, Mr. Larkin is quite ill. No need, perhaps, to tell you that. We'll have to see how he responds to treatment." He paused. "That is, if you have no objection to my offering my services."

"Your fee, sir?"

Mawney smiled. "You needn't worry. Mr. John Brown will compensate me for my assistance."

"Why should John Brown care about Mr. Larkin? He's no relation."

"And why, sir, do you care for Mr. Larkin? I do not understand that he is kin of yours."

Johnny was taken aback for an instant. "He's a shipmate and a particular friend, which is kin enough. And I do believe he saved my life when he brought the brig *Mary Ellen* into Boston after the captain died."

"Reason enough indeed," Mawney replied. "I believe that John Brown took a special regard for Mr. Larkin after their meeting in Boston last summer. I would suspect that Mr. Brown was a grateful as well to young Mr. Larkin for saving his ship, just as you were for his saving your life aboard the ship. Beyond that, I can not tell you why John Brown has an interest in Mr. Larkin anymore than I can explain the interests of any of the brothers Brown. All I know is that their judgments are so very often right that I have almost stopped questioning them." He paused, waiting for an objection from Johnny and saw none.

"I have taken a room at the Mill Stone Tavern and will attend Mr. Larkin mornings and evenings until the crisis is past."

"And how long do you expect that to be?"

"Difficult to say. Perhaps a fortnight, if fortune favors us. Longer if not. Less time, if he turns for the worse. It is hard to predict the course of the illness."

❖ ❖ ❖

John Mawney, good to his word, called on Thom twice the following day and the days that followed. Thom remained in a stupor, tormented by pains in his head and stomach. He cried out when a shaft of sunlight played across him, so they darkened the room with a blanket over the window.

Johnny stayed by Thom's side, leaving only when sent on errands by Dr. Mawney or chased out by his aunt. Aunt Elizabeth would lean into the room. "John Stevens, you look near as bad as young Thomas there. Be gone from that sick room for a few hours or yea'll be afflicted yourself. I'll look after Thomas. I've treated more'n a few fevers in my time. Darn sight more than you have, so get yourself from here 'fore I chase you with a broom like some stray cat."

When Johnny stumbled out into the street, the winter's sun seemed unnaturally bright and the wind tore at his coat. He hurried down the street to Miller's tavern and drank a jar or two of porter before returning to his vigil by Thom's bedside.

After a week, whenever Thom moved, he whimpered in torment. Dr. Mawney noted each symptom, commenting calmly that none was unusual during the progress of the infirmity. Johnny felt like crying out himself in a rage that no more could be done, but he saw that Mawney was doing all within his power. Johnny became his assistant, helping him to bleed and purge Thom, listening with both interest and concern as the young doctor explained the modern theories of medicine, the new techniques to ease imbalances in the fibrous aspects of the blood vessels and nerves while increasing their strength and elasticity and reducing nerve stress and blockages. The breadth of the Mawney's scientific knowledge and understanding gave Johnny some comfort though their combined efforts seemed to comfort Thom little enough.

❖ ❖ ❖

For Thom, the days sank beneath a fevered sea of pain and laudanum dreams. He was tossed like flotsam caught on the tides, swirling in eddies of torment and memory, with neither dusk nor dawn to mark the passage of time. In his delirium, he was back on the *Romney*, chained in the hold only to be yanked into blinding sunlight and lashed to a grating. The cat's tails flayed his skin, back, and chest, somehow all at the same time, Dudingston's leer and Lasco's laugh taunting him as he screamed. Then he was high in the rigging, free in the wind, swinging from top to stay until his hand slipped and he spiraled into space far above the deck, falling fast then crumpling slowly as he hit the oak planks, feeling each bone shatter, each muscle rend and burst, skin and sinew slowly ripped asunder.

His body, a wailing mass, slipped through the main deck and passed like a spirit cross the gun deck, finally to stop where he began, in the dark recesses of the hold, shackled to rusting chain, assaulted by the stench, soothed only by the murmur of bilge water between the ballast stones.

Shadows moved across the hold, the shapes comforting now and he seemed to be back in his father's house, years before angry words had driven him away. He sensed his mother and elder brother, though his eyes wouldn't answer to his helm and he never made them out.

The madness and anguish ebbed slowly, reason returning in slim tendrils, slowly weaving sail enough to catch the cooling breeze. He looked across the small room and saw a tall man looking back at him. His mind said, "Who might you be, sir," though his lips and throat, barren and burning, croaked only, "Who ... " a guttural sound more like that of an animal than his own voice.

The man smiled. "We've spent much time together, Mr. Larkin, yet I haven't introduced myself. I pray that you overlook the oversight. My name is John Mawney, Dr. John Mawney, and you are responding well to treatment. Quite well indeed."

"Where?" Thom croaked, trying to lift his head from the pillow, but finding the struggle too great.

The man pulled up a rough stool in the narrow space between the two cots. "You are in the house of Isaiah and Elizabeth Stevens, uncle and aunt to your shipmate and friend John Stevens."

Thom lifted his head and tried to reply, but his strength had left him and his head fell back against the pillow.

"Rest now, Thomas, you've done quite enough for one day."

Thom slipped again into darkness, but now at least the angry winds had stilled.

❖❖❖

The next afternoon, Johnny sat in a dark corner of the tavern, chased from the house by his aunt's threats. Dr. Mawney came down the narrow steps from his room above the bar. Johnny was struck that Mawney himself looked tired and pale, even for winter. Mawney saw Johnny, smiled, called for another porter and joined him.

"I believe that Thomas has finally seen the worst of it. The greatest threat may well be past. "

"I pray that you are right."

"Yesterday evening while you were on an errand for your aunt, Thomas spoke to me. Asked me who I was. He appears sensible again." Mawney raised his mug and took a deep drink, looking weary, but with a half smile.

"Why that is fine news, sir. Fine news indeed. Sorry I missed you last night so that I could have heard it sooner. Fine, fine news." Johnny's own smile spread fully across his face.

"He has gone through a great ordeal, of course, and may still need some considerable time to recover. Your uncle and aunt have been quite generous in the use of their home though Thomas will need continuing care." He paused. "Prior to my arrival here, John Brown instructed me to offer whatever assistance he could offer. His house in Providence is large and could perhaps provide the quiet and sort of care that Thomas will need if he is to return to us in all his health. "

Johnny knew that he couldn't ask Uncle Isaiah and Aunt Elizabeth to care for Thom indefinitely and come spring, there would be little time with the Newport fleet outfitting for the season. Still, part of him didn't want to let Thom be taken away as if he had a duty to watch over the young man. Yet, for all his watching, Johnny never seemed to be able to make much of a difference. All he could do was watch.

Johnny glanced over warily. "Fair enough. Fancy his house may be, but a ride to Providence be woefully hard on Thom about now."

"I agree. We'll have to see how he fares over the next several days. If he strengthens as I hope, I'll arrange a wagon for transport. Until tomorrow then. I'll stop by in the morning."

Johnny's caution eased as he shook Mawney's hand. Aunt Elizabeth always said, "Look to Providence for succor and salvation," but he knew that she didn't mean the Providence Plantations.

Three days later, Mawney arrived with a buckboard and four fine horses. A frame of pine had been nailed together and covered with painted canvas to form a sort of tent in the back of the buckboard. Thom had begun to revive as Mawney had predicted, but still needed both Johnny and Mawney to help him down the stairs and up onto his pallet in the wagon.

Once Thom was covered with several layers of blankets, Mawney climbed up and took the reins and seemed surprised when Johnny joined him at his side. His questioning look was greeted by a cock of Johnny's head and a glance that clearly said that he wasn't letting his young charge being taken away without being satisfied that Thom's new accommodations were satisfactory. Mawney smiled, nodded and flicked the reins and the loaded wagon clattered off, up the Providence Road.

CHAPTER THREE

Thom felt himself being lifted up, a strong arm around his shoulder, a hand at his back. He seemed to float across the parlor and to drift down the dark tunnel of the stairs, his own frail form pressed against the shadows that carried him, rubbing on either side against the plaster walls. When they reached the door, the sunlight was overwhelming, yet not the torment that it had been in the weeks before.

He was carried through the brilliance and lifted up again into shadows, comfortable to be lying down, sheltered beneath the weight of woolen blankets. He slowly opened his clenched eyes and found himself inside what seemed to be a box. His hand reached out and touched canvas, and he was relieved that the enclosure was not a coffin, or if so, it was a canvas coffin, suitable for burying a sailor, dead or alive, or perhaps lingering somewhere between.

They jerked to a start, bouncing over the wagon-rutted road. A dull ache coursed through his arms, legs, and chest, yet Thom was pleased by the motion, happy to cast off again, free of the room and the pallet that had been his world for what seemed a time beyond years. The buckboard rocked in an uneven rhythm and Thom slipped into a dream, drifting into a realm free, at last, of pain.

When he awoke, he had no idea how long he had slept. Above him glowed a sky of pallid blue and he floated on clouds of warmth and sweetness. A gentle breeze lifted translucent curtains and at a short distance, an angel sat quietly in a gown of pale peach. The light from the window wrapped her in an aurora of gold as she read from a small book that she held in her lap, her dark hair flowing across her shoulders.

The paradise of preachers and propriety was not reputed to favor sailors, but this seemed near enough to heaven. As his head cleared, he was relieved to see that the sky above him was the painted ceiling and that he lay not on clouds but a bed, softer perhaps than any he had known, but a bed, nevertheless. He smiled to himself, doubting that heaven had windows, curtains, walls, or beds. He looked over toward the corner, saw that the young woman he had taken for an angel was still there.

As he looked, she turned her head. "Glad to see that you've awakened. How do you feel, Mr. Larkin? I must say, you looked far better in Boston, when last we met." She laughed. "Do you remember me, by chance?"

He remembered her well indeed, even if he had forgotten how beautiful she was; her smile, so lovely; her eyes, dark and shining. "Tis a joy to see you, Miss Brown. Sorry that I'm..." Thom felt overcome by weariness, not sure quite what he was saying. He rested for a moment. "I regret that I'm not a more presentable visitor." He smiled, pleased that he had finished his thought, and lay his head back against the softness of the bed.

"You've survived your journey, which is more than could be said of many. My father told me the tale that your friend, Mr. Stevens, related to him. Remarkable. I am pleased that you returned to us at all, regardless of how you arrived."

"You are most gracious," Thom replied at little more than a whisper, his eyes leaden.

"We've spoken enough. I'll let you rest," she said and was gone.

❖❖❖

The days that followed were a perplexing mix of wonder and weariness. Thom was cared for by Angela Brown and Margaret, a house servant; with John Mawney visiting every afternoon. Each day Thom felt stronger, only to be struck down by the smallest thing - trying to speak, or sitting up too long at any given time. Mawney cautioned patience while Angela encouraged his efforts. Thom seemed to be tacking against a flood tide, making good distance on each leg, only to be carried back again by the current. He knew that as long as he wasn't driven onto the rocks, he would finally see slack water.

In just over a week, he could sit up on his own, and not long after, forced himself to stand, much to the alarm of Angela when his grasp on the chair back weakened and he slipped to the floor with a graceless thud. She rushed to him as he lay there, chagrined. He hurt, but couldn't stop himself from laughing to Angela's dismay and delight.

The next day, his host and benefactor, John Brown, strode into the room. He was taller than Thom remembered, near enough to a giant from Thom's vantage point. Squarely built, John Brown appeared to be filled with an energy that Thom hoped might prove contagious.

"I see much improvement in you, truly I do. Dr. Mawney told me that you were out of danger, although from your appearance when you came to us, I must say that I wasn't so sure."

"I feel much better, sir. I cannot express my gratitude for your interest and generosity."

John Brown raised his hand. "Speak no more of it. A trifling thing. You returned a ship to us. We certainly can aid in your recovery. "

He crossed his arms and said with a grin, "Although I will warrant that I have all rights to be angry with you. I offered you a position one morning and not the next day do I learn that you've shipped out with another concern."

Thom smiled, "I can assure you, sir, that I would have found far greater felicity beneath your house flag than theirs."

"I have no doubt that you would, sir." Brown's smile drained from his face. " I have seen the scars on your back. Get your rest. We have much to speak of."

One morning, just after breakfast, Angela came to Thom's room and announced, "I believe it is time for an outing, Thomas Larkin. The fresh air will revitalize you, I don't care what John Mawney says. It is too lovely a day to waste after so wearisome a winter."

Thom could only laugh. "I am in no position to argue with you, Miss Angela, and I would enjoy a carriage ride more than anything I can imagine."

Angela smiled. "Then I shall meet you at the stable."

Albert, the house slave, helped Thom dress in a fine linen shirt and breeches with silk stocking and shoes with silver buckles. He swung a tan leather coat with a fleece lining around Thom's shoulders. The coat felt heavy even as he sat in the chair next to the bed.

"There you are, young sir. That'll keep you warm, surely it will."

Albert put a strong arm around Thom and helped him outside to the stable where the coach waited and hoisted him up to the seat across from Angela who nodded and said, "Let us be on our way, Albert." The black man climbed aboard and gave the horse as a quick snap of the reigns.

Angela was right, it was a glorious day for, what? Early March? Thom had lost count of the months. Whenever it may have been, the air was warm and the breeze drifting through the rocking carriage felt fresh and invigorating.

They had gone a short way, leaving the cobblestones and passing onto a dirt lane leading out of town, when Angela leaned over toward him intently.

"Now, you must tell me of your adventures," she said with a gleam in her eye.

"Hardly a tale worth telling," Thom suggested with a shrug.

Angela sat back abruptly. "I'll have none of that, Thomas Larkin. I know you to be no fool and false modesty is not becoming." She arched an eyebrow. "Unless you think that a silly young girl should be spared such things, in which case I'll rid you of such a notion this very morn."

"I cannot say that I've ever considered you to be a silly young girl, Miss Brown."

"Miss Brown, indeed," she replied. "You call me Angela, save when you are mocking me." She scowled at him, barely shielding a smile. "I've turned 16 and I am certain that when my younger brother achieves my age, he'll sail as captain's clerk or maybe even supercargo and then see the Indies and perhaps England or Spain through his own eyes."

"So you wish to sign articles, do you? You'd make a most unlikely Jack Tar if I may be so bold." Thom realized that he was smiling. It felt good.

She huffed, "I am most pleased to be who I am, which doesn't mean that I must hide in my father's house and never look beyond the shutters. So, tell me now of being pressed aboard a man-of-war."

"It's not a pretty story."

"The best tales are often not the prettiest," she replied.

Thom sat back in the coach. "I feel as if I died and went to the devil, only to be cast back and to be reborn in the Providence Plantations."

Angela smiled and tilted her head, waiting for the rest. Thom spoke slowly of Boston and of the *Romney*, of Captain Corner, Lieutenant Dudingston, Bosun Lasco, of poor Michael Skinner and the rest. Her eyes widened to the tale, never flinching or feigning shock as he told of the floggings, of being flogged himself and of the terrible anger that burned in him long after his back had healed.

As he described their escape in the hurricane, she smiled and grew animated as if she was imagining riding a jolly boat down the face of a boiling wave. He smiled back at her, amused by her easy enthusiasm. He ended the tale quickly not wishing to dwell on his illness. "And once my strength returns, I'm away back to sea."

She looked out the window of the carriage. "I imagine that the life of a sailor must be a pleasant one. Once at sea, I mean, and when the winds favor. The captains I know assure me that the gales are not so frequent and on some courses, they don't touch the sails for days at a time."

Thom laughed. "Perhaps if your brother goes to sea, you should join him to see for yourself. The life of a sailor is endless toil, to be sure."

He looked into her eyes, hazel and flashing. The light from the carriage window bathed her cheek and the lovely curve of her mouth in a soft gold. He suspected that she was toying with him, though he didn't care. Her smile barely concealed a smirk, and he wondered whether she knew more than she admitted and only played the ignorant lass. Perhaps she reveled in the naughty pleasure of lowering herself to speak with a common sailor. He chose to ignore whatever caprice she had chosen. Whatever it may be, he would enjoy it.

"What were the sailors like aboard the man-of-war? Mostly pressed men? Or were they all cutthroats and the dregs from the gutter, as some say?"

"Many were pressed. Some were experienced sailors pulled off merchantmen and some were landsmen, caught by chance. The rest were like any ship. A few scalawags, but most were just sailors.

"I was surprised how different I felt from my shipmates. Not John Stevens or the pressed Boston men, but the other foremast hands." Thom looked away from Angela and for a moment was lost in the light streaming through the carriage window. "Sailors are all cut from the same cloth, but still, there was something that made us separate. The Americans stood out. We could jump as fast to an order, knuckle our brows just like any other tar, but the other hands averted their eyes when an officer was near, dropped their heads, and were quicker to accept and go along. The bosun called us his damn colonials because we weren't so fast to bow and scrape."

Thom smiled to himself. "My grandfather told me that the Dutchmen back when New York was New Amsterdam use to call their countrymen born in New Amsterdam - John Cheese, or Yan-Kees, the way they say it as if growing up so far from crown and scepter, made them different. Maybe it does. Maybe we are."

He turned his head back toward Angela, almost as if he had forgotten she was there. "I apologize for rambling on so. I pray I did not offend."

She only laughed. "I cannot speak for those at sea though the English gentry in Providence does seem almost a different race at times. I see it in the way they look at my father and his brothers, men of greater ability and means than they could ever hope to aspire, and yet the aristocrats look toward them with disdain, envious of their wealth and scornful of their enterprise." She tilted her head and smiled, as asking what could be done, then turned and looked out the carriage window once more. The light played across her face in delicate, shifting rays of color and shadow, and Thom found that he lacked the strength to look away.

❖ ❖ ❖

As his vitality returned, he took walks down to the docks and out along country lanes, sometimes with Angela and Margaret and sometimes alone. Inactivity was as hard to bear as the sickness had been. Dr. Mawney called on him, though less regularly, still advising rest and patience. Thom protested that he had had far too much of the first and had wholly exhausted the second. He tried to help Albert with household chores though the old black man shooed him away. "No kinda work for you, Mr. Thomas."

Thom found himself thinking always of Angela. She filled his thoughts, both as joy and torment. What business did a penniless sailor have becoming infatuated with the daughter of he richest man in the colony? What form of madness had taken hold of him that he could not get her out of his mind? He seemed to have recovered from one fever only to be taken by another.

He walked the cobblestone streets of Providence, trying to decide his next course. Once he had recovered his strength he could find a berth on an outbound ship, sail off and try to forget Angela. The life a sailor was the life he knew. He knew nothing of the world of the counting house, of the intricacies of trade, of the ways of merchants like the Browns. Shouldn't he just be happy to live the life he knew? Whenever he was ready to answer affirmatively, thoughts of the way Angela's eyes flashed when she laughed flooded back. He knew he wasn't ready to simply try to forget her.

Should he stay in Providence? Until he was stronger, he had no other choice. And then one afternoon, he found himself walking past the Brown's counting house door. He stopped in the street for a moment. Suddenly, he knew which course he would choose to steer.

The next morning, Thom dressed carefully and walked to the counting house of Nicholas Brown and Brothers. He raised the heavy bronze knocker and rapped at the door.

"Is Mr. John Brown available?"

The clerk looked at him querulously but showed him in. He was surprised that the inner sanctum of the greatest merchant family in Providence was not more grand. A large fireplace divided the room in half. One end was filled by six clerks standing at writing desks, while at the other, the four desks of the brothers Brown faced out. John sat at one desk, lost in correspondence, while two others were occupied by a pair of men who, from the shared resemblance, were clearly his brothers.

John Brown looked up. "Thomas Larkin. Good to see you up and about."

Thom walked over and said, "Mr. Brown, I am deeply indebted to you for your care and generosity, sir." Thom tried to stand as straight as he could and hoped that his voice didn't waiver. "Accepting charity is difficult enough for me, but this idleness is intolerable. Is there any manner of work that I could do that would be of service to you, sir? I would be most grateful for the opportunity, whatever it may be."

John smiled. "Well, you can write. Can you cipher?"

"Aye, sir. I can." Thom replied almost too eagerly.

"Well, then we'll set you to work this very morning, young sir."

John Brown rose as if to lead Thom over to the other side of the room, before stopping. "I should first introduce you to my brothers and partners." He guided Thom to the desk farthest from the door. A slender man with a slightly hooked nose glanced up at Thom, examining him as a hawk might a sparrow.

"Nicholas, may I present Mr. Thomas Larkin, the young man of whom I have spoken. He has volunteered to assist us while he recuperates."

"Thomas, Mr. Nicholas Brown, founder of the firm and my eldest brother."

"My pleasure, Mr. Larkin," Nicholas replied, extending a bony hand, neither rising nor smiling.

"At your service, sir," Thom replied.

John Brown's hand at his back steered him away. "You shall have to make the acquaintance of my other elder brother, James, at some other time," he remarked nodding toward the empty desk. "He is presently at our iron works in Hope. He is the engineer and artist of our family.

"Ah, but there is something that I must show you." He stepped quickly over to what appeared to be a chart table. Plans for a house, or rather a mansion to Thom's eye, were spread across the table top. "My new house on Water Street. Well, it is to be on Water Street. James designed it for me, as he did the Baptist Church and several other buildings of note." John Brown ran his fingers lightly over the plans. "Isn't it grand? A fine house." Thom wondered whether he was being addressed or whether John Brown was musing to himself.

"Pride is still a sin, Brother John. Even for a Baptist," rang a voice behind them.

John turned smiling. "Such disrespect, particularly from a younger brother."

"Moses, may I present Thomas Larkin."

"Thomas, my youngest brother, Mr. Moses Brown."

Moses was shorter than John, with a round and open face and eyes that seemed quick to smile yet sheltered a certain reserve. His clothes were well cut, but severe, of simple black cloth that contrasted with his brother's fine linen. He rose at his desk and extended a hand. When they shook, he said, "I've heard much of thy travels, Mr. Larkin. Pleased to see you've recovered." He smiled then returned to his chair, saying, "But I shall delay thee no further."

"Well then, to put you to work." John Brown looked over toward the rows of writing desks on the other side of the room. "Mr. Rogers?" he said, raising his voice slightly. A slender young man looked up, then scampered over. "Show Mr. Larkin here to a desk and set him to checking manifests." John Brown turned to Thom. "Sorry it's not too diverting an undertaking, but it is a fine place to start."

Abraham Rogers, the young clerk, raised an eyebrow as he glanced at Thom as if a monkey in a breeches stood before him. Rogers was about Thom's age yet appeared younger, his skin fair and pale, unblemished by the sun and wind. Thom smiled to himself knowing that he was indelibly marked as a sailor, even at three years shy of twenty.

"Yes sir, Mr. John. I'll see that he's set up properly. This way, Mr. Larkin."

❖❖❖

As promised, Thom began by checking manifests, tallying the long columns of figures for each of the myriad items of cargo carried in the holds of the Brown ships from the Indies - molasses, coffee, cotton duck, spices, and all the luxuries and necessities from Europe, transshipped through free ports to avoid the duty. Though it felt strange to be a clerk, standing holding a quill pen, the manifests felt familiar, a tie to ships, ports, and cargoes; a world that was once his own.

All the tasks that the other clerks wished to avoid were passed on to Thom as proper employment for the least of their number. Thom was contented to be kept busy regardless of the task and was quietly intrigued to glimpse into a realm most sailors never saw.

The Browns chose not to settle on one cargo or trade but spread the hazard across multiple partners and ventures, trading in oil, candles, molasses, chocolate, and cloth; cargoes of their own and on consignment; agents for a dozen other correspondents.

After a time, Thom saw that the owners of the largest fleet in the colony were as substantial manufacturers as they were merchant venturers. The Browns' spermaceti candles sold well from Bangor to Charleston and fetched a fair price in London and Le Havre. In a few weeks he was given ledgers from the Hope works, of which he had heard only in passing, and was amazed by the quantities of iron cast, scores of tons of gray pigs shipped to England for forging. Of smaller quantity, but no less value, was the chocolate ground at the Browns' mill or the rum from their various interests in distilleries.

Each day standing at his desk, fingers stained from ink rather than tar, Thom was intrigued by the range of the Brown brothers' interests and ambitions. Each brother was so different, conflicting yet somehow complementary. Nicholas, whose name graced the door, was careful, cautious, hedging each venture, happy to take an assured shilling before a risky pound. He didn't seem the sort to build a great enterprise, but could be relied upon to preserve its capital.

John seemed to revel in risk, aware that return and risk were the twin faces of Janus, and to the horror of both Nicholas and Moses, seemed equally fond of either face. Thom couldn't help but like John, perhaps even more for his exuberance and careless arrogance than for the generosity that just might have saved his life.

Thom sensed that Moses was one to be watched, the youngest of the clan and the most complex; a Quaker like his mother, among his Baptist brothers who had accepted their father's faith. Moses was an independent soul who seemed to have taken his lessons equally from Nicholas and John.

And James remained the missing brother that Thom hadn't met, except through his hobbies, or perhaps his work. While James was off at the iron works, Thom knew him only as the architect of John's new house and of the Baptist church where John was an elder. The church was a classical, restrained structure, yet boastful in its expectations. It was capable of seating over a thousand in a town not yet exceeding four, and of as many creeds and beliefs as there were creeds to be had, so the church was rarely more that a quarter full.

The work pleased Thom though he still tired easily. The standing was harder than walking on deck. Still, he was sheltered from the weather and the hours weren't over-long. Slowly he felt his power returning, like the Spring, advancing tentatively though tenaciously, driven back for a time by a late winter storm, only to return warmer and more vibrant when it passed.

He moved out of John Brown's house and took a room in a boarding house close by. Now that he was almost fit again, he couldn't bear feeling like a perpetual guest, an interloper who awoke one day in a feather bed.

To his great pleasure, Angela stopped by to visit from time to time in the early evening, always accompanied by Margaret, finding a reason to call on errands that Margaret's patient smile suggested that she could have done better by herself. At times Angela carried a message from her father or one of her uncles, messages that would have waited for the next day. Thom was overjoyed to see her, trying not to give too much of his joy away whenever they met in public. He felt that they were growing closer, which served as a reminder of the yawning gulf between them, but he also knew that every day he was learning more of the mysteries of commerce and trade. He no longer felt quite the ignorant sailor he once thought himself to be. And as he was learning the ways of this new world, he would steal moments with the raven haired girl that filled his dreams.

Chapter Four

O ne morning in late April, a black-hulled sloop sailed into
Newport harbor. She was one of several early season
arrivals, hardly worthy of note.

The day was clear, cool, but not cold, with luminous sunlight
borne on a moist and gentle breeze. The docks teemed with the
impatient urgency of springtime, a pent-up restlessness bursting
forth after a long winter. The shops of the joiners, braziers, turners
and tallow dippers, recently shuttered against the cold, spilled out
onto the sidewalk, their windows opened wide with goods piled on
tables ready for customers to arrive. Shod hooves and the metal
rims of cart wheels rang on the paving stones, blending a bit
farther down the road with the rhythm of adzes and hammers, and
the calls of the shipwrights and laborers raising their voices freely
again after the winter's long hush.

John Stevens pushed a loaded wheelbarrow down the lane
from the chandlery to the longboat waiting at the wharf. Without
question or discussion, Johnny had set to work for Uncle Isaiah,
taking over the more strenuous chores of the chandlery. His uncle
wouldn't admit that the years had slowed him, but it was clear
enough to John. Time is a pitiless thief, daily lifting only a single
coin, yet relentlessly emptying the purse.

Johnny wheeled coils of hemp rope piled high in the
wheelbarrow, waving and shouting to acquaintances and friends
as they rode or walked by. There was too much to be done to stop
and talk, though the few words exchanged would do as he made
several trips, now loaded with deadeyes and shackles as well as
more rope and seizing to rerig a schooner. He dumped his load on

the wharf, jumped down into the longboat, then swung a coil of rope down with him.

At first, he only just glimpsed the sloop that drew abeam the wharf. He saw it from the corner of his eye, barely noting her, then turned back again and stared. She was small with a black hull, her bulwarks pierced for guns, different from when he had seen her last, but he knew her just the same. The gun ports were new, as were the two brass swivel guns on the stern rail. A slender man paced the after deck wearing a blue jacket, looking over the docks just as Johnny watched the sloop.

Johnny climbed up from the longboat and walked down the wharf to get a better look, sure he was mistaken, while at the same time, knowing that he wasn't. Her stern swung slowly as the helmsman put the tiller over and Johnny smiled bitterly as he read the name on her stern - *Liberty* - John Hancock's little ship, reborn as a revenue sloop. No merchant valuing his health or trade would dare bid on Hancock's sloop, condemned at Admiralty Court, so the Commissioner of Customs must have taken her into their own service.

There had been rumors of a naval patrol to enforce the Molasses Act, to stop "smuggling" as the Parliament would call it, to interfere with honest trade, if the truth were told. Johnny felt a quiet but seething anger. They had taken Hancock's *Liberty* and would use her now to take the liberty of a chartered colony. Damn them all to hell. Johnny turned and walked down the wharf toward the chandlery to spread the word, the half-loaded longboat forgotten for a time.

In the weeks that followed, the *Liberty* and her new captain, a Mr. William Reid, were the talk of the docks, each ship, boat or bark calling Newport bringing new tales of outrages wrought by the Customs sloop. Captains and sailors, stopping in his uncle's store or over a jar of ale in the tavern, told the same stories, of the evil Reid, and of the bitter irony that the instrument of his mischief was named *Liberty*.

Where had the Crown been when the French and Spaniards raided the coast in the late wars all now asked, when French brigands occupied and ravaged Block Island, barely a score of miles to the south? Why now, when peace brought the faint hope of prosperity, did this demon descend upon them?

A Connecticut trader, one Andreas Morton, who had sailed as supercargo on a lumber brig, called on Isaiah's store to purchase stores and joined Johnny for an ale at the Mill Stone Inn. "Any news of the Turk Reid?" Jacob Miller, the innkeeper, asked not long after they arrived.

"Indeed, sir, I have," the trader snorted. "The cursed pirate, for that's what he is, Royal Commission or no. Been stopping and arrestin' everything afloat 'tween New London and Providence. We only just narrowly slipped his clutches. If the wind hadn't shifted and we hadn't nabbed the flood, he'd a catched us sure enough."

With a flourish, he drew a copy of a newspaper from a pocket of his waistcoat. "The *New London Gazette* of this nineteenth of May, sir, I believe says it right true." He looked for a moment, then said, "Yes, here it is." The buzz of conversation subsided, those who couldn't read anxious to hear the news from one who could. The trader cleared his throat with a "harumph" and began.

"We hear the *Liberty* sloop, which sail'd a few days past on a cruize, has taken a prize but of what nation, or whither bound, we have not learned; but imagine her to belong to some of the North American colonies, as the whole naval force of h-s Br-t-n-c M-j-y seems to be principally aimed against those colonies, notwithstanding they are inhabited by the best subjects that ever serv'd a king: most remarkable for the loyalty and yielding obedience to every just and constitutional Act of Parliament."

Miller, the innkeeper, pounded on the bar with his fist. "Hear him. Damn the Parliament and their unlawful laws." A half dozen voices echoed their agreement, most offering their own stories or proclamations to their companions as the hum of jumbled voices rose again across the room along with calls for more ale, sending Miller scurrying off to satisfy his customers.

CHAPTER FIVE

Each morning, as he got to his desk at the counting house, Thom reminded himself of all the reasons that he should be pleased to be a clerk in John Brown's counting house. He was earning his own way at last. He was learning the ways of merchants and traders. He was witness to a world that most sailors would never see and yet dictated the terms of their very lives. Thom was hungry to grasp the secrets of wealth and power, in the faint hope that one day he might have a share of each.

The work itself was not difficult or overly demanding and presented the possibility of bettering his circumstances. He had proven himself to be a worthy scribe and a passable computer. Nevertheless, he was growing tired of tallying endless columns of figures, and neatly copying letters and invoices. Only so much could be learned from repetition.

The one real reason that he was pleased to be John Brown's clerk was that he could see Angela almost daily. Perhaps that was reason enough, yet while standing at his desk a short distance from the richest man in Providence Plantations, Thom wondered what her father would think of his penniless clerk dreaming of an attachment to his only daughter. For a moment, Thom wondered whether Angela was already promised to the scion of some other merchant trader. The thought plunged him into the darkest despair. He forced himself to return to the column of figures that lay before him on the ledger page.

Around mid-morning, a messenger arrived and lay a folded slip of paper before his employer. John Brown opened it, then after a moment, looked up from the note. "Thomas Larkin, if I may have a word?" Thom hurried over to the desk.

"Have you made the acquaintance of Anthony Boskins, mate on the *Hannah*?" He paused. Thom shook his head. "No, I imagine that you haven't. Likely not to make it now either, as he's crushed his foot 'neath a hogshead.

"I own the Providence to New York packet, *Hannah*, and I seem to be short a mate. Would you have an interest in serving in that capacity?" John Brown's face wore a half smile that suggested he was confident of the answer to his question long before he asked.

"Why yes, sir. Definitely, sir." Thom answered almost without thought.

"It is likely only a temporary position. Captain Haney is still a part owner of the packet and he has the final say on who sails aboard her. Still, I suspect that you might enjoy getting out of these offices for a time."

"Yes, sir. When should I call on Captain Haney, sir ?"

John Brown looked over at the clock over the hearth. "If you could present yourself at the dock in a quarter hour, that should serve."

Thom's eyes widened and he mumbled, "Yes, sir" as he rushed for the door and onto the street, not bothering to stop back at his desk. Behind him, he heard laughter, which he didn't mind, as he found that he was laughing as well.

❖❖❖

Captain Joshua Haney stomped from the bow to the stern and back again on the packet boat *Hannah*, keeping one eye on the Salt River wharf, trying to calm himself by focusing on the high clouds drifting across the distant horizon, only to be reminded once more of his own immobility. The deckhand, little more than a boy, knew enough to stay out of the old captain's way, scampering a few rungs up the ratlines to keep clear.

At the stern, the captain peered over the taffrail at the current boiling along the hull and then scrutinized the height of the tide on a piling. They were ready to sail, the mail packet aboard, cargo loaded and secured. All they lacked was the new mate and one passenger. "Won't wait much longer. Tide shan't wait for us," Captain Haney declared to no one in particular, though his voice carried the length of the small sloop.

When he looked up he saw a tall, slender young man approaching, a small seabag slung over his shoulder. He was not much to look at from a distance and was no more impressive on closer inspection. Damn that Anthony Boskins, Haney thought. Barely a decent mate, though likely better than his replacement.

From the dock, Thom called over. "Captain Haney? Thomas Larkin, sir. Mr. John Brown asked that I call upon you."

"Well, get yourself aboard then, an' step lively about it."

Thom hurried up the gangway and presented himself before the imposing gray-haired figure, who scowled at him. For reasons that Thom didn't fully understand, the glowering captain made him want to laugh, to chuckle to himself. He couldn't remember wanting to chuckle for quite a while, yet now he thought it best if he deny himself that simple pleasure.

"Hear you had fever. Strong enough to haul your weight?" Captain Haney gave Thom a hard look. "A'int no pleasure ship, less'n you pay a fare."

Thom smiled. "I'm strong enough, sir. I won't disappoint. "

Captain Haney began to say, "See to it that you don't, and" but was interrupted by the clatter of a carriage pulling up alongside and a florid passenger in a powdered wig disembarking with the aid of a slave steadying his hand. Haney turned and bellowed to the young deckhand, "Mr. Jacobs, help our passenger aboard. See to his baggage." He looked over at the dock then back at the sloop. "Stand-by the hawsers. Matthews, ready the jib, if you please."

The captain glanced back at Thom as if he had forgotten his presence. "Stow your gear below and get up here on the double." Without waiting for a response Captain Haney strode off yelling to the deckhand to loose the gaskets on the boom.

When Thom came back on deck, he stood for a moment at the outboard rail. The young deckhand of perhaps twelve or thirteen helped the bewigged passenger below, then came over to Thom. "Justin Jacobs, the name. You the new mate?"

"Thomas Larkin," Thom replied extending his hand.

"Don't let the capt'n scare ya. He's got a growl on him, but he's the best on the coast."

Captain Haney walked their way. "Jacobs, there's still a trunk on the dock. Ye waiting' for it to grow legs and walk aboard itself?" The boy scurried off to the gangway. "And haul the gangway aboard after ye." As the captain passed Thom, he grumbled, "An' just you stay out of the way till ya' learn the ropes."

"Aye, sir," Thom replied to Haney's back, wondering why he liked the gruff old captain. He bore no resemblance to his memories of his grandfather, save perhaps in age, but he was like several of the captains that Thom had served. Perhaps it was just good to be back aboard ship, a very small ship, but a ship none the less.

An easy sou'westerly was blowing, holding the packet just off the dock. "Cast off fore 'n aft," Haney roared. "Raise the main, Mr. Matthews." The hawsers were hauled aboard, tails dripping from dragging in the water. Matthews and another sailor hauled the throat halyard while Jacobs took the peak. Haney nodded to Thom who took up hauling with Jacobs. With mainsail luffing gently, the *Hannah* slipped away from the wharf, ghosting on the tide, sailing to windward.

"Raise the heads'ls," Haney ordered. With a sailor on each halyard, the jib snaked up the stay, followed by the flying jib at the end of the long bowsprit, flapping wildly, the sheets snapping taut as the sails filled in the breeze.

The *Hannah* was no more than forty feet on deck though her bowsprit stretched for half again as far forward. The sloop's single mast was tall and seemed spindly after the masts of the *Romney* or even the *Black Swan* or the *Mary Ellen*. Above the crosstrees, a topsail yard was rigged, which struck Thom as a lot of sail for the four deckhands to handle in any sort of blow.

And, oh, the *Hannah* could sail. Hanney hauled the mainsheet, and the huge mainsail and the smaller jibs pulling her along into the channel. The wharves on either side of the Salt River slipped silently by as the packet sailed down stream.

Captain Haney walked back toward the helm, his step lighter than Thom would expect of a man of his age, though still not sure what that age might be.

"Hear you're good at navigatin' by the stars." Haney paused for a moment, waiting for Thom's reaction, getting none. "Worth nothing to a coaster man, of course, 'less you know the currents and the tides and every shoal, ledge and rock 'tween here and Manhattoes, might as well stay ashore. And if you think sailing a coaster is any less a task than a ship at sea, you got it wrong, sure as sin." He was surprised when Thom replied with a smile and for a moment, nothing more.

"Sir, I've no doubt that I've much to learn. But I've always been a good student if you'll forgive my vanity for saying so. If ever you do not care to have me aboard, I'll go ashore directly. I'm also a fine swimmer."

At this Haney laughed. He looked over at Thom, the scowl gone if only for a moment. "Well, you got sass. Let's see if you got any brains. Your schoolin' starts now. Take the helm. Matthews get for'ed." The quartermaster grinned at Thom and relinquished the tiller.

Thom cradled the curved spar beneath his right arm, gazed up at the sails then at the channel. If he sailed too close to the wind, the sails would stop driving and luff, and if he sailed too large, they wouldn't clear the wharves on the other side of the channel. From the corner of his eye Thom saw Captain Haney

watching him closely. As they cleared the lee of the town, the
Hannah heeled in the breeze, rounding up slightly in the gusts.
The tiller was light beneath his arm, the helm responding almost
as if to his thoughts, and the smile spread freely across Thom's
face.

The *Hannah* picked up speed, the wake a low hiss behind him
with the shrouds humming, taut and alive in the wind. The docks
had slipped behind them now and the riverbank grew closer on
the bow. Thom glanced at Captain Haney, who appeared
detached almost uninterested as sloop bore down on the muddy
shore. Thom turned forward with a smirk, not about to let
himself be flustered by the imminent prospect of grounding
within sight of Providence. When the reeds on the riverbank
glowed green against the brown, Captain Haney said, "Ready
about," in a voice just loud enough to carry the length of the
sloop. "Ready," Thom replied, shortly echoed by a "ready" from
the deckhands. The reeds ashore now waved distinctly and
individually, the midday sun casting shadows between the
slender stems shifting in the breeze.

"Helms a' lee," the Captain ordered.

"Helms a lee, aye" Thom responded, pushing the tiller down
wind. The *Hannah* spun like a dancer in a flurry of flapping sails,
spars and sheets, settling with almost a snap on the other tack,
quickly gaining way, charging again across the channel. In a few
minutes, they tacked again within what seemed inches of the
other shore and set off on the long tack down the river.

"She sails sweetly, sir."

"That she does," the captain agreed. "That she does indeed."

For a time, the only sound was the wake and wind in the the
rigging until Captain Haney said, "Well, you make a fair
helmsman. Might make a mate if you pay attention, so listen up.
Current in the river floods at a knot and a half, ebbs at two.
Maximum current four hours after high tide. Hear me?"

"Yes, sir. Floods at one and a half, ebbs at two, maximum four hours after high, " Thom said with a nod, repeating it to himself silently.

Captain Haney kept up his instruction all the way to Newport, calling out the names of the islands they passed, Prudence, Conanicut, Rose, Hog, Aquidneck, and all headlands, hills, and coves, commenting on the tide and currents, the shoals and bars, reefs and boulders along their course, until Thom's head spun with names and figures and he wondered if he could possibly learn them all, to know them as a coaster man needed to know them.

Nor did he yet know the *Hannah* well enough to be rated able seaman much less mate, but in the first few hours at her helm, he had already moved from infatuation to admiration and almost to love for the sleek little packet.

❖❖❖

They arrived at Newport late that afternoon. After Thom nearly collided with a schooner heading out of the harbor and came perilously close to the rocks off Fort Point, Captain Haney snorted, "That'll be quite enough. I'll take the helm." Thom skulked off to leeward and Captain Haney brought the packet alongside Long Wharf with a practiced ease.

Alongside, Thom presented himself to Haney. "Sir?"

Captain Haney looked over at him with a sidewards glance. "Be worthwhile to rig the gangway, tend to the passengers and cargo, if you don't mind."

"Aye, Captain." Thom spun on his heel and was pleased to see Justin Jacobs already rigging the gangway and Matthews knocking the dogs off the hatch. Thom hurried to help him as Haney went below, returning an instant later with the bulging mail packet under one arm and the ship's documents under the other. He strode down the gangway and onto the dock, disappearing in the throng of longshoremen, merchants, and teamsters.

"Off to the customs house and to the post," Justin said to him. Thom laughed to himself, chagrined that the ship's boy would find him so lost that he needed to explain the captain's errands.

Thom worked till dusk, unloading Newport trunks and bundles and loading those bound for New York. Esa Matthews had dropped into the hold and was heaving the cargo up to Thom to carry down the gangway to the warehouse. When they were done, Matthews strode toward the gangway.

Esa turned, "Come along for a jar, Mr. Mate?" Thom didn't know him well enough whether to read a jest in his tone, but ignored it, if there was.

"Thankee, no. Some other time. Too tired to lift a tankard. I'll stay aboard." He went into the tiny cabin and fell soundly asleep on the bunk.

❖❖❖

The next morning he woke before dawn to the cadence of Captain Haney's footfalls. Thom jumped up and found that he was almost the last on deck. Haney glowered at him as he called out the orders to get the packet underway. Thom took his place at the tiller, neither quartermaster nor mate, but some of odd amalgam, ready to follow orders and learn as quickly as he could. As soon as they slipped beyond Fort Point, the sails set and drawing, Captain Haney resumed Thom's instruction from the day before without further comment.

The *Hannah* stood down the East Passage on a close reach, hurried along by the tide. Once past Beavertail Light, Block Island Sound opened before them with the long arm of Point Judith pointing seaward, just visible in the morning haze. Captain Haney gestured off to starboard. "Breton Reef's wrecked more ships and reputations than I can name. No reason that you should be near it if you are bound for Race Rock. Homebound in fog, though, easy enough to stand on too far. Once you hear the fog horn on the lighthouse, keep it well to starboard. Rather you ended up in the West Passage than on Breton Reef."

"Amen to that, Captain," Thom replied.

A silhouette took shape off the bow, still distant in the haze. Mathews, on bow watch, saw it first. "Get aloft, Esa." Captain Haney bellowed. "Sing out soon as you make it out. Let me know if its Reid."

Matthews scrabbled up the ratlines to the top, then climbed out on the topsail foot ropes, working his way out on the yard to windward to get a better look.

"Deck," he called. "She's a sloop, inbound. All's I can see."

Captain Haney nodded to himself. From the tiller Thom strained to see ahead. *Liberty* was a sloop, but so were at least half the coaster in the colony. But if it was the *Liberty*, their courses would cross. With Breton Reef to larboard and Point Judith to starboard, there was nowhere else to go, short of turning around and running back into Narragansett Bay. Thom suspected that Captain Haney, like a true packet boat master, would sail straight toward the devil himself rather than fall behind schedule.

The lookout cried, "Deck, there. Setting her topsail."

In the haze, a small white blossom appeared above the sloop's main top, petals fluttering for an instant then opening into a diminutive rectangle. The *Liberty* carried a topsail yard, but again that was not unusual.

Thom knew that there was no contraband aboard. He had helped load the cargo at Newport and had seen for himself. Still, he had heard enough of Reid to know how little that mattered. The customsman mined the Navigation Acts, finding the smallest infractions, the most arcane requirements, ignored by customs and traders for full scores of years. And even if he found no transgressions, a seizure could tie up the *Hannah* for a fortnight. The long tranquil of the Admiralty Court now was overwhelmed by Reid's predations.

Thom strained his eyes to make out the unknown sail but to no avail.

He felt a tightening in his chest. He had escaped death twice in their run from the *Romney*. First in not being in the hurricane and then by surviving the fever. He would have liked to think that he started his life anew, but the arrival of the *Liberty* seemed to say that his past was pursuing him.

"Deck - her hull's blue." Thom took a long, deep breath. It wasn't the *Liberty* unless she'd received a new coat of paint over her black hull.

"Get yourself back on deck, Esa," Captain Haney called.

Concerns about the customs sloop swept aside, Captain Haney turned back toward Thom. "Water stays deep up to the Point Judith shore, though you best stand off a ways when rounding the point. Lots'a rip rap just awash at low water. Rip out the bottom, easy as you please."

"Yes, sir," Thom replied, repeating everything Captain Haney said silently to himself in hope that the repetition would help the flood of facts settle in the backwaters of his memory.

In a few minutes, the blue-hulled sloop passed close aboard. Captain Haney roared, "Packet boat *Hannah*, out'a Providence, New York bound."

"Sloop *Reliant*, New London bound for Newport," came the reply.

"Any sign of Reid?" Haney shouted back at the sloop that was now past them and slipping away quickly. Thom thought he heard the other captain shout, "No," but couldn't be sure over whistle of fresh south-southwesterly wind.

They stood on for another hour until Block Island rose low and blue in the mist. When Captain Haney shouted "Ready about," part of Thom wanted to hold the tiller steady and continue on out to sea, passing Block Island's sandy shore to starboard, bound for the West Indies or Spain, but instead he replied "Ready", and when the order came pushed the helm hard alee.

Somewhere off their bow was Race Rock, marking the entrance to Long Island Sound. It felt odd, being on the second day of a voyage, and yet to be sailing toward shore. Thom always looked forward to getting off-soundings, where the water was too deep for a lead line and the smell of shore was just a memory. But he was a coasterman now, bound to sail the shoreline and to try not fetch up on a rock before they made harbor. Strange as it was, it felt good to be sailing again, back where he belonged, even if he was just learning his way on the little packet.

He also didn't mind sailing a coaster, instead of setting off on a long voyage to the Indies or Spain, because he would be back in Providence in two weeks and would see Angela again. He had grown too fond of seeing her almost daily when he worked at the counting house. Day and night, she haunted his thoughts.

The shore of Long Island rose dimly in the distance to larboard. Captain Haney scanned the horizon. "We'll begin to feel it soon. The current's lifting us along now. Give us a real kick, time we reach the Race." Haney walked forward. Thom was pleased that the captain trusted him alone at the helm, for a short time at least.

When the sun was high above him, Captain Haney called, "Mr. Larkin, you goin' to steer all day or do you want something to eat? Matthews'll take the helm."

Thom dropped below deck where Justin Jacobs stirred a small pot of boiling beef.

"You cook, Larkin?" Jacobs asked. "We take turns cooking, so if you can't, you best learn or this bunch'll toss you overboard."

Thom laughed and took a bite of the beef. "S'pect I can do as well as this anyway."

Young Justin looked hurt for a moment, then broke into his own smile.

When he was finished, Thom returned to the tiller and relieved Matthews with Captain Haney standing just to windward. "We'll see Gull Island on the larboard bow 'fore you see Race Rock itself. Got about a two knot current under us now. Build to four by the Race."

As they approached Race Rock, the water around the *Hannah* chortled in the thousands of tiny waves stirred up by the wind against the tide. The sea began to boil up around them, making smooth patches among the waves, the current welling up, deflecting off the rocky bottom as it shoaled. The Atlantic Ocean was pouring into Long Island Sound, a boundless cask filling a single bottle through a narrow neck. Thom smiled as they flew through the confused waters. He was sure that Haney would be back soon to fill his head with facts about the time of current change and how close to stand off Gull Island. Until then he would enjoy the wild chatter of the water and the warm breath of the south-westerly.

Thom felt alive again and not just to be sailing, but to be free. Whether Captain Haney chose to fire him or make him the packet's mate, he could do no more, and Thom was also free to quit, if he chose. The wages weren't generous except as compared to a man-of-war, where likely as not the crew would never see their wages at all, after deductions and charges were made against the miserly pay by a thieving purser.

Because as there was nothing to stop him from quitting, just walking away the next time the packet touched a quayside, Thom decided that he wouldn't, that he would scramble to be the best mate that he could be until Haney either accepted him or threw him over the side.

With the sounding of the bells for the second dog watch, Captain Haney reappeared, looked around to see that nothing was amiss, then ordered Thom and Matthews below.

"Aye, Captain," Thom replied, grateful for two hours below deck. He went to his sea bag and pulled out a small notebook and started writing down all he could remember of Haney's instruction, the set of the tide, speed of the current, that it turned two hours past high water. After reading back through his notes, Thom stowed the book and lay down on the bunk, slipping into sleep only to be roused by the change of watch in what seemed only a moment later.

Afternoon yielded to evening. The packet was lit by the pale lume of the sunset, glowing off the bow. Fisher Island was a dark shape to starboard and Long Island was no more than a shadow on their larboard beam as the narrow waters of the Race widened into Long Island Sound. Behind him, a quarter moon rose pale against the darkening sky.

Thom stepped toward the tiller, though Captain Haney shook his head. "Want you watching more than just the compass. Justin'll steer. Tide turns in three hours. Call me if the wind, weather, or anything else changes, for that matter. I doubt the pirate Reid is sailor enough to hunt at night, but keep a weather eye. And leave Long Island to larboard." With that he disappeared below, leaving Thom amused at the Captain's small jest – "Long Island to larboard, indeed."

A few minutes later Justin volunteered, "I'd wager he'll keep you aboard, if you don't mind my saying so. If you don't foul up, of course."

Thom smiled. "Guess that remains to be seen, doesn't it."

The sky slipped quickly into blackness. The night was clear and the moonlight shone on the crests of the waves. The *Hannah* moved along easily on a close reach, healed to her lines as if she had worn a track in the water from her repeated passages down the Sound to New York.

CHAPTER SIX

July was hot and stifling with only the suggestion of a breeze stirring beneath the haze. Though still before noon, Johnny's shirt stuck to his back as he pulled at the oars of the skiff, rowing from ship to ship anchored in the harbor. At each, he paused at the stern and sang out, "Ahoy, the ship. Isaiah Steven's Chandlery. Be of service to ye this morning fair? Best stores on the coast."

At a few he was greeted only by silence, and at one or two, a gruff "Be 'way wit' ya," though at most he met a "Good morrow," and a handful of friendly words. He progressed slowly down the length of the harbor, taking orders and trading rumors, retelling the story he had just heard at the last ship, or a tale told over a jar the evening before at the tavern.

More often than not, the face looking down at him over the transom broke into a smile, an old friend from a ship or distant port. One old ship mate cried, "Why John Stevens, haven't seen you since the *Speedwell*. Never thought you had sense enough to be a water clerk."

"Maybe still don't," Johnny answered, grinning, as he pulled alongside.

He kept an eye cocked toward the harbor mouth, enjoying the wharfinger's pastime, watching for new arrivals. There were three that morning, though none a likely customer.

He saw the sloop first, under plain sail, rounding the point carried more by the flood than the breeze. A large brig followed, moving listlessly, topsails alternatively snapping full and hanging slack. Behind them in the haze the small and dark outline of a third vessel took form, a shape that Johnny recognized. He knew then, that the sloop and brig were the sheep driven by the wolf, William Reid.

Johnny leaned on the oars and swung the skiff about, following the new arrivals at a distance. The sloop anchored near Long Wharf, with the brig some way astern. The *Liberty* rounded up and anchored smartly between them. He didn't know the sloop, named *Sally*, hardly bigger than the *Liberty* herself. He smiled bitterly as the brig's stern swung his way and he saw that it was the *Standfast*. If Joe Packwood was still captain, he wasn't likely to go meekly and for a moment he worried for Packwood's safety and then for an instant Reid's.

Captain Packwood was a New Londoner, though known well enough in Newport. He was a large and oft times loud man who Johnny had met years ago in a Surinam tavern, when Packwood was still a bosun on the *Standfast*. An occasional customer of Uncle Isaiah, Packwood was a friend to Johnny, even though he was now captain and a minor merchant in his own right. He wore his change of situation as lightly as a new coat, easily enough cast off or replaced by another. Silk or homespun, a coat was a coat and didn't effect the man who wore it.

A longboat set off from the *Liberty*, four men at the oars with William Reid in his blue coat sitting in the stern. At almost the same instant, a boat pulled clear of *Standfast* with Captain Packwood in the bow, shouting toward the *Liberty*'s boat. Johnny chuckled and hauled harder on the oars, eager to get ashore.

Captain Reid and his escort marched off down Long Wharf with Captain Packwood and one other man following close behind. As Johnny watched them disappear down the wharf toward the Customs House, another boat tied up and a scowling man clambered up onto the dock, cursing to the morning air. "Bloody corsair, nothing more than a picaroon, damn his eyes. " He strode off alone and the boat pulled back to the *Sally*.

Johnny sat at the oars for a moment, ready to follow the small procession down the dock, then thought better of it. He still had half the harbor to call and anyone who hadn't seen the *Liberty*'s latest catch would hear of it presently - Johnny would make sure of that. Behind him, the *Liberty*'s other boat was loading the crew of the *Standfast* under the watch of four men with muskets.

By early afternoon, Johnny had spoken to every ship, boat and bark from the tip of Goat Island to the end of Breton Cove and many had sent boats ashore to attend to the Commissioners of Customs. Tired, though pleased with his labors, Johnny pulled toward the wharf to join the growing crowd.

There was barely space to stand outside the Customs House. Occasional faces would appear at the windows, then draw back quickly in what seemed great fright. In time, the heavy door opened and Commissioner Charles Collins filled the threshold. His wig was freshly powdered and gold buttons shone brightly on his white linen coat. The crowd hooted as he pounded his heavy cane against the Custom House steps.

"Be still ye," he bellowed and gradually the din subsided. "You are blocking the lane. Be gone. To your homes or ships, like honest men."

"Hah," Welcome Anderson scoffed, stepping from the crowd. A merchant and owner of two small sloops, he stared at Collins with unbridled contempt. "Blocking the lane, ye say. How dare ye. A pirate blockades our coast, seizing ships from honest men, taking shelter behind your very robes and you bid us go home. "

Commissioner Collins cleared his throat with a 'harrumph.,' "Captain Packwood, late of the *Standfast*, and Captain Finker of the *Sally* will be fairly heard. If the evidence indicates contraband, their ships shall be sold at Admiralty."

"They bear no guilt," came a voice from the crowd.

"If that be true, then they shall be sent on their way," replied the commissioner, his voice rising to crest the noise.

"Just you see to it that they are, Charlie Collins," Welcome Anderson said in a low but menacing tone. The commissioner rapped his heavy staff once more against the flagstones, turned on his heel and shut the heavy door with a slam, setting off an angry cheer from the crowd, which slowly dispersed.

The next day was a copy of the day before, stifling heat and little wind. The *Liberty*, *Sally* and *Standfast* wandered carelessly at their anchors, minding the twisting currents of the harbor more than the feeble breeze. Eyes from more than three dozen ships anchored close by watched the two sloops and the brig in their leisurely dance, while from the shadows of the warehouses along the wharves, more eyes watched, waiting, though the true action should have been taking place inside the Admiralty Court.

By sundown, the taverns filling with a flood of sailors and longshoremen, the word went out that nothing had happened. Rumor held that Captain Reid asked for time to gather his evidence as none could be found to condemn either ship from their logs or manifests. All cargo had been duly declared with no hint of deception.

Late in the evening, Captain Packwood roared into the Mill Stone and ordered a pint. He saw Johnny and waived him over, a unnecessary act as Johnny had been moving toward him since he came in the door, as had all who could claim the captain's acquaintance and several who could not.

With Johnny by his side and most of the tavern clustered about them, Captain Packwood took a deep drink of ale and then turned and growled, "Do you know what that bastard tried with me? This very afternoon, in the bloody Admiralty coatroom, he comes up to me and says that if I pay a fine for smuggling, he'll have charges dropped. For five hundred pounds slipped in his pocket, I get *Standfast* back. Goddamn thief." Packwood took another deep drink of ale as angry murmurs filled the tavern.

"So will you pay him?" Johnny asked, sure he knew the answer, but having to ask all the same.

Packwood smiled. "Told him I'd see him in hell 'fore I paid him a penny. Got no evidence against me and he knows it truly." Approving voices and a slap on the back from an unseen hand greeted his response. Tankards of ale appeared on the bar, gifts from new and old friends and Captain Packwood drank toasts to English Liberty and confusion to Reid and his damned *Liberty* sloop, as he slid sloshing tankards over to Johnny with a smirk. John Stevens, never one to turn down a gift of ale, joined heartily in the toasts.

The next day Johnny waited, with what seemed to be all of Newport, for a ruling from the court, though none came. By two hours past noon, Captain Packwood announced that he had waited long enough and would at least get his personal effects that had been taken to the *Liberty*. The Crown had no right to them no matter how the court ruled. He rowed himself out and was met by the *Liberty*'s bosun at the gangway. Johnny and a milling crowd watched as the bosun challenged Packwood only to be knocked aside as the captain bounded on deck. The bosun, temporarily in command of the sloop, swore violently at Packwood who disappeared below deck to the cabin.

In a few minutes Captain Packwood returned, holding his sword and scabbard and a small pile of linen. "You thieving bastards," Packwood bellowed. "Me' best shirts and coats are missing. They're my private gear and I demand that you give 'em back."

The bosun puffed up like a toad in the hot sun and at almost a shout replied, "I'm in command and I'll do whatever I want with anything on this here ship and there's nothing that you can do about, you smugglin' son of a bitch."

Johnny saw the bosun glance over toward the wharf with a smirk, well aware of his audience and enjoying holding center stage. When he looked back at Packwood, the point of the captain's sword suddenly held his attention, as it now hovered an inch below his chin. Johnny couldn't hear the rest of the conversation though a seaman appeared promptly with Packwood's gear. The captain sheathed his sword and dropped down to his boat with his sword and linen beneath one arm.

The bosun regained his composure and shouted to his crew, "Fire on that boat."

Two customsmen on the *Liberty* shouldered muskets and a third pulled a brace of pistols. They fired in a ragged volley at the skiff and while the range was point blank, the balls splattered in the water around the boat. Packwood jerked, apparently from the surprise of not being hit rather than from the impact of a ball.

Johnny could hardly believe what he saw. "God damn cowards. Lowly whore's sons." His voice blended with the cries of others shouting at the men on the *Liberty*. When Captain Packwood made it ashore, the crowd parted to let him pass then followed, an incensed mob trailing behind as he went to rouse the constable.

Word of the shots fired at Captain Packwood echoed across Newport and the crowd waiting near Long Wharf grew as if summoned by the sound of muskets. "Where is Reid?" The one question asked over and over again. "Where is the pirate?" He wasn't aboard the *Liberty*, nor the *Sally* or the *Standfast* - that much was known to all. Johnny heard some suggest that he had fled to Boston or back to New London, or went to marshal reinforcements, among a dozen other wild stories.

Only once the deep shadows slipped into darkness, blues turning purple and then black, did Captain Reid return, almost passing through the crowd but for his own impudence, raising his voice and cursing at a sailor to clear the way. The sailor turned and the rough torch he held in his hand threw light on Reid's fancy blue coat and dark eyes.

"You bastard," he cried. "It's Reid." His voice shouted louder. "Reid."

Captain Reid stood still, startled by the sailor bellowing his name until the crowd encircled him, shouting, a hundred voices howling at him in a deafening incompressible din. Jeremiah McAndrews, Newport constable, forced his way through the crowd.

"Your crew tried to murder Captain Packwood this very afternoon. Best we talk inside," McAndrews said, motioning with his head toward the Customs House, a light still burning in one window. "Make way. Make way," the constable shouted and the crowd parted with a grumbling reluctance.

At the Customs House, a confused clerk tried to bar their way but fell back frightened by the multitude behind the constable. Captain Reid stepped quickly into the shelter of the stone walls, though McAndrews stopped. "Where is Packwood? Who witnessed the attack?"

A dozen voices answered, though Johnny who stood near the door, stepped forward. "I had a good view. Saw it all clear." Another man stepped up. "Saw it too," he said.

"Then get in here both of you," McAndrews replied. He turned toward the crowd. "Find Packwood," he said as he closed the door.

"I will not stand for this outrage, sir." In the safety of the custom house, Reid regained his voice. "I demand that you call out the militia to disperse that mob."

At this Jeremiah McAndrew's stern visage crumbled. He looked toward Reid and laughed freely and heartily, much to Reid's consternation.

"There is no need to call out the militia, sir. I saw a good many of their number just outside. They seem to have been joined by a legion of volunteers. That mob is the militia and the militia, the mob." All trace of humor fled McAndrews face and he looked sternly at Reid. "If you wish, I could bid them home to fetch their muskets, powder and ball, if that would add to your comfort, sir." He waited for a response and received none save a glowering glance from the captain.

The constable turned toward Johnny. "For the record, sir. Your name and your best recollection of the events of this afternoon. "

"My name is John Stevens. Nephew of Isaiah Stevens. I was on Long Wharf two hours past noon and saw Captain Packwood row out to get his gear. The bosun swore most crudely at him, but he got his kit and was rowing back, when the bosun yelled at his men to fire on the captain. Three blackguards shot at him, two with muskets, the other with pistols. If they'd been decent shots would have blown his head off, but all missed."

McAndrews turned to the other man who took off his cap. "Seth Phillips, sir, teamster. Mr. Stevens here spoke true. Saw the same thing, I did. I was loading my cart an.."

A loud pounding at the door interrupted him. The customs clerk cringed at the sound and stepped back from the barred door. A voice on the other side of the door rang out. "It's Captain Packwood! Let me in! Need to see the constable!"

"Unbar the door." The clerk, who seemed to be trying to disappear into the shadows, stood like a frightened animal until a hard look from McAndrews bade him move. The door unbarred and opened a crack, Captain Packwood pushed his way in followed by two sailors. Reid's composure seemed to falter at the sight of Packwood, his sword buckled at his side. Then Johnny saw that Reid was looking instead toward the two men standing behind him.

"Evening, Jeremiah, Johnny. May I have the pleasure of introducing two of my crew, good and loyal sailors both - Allen Summers and Ethan Baker." He paused and looked over toward Reid. "This scoundrel offered each of 'em ten pounds sterling if they would testify that we broke bulk off Montaulk, swear to it that we were smuggling, unloading along the coast. That's the truth, isn't it." Both sailors spoke almost in unison. "Aye, Capt'n."

"Should have offered thirty pieces of silver," Packwood growled at Reid who was beginning to quake before his towering accuser.

Packwood drew his sword and strode toward Reid. With his free hand he grabbed the Customs captain's collar and lifted him so that only his toes still touched the flagstone floor. Reid gasped, looking wildly at Packwood and then at the window where the light of torches flickered on the glass. The haughty sneer had drained from his face, replaced by dread and panic.

Packwood looked at Reid with a bold smirk. The demon who seized his ship, deprived him of his livelihood under the protection of guns and swivels, was now in his grasp, a small man cringing in fear. With a look that shifted from boundless disdain to a contemptuous dismissal, Packwood opened his hand and Reid slipped backward, almost falling down.

"Arrest this man, Jeremiah, or else turn him outside and we'll see if we can find some hot tar and goose feathers for his entertainment."

Reid rushed toward the constable and fell on his knees, his face now wholly ashen. "Preserve me from these ruffians. As an officer of the Crown, I beseech ye."

The constable looked down with scorn. "Get up, you whining son of bitch. If you attempted to bribe Captain Packwood's crew, it is no concern of mine. Save it for Admiralty court tomorrow, and if it proves true, I hope they act most harshly." He paused and looked toward Packwood. "Can you identify the men who shot at you?"

Packwood shook his head. "Only the whore's son who gave the order. The others were over my shoulder. Didn't get a good look."

The constable turned to Johnny and Seth Phillips. "Can you identify the men who shot at Captain Packwood?" Johnny nodded, "Believe I can." Seth agreed. "I'd know 'em."

McAndrews looked toward Reid who had risen and backed away. "Order all your men ashore, off all three ships. We'll have a look at every man-jack of them."

Reid's crew were rousted from their berths, rowed ashore and lined up in front of the customs house. A dozen torches lit the darkness and Constable McAndrews, Johnny and Seth Phillips walked up and down the line. They both identified the bosun who had ordered the shooting, and while Johnny and Seth identified men that they believed that they had seen firing from the *Liberty*, they each picked different men. Other witnesses came forward with differing accusations until it seemed that every member of the crew, save perhaps the cook, was charged with shouldering a musket.

As most eyes looked toward the misbegotten crew lined up like birds at a turkey shoot, Johnny saw motion over his shoulder in the darkness. Boats full of dark shapes were rowing for the *Liberty*. In a moment, they swarmed over the revenue sloop. A shadow swung out over the bow, sawing at the anchor rode. The sloop swung free, and three longboats towed her toward the wharf. Johnny smiled, then turned back to the constable. "Why don't I take another look. See if my recollection's any clearer."

He walked the line again, though he, Seth, and the others couldn't agree on the assailants. "Nothing more to be done then, " Constable McAndrews said. "Time to be going home."

Captain Reid and his crew stood there, blinded by the torches, still surrounded by the mob, not sure what to do. Then slowly, with parting jeers, the crowd turned away from them as if heeding the constable's advice to repair to their homes.

A moment later Reid gasped in horror as he saw the *Liberty* was now alongside, sailors swarming over the deck. A dozen other men were pulling the ship's longboats up onto the wharf. They dragged them up across the cobblestones, the iron shoes on their keels leaving a trail of fiery sparks on the street as the men whooped and yelled in triumph, dragging the boats ever faster.

Johnny who had been watching Reid, turned and hollered along with the celebrants. When he turned back, Reid and most of his crew had melted away into the darkness. Johnny watched the trail of sparks from the longboats up the street toward the Common. The boats would make for a fine bonfire.

Behind him he heard the rhythm of an ax and he turned to see the *Liberty*'s mast waiver, then fall. Everything of value was being carried off, from cordage to ironwork to canvas. Johnny turned and walked quickly back to the chandlery. He returned with a bucket of whale oil sloshing as he walked.

"Might you have use for some good brown oil, friend?," Johnny called out as he reached the sloop.

"Come aboard, fine sir," one sailor replied, offering a hand. Johnny clambered up over the gunnel spilling half the oil on deck. As soon as he was aboard he sloshed the rest of the bucket across the planks. The sailor who helped him aboard laughed. "Be a warm night tonight, I 'spect."

❖ ❖ ❖

The next day as the *Hannah* pulled Goat Island abeam, Thom saw the smoke. They rounded the southern tip of the island where a blackened hulk, on her beam ends, lay on the beach, without masts, stripped of everything save her timbers, still smoldering, with part of her deck wholly consumed by flame and the rest badly scorched. Her stern no longer bore her name though Thom recognized what was left of the *Liberty*.

Captain Haney glanced over at the derelict. "Had to happen sooner or later. Time they learned that we don't take too well to bullyin'."

"May liberty like a phoenix rise," Thom said softly.

Captain Haney just snorted. "Be minding your course, now. One wreck in Newport harbor is quite enough." Thom smiled and eased the helm a touch.

Haney looked forward. "Mr. Jacobs, rouse yerself. Get that mainsail down. Lively now."

When they were alongside, Thom saw Johnny with his cart on the dock.

"A new landmark on Goat Island, I see," Thom called out, leaning on the bulwark.

Johnny walked over the *Hannah*'s side. "Yeah. End of the island where they used to bury murderers."

"What happened?"

Johnny shrugged, adopting a look of bemused innocence. "Nobody knows. Someone cut the cable and set her afire. Terrible, terrible thing," he said with a smile, as he rolled his cart off down the wharf.

Two hours later, the passengers and cargo were unloaded, new cargo and the mail packet aboard, hatch battened, sails furled, hawsers coiled. Thom looked across the *Hannah*'s deck, wondering what was left undone. "Get ashore, if you want," Captain Haney grumbled. "Tide turns two hours past dawn. Just be back four hours 'fore that, hear me?"

"Aye, Capt'n," Thom replied lopping down the gangway and on to the dock. He found Johnny at a back table in the Mill Stone.

"You missed a fine night, Thomas. Bible says, 'Wickedness burneth as the fire, and shall mount up like the lifting up of smoke.' Well, the wicked burned last night and the smoke, sure as hell, lifted up." He emptied his tankard and called for two more, one for Thom and one for himself.

"So, will your Uncle be offering Reid's blocks, deadeyes, and ironwork for sale?" Thom asked, one eyebrow raised .

Johnny looked up with a half grin. "Another fellow must'a got 'em." He lowered his voice. "Though I nearly tripped over a four pound cannon in the back of the store room this morning."

Thom laughed in spite of himself. "I meant it all in jest, John. A cannon, lord in heaven, what will your uncle do with a cannon?"

"Ah ha, he doesn't have a cannon." Johnny lifted his tankard and took a swig. "He's got six cannon, all lined up like he was to fire a broadside through the side of the house, though I 'spect by now he's got 'em all wrapped in oil soaked canvas and buried somewhere for safe keepin'.

"I asked him myself, 'What do you propose to do with this bloody arsenal? Not like you can sell them as cauldrons or cooking pots, now can you?"

"He just looked at me and said, 'The time may be coming, John. The time may be coming. An' I got 'em at a good price besides.' Course my uncle doesn't oft' make a poor trade, so I'm not about to call him fool. Least not to his face," Johnny said with a chuckle.

Thom drank and as he put down the tankard, his smile faded. "What'll happen now? I doubt that Royal Customs will favorably consider having one of its sloop reduced to timber and ash."

Johnny shrugged. "Naught to be done. The complaints were registered, evidence offered and still the colony posted no sanction against Reid. When there is no justice in the law, the people take their own."

"Truly. Tis the common law, though the point remains, Royal Customs has lost a sloop, and can be none too happy."

"Back in '65, the *Maidstone* was fired on and her boats burned . A 'commission of inquiry,' was called." John stressed each syllable with mock regard. "An' they found that persons of the meanest sort -- sailors and Negroes, went on a rampage, or some other rubbish. Imagine they'll do the same again. An' witnesses will be as hard to find as virgin whores or admirers of Billy Reid. Not that everyone from the governor down through the legislature isn't as pleased as the rest of us at being rid of the *Liberty*. Every storm passes, and so will this."

Thom looked off across the room. "Sometimes, I get the same feeling that I got in the pit of my stomach at St. Kitts, that the storm glass is falling, has been falling for a long time, and that a devil of a storm is blowing up someplace over the horizon that will make the little hurricane we rowed through seem like a squall on a summer afternoon."

Johnny shrugged and raised his tankard in a toast. "Well then, may the likes of Billy Reid be 'as stubble 'fore the wind and chaff carried away by the storm."

CHAPTER SEVEN

Thom had expected an outcry from the burning of the *Liberty*, yet none came. Some said that Lord North was negotiating the repeal of the hated Townsend Acts and that no one wanted to disturb the delicate talks. Others thought the Admiralty was waiting for more evidence to be found or purchased, while some swore that everyone knew that formal charges against anyone were a waste of time and colony money. Thom listened to the theories intently over pitchers of ale, and had no confidence that any one rumor held more truth than the next.

The life of a packet boat mate settled comfortably into routine. On their arrival in Providence, Thom would walk the two blocks to the Royal Post Office with the mail packet under his arm. Often as not Angela would find a reason to be passing by as he waited on the rough bench just outside the door. They would talk for a few minutes while the postmaster's clerk sorted the Providence mail. Those few moments were unquestionably the best part of his week.

When the clerk was finished, Angela continued on her way and Thom took the New York and Newport mail packets as well as the bundle of correspondence bound for Nicholas Brown and Sons. One of the benefits of owning the packet boat, John Brown received his mail before anyone else in town.

❖❖❖

One afternoon when he delivered the bundle at the Brown office, John Brown took up his cane and offered to walk back with Thom to the dock.

"Could use the exertion. I pray that you do not mind my company, Mr. Larkin?"

"No sir. Most happy for it."

"Then let us not delay good Captain Haney, shall we?"

Thom only smiled and kept pace beside John Brown who walked briskly, swinging his cane in bold arcs as he strode down the street. The oak staff with a bronze grip looked almost like a scepter in the hands of a young merchant prince.

A short way from the docks, Brown stopped suddenly. He reached beneath his collar and pulled out a small pendant on a silver chain. "Do you perhaps, recognize this?"

Thom nodded. His grandfather had owned a similar pendant. "Worn only by a high Son of Liberty, sir."

"As I remember Thomas, you once mentioned an acquaintance with your grandfather's friends in New York. Have you met Isaac Sears, John Lamb or Jacob Gingham by any chance?"

"I've been introduced to the gentleman, sir. I was quite young when I accompanied my grandfather to meetings at Gordon's Coffee House during the Stamp Act troubles, so it is not likely that they should remember me, but they may recall my name."

"That should suffice. I have a task for you, should you agree to undertake it." Brown turned to Thom with a questioning look. "The Providence merchants have joined in a non-importation agreement, along with those of New York and Boston. If the Townsend Acts shall tax what we import from our mother country, then we simply shall not import their goods. Let their workers and craftsmen feel the wrath of an unhappy customer and then let them pay their regards to the lawless lawgivers in Parliament." Brown smiled, as if to himself.

"But it shall work only if we unite and act together. I need a courier. Not just one to carry correspondence, but someone to listen carefully and relate his honest impressions. More of an agent, a confidential aide."

"Do you believe, sir, that your correspondents would be candid with a messenger such as myself?"

"Your youth and family ties may encourage their candor, lower their guard." He paused. "So will you do this for me?"

Thom felt that he couldn't refuse, even if he had objected to the assignment, which seemed quietly thrilling. "With pleasure, sir. I only hope that I shall be suitable to the task."

"Oh, I'm sure you shall." Brown reached inside his waist coat and drew out a small leather pouch. "When next you call in New York, please be so kind as to attend Mr. Isaac Sears on Water Street. The letter inside explains that you act on my behalf and that you shall wait upon Mr. Sears's response, should he care to reply."

He handed the pouch to Thom who was surprised by its heft. Brown smiled. "Oh, yes. The pouch is weighted. Should the *Hannah* be intercepted, please deliver the pouch and its contents to the Lord Neptune. I would prefer he reads it before the Lord Admiral. And under all circumstances, I ask that our arrangement remain strictly confidential."

Once Thom tucked the pouch safely away, John Brown resumed walking, speaking while looking straight ahead. "We have so long squabbled like children, one colony against the next, near enough to warring with our brothers while our true foes profit from our discord. We must now strive as one. I wish that I believed us equal to the enterprise." He stopped again, turned to Thom and held out his hand.

"Fair winds to you, Thom Larkin. I shall take my leave from you here."

Thom shook his hand, then watched John Brown's back as it disappeared back up the street. The pouch seemed heavy in his pocket as he turned and walked the last quarter mile to the dock.

The two-day trip to New York seemed interminable, with every sloop on the horizon sure to be a customs man, every ship a man-of-war. When they were finally alongside again in Manhattan, Thom relaxed. He walked quickly to drop off the mail packet and then hurried along to Isaac Sears' counting house.

Thom had walked these streets before as a boy of twelve, one of the multitude, tagging along with his grandfather during the Stamp Act troubles four years before. The Sons of Liberty had called the town to rise and by and large the town had risen, from sailors to merchants to the gentry, all to resist the insidious stamps.

Captain Sears was one of the mob leaders and one of his grandfather's friends. He was a prosperous merchant now with a balding pate and ample girth but, like Thom's grandfather, he had risen from the fo'c's'le to the captain's cabin and bore no shame for his humble beginnings.

"Mr. Sears, sir. I'm Thomas Larkin. Perhaps you remember my ..."

"Lord in heaven." Sears rose from his desk and walked over to take Thom's hand.

"Caleb Larkin's grandson, Thom. Grown to a man since last we met."

"It does seem like an age ago, sir."

Sears laughed. "The gift of youth. The days still pass slowly. For me, it was but yesterday. So tell me of yourself, young Thomas," Sears said showing Thom to a chair.

"I'm mate on the Providence-New York packet *Hannah*, owned by John Brown. He asked me to bring a message to you." Thom pulled the pouch from beneath his shirt, opened it and handed Captain Sears the letter.

Captain Sears chuckled. "Working for the Brown brothers, are ye? Watch yourself, young man. Rogues Island's full of sharp dealers and half learned their tricks from John Brown himself."

Thom smiled. "I'll be on my guard, sir."

Sears sat reading Brown's letter then looked up. "Bout time Providence fell in line. Now if Newport'll do its part, the entire coast'll be locked up to British goods. Show 'em we can do more than march and burn straw men before a liberty pole.

"In the Stamp Act days, you know, we almost lost all, just as we grasped at victory. The burning of houses, the violence could have brought a far greater brutality down upon us. But now we shall show them our strength simply by withholding our hand. Just by closing our purse. Let 'em see what happens when three million Americans deny custom to their goods rather than pay Charlie Townsend's bloody duties.

"Yes, sir," Thom replied feeling that he walked in half way through a conversation.

"I've some thoughts to pass on to your employer. Why don't you shove off and have a pint at Jasper's Tavern. You know the place? Good. I'll meet you there when I'm through. Hoist a glass together."

"Be my greatest pleasure, sir."

❖❖❖

Thom strolled the two block to Jasper's tavern on the docks, smiling to himself. Isaac Sears was too good a merchant not to steer business to his father-in-law's tavern. As he was about to reach the tavern door, he paused and looked out at the East River as it emptied into the harbor. The shores on either side were a forest of masts, and from each, ferrymen in their launches, bent at their their oars, fought to stem the current and dodge the river traffic.

From his left, a black armed schooner cut across his field of vision, sailing close to the seawall, riding the ebb tide down river. It was trim and well kept with a pair of polished brass swivel guns forward. On the small quarterdeck, just aft of the helmsman, stood a tall ruddy faced officer in a fine blue jacket with shining brass buttons and wearing a hat fit for an admiral.

Suddenly, Thom couldn't breathe. It was William Dudingston, looking downstream imperiously, unquestionably in command. As Thom stood there stunned, the schooner slipped past, turned onto a broad reach and sailed out into the harbor. Thom could read the name of the stern under the fluttering Royal Navy Jack - "*HMS Gaspee*". He stood watching until the *Gaspee* disappeared wholly into the haze.

He caught his breath, but felt himself shaking with rage. He stood watching the swirling water for a moment before taking another deep breath and stepping into the shadows of the tavern.

The afternoon was still early and the inn wasn't yet crowded. A lanky man came in, cast off his hat and settled heavily in a chair near the door. The barman looked up and called out, "Good morrow, Captain Johnson. What news bring ye from Philadelphia?"

"Afternoon, Michael," the man said wearily. "Three days of fickle winds and seams opening up. A sorry trip, if ever there was one to be had." He looked over to the serving girl. "Darling, could you bring over a pint to a thirsty man, and be quick about it?"

The girl snorted but brought over a brimming tankard and put it down before him.

"That's better, sure enough. No good news from Philadelphia nor the Chesapeake neither. A pirate flying the King's flag's been chasing anything afloat. Remember, Ez O'Donnell and the *Bold Venture*? Seized with a cargo worth fifteen thousand pounds."

The barman shook his head. "Who is it? Customs?"

The captain looked up from his tankard. "Worse. Royal Navy."

Thom looked over and tried to keep his voice steady, "Scuse me, friend, would that be the schooner *Gaspee* commanded by Lieutenant Dudingston?"

"Yah, the *Gaspee* that is the name. And the captain is a Scotsman, a fair haired, arrogant son of perdition, acting like he was lord high admiral his'self."

"That's him," Thom nodded.

"You know him?"

"Better than I'd like. Grieved to hear he's on the coast."

"Well, the coast's aggrieved as well, from 'Napolis to Philadelphia. But I hear he is bound for Boston, so maybe the Chesapeake's seen his stern for a spell."

Thom again felt an odd mix of anger and fear. The rage within him wanted to sail out and find Dudingston and end it once and for all, while the fear wanted Dudingston and the *Romney* to simply disappear forever, from his present, past and even from memory. The first choice was mad and the second unlikely. Either way he would need to keep a weather eye out for Dudingston.

A few minutes later, Isaac Sears joined him for a drink, passing along a sealed letter to John Brown. Thom saw no need to speak of Dudingston, nor of how he knew the apparently now infamous officer, so he happily listened as Sears spoke of grandfather and their days together.

❖❖❖

The voyage back to Providence was uneventful. If Dudingston and the armed schooner *Gaspee* were cruising for prey, Thom, happily enough, missed them.

Once again, the past that he thought that he had left far astern seemed to be in full pursuit. First the *Liberty* and now Dudingston and the *Gaspee*. When he delivered the mail to John Brown on his return to Providence, he waited before his employers desk.

"I have a favor to ask of you, sir, if I may."

"If it is in my power," John Brown replied with a quizzical glance.

"I hesitate in asking, sir, you've done so much on my behalf already, but.."

"Nonsense. What is it?"

"It is a trifling matter, but it has troubled me. I wonder how Mr. Stevens and I are viewed by the Admiralty. I suspect that we are marked drowned in the hurricane off St. Christophers, but I cannot be sure. It is possible that we are marked deserters and therefore may yet be at some risk.

"I thought perhaps, sir, that if it didn't cause undue inconvenience, that you might inquire through your London correspondents as to our status with the Royal Navy. The Admiralty maintains records and I understand that such a request may not be unusual from a ship owner who employed the sailors before being pressed. "

In the moment of silence that followed, Thom wondered whether he had overstepped his bounds, but a suggestion of a smile on Brown's face put him at ease. "I shall make inquiries on your behalf."

"Thank you, sir. I was listed on the muster book as Thomas Lewis and Johnny was Jonathan Saunders. And if you wouldn't mind, sir, there was another pressed man, Michael Skinner, a weaver with a young son, pulled from the street by the press. I would be most pleased to hear of his fate, as well.

John Brown took up a pen, dipped it in the well and made note of the names. "Would you perhaps like me to petition for unpaid wages as well, or do you prefer to keep matters quiet, Mr. Larkin?" he asked with a wry smile.

"No, sir," Thom laughed. "A quiet inquiry is all I seek, thank you."

❖❖❖

The patterns of the packet became as relentless as the tides. When he saw Angela in Providence, he was lifted to the clouds. The trips when he didn't were an agony. Then to his horror, on a fine September morning, when he called on Providence, he found Angela on the arm of a young man.

"Thomas," Angela called out. "It is my great pleasure to introduce, John Francis, of Philadelphia. Son of Trench Francis, one of my father's oldest correspondents and partners."

Thom had read the name on the ledgers when he worked in the counting house. Trench Francis appeared to be as rich a merchant as John Brown, perhaps more so, if only by virtue of being in the grand city of Philadelphia rather than the backwater of Providence. His son John Francis was the merchant prince. He appeared to be around twenty, finely attired and graced with the self assurance that being the son of wealth imparted. To Thom's eye, he was also annoyingly good looking.

"And John, this is Thomas Larken, ex-captain of the *Mary Ellen*, currently of the packet *Hannah*."

"A pleasure, sir, " Thom mumbled as he shook the offered hand. "If you will excuse me, I must deliver the mail packet."

❖ ❖ ❖

The next voyage was intolerable. Thom tried to keep a weather eye out for the *Gaspee* and tend to his duties on the *Hannah,* yet all he could think of was Angela and John Francis. He was suddenly sure that Angela would be married off to John Francis. Thom knew that he loved Angela with all his soul and he was sure that she cared for him, yet did any of that matter? What role did love play in commerce? A marriage between the Browns and the Francis trading houses would no doubt benefit both. Was the match already arranged? Angela and John seemed so at ease together.

He didn't know what to think. Had he been a fool imagining that the penniless mate of a packet ship might woo the daughter of the wealthiest man in the colony? Should he accept the reality before him, wish them both well and give up all his hopes?

On his return to Providence, he longed to see Angela and dreaded the prospect with almost equal measure. After retrieving the mail packet he caught a glimpse of her dark hair rounding the corner of the lane, followed closely by Mary, her maid. Despite himself, his heart soared. He rose from the bench and smiled as she turned his way.

"I hope that the day finds you well, Master Thomas."

"Quite well, Miss Angela. And good morrow to you, Miss Mary".

Mary curtsied and Angela laughed the quiet easy laugh that at first Thom was afraid was mocking.

"If you are bound for Water Street, it would an honor to walk with you along the way," Thom said, with more formality than he intended.

"It would be a pleasure," Angela replied.

Thom tucked the packet beneath his arms and they walked up the cobbled street. Mary retired some distance, behind them.

"And how was your passage?" Angela asked.

"Fair weather, inconstant winds." Thom replied. "It was a pleasure to meet Mr. Francis. I hope your visit was a pleasant one."

Angela smiled. "It is always a pleasure to see John. He summered here when I was growing up."

So Angela and John had known each other for most of their lives. What better match could be made? Long-terms companions, both scions of established trading houses. He felt crushed beneath a wave of despair. Should he simply keep walking, exchanging pleasantries? For a moment he wasn't sure he could. He stopped.

"Is something wrong?" Angela asked.

"I care deeply for you, Angela." Thom replied, not knowing what else to say. "I only wish you all happiness."

She looked up into his eyes, intently, searching. "And I care for you Thom. More than I can say."

Thom felt confused, dazed. "But, John Francis?"

The expression on Angela's face shifted from from questioning, to irritation, to amusement.

"Are you jealous of John Francis?" She smiled. "Don't be. He is like an older brother. I could never care for him as I care for you."

"But, he is the son a merchant like your father. I thought that he might be considered a better match..." Thom's voice trailed off.

At this, Angela laughed. "Firstly, I am too young to marry and when the time comes that I do wed, I shall choose my husband. I will not be bartered off like a cargo of molasses."

"But, your father?"

"I am my father's daughter, and if there is anything that he has taught me it is to think for myself."

Then to Thom's wonder and amazement, Angela put her hand on his cheek and reached over and kissed him.

CHAPTER EIGHT

After a wearisome winter, Thom was anxious to ready the *Hannah* for the season. The wind was still bitter when he climbed the rigging, looking and finding, just as he'd expected, rot in the base of the topmast. He rove the halyards, and inspected the shrouds and stays, set the carpenters and caulkers to work, spoke to the riggers about the new section of mast, and hired the laborers to shift the ballast stones to get a look at the planking beneath.

Captain Haney wasn't there. The first week, his absence hadn't bothered Thom, but after a second, it was difficult not to be concerned. Thom considered stopping by Captain Haney's house, but that seemed too great an intrusion. At mid-day one Tuesday, Thom saw Captain Haney walking down the string-piece. He carried a cane and moved more slowly than Thom had come to expect from the captain. Thom put down his caulking hammer, wiped the grime from his face with a rag, and walked over to the gangway.

"Got 'er in shape yet?" Captain Haney called out.

Thom smiled. "Another week and we'll be ready to get underway."

Captain Haney nodded and made his way up the gangway. He looked around the deck, slowly and carefully, then instead of pointing out the deficiencies in Thom's work, he said quietly, "I'll miss this old lady. Though she's far younger than I, to be sure." He looked over toward Thom. "I'm going ashore. Sailed long enough."

Thom wasn't sure what to say.

"I told John Brown that you'd make a decent captain, should he want ya and should you want the job."

"And what did Mr. Brown say?"

"He seems to hold you in high regard. Course, I never told him 'bout how you nearly collided with a schooner your first trip into Newport." Captain Haney smiled. "Well, ya' want the job or not?"

"Happy to have it, sir," Thom replied.

"Good, now you'll need a mate. I'm sending Isaac Rollins round to see Mr. Brown. Hear he's on the beach. A Providence man and a good coasterman to boot. 'Bout time the *Hannah* had a decent mate."

"Yes, sir," Thom laughed. "About time."

"Captain Haney, I want to to thank you for everything. All that you taught me. I sincerely appreciate it," Thom said reaching out to take his hand.

The captain shook his hand. "You are a quick learner. I was pleased to have you aboard. Well, good luck, Captain Larkin. Keep her off the rocks, if you can."

"Aye, Captain. Do my best."

The season began as the past two had begun, in a rushed jumble of repairs and outfitting that couldn't possibly be completed to meet the schedule, but Thom, with the help of his new mate, somehow saw that it could. It felt odd not to have Captain Haney aboard, but otherwise being back sailing the *Hannah* felt like returning home, except that now he was the master and not merely the mate.

When they called on Newport on the second trip of the season, Thom was pleased to see Moses Brown stride up the gangway. He wore Quaker black. The round brim of his hat mirrored his healthy circumference. Moses, the youngest of the brothers Brown, was always the most congenial, the quickest with a smile or a wink. Thom knew him to be just as sharp and wily as any of his brothers, perhaps the only one who could match or even best John.

"Captain Larkin, a most good afternoon to thee, sir. I hope thee will not mind my addition to your passenger list."

"Tis a true joy to see you, sir. I am pleased we can be of service. Do have luggage to be put aboard? "

"Thankee, no. I was carried to Newport by coach this very morning and I fear my back would prefer avoiding the rutted roads twice in the same day. Travel by packet is so much more amenable."

"Well, pleased to have you aboard, sir. If you would care for some coffee, I believe Justin just fixed a new pot."

Moses raised a hand. "Worry not about me, Captain. I shall not keep thee from thy other duties."

Two more crates were loaded aboard, the hatch sealed, and lines cast off. The gaff and main sail snaked up the mast to the chattering of the jibs and the *Hannah* slipped out of Newport, settling in on an easy broad reach up the bay.

A scant three hours later they rounded up to make the turn into the Providence River. They jibed around Conimicut Point and set a course upriver against the ebb. The sun rays were low and golden and the *Hannah* cast a long shadow on the deep blue waters. Thom stood aft next to Justin who had the helm. The cool breeze was tempered by the warm sun and Thom gazed over toward Namquit Point, a golden spit of sand with the deep green farmland beyond. Suddenly he found himself face down on the deck which seemed to have risen up to meet him.

"Captain, how fare ye?"

"Son of a motherless whore." Thom forced himself up and looked at Justin who was clinging to the tiller as if his entire life depended on it. "Get for'ad. See if anyone is hurt. No need for a helmsman when hard aground."

Wilton and Rollins rushed back to the quarterdeck. "Mr. Wilton, get the line and sound around us. And Mr. Rollins launch the boat. If we can row out an anchor, we may yet be able to kedge ourselves off." Thom looked up at the sails, the mainsail still drawing, holding them on the bar. "And get the sails down."

"Aye, sir." Both Wilton and Rollins looked ashen. Thom walked down the deck, feeling equal parts stunned and mortified. The *Hannah* lay absolutely still except for the flapping of a jib.

Justin met him. "No injuries, sir."

"Good. I should speak with our charges." That was exactly the last thing that Thom wanted to do, but he was, at least for a time yet, still captain and the packet was too small to find a place to hide. Moses Brown was sitting on the hatch coaming talking to a Fergus Greene, a fellow merchant. Moses looked up on Thom's approach.

"I pray that you gentlemen were not injured in the grounding." On hearing assurances that neither were, Thom said, "We are attempting to kedge her off the sand bar. I'll be sure to keep you advised of our progress." The words almost stuck in his throat. While the *Hannah* was motionless, the current was not. The tide was ebbing and their prospects ebbed with it. "Gentlemen."

Thom turned and strolled aft trying not to walk too slowly or too fast. Wilton was still casting the line. Rollins and Justin had wrestled the mainsail down and were readying the boat. The deck sloped upward and just slightly to larboard.

"Looks like we just clipped the bar, sir. Shoals ahead but deep water to larboard." Wilton stood before him, the sounding line coiled and looped over his shoulder, dripping, leaving a small puddle at his feet.

"Thank you. Please assist Rollins with the anchor."

They set the anchor to larboard and lead the rode through a block at the masthead to the windless. All hands, Thom included, raced to haul the packet over in the faint hope that hove down she might float off and slip back into the channel. But, it was not to be. They had lost the race with the ebbing tide. The packet was laying over on her own accord as the tide dropped.

Once again, Thom went to speak to his two passengers. Now the deck was hard to walk on. The packet was on her bilge and the deck sloped a good ten degrees.

Moses Brown and Fergus Greene were as he left them, both now sitting on the hatch coaming.

Thom cleared his throat. "Gentlemen. It appears that we must wait out the tide. If you would like, we will have you rowed ashore where we will endeavor to arrange a coach to take you the rest of the way to Providence."

"Mathers Phillips has a house nearby and he keeps a surrey. I am sure he will be able to accommodate us," Moses replied.

Rollins had the boat alongside in a moment. Thom stepped up to Moses Brown. "Sir, I do wish to say that it has been a true pleasure in being in the employ of your family these few years and that I only wish you all the best. I could understand if your brother might wish to find a new captain for the packet."

Moses raised an eyebrow, which seemed also to draw his mouth into a smile and then, an instant later, into a laugh. "I have learned years ago never to speak for my brother so I will say nothing on that matter.

"You are still a very young man, Captain Larkin. You should learn two lessons from this misadventure. The first you know well enough. Sandbars tend to move from one season to the next. But you know that firsthand."

"Yes sir. I believe I do. And the second lesson?"

"The second. Yes, this is a bit more subtle. Wisdom and folly are rarely original. Do you think that you are the first packet captain to find this sandbar?"

Thom stood silent.

"I am sure that Captain Haney gave you fair warning about Namquit Point. Warning which you now wish you gave greater heed. How do think Captain Haney learned of Namquit's hazards? Direct experience is always the best teacher. And how do think I learned of Mathers Phillip's surrey? This is not the first time my trip was interrupted by that particular spit of sand. By my reckoning you should float free by an hour after midnight. Depending, of course, on the moon."

❖❖❖

True to Moses Brown's estimate it was roughly a quarter past one in the morning when the tide lifted the *Hannah* free. The wind had died so it was not until three that they were finally alongside in Providence with the sails furled. Thom managed only an hour or two of sleep before the dawn called him back on deck. He fixed himself a cup of coffee and with the further fortification of a stale biscuit, set off to present himself to his employer.

John Brown was already at is desk when Thom arrived. "Sir, I regret to advise you that I ran the *Hannah* aground."

"Yes, yes, heard all about it. Namquit Point can be tricky. Any damage? Seams tight, no leaking?"

"Ah no sir. She's tight as a drum. No damage."

"Fine, then we need speak no more of it. Captain Larkin, there is a saying that a coasterman is not an experienced sailor unless he has run aground at least once. Let us consider you sufficiently experienced, that no repetition is necessary. "

"Yes, sir. Absolutely, sir."

❖❖❖

The *Hannah* called on New York and had to wait for the morning tide to venture back up the East River. Thom lingered at Jasper's Tavern into the early evening, enjoying both the ale and the company. He made his way down the dark alley that he had walked a dozen times before, his feet following his memories more than the dim light from the high windows and occasional doorway.

The roll of the drum startled him, commanding his heart and lungs before the warning reached his brain. An instant later a pair of fifes began the introduction to "Heart of Oak." Save for the surroundings Thom felt as though he was aboard the *Romney* and the drum were beating to quarters. He glanced up and down the alley, expecting fully to see a press gang sweeping the street, dragging away all in their net. His heart raced and he could barely breathe. The confidential letters for John Brown felt heavy in his breast pocket. His eyes searched vainly for an escape and saw none.

He stood for a moment and realized that he was alone. There was no one else in the alley. No officer or bosun, no band of sailors running toward him wielding belaying pins and clubs. Only the sound of the drum and the fifes. Then a voice boomed out in song, but not the high pitch of Midshipman Paulings that lived in his memory. Nor was the singer singing the lyrics that Thom expected, the lyrics that he so hated, "*to honor we call you not press you like slaves, for who are so free as the sons of the waves?*" Instead they were new words, different, strange, yet stirring from what he could hear.

"*Come join hand in hand, brave Americans all,
and gird your bold hearts at Liberty's call.*"

The next few lines he couldn't quite make out, but the chorus rang clearly enough.

"*As free men we're born and free men we'll live,
Our heart and hands are ready, Steady boys steady,
For justice and freedom our all we shall give.*"

Thom turned and walked toward the smoky light of an open doorway just around a far corner, drawn by the song and roll of the drum. In the tavern, a drummer, a boy barely larger than his drum, and two pipers were wedged next to the door with a barrel-chested singer stomping out the glorious song.

The tavern was crowded with sailors, tradesmen, and mechanics of a lesser sort, all drinking and singing along when the chorus came back around. As he elbowed his way to the bar and shouted his order to the bar maid, Thom joined in the song, *"Free men we're born, An Free men we'll live..."*

The crowd sang boisterously, either enjoying the lyrics or more likely the tune, that Thom had cursed ever since they made good their escape from the *Romney*. The song, *Heart of Oak*, had haunted him, returning at odd times, refusing to leave him alone. *"Heart of Oak are our ships, Jolly tars are our men."* It was a damned lie that wouldn't take its leave and yet until it did, his escape from the *Romney* wasn't complete. He was always drawn back to the gun deck for muster, neither a jolly tar or called to honor, but a pressed man, no more than a slave.

Now it was all different. The simple change in the lyrics felt like a shackle broken. He loudly sang with his fellows, *"brave Americans all."* *"Freemen we're born and freemen we'll live."* Thom sang the chorus, now just another brave American singing, shouting joyously till he felt hoarse.

The drum rolled and the pipes squealed as all joined in the final chorus, ending with a great roaring shout. The young drummer put down his sticks, unharnessed his drum, doffed his tricorn hat and passed through the crowd catching the copper coins cast his way. The singer, bellowed, "Gentlemen, the *Liberty Song*, by John Dickinson of Pennsylvania. An' if you like the song, the words and music are but three pence." He shook a sheaf of broadsheets in his thick hand.

In a few minutes the noise of the crowd diminished and the drummer, dumped the coins into a mug next to the singer, strapped on his drum and readied his sticks. The pipers lifted their fifes and the singer announced, "A tune on the same sort of feeling, gents. *Free Americay*, by Dr. Joseph Warren of Boston."

The drum rolled and the fifes picked up another familiar tune that Thom had heard the morning that Boston was occupied. The Grenadiers had marched with their banners flying to the tune that bore their name, *"The British Grenadiers."* So proud and haughty yet now the melody had new words and another sort of pride.

"Torn from a world of tyrants,
Beneath a western sky,
We've formed a new dominion,
A land of Liberty.
The world shall own we're free men,
And so shall ever be,
Hurrah, Hurrah, Hurrah, Hurrah,
For Love and Liberty."

Thom made it back to the *Hannah* happily intoxicated by both the music and the porter. In his pocket he carried the broadsheets with lyrics for the *Liberty Song* and *Free Americay*. If he crossed paths with the *Gaspee* on the return trip, he might not be able to match broadsides with broadsheet, but at least he could sing his defiance.

❖ ❖ ❖

When he returned to Providence, Thom placed the bundle of mail on John Brown's deck, his employer looked up with a smile. "I have news for you, Mr. Larkin. I've received word from my correspondents in London. They relay a sad account. According to Admiralty records Thomas Lewis and Jonathan Saunders were lost at sea off the HMS *Romney* last year. Sad, sad news," he said with a smile.

"Yes sir, sad indeed," Thom replied, beaming.

"You made good your escape, even on the records. You are to be congratulated. Oh, yes, your friend, Michael Skinner, may have escaped as well. He is also marked 'lost at sea.'"

Thom's face fell and he shook his head. "His only escape was to his maker, sir. Was a weaver, out celebrating the birth of his first born son when the gangsters caught him. Had no business being on a ship. Press gang killed him as sure as the storm. Bloody bastards."

"It is a sorrow to hear."

Thom forced a smile. "Thank you sir for your efforts. It is good to be dead in the eyes of the Admiralty."

"May we all be dead in the tyrant's eyes," Brown replied.

❖❖❖

On the next voyage when the *Hannah* arrived in Providence, Thom was surprised to see John Brown on the dock. He walked with Thom to the postmaster's. Thom saw that he was troubled. His gait seemed almost angry and his jaw remained clenched, but his eyes suggested less rage than sadness. They walked for a time, neither speaking until Brown stopped.

"My brothers and I are dividing our business ventures. We've been unable to agree on our" he paused, "our principles and practices. My eldest brother finds my ambitions reckless and my youngest judges me to be immoral." He looked off toward the docks. "So, I shall be establishing my own office at 140 River Street.

"It is my sorrow that my association with my brothers is ending thus. I know little of importance beyond my family, but so be it. Our relationship, Thom, is, of course, unchanged, or may perhaps grow in importance. My need for information and communication has grown, so I value your service all the more. You are my good eyes and ears, and a most worthy captain, as well."

Thom didn't know what to say. He mumbled "Yes, sir. Thank you, sir," and wondered whether John Brown had intended to be so candid, but he seemed relieved to be able to speak freely. They walked for a bit more in silence until John Brown chose to speak again.

"I can understand Nicholas's caution, while I don't share it, but I cannot abide Moses's righteousness. Our mother was a Quaker, you know, and Moses decided to follow her course rather than our father's and uncles'. He was always like that, independent of mind, quick and bright, my favorite, if truth be told, yet now he damns me as in league with the devil.

"He is a hypocrite, you know, but completely unaware of his hypocrisy. He damns the slave trade as unholy and corrupt, yet profits from it, as do we all. He sells candles and tobacco in the Indies for molasses, never once asking how the sugar cane for the molasses would be raised without slaves. How they can afford the bills of exchange to buy our fish, tobacco, or ironwork except by the sweat of slaves? He sells the molasses to distillers of rum, blissfully untroubled that next season that rum will serve as currency to buy black men on the beaches of the Guinea coast. This entire colony depends on the Guineaman trade, one way or another. It is commerce, nothing more."

He stopped speaking and looked at Thom. John Brown seemed to have the capacity to reach into his thoughts, a capacity that always amazed Thom and that now he regretted.

"Or perhaps you agree with my brother, Moses?"

Thom thought for a moment. He had to concede the truth in what John Brown had said, yet was unable to accept his conclusion.

"When I was kidnapped by the press gang, I only spent a few days in irons in the hold of a ship. I cannot imagine the torment of Africans stolen from their homes, in irons for months in the Middle Passage. When I sailed home on the *Black Swan,* I heard the shackles rattle as she rolled. My dreams were haunted by the cries of the bondsmen. I do not disagree with you about molasses or trade, but neither can I disagree with your brother."

He had expected anger. John Brown rarely brooked disagreement with grace, yet now all Thom saw was sorrow and a weariness that he had never seen before in his employer. Some of the irrepressible energy that almost defined the man had been drained away.

"Then shall you part with me as well?" The question sounded almost like a plea, the cry of a wounded man.

"No, sir. I'm most pleased to stay in your employ, if you'll have me."

John Brown smiled. "Good." He slapped Thom on the back and returned to their stroll. "Now tell me. What rumors have you heard in New York. What course will the Yorkers steer?"

Thom smiled, pleased to see the man that he knew return to himself again.

"I believe they're split. 'Bout half want to ship goods as fast as they can to London to catch the season and the other half seems to think that the Indies is the better chance. And at least a few bear a grudge against Rhode Islanders, thinking that we played the agreement to our advantage, so that maybe by trading south they can rebuild their commerce and take back a bit from this colony at the same time."

"So, we'll see competition in both London and the Indies. Well, we've faced worse and fared well enough. Likely do as well this time."

❖❖❖

The season ended with a mild autumn and a temperate winter. When the snows finally came, Thom felt, for the first time in what seemed to be a very long time, a sense of peace and a wary confidence that winds again had shifted in his favor. While he mentioned it to no one, and had managed to deflect Angela's inquiries regarding specific dates, as of the last week of August, he had finally turned twenty.

It felt important, yet Thom was not quite sure why. His pocket held no more silver at twenty than at nineteen. He had acquired no more wisdom and likely possessed no less folly than in the year before. Yet somehow, riding the inexorable procession of time itself felt like a victory. He had escaped the *Romney*, survived both a hurricane and a fever, had begun to learn the ways of the merchant class, and ended up sailing as a captain, even if only on a packet boat of little consequence.

And then there was Angela, on whom all his unspoken hopes, dreams, and desires rested. Dear Angela.

Everything seemed to be changing with the season. His good friend, John Stevens, announced that he was to be married to a lovely young Newport lady of long acquaintance, a captain's daughter. Perhaps, despite all his denials, Johnny was finally settling down.

All seemed well even as the winds blew cold off the Narragansett. The one dark and dangerous storm cloud lingering on the horizon was the certain knowledge that his past would never quite set him free. He would have to keep a weather eye out for Dudingston and the *Gaspee*, which had ranged between Massachusetts and the Chesapeake. One day their wakes would yet cross.

CHAPTER NINE

The *Hannah* had just cleared the East Passage. Block Island Sound and the open Atlantic spread out off to the south, shining silver in the morning sun. Thom hooked an arm around a shroud and pulled the collar of his coat tighter about his neck. It was the first voyage of the season and the early spring breeze was bitter but bracing, setting up a short, steep chop; the wave crests, a brilliant white against the blue of the sky and the deeper blue of the bay.

Were he not occupied checking the rigging, Thom might have lost himself in the morning, finally freed from the chains of winter, as the miles slipped magically by beneath them, the rigging humming, alive in the wind. He paced the deck, his eye following the line of the mast, stays and shrouds, carefully examining each fitting and deadeye, one more time. Early spring was always treacherous. If anything was to let go, it would be on the first trip or two. As he reached the bow, pitching gently in the chop, all seemed in order.

On the horizon, the masts and topsails of a ship, still hull down, rose from the sea and Thom watched idly as the ship grew from the haze. She was most likely a homebound trader from the West Indies. Watching her, he recalled the wild anticipation of landfall that he always felt after a foreign voyage. Part of him wished that he was sailing on the northbound ship. By now, he had lived just long enough with that longing to put it aside.

After a half an hour, he could make the ship out, a fine barque, deeply laden. In another hour, they crossed, Thom shouting, "Packet *Hannah*, from Providence, New York bound;" the captain on the barque answering across the wind, "*Dauntless,* homebound for Bristol, from St. Barts". Thom waived as she passed, then scanned the horizon, watching the high wisps of clouds, a sure sign of fair, dry weather.

Perhaps twenty minutes later, the distinctive thud of a ship's gun set Thom spinning on his heals. Only a silhouette against the bluffs ashore, a schooner sailed on a closing course with the barque. A small cloud floated just off her bow, fading as he watched. The schooner was dark with dull yellow topsides and cannon ports that appeared painted on her bulwarks. The ports seemed almost comical. Many a merchantman had painted gunports so that at a distance they might pass for a man-of-war, but no one would mistake this schooner for a frigate. The ports appeared to be open, with gun barrels, diminutive but distinctive, peaking out from the bulwarks. Again, a small cloud appeared off the schooner's bow followed immediately by the distant thunderclap.

Thom hurried back to the quarterdeck where Rollins studied the schooner through a spy glass. "She put a shot cross the bow of the barque. Flying British colors. An' look at the pennant on her stern," he said handing the glass to Thom.

Thom focused on the distant schooner and saw a fluttering Royal Navy pennant. "Bastards," he muttered. He knew the schooner. He had seen it once briefly in New York harbor. It was the *Gaspee.* The past had returned to find him. Dudingston had finally arrived in Narragansett Bay. For a moment, Thom felt as if the wind had been knocked from his lungs.

He took the glass from his eye. "Nothing to be done for the barky." Hope he's paid the duty on his molasses. He thought darkly, knowing full well that any cargo from St. Barts was French, lifeblood of the colony and contraband to the Crown. "Bastards," he repeated. He wanted to change course and give a warning back in Newport but knew the word would spread soon enough. Instead, he glanced up at the sails. "Believe we could use a reef in the topsail 'fore the course change."

"Aye, Capt'n," Rollins replied nodding toward Wilton who eased the halyard, before clambering up the ratlines to reef the sail.

❖ ❖ ❖

When Thom returned to Newport he found Johnny at the chandlery. "Saw the *Gaspee* take a barque, the *Dauntless*, inbound off Point Judith. What news have ye?"

"Took the *Dauntless*, the *Lucinda* and four other ships in less'n a week," Johnny replied. "When Captain Johnson called him a pirate, the bastard opened his cheek with a cutlass. And he fired straight into a sloop when she was slow to heave to.

"Billy Dudingston was a right foul son-of-a-whore as a First Lieutenant on the *Romney* and if anything, seems he's got worse with his own command." Johnny shook his head then grinned. "Been wonderin' whether he'll recognize his old ship mates?"

Thom stood silent for an instant, breathing deeply to control the anger that that well up within him. "More important that we recognize him. Besides, the shipmates you mention are dead, drowned in a hurricane, as I recall. Pity he didn't find the same fate."

❖ ❖ ❖

That evening Thom and Johnny were joined at the Mill Stone by friends, fellow sailors and merchants, drinking and listening to what news there was of the *Gaspee*. Rumor was that the *Beaver*, a sloop of war of sixteen guns, would join her within the fortnight to patrol offshore, while the *Gaspee* prowled the bay. "Like trying to lock us in a cage," one of the captains commented.

As the evening wore on, the crisis, while no less grave, grew more distant. "Tell us again 'bout when you and young Thomas slipped outta the bastard's clutches in the storm. Always liked that story."

Johnny smiled, flushed in the glow of the fire and warmth from the ale, at first shaking his head, no. "Go on, John," Thom said. "I won't call you a liar, whatever yarn you spin."

With that John sat back and told the tale, slowly, being led on by those who had heard it before. It felt good in the telling, reminding all that he and Thom had escaped Dudingston's grasp once before and that they all yet might do as well, or better.

On the far side of the room, Samuel Martin leaned over his tankard. The rough wood columns in the tavern put Thom and Johnny's table almost out of sight, but not out of earshot. He listened to Johnny's story and seethed to himself. He'd been made a fool of by those two, when he was the mate on the *Black Swan*. Traveling merchants indeed. The large one had shamed him before the crew. If he hadn't, the bosun would never have dared tell the captain that he had been stealing wine from the spirit locker, and the captain never would have fired him. So, Thom and Johnny, their real names were. Well, Thom and Johnny, your time will come, Martin swore to himself.

❖❖❖

The next afternoon, when Thom dropped the mail at John Brown's counting house in Providence, his employer was in a rage, looking down at a note on his desk.

"I've received word that the *Elizabeth* has been taken. That bloody bastard Dudingston is naught more than a brigand. He hasn't presented his commission to the governor, did you know that? Charges into the bay taking every ship that crossed his hawse. How do we know that he has any authority at all? I'll call on the governor myself, for this must not stand. We cannot have a renegade spreading terror in our own waters. We still have every right to hang pirates, you know."

The *Elizabeth* was one of John Brown's newer ships and Thom knew that the Browns were relying on the proceeds from her last voyage to cover the costs of an upcoming trading venture. Thom shared his anger and did his best to control his ire whenever he heard the name Dudingston or *Gaspee*.

"I know William Dudingston too well. He is a greedy and arrogant bastard, if ever there was one," Thom said.

Brown shook his head. "This will not serve. This will not stand."

Shortly before the *Hannah* was due to sail the following day, Thom was surprised to see a carriage pull up. John Brown got out and strode up the gangway.

"I believe you have room for another Newport passenger."

"Yes, sir. Welcome aboard."

Brown lowered his voice. "I carry a letter from Lieutenant Governor Darius Sessions for Governor Wanton, which I will deliver to the governor personally. I will also give the governor my own thoughts."

Thom wondered why John Brown chose the packet for his transport. It was certainly more comfortable than a carriage, but as they were bound for New York, Brown would either have to arrange a way back to Providence or wait ten days for the packet. Thom smiled to himself. If he knew John Brown, he was hoping that Dudingston would stop the *Hannah*. Against John Brown's will, Thom wondered whether the *Gaspee*'s guns would suffice.

"I wish you good fortune, sir." Thom turned. "Justin, help Mr. Brown with his bag and make him comfortable in the cabin."

❖ ❖ ❖

The trip to Newport was uneventful. John Brown stood on the quarterdeck, telling Thom of his days as supercargo for his Uncle Obediah. He was sufficiently caught up in his tales that he hardly seemed to notice the other traffic. Thom, in contrast, scrutinized each schooner they past, watching for the *Gaspee*. When they arrived in Newport, Brown was the first down the gangplank, marching as if to war, to make his case to Governor Wanton.

Thom stepped ashore briefly to check on the latest rumors of the *Gaspee*. Narragansett Bay had three entrances and myriad islands where a single schooner could slip by unnoticed. A fine bay for smugglers. Now the Crown had turned the geography against them by sending in a shallow draft schooner in search of prey.

The *Hannah* sailed from Newport on schedule but didn't see the *Gaspee* on its way to New York or on the return trip.

When they arrived back in Providence, John Brown was waiting for him. "Any sign of Dudingston?"

"Ah, no sir."

"When we sailed for Newport together, the scoundrel snapped up two Bristol ships, then a Providence sloop in the West Passage. We were lucky to have missed him." Brown smiled bitterly. "He's even taken to stealing hogs and cattle to feed his crew. They come ashore like any band of brigands and promise to burn down the farmer's house should he resist their thievery. And I hear reports that they came ashore Friday last on Gould Island and cut down seven of Joseph Wilton's best chestnut trees for firewood.

"Dudingston will answer. We're a chartered colony, after all. We elect our governor. Not like Massachusetts with a lickspittle appointee from London. I have assurances from both Darius Sessions and Governor Wanton himself, who is writing to Dudingston in the strongest terms. If that doesn't cease his banditry, he'll write to his commanding officer. That'll reign in the brigand."

"Lord willing," Thom replied, not as sure that mere ink on paper would stop William Dudingston.

❖❖❖

One late afternoon, when pushing his uncle's cart made for thirsty work, Johnny stopped at the Mill Stone for an ale. As soon as he walked through the door, Jacob Miller called him over.

"Don't know what it's about, but had two Royal Navy sorts in here asking about a Thomas and a Johnny. The men they described fit your descriptions, more or less. They weren't too sure of the last names. Saunders and Lewis, I think they said. Came dressed as gentlemen, but I knew 'em for Navy sure as they're born. *Gaspee* was at anchor and I 'spect these two were from the prize crew off the schooner they brought in.

"And what did you tell 'em?" Johnny asked.

"What do you 'spect I told 'em? Told 'em never heard of either of the gents. Asked them why they wanted to know, but they weren't so talkative and left after a pint."

Johnny raised an eyebrow. "Anybody asks, John Saunders and Thom Lewis were lost at sea in a hurricane. That's what the Admiralty records say."

"Who do you think tipped them off?" Millers asked.

"Don't know. I've told that story more'n I should'a, I'm sure. You have a guess to offer?"

Miller thought a moment. "Coupla nights ago had to throw Sam Martin out'a here, sufferin' from the drink. Thought I heard him mumble something 'bout you and Thom, but can't be sure. Sent him off with that dog of his, that he keeps tied in the ally. He's a worthless sod, but might be dangerous when he's sober."

"I'll watch out." John repled. "Thank's for the warning."

Miller smiled. "Well, what'ya have?"

"A pint 'o porter'll be fine."

❖ ❖ ❖

When Thom entered the office, John Brown was smiling broadly. He rapped his desk soundly with his fist. "He's finally gone too far, too far by half. Have you heard? The pirate Dudingston took the *Constance* with a cargo of molasses and because the Admiralty Court in Newport is no longer dancing to his tune, the bastard sent the sloop to Boston Admiralty Court, in clear violation of the law. Every ship seized within a colony must be adjudged in the colony.

"Nathaniel Greene owns the *Constance* and her cargo, and he's had a warrant sworn out for the arrest of Lieutenant William

Dudingston. That will get the bastard. He lacks all allies now, save his crew and I doubt not that many of them would choose to desert, had they the chance. Even the commissioners of customs detest him."

"Why don't the customs men support him?" Thom asked.

"Because greed's a poison. If customs makes the seizure, a third goes to the commissioner, a third to the governor and a third to the colony. If the seizure is at sea, half goes to the Admiral and half to the ship. Dudingston is filling his pockets and cutting out the customs men, who are now all sharpening their knives for him. He won't send his prizes to Newport and the warrant will take him in Providence."

"If he should choose to go ashore in Providence. He may not oblige you," Thom suggested.

"We'll stop him. One way or another."

❖ ❖ ❖

Whatever hopes John Brown had for the warrant, it remained unfilled. If anything conditions had grown more grave. Dudingston continued raiding the bay, while a sloop of war, HMS *Beaver,* had arrived to cruise offshore. Dudingston was now sending every ship seized either to Boston or Halifax manned by a prize crew, further enraging both Newport and Providence.

Angela now made a point of meeting Thom on each arrival in Providence. She smiled at him bravely and never spoke of her fears but they were clear enough in her expression. Likewise, Thom chose not to speak of the lingering dread and the rising anger that he felt. There seemed to be no obvious answer, except to keep a sharp weather out for a black schooner.

One afternoon after arriving in Providence, Thom stopped for a pint in Sabin's Tavern, which was unusually crowded. Captain John Hopkins was holding forth, sure that he had the answer to Dudinston's depredations. The oldest son of Ezra Hopkins, Brown's most senior captain and nephew of the five-time governor, Stephen Hopkins, John Hopkins was captain of John Brown's *Pretty Polly* carrying cargo between Providence, New York, and Philadelphia. He sat surrounded by fellow captains and officers after several pints of porter.

"The *Polly*'ll carry six pounders on deck. Get across the *Gaspee*'s hawse, we'll send her to the bottom." His audience, initially reluctant, seemed to warm to the idea, so Hopkins continued.

"Tis the only way. All legal means have been undertaken, remonstrances ignored, the governor insulted by a lowly lieutenant. Time to stop talking and act like the men we are -- Sons of Liberty, true and strong."

A dozen voices shouted agreement and only when the noise diminished did Captain Abraham Whipple, sitting at a nearby table, raise his voice.

"I would hope that you have a greater wit than that, John Hopkins. Everyone on the coast from Pennsylvania to Massachusetts knows both you and the *Polly*. I'm sure that the son-of-a-bitch Admiral Montague would love to see you arm the *Polly* and sink one of his Majesty's schooners. Would nab you and as a special prize snare John Brown and maybe his brothers and your uncle besides. The first families of Providence sunk by your puny six pound guns."

The tavern was quiet for a moment till Hopkins piped up, "So we find another ship. Something's to be done. If we don't resist we are naught but sheep."

"Better to choose the chance with care than to rush in and be slaughtered like sheep," Whipple suggested before rising and leaving the inn.

❖❖❖

Johnny hailed Thom as he came down the gangway. "What news from Providence?"

"Little enough. Anger's high, but nothing to be done. How fare's Newport?"

"Not so different." He stepped closer to Thom, his voice low. "Watch yourself. Two Navy men, likely from the *Gaspee* or the *Beaver* came to Miller's asking 'bout John Saunders and Thomas Lewis. I think that whore's son Sam Martin turned us in, probably for the price of a drink. Miller said that he never heard of Saunders or Lewis and I told him, if anybody asks again that they're both dead, drown in the Indies."

"I'll be careful."

"Do you think that the *Hannah* might not be a safe berth for you right now?"

"I'm not about to run away, if that's what you mean."

"No, that's not what I meant," Johnny replied.

Johnny noticed a pistol stuck in Thom's belt. He nodded toward it. "And what's that for?"

"Wharf rats. Seem to be a lot around these days."

"And some carry guns. Don't try to best three pound guns with a three ounce ball."

Thom smiled for an instant but spoke no more of the pistol. "Did you hear about Josiah Peters? Old man, a woodcutter, rowing firewood to Bristol, was stopped last week by the *Gaspee*. They threw his firewood in the water looking for molasses of tea or some sort of contraband hidden in his boat, but don't find any, so they sank his boat and put him ashore a full score miles from the nearest farm. Near death when folks found him. He's a poor man and without his boat he'll either starve or have to beg for charity."

Johnny just shook his head and walked back to the chandlery.

A few days later, Johnny heard of a meeting called at the Mill Stone Tavern. The rumor was that the legislature was to do something about the *Gaspee*, but it was far from clear what that might be. When Johnny arrived not long after dusk, the tavern was crowded. In a few minutes Jacob Miller pounded on the bar.

"First order of business," he shouted over the din of voices. "Does anyone need an ale?" When his customers were well served, he continued.

"I have here the *Newport Mercury* for this day May 12, 1772. Thought you might want to hear what's transpired, if ya' haven't heard already. Governor Wanton requested that the pirate Dudingston present his commission and was sorely rebuffed. Admiral Montague then wrote a scandalous and disgraceful letter that our good governor has seen fit to set before the legislature. An' the legislature has resolved to forward it all to the Secretary of State, asking the Royal Navy and one admiral in particular be taught some manners. The letters are all printed here in the paper."

"So, stop flapping your jaws and read it, Jacob," came a voice from the crowd followed by a murmur of agreement.

"All right, if you insist," he said, rattling the paper.

"To the commanding officer of a schooner near Breton's Point. Newport, Rhode Island March 22, 1772.

"Sir: A considerable number of the inhabitants of this colony have complained to me of your having, in a most illegal and unwarranted manner, interrupted their trade, by searching and detaining every little packet boat plying between the several towns."

Voices from the crowd shouted agreement. Miller looked up then continued.

"As I know not by what authority you assume this power, I have sent off the high sheriff to inform you of the complaint exhibited against you, and expect that you do without delay, produce your commission and instructions, if any you have,

which is your duty to have done when you first came within the Jurisdiction of this Colony. I am your humble servant, J. WANTON"

"Rightly said," shouted a sailor from the tavern.
"To which the pirate replies:

Gaspee, Rhode Island, March 23, 1772
Sir: Last night, I received your letter informing me that a "number of the inhabitants of this Colony had complained" to you of my having "in a most illegal and unwarrantable manner interrupted their packet boats plying between the several towns."
In answer to which, I have done nothing but what was my duty, and their complaint can only be found in their ignorance of that.
Sir, your humble servant,   W. DUDINGSTON.

"Useless whore's son," and a dozen other curses filled the air. Miller waived his hand to still the crowd before continuing.
"An' the governor writes back:

To Mr. W. Dudingston, of the Schooner Gaspee Newport, Rhode Island March 23,1772
Sir: Yours of this day I have received, which does not give the satisfaction I have the right to expect; ... I expect that you do without delay, comply with my request of yesterday, and you may be assured that my utmost exertions shall not be wanting to protect your person from any insult or outrage on coming ashore. I am your humble servant, J. WANTON"

Miller stopped and took a deep swig from a tankard. "Thirsty work, reading." He raised his voice. "Now any righteous man would have shown his commission to our honorable governor. But Dudingston complains to his admiral, he does. Here's the letter from Admiral Montague." Miller looked down at the newspaper again and started to read.

"Boston, 6th April, 1772
Sir: Lieutenant Dudingston, commander of his Majesty's armed schooner and part of the squadron under my command, has sent me two letters he received from you of such a nature I am at a loss what answers to give them and ashamed to find they come from one of his Majesty's Governors."

Shouts from the tavern nearly drowned him out, but Miller raised a hand until the protests died down and he started again.

"He, sir, has done his duty and behaved like an officer, and it is your duty as governor, to give him your assistance, and not endeavor to distress the King's officers for strictly complying with my orders. ... I am also informed, the people of Newport talk of fitting out an armed vessel to rescue any vessel the King's schooner may take carrying on an illicit trade. Let then be cautious what they do; for sure as they attempt it, and any of them are taken, I will hang them as pirates."

"Just let 'em try," a dozen voices shouted. "Pipe down," Miller replied, "less'n you want me to stop now." He paused for a moment then satisfied, he started again.

"I shall report your two insolent letters to my officer, to his Majesty's Secretaries of State, and leave them to determine what right you have to demand a sight of all my orders I shall give to all officers of my squadron, and I would advise you not to send your Sheriff to board the King's ship again, on such ridiculous errands. I am your most humble servant. J. MONTAGUE"

Jeers and taunts filled the tavern till Miller pounded on the bar.

"Now Governor Wanton wouldn't let those insults stand. He writes back:

Rhode Island, May 8, 1772
Sir: Your letter dated April the 8th at Boston, I have received. Lieutenant Dudingston has done well in transmitting my letters to you, which I sent him.... You say 'he has done his duty and behaved like an officer.' In this I apprehend you must be mistaken, for I can never believe it is the duty of any officer, to give false information to his superiors. He, at no time, ever showed me any orders from the admiralty or from you, therefore it was altogether out of my power to know, whether he came hither to protect us from pirates, or was a pirate himself."

The crowd burst into a roar of agreement. "He said it truly, yes he did," Miller agreed. He cleared his voice and read on.

"I am greatly obliged for the promise of transmitting my letters to the Secretary of State. I shall also transmit your letter to the Secretary of State, and leave to the King and his ministers to determine on which side the charge of insolence lies."

The noise overwhelmed Miller's voice. "Quiet down now. I'm almost through. Now where was I ?

"As to your advice not to send the Sheriff on board any of your squadron, please to know, that I will send the Sheriff of this Colony at any time, and to any place, within the body of it, as I shall think fit. In the last paragraph of your letter you are pleased to flatly contradict what you wrote in the beginning; for there you assert that Dudingston, by his instructions, was directed to show me the admiralty and your orders to him, and here you assert, that I have no business with them, and assure

me that it is not his duty to show me them or any part thereof. I am, sir, your humble servant, J. WANTON."

Miller's patrons drank toasts to the Governor and to the King until late into the night. When Johnny made his way home, it occurred to him that while the Governor may have assured his re-election, nothing had been done to stop the *Gaspee*.

CHAPTER TEN

On the ninth day of June, just before midday, Thom picked up the *Hannah*'s papers from the customs house in Newport and stepped back aboard the packet. "Mr. Rollins," he bellowed to his new mate, "Prepare to get underway. Tide won't wait for us." He caught the grin on Justin Jacob's face and for a moment felt foolish, then pleased with himself. If he sounded like old Captain Haney, well, so be it.

With the gangway aboard and the hawsers hove short, he shouted, "Cast off. Raise the main." Rollins took the throat halyard with Justin on the peak and the main rose, luffing in the nor'westely breeze. "The jibs, Mr. Rollins. Smartly now." The jibs rose, flapped then filled, pulling her to weather.

The helmsman stood nervously at the tiller. It was only his second trip. Thom stepped over and motioned him aside. "I'll take'r out of the harbor, if you don't mind." The green sailor stepped aside, appearing grateful.

Thom was fond of his hand on the tiller, maybe more than was proper for a captain. But propriety be damned. He smiled as he felt her respond to the helm.

"Sheet her flat, Mr. Rollins," Thom said in a tone suggesting that he shouldn't need to be told. They sailed the length of the harbor before bearing off. This time, the mate anticipated him and the sheets were eased as soon as he put the helm over.

"Mind the main now. Ready for the jibe, " Thom said with half a smile. They ran along the island shore and then rounded up again at the harbor's mouth, slipping between Breton's Point and Goat Island.

Thom's smile faded and his jaw clenched when he saw the schooner *Gaspee* sailing up the East Passage. Dudingston, in his fine blue coat and a hat fit for an admiral, was yelling something at the crew and didn't see the *Hannah* till the ships were abeam, slipping quickly by on opposite tacks.

Lieutenant Dudingston looked over and fixed Thom with a stare, that Thom answered only with a nod of his head. Even at a distance, Thom could see the the scowl that spread across the lieutenant's face. Thom felt a cold hatred rising within him and forced himself to look away.

Goat Island slipped astern and he brought the *Hannah* closer to the wind, the deckhands trimming the sails till the sheets were bar tight and sloop heeled smartly in the nor-westerly breeze.

Justin Jacobs stood looking first at the *Gaspee* then back at Thom, who seemed almost to have dismissed the inbound schooner.

"Captain, sir? Beg your pardon, sir?" Thom glanced over at the young man. "Peers they're comin' about, sir."

Thom looked over his shoulder and saw that the sails of the *Gaspee* were luffing. An outbound bark blocked the schooner from turning so she sat in irons, all sails flapping, sheets flailing, while the bark made its way past.

"Mr. Rollins," Thom shouted with a greater urgency than he intended, "Set the topsail, if you please." Thom steered close to Rose Island, the wind easing slightly in the lee as the hands cast off the gaskets from the topsail and slacked the bunts and clewlines. The sail rose slatting back and forth while the halyard was hardened up. The deckhands hauled the weather brace and the sail filled just as they cleared the island. The *Hannah* settled in, with the water rushing along her lee rail and the northerly whistling in the rigging. Thom spread his legs slightly to balance as the heel increased, the deck sloping like the side of a mountain down toward the water boiling along the rail.

Thom looked aft. The *Gaspee* was just clearing the harbor and also setting her topsails. Thom took a deep breath. He couldn't take his eyes off the schooner gaining weigh and clearly in pursuit. This was the day of which he had dreamed for so many years, day and night. It had been, in turn, a nightmare and a dream of redemption.

From many of his dreams, he had awoken in a sweat, shaking with fear, dreaming of being dragged back to the *Romney* by Dudingston and a press gang — back to bondage, the lash, and oblivion.

He had also wakened triumphant, dreaming of confronting the arrogant lieutenant. Sometimes, they fought with swords, sometimes with pistols and sometimes with bare hands. In those dreams, his anger and righteous rage made him mighty, and they always ended with Thom standing over the Dudingston, sometimes dead, sometimes alive, but always, utterly defeated.

Now, Thom was not dreaming. His old foe was in pursuit in an armed schooner. Thom rested his hand on his pistol at his belt, the only weapon aboard the packet. For an instant, he suddenly felt foolish and helpless.

He took his eyes off the *Gaspee* and looked up at the *Hannah*'s mainsail, full, white and taut against the brisk nor'westerly wind. The wake hummed and sang to him and the clear blue sky above was soothing. The feeling of helplessness slipped past with the rushing water. Listening to the wake and watching the curve of the sail, he felt neither fear nor rage, but a calm, if grim resolve. He wasn't sure how, but whatever the outcome and at whatever the cost, he knew that he wouldn't let himself be taken.

"Think they're after us, sir?" Justin asked.

Thom smiled. "Could be. Maybe they are bound for Providence and just care to give us a race. We'll ask them their intentions, if they happen to catch us." Thom glanced back at the schooner then at Justin. "Which barky do you think is faster, *Hannah* or the *Gaspee*?"

The boys eyes widened as he looked back at the schooner. Receiving no response, Thom went on. "Myself, I'd say that the

Gaspee might have the edge on most points. She's longer, carries more sail. Not to be hard on the fair *Hannah*, mind you." Thom paused and looked along the rail. "Of course, to weather's a different matter. *Hannah*'s faster to weather I expect. Wind for'ard the beam, a sloop'll always take a schooner, don't you agree, Mr. Jacobs?"

"Ah, yes sir," Justin replied his hands grasping the rail tightly.

Thom forced himself to turn away from the pursuing schooner. His heart raced and he knew he needed to stay calm. He peered ahead at the rocky shore of Conanicut Island looming gold and green on the bow, Freebody Hill rising above Taylor Point. They were two hours before high tide and the flood current was carrying them smartly up the bay. They just might clear the point on one tack.

Thom looked back at the *Gaspee*, her topsails visible behind treeless Rose Island. Oddly, some part of him felt relieved that the final confrontation with Dudingston and own his past had finally arrived. The dread and the anticipation were over.

He turned back and stared ahead. They were nearing shore now, but he could wait. The water was deep up to the beach. Justin looked at him anxiously. Thom waited a moment more. "Ready about, "he yelled. "Ready," came the echo from the mate. "Helms alee," Thom shouted and pushed the tiller down. The crew hauled the sheets and braces and just like the graceful lady that she was, the *Hannah* pirouetted, her skirts fluttering as she settled in on the other tack.

From the low hill that rose from the wharves, Johnny saw *Hannah* cast off and sail, as if leisurely touring the harbor. He smiled at the sight of the sloop, as lithe and graceful as any packet boat should be, all the more lovely as most were neither.

His reverie ended when he spied the *Gaspee*. She was inbound and sailing alone. No prey for the jackal today, Johnny thought and looked away for a moment. He looked up again and Johnny realized what was happening. The *Hannah* was well clear of the harbor, charging to windward up the bay, and the *Gaspee* and the whore's son Dudingston with his three-pound guns primed and loaded was giving chase.

He dropped the parcel slung over his shoulder and ran down the rise toward his uncle's. "What's the hurry, John?" Isaiah called out as his nephew ran up the stairs. Johnny grabbed the musket from over the hearth and yelled back down, "Where do you keep your powder and shot?"

"What?" Isaiah yelled back.

"Powder and shot. Where d'ya keep it?"

"In the chest, foot ta' bed," Isaiah shouted, bewildered.

In a moment, Johnny ran down the steps again, musket and cartridge box in hand. "I need a horse. I must away this instant."

Isaiah looked at him querulously then said, "Jeb Thompson, the sailmaker. Got a good horse and he owes me money. Call on him."

Johnny ran around back of the Thompson's shop to his stable. A dappled mare snorted at him from behind the fence. "Jeb, need ta' borrow your horse, " Johnny shouted. In a few moments, Jeb Thompson came out the back door.

"What you hollerin' about?"

"Need to borrow your horse, Jeb. Tis most urgent."

The sailmaker raised an eyebrow. "That horse cost me dear. Fine Surinam filly, that one. Not sure that I want to just hand it off."

"I'll hire her from you, against your account with my uncle."

A smile creased the sailmaker's face. "You'll need the saddle," he said, disappearing into the rear of the small stable. He saddled the horse and led him out.

"Done much riding, Johnny?"

"Enough," Johnny said, hoping that that was true. The horse seemed awfully tall close-up. He handed Jeb the musket and slung the cartridge box over his shoulder, then had to think for an instant which foot to put in the stirrup. That resolved, he hoisted himself on the mare and Jeb tied the musket across the back of the saddle.

"Her name's Delores," Jeb said with a nod. "Nice and gentle, she is."

With that, Johnny took the reigns and kicked his heels against Delores's flanks. The horse took off with a start, knocking Johnny back in the saddle. He pulled himself upright and pulled the reigns over, turning Delores down the lane. He kicked again as the horse slowed to a walk, working up to a canter, then a gallop, bouncing off toward the Providence Road.

❖❖❖

The *Hannah* made good distance on the next tack, slipping under Gould Island and charging toward the wooded Aquidneck Island shore. Thom glanced back at the *Gaspee* from time to time, watching carefully only as the schooner prepared to tack. Would she stand in close to shore or stay well off? It was hard to judge the distance, but she seemed to stay clear, tacking well before she absolutely had to. It looked to Thom that either Dudingston or his helmsman wasn't too sure of the waters. Thom smiled and silently blessed Captain Haney.

With the wind against the current, a chop was building and the *Hannah*'s bow slammed into the short, steep seas. Curtains of spray flew into the air, bursting off the bow into a myriad of tiny diamonds sparkling in the afternoon sun, then disappearing against the surging blue water. Heeled over on her lines, the masthead angled off to leeward, Thom looked and saw only the clear and crystalline sky, the high cirrus clouds like delicate wisps of cotton, the gift of a nor'westerly breeze. A day such as this, as glorious a day as can be, Thom thought. Then he laughed at himself, not having to be reminded of the armed schooner in pursuit and the devil in command who likely bore no mind to his joy at the beauty of the afternoon.

They tacked when Aquidneck Island was close aboard and set off toward the tip of Prudence Island. They were sailing into ever more confined waters, toward the mouth of a funnel that was the Providence River.

He chose the eastern channel, almost to show off how the *Hannah* could dance, each tack as graceful as the one before, sure the *Gaspee* was no match on the narrow dance floor. They short tacked up past Hog Island, crossing a cutter and another schooner, both bound for Bristol. For a moment, Thom wondered whether Dudingston might prefer these as prey, but dismissed the thought, somehow sure that the *Gaspee* would follow them like a hound after a pheasant. Past Bristol, the bay widened slightly as they tacked toward the northern end of Prudence Island. Ahead lay Warwick Neck and beyond, the river and Providence.

❖ ❖ ❖

Johnny held tight as Delores seemed to do her best to be rid of the irritant on her back. They had left Newport town behind and were on the coast road, Johnny trying to catch sight of the packet between the trees. He kicked the horse again and she bounded off then slowed. At a gallop, he could easily outdistance the sloop and the schooner, but Delores seemed to prefer a walk. Johnny kicked again, wishing with all his heart that he was on the *Hannah* rather than chasing her on the old nag. With each bump down the rutted road, his hips, legs, and buttocks cried out from ill use.

At a rise in the road, where the trees parted, he saw the *Gaspee* clawing to weather with the *Hannah* well ahead near the far shore. He regretted that he had no spurs on his boots, but kicked the horse's flanks, spurring Delores along the best that he could. At the end of the island, he stopped and happily saw that *Hannah* was still well ahead of the *Gaspee*, sailing a half point closer to the wind than the schooner.

He rode on only to find the Bristol ferry on the far shore, so Johnny blew the cow horn tied to the post at the landing and shouted to the boatman, but he was too far for the words to be sensible. The ferry master raised a hand to acknowledge that he heard the summons and cast off from Bristol Point, manning one long sweep, with a deckhand, looking to be only a boy, manning the other. Each walked slowly across the deck of the ferry, hardly more than a small barge, square at each end, pushing the heavy oar, steering a bit downstream to counteract the flood current, trying to carry them up into Mount Hope Bay.

Their passage seemed painfully slow and Johnny watched anxiously for the *Hannah* or the *Gaspee,* but both were too far down channel to be seen. When the ferry finally made its way across, Johnny paid the ferry master, led Delores aboard and tied her to the rail. They cast off, but the northerly wind seemed stronger than it had just moments before and they made slow progress back toward Bristol Point. Johnny took the sweep from the boy and pushed against the long oar, swearing oaths under his breath at Reid, Dudingston, and all of their like. The ferry master, a weathered soul of indeterminate age, glanced over at him but paid him no particular mind.

When they finally rowed the half mile across, Johnny feeling winded and breathless, nodded to the ferry master and led Delores off. From the landing, he could now see the *Hannah*, rail down, her bow wave gleaming white, seeming to be heading straight for them. She stood on close to the shoals off Hog Island before again tacking northwest. Johnny let out a yell, a joyous "yip", on seeing the *Hannah* come about so graciously with the *Gaspee* slipping what seemed to be ever farther behind. With luck Thom would be safe and ashore long before the *Gaspee* fetched the Providence docks. He mounted Delores and galloped up Bristol Neck toward Providence. He wanted to be on the dock to meet the *Hannah* when she arrived.

Justin Jacobs kept a vigil at the weather rail of the *Hannah*, watching, studying, their pursuer. "Captain sir, if you don't mind my saying so sir, I think they're a touch over canvassed, sir. Might do better without the fore topsail."

Thom glanced over and laughed. In the freshening breeze under full sail, the *Gaspee* was dragging her lee rail and rounding up in the gusts.

"Just glad you're not sailing master on the *Gaspee*, Mr. Jacobs. Might be catching us now, if you were."

Justin's face colored. "Didn't mean to be out 'a line, sir. Not my place and all..."

Thom smiled. "Nonsense, Mr. Jacobs. And I think that you're right. Fore tops doing him more harm than good. He's acting like he's back on the *Romney*, not on a Marblehead schooner."

Justin looked over at Thom. "Yes, Mr. Jacobs?"

"Nothing, Captain," he replied but maintained his gaze. Thom wondered how widely the story of his impressment and escape had spread. He knew now that it had surely gotten to the fo'c's'le of the *Hannah*. Just as well.

"I think the *Hannah* will carry her topsail a while longer. What do you think, Mr. Jacobs?"

The boy stammered. "Ah...ah, yes, sir."

Thom strained to make out the landmarks. The bay was growing narrower and shallower, and now of all times, he needed to be careful. They were an hour past high tide so they had an extra four feet of water under the keel which they could always use, even if it made grounding more dangerous.

Off the bow, he made out Rocky Point and stood on until Nayatt Point on the far shore began to pull abeam. "Ready about", he called. "Ready," came the response. "Helms alee."

As they tacked, the wind shifted, heading them, making them fall off, steering broader than Thom would have liked. He glanced back and saw the *Gaspee* on the opposite tack, sailing closer to their course now, gaining from the wind shift even as the

Hannah was set back. They stood on close to the shore then tacked again, hoping that the wind wouldn't shift back.

As he pushed the tiller over and *Hannah* danced across the wind, he laughed to himself. The *Gaspee* had gained on them but it didn't matter. They had spent the afternoon tacking up the bay and now the packet boat, its crew, and captain all seemed part of the same grand creature, neither fish nor fowl, but some wondrous thing with wings spread like an eagle, surfing through the waters like a dolphin. Thom knew that this was his place and his time, whether he lived for four score years or only for this day, it was the only place that he wished to be. He looked back at the *Gaspee*, then again up at the great arc of the *Hannah*'s sails against the sky.

"Mr. Jacobs, appears to me that they have struck the fore topsail. I believe that you spoke too loudly. They must have heard your recommendation."

Justin Jacob looked back and laughed. "Yes, sir. I'll speak softer in the future, sir."

"See that you do, Mr. Jacobs. See that you do."

The western shore grew close and Thom, hoping that they could clear Comnicut Point at the mouth of Providence River in one tack.

They tacked again and again, the ebb tide just beginning to slow their progress. Ahead lay Namquit Point. Namquit Point - his old nemesis. Thom tacked again to favor the east side of the channel.

Then in an instant, he knew what he needed to do. The time for running was past. It all became clear. He wanted to shout in jubilation but knew that, now of all times, he must keep his focus.

With the point falling just astern, Thom called out, "Mr. Rollins, prepare to heave to."

The mate looked up, as did every member of the crew. The looks on their faces ranged the narrow spectrum between disbelief and amazement. For a moment there was silence.

Rollins looked aft and the *Gaspee* suddenly didn't seem so far astern.

"Sir?" Rollins asked, his face begging for an explanation.

"Heaving to," Thom called out, with no expression save the look of a calm determination in the muscles of his jaw. He shoved the tiller over. The bow swung and the jibs and main came about, as the topsail, held by the braces, fluttered then backed. With the topsail trying to push the *Hannah* backward and the rest of the sails trying to draw her forward, she sat almost perfectly still in the river, drifting slowly westward, untouched even by the current, swirling in an eddy off the point.

Rollins charged back to the helm. "Excuse me, sir, but I am at a loss to explain your actions."

"We are heaving to, Mr. Rollins," Thom replied coldly.

"I can see that sir, but why? Once we get to Providence we are safe. Dudingston daren't come ashore with a warrant for his arrest outstanding."

Thom took a breath. "If I know Billy Dudingston, he has more faith in his guns than he fears a warrant," Thom replied. He turned and looked over toward the *Gaspee* growing ever larger as they spoke. "His vanity exceeds his virtue. It is time we taught him a lesson about sailing these waters."

Rollins looked at him as though he had been struck mad. "But sir, we can still..."

Thom cut him off. "Speak no more of it." His hand rested on the butt of his pistol. Rollins stood staring at Thom then at the *Gaspee*. The eyes of the entire crew had swung from the quarterdeck to the approaching schooner.

For a time, there was silence. The schooner's bowsprit pointed directly toward them then swung off on the other tack. Each time she came about, the details of the schooner became clearer, the dolphin striker, the rigging of her bowsprit, the ugly black muzzle of a gun protruding from her fo'c's'le head, growing more distinct and menacing.

"They'll think that we are surrendering," Thom commented calmly. The crew all stared at him, their eyes asking, "well, aren't we?"

The schooner bore off, then came about one last time. On this tack, she could reach the *Hannah*. Thom saw a tear tumble down Justin Jacob's cheek.

The bow wave of the *Gaspee* shone white against her dark hull. She was so close, well within the range of her bow chaser. Within pistol range, Thom thought, his hand still grasping the butt of his pistol, fearing that it might tremble if he released his hold. He was an unpracticed shot and wondered idly whether he would be able to hit what he aimed at, if it came to that.

Thom watched mesmerized, trying to gauge the distance from the schooner to the point, finding himself unable to look at anything beyond the schooner in her relentless approach. She was so very close now, every aspect clear and sharp.

He was admiring the scroll work on the *Gaspee*'s cat head when the schooner suddenly lurched skyward. Her bow lifted, as if plucked up by an unseen hand. The gunner at the bow chaser flew over his gun and landed in the water, the gun pitching forward, as if to follow. The entire rig flexed toward the bow with a rending crash. The masts tried to rip themselves from the deck, the timbers and keel screaming in their own wail of pain. The gaffs swung around, striking the shrouds and both topsail spars carried away with a rapid fire crack, crashing to the deck in a tangle of shredded sails and rigging.

The silence afterward was almost as startling as the noise of the grounding. The *Gaspee* sat motionless on the bar, healed slightly to larboard with her bowsprit pointing oddly upward, her deck lost in canvas and cordage. Her guns, aiming only at water and sky, could now do the *Hannah* no harm.

The only sound that Thom heard was the insistent beating of his heart, that seemed as loud as cannon shots, and the gentler hum of the wind in the *Hannah*'s rigging. He looked over at the mate. "Mr. Rollins, a lesson we have all learned, but worth repeating nevertheless. Be careful rounding Namquit Point. It is an easy place to fetch up aground."

Justin Jacobs piped up. "Three cheers for Captain Larkin. Hip hip hooray."

Thom stopped them on the second cheer, though a broad smile stretched his face. "Enough of that. We're due in Providence. Hate to have to explain to the owners why we were late."

"All hands to your stations," the mate bellowed. "Ease off the topsail braces." With the topsail luffing, Thom eased the helm over and *Hannah* got underway, heading upstream to Providence.

CHAPTER ELEVEN

The short sail up the river to Providence was agonizingly slow on the falling tide. Thom was filled with a restless energy, but all he could do was grip the tiller tighter and watch the set of the sails. As the river bank slipped past them on either side, he recalled the grounding in his mind, the look of the *Gaspee*'s dark hull and golden masts, the bowsprit seeming to leap skyward as the keel struck the bar, the terrible rending crack of shattering spars, the taut sails suddenly billowing out and up, starkly white against the deep blue of the sky. Over and over he called the image back, turning it again and again in his thoughts until the memory was polished smooth and seamless as a stone tumbled by a stream. Finally, the shattering rig and billowing sails seemed less a Royal Navy schooner striking a sandbar, than a wooden cage being cast asunder, setting free a great white bird, soaring bold and proud into the heavens. An odd image, yet somehow calming, helping not so much to quench as to bank the fire that he felt burning inside. He held their course in mid-stream and casually scanned the late afternoon sky as if to catch a glimpse of the great white wings wheeling across the high and wispy clouds.

"You may take the helm, Mr. Rollins." There was no need for him to steer now and he felt the need to walk the deck.

"Aye, Captain," Rollins replied, almost springing across the quarterdeck to grasp the tiller.

Thom strolled to the waist, looking toward the incredible blue of the sky. Without being fully aware a few words of an old song came to his lips.

"Torn from a world of tyrants..." He smiled to himself, still gazing up beyond the rigging. *"Beneath a western sky. We've formed a new dominion, a land of liberty."*

He sang softly, not in the cadence of fifes and drums, but the slower pace of a hymn.

"The world shall know we're free men, and so shall ever be.
Hurrah, hurrah, hurrah, for love and liberty."

When at length the *Hannah* was finally alongside the Providence wharf, a lone horseman was waiting, the horse pacing one direction, only to be yanked back clumsily by his rider, before traveling again in the other.

"Johnny Stevens!" Thom called out. "You make a most unlikely dragoon. What brings you to Providence?"

Johnny laughed and stared down river. "The *Gaspee*. Did you leave her so far behind that she gave up the chase?"

Thom began to speak, but Rollin's tongue was quicker. "Captain Larkin left 'em aground on Namquit Point, on a falling tide. Tricked Billy Dudingston, he did. Fetched her up full standing. Was a glory to see."

Thom gave the mate a sidelong glance, his face wearing a wide grin. Johnny let out a wild whoop, bold enough to startle his horse, who lurched and almost cast his from the saddle.

Thom looked over the packet, from bow to stern. "Justin, take up on the forward spring line and get the gangway ashore, if you please. Mr. Rollins, look after the cargo and customs. I've an errand ashore to which I must attend."

With that Thom leaped, one foot on a bollard, the other on the bulwark and hurdled onto the dock, almost tumbling across the paving stones, then rising and breaking into a trot, his entire body rejoicing in the exertion. Over his shoulder, he yelled, "Come along, Johnny. Still much to be done." Johnny kicked Delores and followed Thom. With no one aboard to stop him, Justin Jacobs again shouted, "Three cheers for Captain Larkin! Hip hip hooray! Hip hip hooray! Hip hip hooray!" Johnny joined in on the last hooray as he followed his young friend up the street.

Thom stopped at the door to the John Brown's counting house, gasping for breath. He pounded with the large brass door knocker until the door swung open and an irritated clerk peered out at him and at Johnny, three paces behind still on horseback.

"Oh, hello Thomas."

"'Lo Eb, must see John Brown," Thom rasped, more a statement than a request, stepping through the threshold and into the counting house. He walked straight into Brown's office, interrupting him writing at his deck.

"I bring great joy sir," Thom blurted out. "The *Gaspee* is yours, sir, if you wish her. Chased the *Hannah* from Newport. We left her hard aground on a falling tide. At Namquit Point."

John Brown rose, his face changing from annoyance, to surprise, to glee in an instant. "The *Gaspee* aground? God bless you, Thomas Larkin! Bless you indeed. The *Gaspee* aground! Aground at Namquit Point!" He said the words almost like lines from a gala, and for a moment, Thom thought that he might rise to dance a few steps of a jig. Then, as quickly as the joy swept over him, it passed, replaced by contemplation.

He looked at Thom in earnest. "Will she float off? When is the next tide that will carry her?"

"Way I figure, sir, can't be before three hours past midnight and the way she hit, full standing, maybe not then."

"Time enough. Time enough. Find my captains, you'll know where. Whipple, Hopkins, the rest. And get boats, the largest boats you can. Six, no eight if you can fetch them." He continued giving directions, calmly as if giving instructions to a captain or agent for a business venture, a consignment of iron or spermaceti candles. Only when he was finished did he smile and his eyes flashed. "Like to lead one of the boats yourself, I imagine. Until this evening then, young Thomas. You've done well. Now to finish the venture."

Thom stepped into the street, his head spinning, and heart beginning to race once again. Johnny waited, this time on foot, holding the reins of his horse.

"You say the *Gaspee*'s aground?"

Thom smiled realizing how many times he would be called on to tell the same tale.

"Hard aground on Namquit Point. Not likely to get off 'fore the high tide three hours past midnight.

"There's much to be done and I have a favor to ask. You're acquainted with Andrew Rollins, my new mate?" Johnny nodded. "Good. He's a Providence man. If you would ask him to seek volunteers from the *Hannah* and inquire after a longboat, largest he can find. Have him bring it to Talbot's wharf, across from Sabin's tavern. Repair to the tavern yourself if you wish for a lively evening's work."

"I'll call on Rollins, and see you at Sabin's," Johnny said with a wide grin. "'Tis a night I wouldn't care to miss."

"Nor I, " Thom replied. "Make haste. We've not a moment to spare. As Captain Haney was wont to say, 'The tide won't wait.'"

❖❖❖

"You'll know where they are," John Brown had said, almost in passing. Thom had found Captains Greene, Tillinghast, and Anders, but couldn't locate Whipple, nor Hopkins, both of whom he knew to be in town. He had sent word by as many sources as he knew, messages at taverns, churches, and the captain homes. In the meantime, those that he had reached were organizing the boats.

Exasperated, he trudged to Sabin's Tavern, only to find the missing captains waiting for him there. They sat at a table facing the door, Abraham Whipple's gray hair and ample girth a contrast to John Hopkins who always seemed younger than his years and rail thin. They rose and almost dragged Thom to the bar, vying for the honor of buying him a drink. "No, thank ye," Thom protested. "Far too much to be done. No time to be lost."

"All is in hand, young sir," Captain Whipple replied. "Everthing'll be ready, I'll vouch for that. An' any captain that can disable an armed schooner with an unarmed packet deserves, at least, a drink 'fore the final blow be struck. So sit yerself down now." Thom finally smiled and grabbed a stool.

"My ship's boy will be round soon. Sent him home for the drum he beats for the militia." In a few minutes, the boy, twelve, if he was a day, appeared at Sabin's door with a kettle drum that seemed half his size. He was wearing his best coat and a tricorn hat with a bold feather that added to his stature, if not greatly to his height.

"You know your duty, Jeremiah."

"Aye, Captain," the boy said in earnest. He turned and marched down the street, beating his drum. As he marched he sang out in a voice, high but clear:

"Let all true Rhode Island men
come hear me on this day,
Repair to Sabins 'ere this eve
to take the damned Gaspee."

He marched on a few more paces to the sound of his drum before singing out again. Thom and Whipple rose and watched him from the tavern door. "That un'll raise the town. Needn't worry about that," Whipple said with a chuckle.

Thom finally allowed himself an ale. Captain Whipple and Hopkins sat at each elbow and talked around Thom who seemed almost struck dumb, enjoying listening to their stories.

Sabin's filled like the tide, slowly at first, a few men trickling in, calling out to shipmates, some carrying muskets, most barehanded. Steadily the flow increased until there was little room to stand. Those with firearms retired to the kitchen to cast lead bullets over Sabin's stove.

At around sunset, Johnny elbowed his way into the tavern, followed by Rollins and the rest of the *Hannah*'s crew close behind.

"Every things ready, Captain," Johnny roared over the din of the voices.

Thom looked toward Whipple and then Hopkins. "Meet you gentlemen outside then. Could use the air."

The two captains nodded and drank from their tankards, emptying them. As Thom made his way out, flanked by the *Hannah*'s crew he heard Whipple, then Hopkins and then the voices of captains that he didn't recognize call out to their crews.

Rollins lead them across the lane to Talbot's wharf where eight longboats lined the dock.

"My cousin, Anthony Baines," Rollins said, nodding toward a tall man waiting in one of the longboats. "He fetched the boat."

Rollins called down, "Anthony, may I have the pleasure of introducing Captain Thomas Larkin of the packet *Hannah*.

Thom smiled. "My thanks for the use of the boat, Mr. Baines."

"And thankee for running the bastard aground," Baines called back.

Behind them the lanes filled with men, dividing into crews following their selected captains. Thom saw Andrew Whipple and made his way over.

"Their three pounders shouldn't bother us, but they've a bow chaser and a swivel on the stern to watch for."

"And muskets, " Whipple replied raising an eyebrow. "Ha'fta see how close we can get 'fore they see us. Just make sure your oars are muffled." Then he smiled. "If they were good as they thought, they wouldn't be where you left 'em." He turned and walked off to speak to the other captains.

Thom turned back toward his boat and was surprised to see Angela Brown standing on the dock. He rushed over to her.

"Angela, why are you here. This is hardly your place..."

She smiled. "And when have I paid attention to such things? Besides, I accompanied my father."

Thom shook his head. "Your father is here as well? He should not be connected to what takes place this evening."

Thom heard a voice behind him. "I do believe Thom Larkin that you are the only soul in Providence with the temerity to try to tell me where I should be, even if many would suggest where I should go, once my back was turned." Thom turned to find John Brown, laughing heartily.

Thom reddened. "I meant no disrespect, but with your position ..."

Brown stopped him. "This is my place and it is precisely because of my position that it should be so. Besides, I was never one to miss out on the fun. Now get to your boat, young captain."

Thom saw no reason to argue the point. If Brown wished to see them off, that was his choice, but he wondered if Brown understood the undertaking that he referred to as "fun". Thom turned back to Angela who took both his hands in hers and said, "Take care this night. Return to me safely."

Thom smiled. "I shall. You may count on that. Now, I must go." He turned and almost bumped into John Mawney.

"And you too, Dr. Mawney? What brings you out this summer's eve."

"Mr. Brown suggested that a doctor on hand might be prudent."

Thom nodded. John Brown understood more than he let on. "Just keep your head down, doctor."

Thom looked back at Angela, who bade him farewell with a worried smile, before making his way through the throng to his longboat.

Chapter Twelve

Slowly men clambered down into the longboats. Whipple paced back and forth on the dock until he was satisfied with all he saw, then climbed into a boat himself. Each longboat had eight men at oars with a coxswain at the tiller and a captain at the bow. Several boats packed additional men forward and aft while one boat swung only six oars.

The last lume of the sunset had vanished from the treetops on the western shore and the strongest lights were from the tavern door and the glow from windows of houses across the river.

"Let's finish the job," Whipple roared. Thom's own "Wahoo," blended with with a chorus of cheers and whoops and the rattle of boats being cast off. In a moment, the shouts were replaced by the quiet sound of two score pair of oars, dipping and hauling in the stream, a soft drumbeat quickly lost in the evening breeze.

The tiny flotilla paused at Lambert's Dock and sailors scrambled up in the darkness and handed paving stones and staves down to their fellows. Fully, if haphazardly armed, the boats resumed their progress downstream, fighting the flood, the rising tide that would float the schooner free if they didn't reach her first.

Once they slipped past the town, the river widened and the boats spread out in a rough chevron, looking like a ragged flock of geese casting dark shadows on the dull silver of the river, reflecting the quarter moon that in turns shone and hid behind the scattered clouds.

Thom looked over at the backs of his crew, bent low as they reached out with their oars, then hauled back as they pulled in unison. The buoyant camaraderie of the ale house was behind them, left on shore with wives and sweethearts. They rowed in silence, save for the hiss of the oar blades biting the water and the muffled creak of the oaken thole pins wrapped in rags against the pull of the pine oars. Johnny Stevens grinned at him from the stern, grasping the tiller with a casual ease. Thom smiled and nodded back before turning and once again scanning the dark horizon. For a moment Thom wondered if it was all just madness. Rowing out to face the guns of the *Gaspee* armed mostly with sticks and stones. He pushed the thought aside. He has armed with less when last he faced Dudingston.

They rowed for two hours before the shadow of the *Gaspee* grew from the darkness, a distant smudge off the southern bank. In a few minutes, he could make out the shape of her masts and the line of her deck. The wreckage had been cleared away and had it not been for her dramatic list to starboard, nothing would seem amiss.

The boats split into two groups, one in a wide turn to approach the bow and the other sweeping aft. Thom motioned to Johnny to follow Whipple's boat swinging off for schooner's broad stern.

The *Gaspee* lay silent as if abandoned until the boats were within fifty yards, when a voice rang out, "Who goes there?" The only response was the relentless dip of the oars, which somehow seemed louder now, or perhaps the night more still. He looked up at the clouds and prayed that the moon would remain within their embrace.

The distance to the schooner shrank by another ten yards when the flash from a musket shattered the darkness. Thom could see sailors moving on the deck now, apparitions along the rail. His heart began to race. From the bow and stern more muskets flashed in a ragged cacophony. Thom tried not to flinch at the sound and looked away from the flashes of light.

The distance fell from yards to feet as the glow of a quick match arced toward the touch hole of a swivel gun on the stern quarter. Thom grasped the gunnel tighter and held his breath, bracing for a blast of grapeshot. The touch hole flared feebly and

Thom exhaled when the only sound from the gun was the swearing of the gunner at the misfire.

Captain Whipple's boat bumped against the schooner's starboard quarter and was greeted by a bellow, "Stand off!"

At the rail, Lieutenant William Dudingston stood, shouting, as if his voice alone might succeed where the muskets and the swivel had failed. He wore a fine white linen shirt with a brace of pistols on his belt. He had surely been taken by surprise, as he had not had time to put on his pants.

There he stood, the ex-first lieutenant of HMS *Romney*, Captain of the *Gaspee*, terror of the coast, the almighty William Dudingston bellowing in his night clothes on the deck of the armed schooner, lying helpless on a sandbar. Thom smiled then despite himself, began to laugh.

Captain Whipple stood up in the bow of his longboat and yelled back at Dudingston. "I am the sheriff of Kent County, Goddamn your eyes, and I've come for the commander of this vessel. And alive or dead, I shall have him."

Dudingston turned first toward Whipple and then toward the sound of Thom's laughter. His eyes fixed on Thom and he reached for a pistol on his belt. Thom's laughter died in his throat and he reached frantically for his pistol but was an instant slow. Dudingston's arm arced toward Thom, the black barrel aiming down toward the longboat. In that instant, Thom saw only death in the black barrel of the gun. Thom aimed back, the pistol feeling heavy in his hand, his arm moving not quite fast enough. Just as he expected to receive the blast from Dudingston pistol, his mind racing, not quite believing that it would all end like this, a musket shot rang out from behind him. Dudingston's pistol fired at almost the same, the two blast echoing in Thom's ears. Dudingston's shot was wild. The musket ball found its target and Dudingston spun then crumpled to the deck. Thom glanced down at this shirt, just to be sure that he hadn't been shot, but saw no stain of blood. He breathed deeply for a second then turned and saw John Stevens, standing holding a smoking musket.

"Thankee, John. A fine shot."

Johnny smiled. "My pleasure, Thomas."

Whipple shouted, "Spring to your oars." Thom screamed, "Come on." A last pull on the oars drove the longboat against the side of the schooner and Thom leapt for the rail, pulling himself aboard, with one hand tying the long boat's painter to the bulwark as Rollins and Anthony Baines and the rest scrambled onto the deck. The air was full of the raiders screaming and whooping, a ghastly war cry as they clambered aboard bow and stern, driving the defenders back toward the masts.

Thom looked up to see two British sailors running at him, one with a cutlass raised above his head and the other swinging a belaying pin. Rollins swung his cudgel and caught the tar across the stomach, doubling him over, the cutlass clattering to the deck. Thom pulled back as the belaying pin whizzed past his head, then swung his pistol striking the sailor across the bridge of his nose with the barrel, sending him reeling backwards in the darkness.

Thom saw a glint of steel and spun only to stop when he saw it was Johnny Stevens who had picked up the cutlass. Thom turned and with a furious shout, charged toward the remaining defenders, Johnny and Rollins catching up on either side. With the rest of the *Hannah*'s crew close behind and men from other boats pouring aboard, they formed an angry wall surging toward the *Gaspee's* sailors.

The few who chose to fight back were knocked down and pushed aside, while the rest dropped their belaying pins, boarding axes and muskets and stood in clumps facing their captors. In a few bewildering minutes, it was over. Thom could still hear fighting forward, but the outcome was no longer in doubt. The blood pounded in his ears and for a moment he felt in a daze.

"Get their weapons," Thom called out. He looked around. A Providence man that he had seen around the docks held a flintlock.

"Would you mind tending the flock, good sir?"

"My great pleasure, Capt'n" the man replied lowering the barrel of his gun toward the British sailors.

Thom looked aft and was shocked to see John Brown striding down the deck in the darkness.

"Mr. ...."

"No last names, Thom. Just call me John, if you please."

"I was concerned that you attended us on the dock. I had no idea that ..."

"Doesn't matter and we've no time. Find John Mawney. There's a man bleeding to death below decks."

Thom ran forward. Mawney was just pulling himself aboard, soaking wet below the waist having missed his footing when leaving the longboat. When he saw someone coming towards him, he stumbled to his feet, grabbed a cudgel and raised it above his head.

"Put down that blessed stick, Doctor. It's me, Thom. We have need of your services aft."

Mawney pulled up with a start. "I could have crushed your skull, Thomas. Thank goodness that you stopped me." Thom chuckled and lead the doctor aft.

They made their way down the deck, crowded with raiders and captive British sailors, to the small quarter deck. Thom stopped at the companionway while Mawney dropped down the ladder into the cabin. In the lamplight, Dudingston sat on the cabin sole propped up against a chest, wounded in the arm and the leg. A pool of blood lay on the deck near his left thigh and his face was contorted in pain.

"First to stop that bleeding," Mawney said, as if to himself. He pulled out his shirt and ripped a section of the tail for a bandage.

Dudingston looked over toward the doctor. "Pray don't rip your shirt, sir. There is linen in the chest next to the bunk."

"This will serve well enough." Mawney pulled a small knife from a scabbard and cut away the lieutenant's silk hose, folded the torn piece of shirt into a pad and pressed it against the wound. Dudingston gasped, then grit his teeth. Mawney looked up the companionway ladder.

"Thom, I could use your assistance, if you don't mind." Thom paused for a moment, then dropped down the ladder.

"In the chest by the bunk. Find the linen and scrape lint. Good for staunching the bleeding."

Thom looked toward the crumpled officer on the deck who seemed to take no notice of his presence through a veil of pain. He went to the chest, found the linen and pulled out his knife from its sheath. For a moment he looked at the blade then at Dudingston, then began scraping the fabric as requested. He had been at if for a few moments when Captain Whipple climbed ponderously down the ladder.

"Will the patient live, doctor?"

"God willing, sir." Mawney replied.

"And now where are the spirits? Got to be in the captain's cabin."

Dudingston, who had looked away, now glanced at Whipple with a touch of a sneer.

"The rum is in the cabinet if you really need a drink so badly, good sheriff."

Whipple ignored him, opened the cabinet and proceeded to smash a dozen bottles of claret, brandy and rum. His task finished, he looked down at Dudingston dismissively, then glanced at Mawney. "Spirits'll cause no mischief now."

Whipple turned toward Thom. "And what shall we do with this cur? We bandage his wounds and he accuses me of robbing the spirit locker. Useless bastard."

Whipple turned back to Dudingston and rumbled, low and angry, "Present your commission, you son of a whore, or else we'll hang you like the pirate you are. An' it'll be fine and legal, for we've every right under the law to hang pirates who prey upon these shores." Whipple pulled out a large sheath knife from the back of his belt. "'Course maybe a rope's too good for your likes." Whipple looked again toward Thom. "Ever tell you how I learned scalping from the Narraganset? Maybe I should take this bastard's pate as a souvenir." He glanced at Thom. "Unless you want to do it. You may have best claim of all."

Dudingston's sneer vanished, replaced by simple and sullen fear. He looked toward Mawney then Whipple, then Thom, then back to Whipple's blade, shining in the lamplight. His face, already pale from loss of blood, grew ashen and his eyes widened, pleading before his lips moved to speak. "Pray sir. Spare my life. For the love of God, spare me. For the love of God, I beg you. My commission is in the cabinet by the berth."

Whipple sheathed his knife and laughed. "Not so high and mighty any more, are ye'?" he said as he opened the cabinet and found Dudingston's orders. "Should burn these an' claim you never had 'em. A picaroon but for a scrap of paper." He dropped it on the desk and left for the deck.

Thom stood still for a moment. In one hand he held his knife and in the other a large handful of lint from the cloth. To kill or heal, he weighed his choices, before bringing the lint over to Mawney. "Will this suffice, John?"

"Quite nicely, thank you."

Dudingston looked over at Thom, now within a foot of him in the lamplight. Recognition glinted in his eyes, yet Thom saw none of the imperious arrogance that he so hated while on the *Romney*. Now the eyes seemed merely pained and weary.

His voice was weak, though clear. "You, sir, are a deserter."

Thom still held his knife in one hand. He gripped the hilt tightly, lifted it slightly, then slipped it back into its sheath.

"No, sir," Thom replied with resolution. "You are mistaken. I am a free man and shall remain so. If a pressed man once resembled me, he is drowned in a storm. Marked 'Discharged – dead -" by the first lieutenant, or so I'm told." A half smile crept across Thom's face, but his eyes remained hard as iron.

"And you, sir, are our prisoner. If you should live, then you'll have to explain to your masters how you lost the King's fine armed schooner to a packet boat and a sandbar." Thom saw only resignation in the lieutenant's eyes, a bitter acceptance of disgrace.

Whipple looked down the companionway. "Can he be moved? Or shall we leave the bastard to the flames? Want to get the crew ashore soon as possible. Lot to do before sunrise."

"He'll be all right." Mawney turned to Dudingston. "Is there anything you wish to take with you?"

"Is my clerk still aboard? He'll know my needs." He lowered his voice and turned to Mawney. "Sir, you have shown me great kindness, certainly you've saved my life. In the dresser by the berth, there is a silver buckle that I wish you have. A token for your good service and kindness."

"I am a doctor, sir, but I rowed out with the rest to take your ship and take it we did. I shan't also take your silver. Now take my hand. I'll help you to your feet."

Thom followed Mawney and Dudingston up to the deck. A voice called out. "Thomas."

Thom looked and saw a longboat packed with British sailors, their wrists bound behind them, with half of *Hannah*'s crew at the oars ready to pull away from the schooner.

Johnny Stevens sat at the tiller and yelled, "Lost sight of ya. Glad to see that you're well." With that, he said a few words to the men at oars and the longboat disappeared into to the darkness, pulling for the western shore.

Captain Whipple stood a short way away, speaking to John Brown. Thom walked over.

Brown glanced over at Thom. "I hadn't allowed for the time to get the crew ashore. The dawn is too soon upon us. I would have liked to have taken the guns and powder. Might have a use for it one day."

Whipple chuckled. "Shame we couldn't just let the crew swim to shore. "

"Where are they being taken?" Thom asked.

"Pawtuxet. Asked Joe Rhodes to look after them till morning, then let them go wherever they please. 'Spect a fair share to desert."

Within two hours all the boats had returned and the remaining raiders on the *Gaspee* climbed back into the longboats. As they all pulled away from the schooner, the eastern sky began to flush in pale tones of purple and gray. Whipple's boat was the last to leave and as they cast off Thom saw smoke beginning to rise from the *Gaspee*'s deck.

The flames spread quickly across the length of the schooner, snaking up the masts as the sails caught fire. Soon the *Gaspee* was a distant glow on the river, a small sunrise rivaling the lagging dawn. She burned steadily until the quiet morning echoed with an thunderous explosion that reduced her planks to kindling as the fire reached the casks of powder. An enormous cloud of black smoke hung above the water, clearing to reveal the schooner gone, with only fractured frames piercing the surface, each still burning like an individual torch.

Thom thought that he should have felt relief or joy or a sense of triumph now that his foe lay vanquished and possibly dying, yet all he felt was a weary but quiet calm. One part of his life was closed, a wound finally healed. And there was something else too, something larger, a sense that they had all passed a threshold, that his small ending was perhaps just a greater beginning. Where it would all end was still hull down on the horizon, far beyond the smoldering wreckage of the *Gaspee*.

CHAPTER THIRTEEN

The eight long boats returned to Providence as quietly as they had departed, the men at oars tired from the night's work and the long pull against an ebbing tide. With few words exchanged, the boats parted, spreading out along the warren of docks and wharves that lined the riverfront. The crew of the *Hannah* rowed toward Lewis' dock, returning their long boat to Anthony Baines, Ezra Lewis's partner.

Thom was surprised and pleased to see Angela waiting for him. She looked wan, standing alone on the wharf, but her expression changed the moment that she saw him and her face was lit by her smile.

The crew of the longboat clambered up onto the dock. A few of the crew wandered home while the rest went off to find breakfast in the just waking town. Thom stood holding Angela's hands in his as the crew flowed around them.

When they were almost alone Angela said, "I am overjoyed by your deliverance."

Thom merely smiled and and looked into her shining dark eyes. "I am fine." As he spoke the memory of staring up into Dudingston's gun barrel reminded him how close he had come to never seeing her again. Death seemed less fearful than the prospect of forever being separated from Angela. He pulled her closer to him and, there, on the dock, he kissed her and held her close, as she kissed him back and held him in the same desperate embrace.

She buried her head in his shoulder and kept holding on until finally she looked up at him again. "You should go," she said. "Your crew is waiting for you. I will see you anon."

Reluctantly he let her ago, watching as she turned down the lane and disappeared and he walked off to find his companions.

❖❖❖

Rollins and the rest of the crew had roused a tavern owner who warmed bread and porridge for his early morning customers. Thom joined them again, to a hearty greeting. Over mugs of coffee and tea, they drank toasts to liberty and the King, but took care to say nothing more of their evenings endeavors.

Before the others were finished, Thom walked back to the *Hannah* and found sleep a willing mistress. He had slept for what seemed like only moments before a booming voice from the dock woke him. "Capt'n of the *Hannah*, ye aboard?"

He came on deck only to find two of Whipple's crew, one holding Justin Jacobs by the collar, nearly lifting him from the ground. Squashed sideways on Justin's head was a fine beaver hat fringed with gold tassels.

"This one of your'n?" the sailor holding Justin asked.

Thom felt too tired to laugh and only nodded.

"Found him on the Great Bridge with Dudingston's cursed hat on his head, bragging 'bout burning a certain schooner."

Thom shook his head. "Justin, you goddamn motherless fool. Boasting of a hanging offense. If the Crown didn't catch you, you're lucky that these fine gentlemen didn't string you up just to keep you quiet." Thom looked back at the sailors.

"Thankee good sirs for returning this wastrel. Reckon I'll take him, though I can't say quite what I'll do with the scoundrel."

The sailors smiled and the one holding Justin released his grasp, letting the young man fall flat on his backside on the dock.

Thom looked down at Justin splayed on the ground. "The crew's having breakfast at Fisher's. Join 'em if you want to eat.

"An' get rid of that bloody hat and mind your tongue or I'll personally cut it out for ya."

Thom shook his head as Justin skulked away. He went below, wondering how Justin managed to get the hat ashore without his noticing, wondering what else he may had missed in the confusion of the long night, which seemed more distant than a mere few hours past. "Heaven help us all," he thought.

❖❖❖

Late that afternoon, feeling better after a full watch's sleep, Thom walked to John Brown's counting house where he found his employer also feeling the effects of the night before, yet still buoyed by his own ebullient energy.

"Ah, Mr. Larkin. I can credit Poor Richard's wisdom. 'Early to bed and early to rise makes a man healthy wealthy and wise,' I believe it was."

Thom laughed. "I truly feel neither on this day."

Brown smiled for a moment then said gravely, "I have come to learn that a King's ship was attacked and burned last evening by parties unknown. The captain was wounded, I'm told. Dreadful, dreadful business. Our Lieutenant Governor, Darius Sessions, called on the young officer this morning and offered him all the possible assistance of the colony."

He paused for a moment. "The poor captain is in considerable pain, I'm told. Curiously, he chose not to tell Governor Sessions how he came to be wounded nor any part of the affair, for that matter. Nor will Lieutenant Dudingston be attending to any investigation. His only wish was to return to London, leaving his chief mate to assist in whatever inquiries there may be. He said that if he died of his wounds, he wished the shame to die with him." Brown's expression suggested concern, though his eyes still smiled. "I understand that he'll be sent home on the *Beaver* as soon as he is fit to travel, to answer for the loss of his command. Can't say as too many will mourn his departure."

CHAPTER FOURTEEN

Later that afternoon the *Hannah* sailed only a few hours later than usual, cargo and passengers loaded, in the same comfortable pattern that Thom now knew without thought. Only as they ghosted by the burnt timbers on Namquid Point did the truth of the previous night come back to him. Thom suddenly felt uneasy, sensing that he had crossed the tide line without knowing where the current would set him. Would the ebb hurry him on his way or pull him toward the shoals? It was more than just himself now. The forces that swirled around them all were irresistible, carrying them where no one knew, toward freedom or destruction, somewhere off beyond the horizon's razor line.

Thom was the first to bring the news of the *Gaspee*'s demise to their friends in New York, pleased to tell of his part in the grounding, omitting any knowledge of the events which followed, though from the wry smile on Isaac Sears' face, Thom knew that he had his suspicions.

On his return to Providence, Thom was greeted by the inevitable news from Boston. Never before had a Royal Navy ship been destroyed in American waters except by the French in war. The *Liberty* had been a customs sloop, a government vessel, but not a King's ship. And on the *Gaspee*, a naval officer had been wounded near to death. It could not go unanswered.

"There will be a commission of inquiry to find those responsible." John Brown said, almost casually. "The good Admiral Montegue will attend Newport within the fortnight to begin the proceedings. "

"Are we at risk, sir?"

"As long as we breathe, we are all at risk, young Thomas, but I wouldn't let these matters concern you. If there is cause for concern I shall hear with ample warning for us all. In the mean time, our enterprise must carry on." John Brown smiled. "I am led to believe that Stephen Hopkins will direct the commission on behalf of the colony."

Thom grinned, in spite of himself. Stephen Hopkins, the five time governor, was one of the most respected men in the colony and a wholly reasonable selection to head the commission. He was also the brother in-law of Captain Whipple, John Hopkin's uncle and a close friend and business partner of John Brown, as well a friend or relation of another half dozen of the raiders. Hopkins knew exactly whom to protect.

❖❖❖

When Thom arrived in New York the following week, Isaac Sears sat in the corner of his inn, his face dark and choleric. "How dare they, the goddamn bastards," he growled as Thom joined him at the table.

"And a fine morrow to you too, Captain Sears."

"More cheery than the day warrants I'd contend. Haven't you heard of the commission to be paneled in Newport?"

"And what of it? There have been commissions of inquiry before -- all bluster, bluff and bad wind."

"Ah, then maybe you haven't heard the lot. This commission 'll point out the rogues and send 'em to England for trial. Use'n the Ports and Shipyard Act for their treachery, the blackguards."

Thom sat silent for a moment. A trial in England meant a sure conviction. "So the danger's greater than just for those who set torch to the schooner. The *Gaspee*'s but an excuse."

"An excuse, aye. Perchance they believe that a firm hand'll bring obedience, the greater fools. What does English liberty mean if we've no right to a trial by a jury of our peers, but are bundled off to a Star Chamber near a thousand leagues cross an ocean, our cause forfeit as soon as we are put aboard the ship? A

New York or Rhode Island jury would see to justice, whatever the Admiral's wish, but what of London? A jury of toadies or drunkards paid for their time would condemn any innocent, if that was what their masters ordained. "

Sears took a swig from the tankard on the table. "If they can do it in Rhode Island, who in the colonies is safe? I'm sure Hutchinson in Boston would love to see Sam Adams arrested and shipped off for trial and hangin', an perhaps Hancock or Otis, as well. I can think of a dozen or so fine gentry on this island alone who wouldn't mind see'n myself in chains with no prospect of salvation. An' what of Henry in Virginia, or Dickinson in Pennsylvania, or a score of others?"

Sears looked up and half smiled. "This time, Thomas, it's not Rhode Island or Massachusetts, or Virginia or New York. It's all of us. A blow to one is a blow to all."

❖ ❖ ❖

On the trips that followed, Thom watched for the Admiral's flag as he sailed the *Hannah* into Newport, and was surprised that it was almost two months before the flagship arrived. Finally in mid-August, Thom sailed by the man-of-war flying the admiral's broad pennant, anchored under the guns of Fort George off Goat Island.

"Tis a true shame you missed the performance," Johnny told Thom over a tankard of ale. "When the admiral arrives, he's waiting for a proper salute from the town, which completely ignores him. He sends a protest to Governor Wanton who writes back that they had not been notified of the admiral's arrival date so they had not been able to prepare the salute, as if they hadn't noticed a bloody seventy-four gun ship anchored in the harbor or maybe just forgot how to fire a cannon. Admiral Montague was furious, hear tell."

"Good start for the commission of inquiry," Thom commented. "I'm told that Darius Sessions has sought Sam

Adam's counsel and New York has established its own Committee of Correspondence, like Massachusetts and Rhode Island. They say that Virginia, Delaware and the Carolinas have joined in and more are likely to follow. By the new moon, all the colonies will stand together. And ain't that a wonder, in its own right? Took a burned schooner to unite us."

"From all the fuss almost sounds like the Crown burned a colony's schooner, not the other way 'round," Johnny chuckled.

Thom shrugged. "Feels like the Stamp Act days all over again, but with twice the fire. All united over the ashes of the *Gaspee*."

"To the ashes of the *Gaspee* then," Johnny said lifting his tankard.

"To her ashes," Thom replied.

❖ ❖ ❖

One afternoon in late August when Thom arrived in Providence a messenger bade him attend John Brown.

"Captain Whipple is setting forth on a trading voyage to Surinam and he needs a good mate. He asked if you might be available?"

For a moment Thom was silent. "And what did you tell him?"

"That I would speak on his behalf, of course. It might be an opportune time for you to refresh yourself on a foreign voyage, that is, if you can still remember how to navigate."

"I believe that I do, sir."

"Good. Do you find Michael Rollins suitable as captain of the *Hannah* in your stead?"

"A good mate. Should make as good a captain."

"Splendid. Splendid. Whipple says that he could also use a good bosun. Do you think your friend Mr. Stevens might have an interest in the berth?"

"I'll be sure to ask him. He's married now and says that he's taken well enough to the settled life though he might find an ocean voyage to be to his liking."

"Good. It is likely that you were to be called before the commission of inquiry given that the *Hannah* witnessed the unfortunate grounding of the *Gaspee*. Should that come to pass we will advise the commission that you are unavailable and not likely to return until after the proceedings conclude. Might be best for those involved," he paused, "in the events of the night of June 9th last, to be some distance from Newport in the next few months."

Thom smiled briefly, feeling like a chess piece being moved across a board, then asked in a low tone, "Are you in any peril, sir? I hear the governor has placed a reward for the apprehension of the leaders of the raiders, with full immunity and prince's ransom for the turning over the 'Captain' and the 'Sheriff', whomever they may be." He knew, as did most of Providence, that the "Captain" was John Brown himself and the "Sheriff" was Captain Whipple.

Brown smiled. "And why should I be in peril? It appears that no one in Providence saw who the raiders were, or from whence they came. It was a very dark night, I'm told. A very dark night. I doubt the governor's reward will be claimed. One thousand pounds, I hear. An admirable sum, though in the end naught more than thirty pieces of silver. I'm perfectly certain that Providence harbors no Judas Iscariot."

Thom shook his head. One thousand pounds. A man could work a lifetime for such a sum. The entire colony knew of the night the *Gaspee* burned and thousands knew at least one of the raiders. If the protection of the King's warships in Newport harbor and a stack of gold coins wasn't enough to free a single tongue, what loyalty could the Crown expect if one day, it came to blows? It occurred to Thom that whatever the future might bring, the Crown had already lost the struggle.

When the commission began its inquiries, there was only one witness – Aaron Briggs, a frightened and abused slave boy who had the misfortune of trying to escape his master by taking a rowboat on that dark night in the river. He had fallen in with the raiding party but had no clear description of anyone. His testimony had been compelled by beating or the threat of the same and immediately a dozen witnesses appeared who all swore that they had seem Briggs far ashore that same night. Reading of it in the newspaper, Thom was pleased that by the time his name was called by the commission, he would well off to sea.

❖❖❖

Thom bade his respects to the crew of the *Hannah*, wished his best to Rollins and suggested that he might choose not to remember much of the grounding.

"To which grounding do you refer, sir?" he replied with a smile.

"Good winds to you, Michael."

"And to you, Thomas."

Thom had gathered his gear in a small sea chest. He hoisted it to his shoulder and walked toward the dock where Whipple's ship, the *Bonaventure*, was fitting out. Johnny Stevens was unloading his gear from a buckboard and waved.

"I see that you're signing articles. When I sent the message, I thought that you might stay ashore. A new wife and all. How does she regard your departure?"

Johnny grinned. "She knew she was marrying a sailor, an' I'm not altogether sure that she isn't as happy to see me on my way for a time. Been married for near two years. Just might use some time away."

Thom laughed. "Well, be a joy to be shipmates again."

"Aye, that it will. An' look at this." Johnny opened a walnut case. A well used sextant shone from its velvet cushion. "Perhaps we may continue my instructions."

Thom arched an eyebrow. "And what use has a bosun for a sextant?"

Johnny straightened his back and replied, "If the captain should fall ill and the mate be struck down by fever, the ship's people may value a bosun with a sextant." He grinned. "I once't heard a tale of a boy sailor brought a ship into Boston 'cause he could navigate."

Thom laughed. "Seems like an age ago, doesn't it? Best we get aboard before Whipple changes his mind and gives the berths to Providence men."

❊ ❊ ❊

With his gear stowed, there was one task that required Thom's attention. The walk up the several blocks to John Brown's house seemed longer than ever before. He stood outside the front door for a time before he could get himself to pull the bell.

"Is Miss Brown present? It is Thomas Lar..."

"Pshaww. I know who you are, young sir," replied the servant Marcus. "Wait in here."

Angela greeted him with a warm smile. "I would not let myself believe that you could depart without saying goodbye, Thomas Larkin."

Thom smile was pained. "Shall we take a short stroll? Have a few words?"

Angela nodded. "Of course, I would have a few words with you as well." Marcus gave Angela a questioning look, though Angela shook her head almost imperceptibly. "Shan't be long, Marcus."

They had walked a short distance, when Thom said, "As you know, I shall be away for some period. You know as well as I that I will miss you greatly. I realize now how your very presence seems to have given me a new life. Were it not for your care when I arrived, I might not have recovered from the fever. I have greatly esteemed your friendship these several years. Which I believe has grown to more than friendship.

"I have invested my savings in this voyage and hope to return in a somewhat less penurious state so that one day I may ask your father for your hand, if you will have me."

Angela stopped and turned to Thom.

"Oh course, I will have you. I will have none other. I do not love you for thy purse, Thomas, be if empty or bursting." She smiled and looked up into his eyes.

"I'll speak plainly. Do not worry about your station. My grandfather was a ship's captain, as was yours, and your father is a man of some property, though you be estranged. We are not so different as you say. You are no Jack Tar lacking in prospects. You are as worthy as any man to be at my side. And I am honored to stand by yours."

She paused and just looked at him for a moment, her eyes seeming to reach directly to his essence. When she spoke again, it was with a quiet fire.

"I have faith in you, Thomas Larkin. You rode a jolly boat through a hurricane rather than remain a bondsman and you destroyed a ship of war with an unarmed packet and a sandbar. If you apply that courage and will to commerce, you shall not die a pauper." She reached inside the pocket of her vest, withdrew a bundle of paper and handed it to Thom.

"What is this?" he asked.

"Dutch bills of exchange, worth two hundred pounds lawful money. Add these to your savings and buy trade goods. If you sell them in Surinam you'll return with half again as much and another few voyages could give you a proper start. Then no one, not my father, my uncles, nor any in the colony could say you are not a fit match for Angela Brown."

Thom was stunned. He looked down at the bills and then at Angela. "I cannot take charity, especially from....."

"Charity?" Angela's brow furrowed. "If our hearts are bound, then we are truly partners. That is my money, given freely by my Uncles Moses, a dowry gift of a sort, and I shall do with it as I see fit. If you do not wish to be my partner in this and all other enterprises, then perhaps I have misjudged you and should seek another." Her words sounded harsh, though her gaze was hopeful.

"I love you, Angela Brown." He was almost surprised by how easily he said the words, though they were as true and natural as anything he knew. Tears welled in her eyes as he embraced her, holding her for a long time, not wanting to let go.

❖❖❖

The week that followed was a blur of activity, the final loading of Rhode Island tobacco and horses for the Surinam market on the Bonaventure, a score of shipboard tasks had to be completed and another score of problems to be resolved. With Captain Whipple's help Thom made his own purchases, in what little time he had, trying to spread his risk across commodities, against the certainty that the price for candles might be weak, while tobacco remained strong, and rum could be middling or some other combination than no one could ever predict.

Finally, on their sailing day, with hatches battened and all stores aboard, they slipped their moorings. John Brown and Angela came to see them off. John Brown boomed, "Fair winds and good fortune," while Angela raised her hand to wave. She smiled brightly, yet her cheeks were wet with tears. Her father put his arm around her and said a few words that Thom couldn't make out. Thom waved back, missing her already, then turned, shouting to the deckhands to get the lines aboard, coiled and stored.

They set off down the river into the ever widening waters of the Narragansett, and finally into the boundless expanse of the Atlantic. Thom was glad to leave the complications of the shore astern, to be once again trapped aboard the ship, and thus set free by the confinement. He felt the pain of Angela's absence the moment he lost sight of her waving from the dock, yet now, at least his emotions were simple, as certain as any man could be that she would be waiting for him on his return.

Three days into the voyage, Thom paced the quarterdeck in the moist darkness of the morning watch. Johnny strolled aft.

"Morning, Mr. Mate."

"Morning, Bosun. How fare ye?'

"Well enough, sir."

Thom laughed. He lowered his voice. "Sir, is it, now? Been a fair number of years but we're still shipmates. Damn, but it feels good to be at sea again. Wasn't so sure it would, but it does, true enough."

The eastern sky was lightening, a muted flame spreading across the horizon.

"Morning red. May be due for some dirty weather," Johnny commented.

Thom looked off at the bloody dawn. After the *Gaspee*, he found himself wondering if there might be a far greater storm brewing. A storm like none they had ever seen. A storm to make the hurricane at Statia seem like an afternoon shower. He could feel it coming. The longer the weather glass fell, the greater the blow and the glass had been falling for a very long time. A storm to blow the old world away.

Thom looked back at Johnny. "Yes, a squall's coming. We'll set a reef in the topsails at change of watch. Best tell the captain about the weather coming. Good morning to you, Mr. Stevens," he said with a nod and went below deck.

ABOUT THE AUTHOR

Rick Spilman has spent most of his life around the ships and the sea. Professionally, he has worked as a naval architect (ship designer) for several major shipping lines. An avid sailor, Rick has sailed as volunteer crew on the replica square-riggers "*HMS Rose*" and "*HMS Bounty*," as well as sailing on modern and period vessels along the New England coast, the west coast of Florida, the Caribbean, the Great Lakes and the southwest coast of Ireland. He is also an avid kayaker.

Rick's novel, *Hell Around the Horn*, is a nautical thriller set on a British windjammer in the brutal Cape Horn winter of 1905. Based on an actual voyage, it is a story of survival and the human spirit against overwhelming odds.

The Shantyman, Rick's second novel, is set on a clipper ship in 1870. A crew member carried aboard paralytic drunk turns out to a skilled shantyman. He may be able to save the ship and her crew, but will he be able to save himself? *The Shantyman* was selected as one of Kirkus Reviews' Best Indie Books for 2015.

Rick is the founder and host of the Old Salt Blog, (oldsaltblog.com) a virtual port of call for all those who love the sea. He is a also a partner in Old Salt Press (oldsaltpress.com). He has been published in the Huffington Post, gCaptain, Forbes online, and several canoeing and kayaking print magazines. He was also a Cooley Award Winner in short fiction at the University of Michigan. His video has appeared in the Wall Street Journal on-line and in National Geographic Traveler.

Rick lives with his wife and two sons on the west bank of the Hudson River.

AUTHOR'S NOTES

*E*vening Gray Morning Red is a work of historical fiction. The key events and many of the characters are taken directly from history. Thomas Larkin and John Stevens are wholly fictional but many of those around them are not. I have tried, nevertheless, to stay as true to the history as possible, while taking liberties to suit the plot and the characters when necessary. I hope that I have struck a fair balance between the two. A few comments on the history behind the novel:

The Young Navigator in the Fog

The opening chapter where Thom finds himself the only one aboard the ship who knows how to navigate may seem unlikely, but turns up several times in colonial history.

The best known account is of John Paul, a Scottish sailor of 21, who served as a second mate on the brig *John*. On a voyage in 1768, both the captain and first mate died of yellow fever. John Paul navigated the ship safely into port. The owners of the ship were so grateful for its safe return that John Paul was made the ship's master and rewarded with 10 percent of the cargo.

In *Evening Gray Morning Red,* the ship's owners were not as generous to Thomas Larkin as the Scottish ship owners had been to John Paul. I decided that, as a work of fiction, that that level of generosity might not be wholly believable, despite being based on history.

Captain John Paul would later change his name after he was charged with the murder of one of his crew during a failed mutiny. He took the last name of Jones and is remembered today as John Paul Jones.

Impressment and the Liberty Riots

Impressment was the seizure of merchant seaman to serve on Royal Navy ships, effectively a form of legal kidnapping. In the British American colonies, naval impressment was extremely unpopular.

In *Evening Grey Morning Red*, Thom's capture by a press gang from HMS *Romney* is based on history. The impressment of sailors in Boston by a press gang from HMS *Romney* in May of 1768 mobilized the Boston mob. When, only days later, the customs men seized John Hancock's sloop *Liberty*, the Boston mob was already on the streets. The Liberty Riots that resulted led directly to the occupation of Boston by British forces in October of 1768.

The hostility to impressment was well established in Boston. Two decades before, in 1747, three days of anti-impressment riots broke out after 49 Bostonians were pressed under the orders of Admiral Charles Knowles, commander of a British naval squadron anchored in the harbor. Thousands of Bostonians effectively shut down the colonial government and seized a number of naval officers as hostages. Admiral Knowles threatened to bombard the town if the officers where not released. Ultimately, a deal was struck to free the impressed sailors in exchange for the release of the hostages.

Opposition to impressment was central to the principles underlying the American Revolution. During the Knowles Riots, a young Samuel Adams, in his newspaper, *The Independent Advertiser*, invoked the ideas of John Locke to defend the rioters. He praised them as citizens defending their natural rights to life and liberty when the government failed to do so.

In the days surrounding the Liberty Riots, Sam Adam's brother and attorney John Adams spoke out forcefully against impressment. A year later, he would successfully defend a sailor who killed a British officer from HMS *Rose*, during an attempted impressment. John Adams, of course, would become a leader of the American Revolution. He would go on to sign the Declaration of Independence and be elected the second president of the United States.

The Brown Brothers of Providence

I hope that I have done justice to the Brown brothers of Providence in my portrayal of them in *Evening Gray Morning Red*. John and Moses Brown, in particular, were fascinating and complex characters. With their brothers, Nicholas and Joseph, they built a substantial trading business, some of which survives to this day.

I have taken several liberties with the Brown family. John and Moses were in conflict over slavery for many years. John considered the slave trade to be just another form of business, whereas Moses became a Quaker and an abolitionist. When we meet Moses in 1769 in *Evening Gray Morning Red,* he is already a Quaker, when he actually did not convert to the faith until 1773.

John Brown actually had three daughters – Abigail, Sarah and Alice – but no Angela. Sarah married Charles Frederick Herreshoff, the grandfather of the famous yacht designer Nathaniel Greene Herreshoff. I modeled Angela Brown, who is wholly fictional, after the vivacious "Caty" Greene, the wife of Nathaniel Greene, George Washington's favorite general and a close friend of the Brown family.

In 1797, John Brown was the first American to be tried in federal court under the Slave Trade Act of 1794, which prohibited the making, loading, outfitting, equipping, or dispatching of any ship to be used in the trade of slaves. Brown was convicted and was forced to forfeit his ship *Hope*.

John and Moses Brown helped to found the College of Rhode Island, later renamed Brown University. In 2007, a number of Brown University students became alarmed to learn that the institution had been funded, at least in part, from the profits of the slave trade.

In 1791, John Brown founded the Providence Bank - the first bank in Rhode Island. Over time, through multiple acquisitions, Providence Bank became FleetBoston Financial, which was acquired by Bank of America in 2004.

Moses Brown established the New England Yearly Meeting School in 1814. He served as school treasurer until shortly before his death. The school, surviving to this day, was renamed in his honor in 1913 as the Moses Brown School, and remains a leading preparatory school in the U.S.

John Brown died in 1803 at the age of 67. Moses Brown lived to be 98, dying in 1836.

Lieutenant William Dudingston

William Dudingston was born in Scotland in 1740, the son of landed gentry. HMS *Gaspee* was his first command. My placing him aboard HMS *Romney* in Boston was entirely fictional. The frigate *Romney* was indeed in Boston in 1768 under the command of Captain Corner but Dudingston was not the first lieutenant.

In October of 1772, William Dudingston was acquitted by Court Marshall of any responsibility for the loss of HMS *Gaspee*. After at least partially recovering from his wounds, he returned to the rebellious colonies during the war in command of the sloop of war, HMS *Senegal* in 1776. He would go on to command the sloop of war HMS *Cameleon* and the frigate HMS *Boston*.

William Dudingston retired as an admiral and died in Earlsferry, Fife at the age of 76.

Abraham Whipple

Abraham Whipple was a remarkable merchant captain, privateer and ultimately a naval commander during the Revolutionary War. While he was never charged with the burning of the *Gaspee,* his actions were widely known.

In June 1775, Whipple was in command of the sloop *Katy,* owned by John Brown and chartered to Rhode Island. Whipple caught and destroyed the armed sloop *Diana,* a tender to HMS *Rose.* Captain Wallace of the *Rose* sent Captain Whipple a message: "*You Abraham Whipple on June 10, 1772, burned his majesty's vessel the Gaspee and I will hang you at the yard arm!*"

Whipple replied to Wallace: "*Sir, always catch a man before you hang him.*"

After the war, Whipple moved to Marietta, Ohio, took up farming and died at the age of 85.

The Grounding and Burning of HMS Gaspee

The grounding and burning of HMS *Gaspee* in *Evening Gray Morning Red* follows the accounts in William R. Staples, <u>The Documentary History of the Destruction of the Gaspee</u> of 1845. The accepted history is that the *Gaspee* ran aground on Namquid Point (now Gaspee Point) when chasing the packet boat *Hannah* under the command of either Benjamin or Thomas Lindsey.

Another version of the story was told by William Dudingston at his Court Marshall, where he makes no mention of chasing a packet boat but says that he had anchored the *Gaspee* near the point and the schooner went aground when the tide went out. Dudingston's version seems unlikely, but we will never know. The accepted version of the grounding as the culmination of a chase makes a much better story.

The *Gaspee* was burned by raiders from Providence led by John Brown and Abraham Whipple. Joseph Bucklin is said to have fired the shot that wounded Lt. Dudingston, rather than the fictional John Stevens.

The Ships and Boats of
Evening Gray Morning Red

HMS *Romney*

HMS *Romney* was a 50-gun fourth rate Royal Navy ship-of -the-line. Built in 1762, she had a 42 year career, serving during the American Revolutionary War and the Napoleonic Wars before being lost in 1804 due to a grounding.

Sloop *Liberty*

John Hancock's sloop *Liberty* was probably typical of the sloops trading in wine from the Madeira Islands off Africa to the American colonies. Most of the better wines in the colonies were fortified Madeira wines. The long transit times, heat and motion of the ships of the day would often damage European wines. Madeira wines generally were better at surviving the long voyage.

John Hancock was a notorious smuggler. As one of the richest men in the Massachusetts colony, he was a target for the Commissioner of Customs. Legend has it that the sloop *Liberty* was named in honor of the British radical John Wilkes, who had been arrested for seditious libel for criticizing King George III. Some have suggested that the rallying cry "Wilkes and Liberty" may have been the basis for the sloop's name.

After the *Liberty* was seized by the Crown in Boston, she was put up for auction but no one would buy Hancock's sloop. She was put into the Custom's service under the command of Captain Reid and was indeed burned by a Newport mob a year later.

HMS *Gaspee* and the Marblehead Schooners

Around 1764 the British Admiralty purchased six Marblehead sloops and schooners -- *St John*, *St Lawrence*, *Chaleur*, *Hope*, *Magdalen*, and *Gaspee*. The name "Marblehead" is generally accepted today as referring to the type of small sailing ships built in Essex County, Massachusetts. The sloops and schooners were intended specifically to crack down on smuggling on the American East Coast. Their relatively small size and shallow draft allowed them to chase the smuggler's craft into the bays, coves and rivers where the smugglers often sought refuge when pursued by the larger Royal Navy sloops of war or frigates.

The *Gaspee* is believed to have been just over 100 tons and roughly 68 feet on deck.

Packet Boat *Hannah*

The packet boat *Hannah* was operated by the brothers Benjamin and Thomas Lindsey and sailed between Providence and Newport, Rhode Island. Most accounts have the *Hannah* under the command of Benjamin Lindsey when the *Gaspee* was lured aground. One version has Benjamin's brother Thomas Lindsey in command. The character Thomas Larkin was initially inspired by Thomas Lindsey, although Thom Larkin is otherwise entirely fictional. The *Hannah*'s trading between New York and Providence is wholly fictional as well.

I hope that you have enjoyed *Evening Gray Morning Red*. Your comments are always welcome and appreciated.

If you feel so inclined, I would also greatly appreciate a brief review of the novel on Amazon, Barnes and Noble, Goodreads or wherever you feel is appropriate

Thanks.

Rick Spilman
rick@oldsaltpress.com

GLOSSARY

AB – Able seaman, able to hand, reef and steer

Amidships – the middle section of the ship

Anchor, catting – to secure the anchor to the cathead, typically for a short or coastal voyage. For longer voyages, the anchor would be hoisted onto the deck and lashed securely.

Apprentice – a young man who signs on for a four year training period, a ship's officer in training.

Armstrong Patent - slang, a ship with few winches or other mechanical labor-saving devices, where the strong arms of the crew were all that raises, lowers and trims the sails.

Articles – short for Articles of Agreement, a contract between the captain of a ship and a crew member regarding stipulations of a voyage, signed prior to and upon termination of a voyage.

Athwartships – perpendicular to the centerline of the ship, across the width of the ship

Barometer – a device to measure the barometric pressure. A rising barometer suggests good weather whereas a falling barometer indicates increasing storms.

Barque - a sailing ship of three or more masts having the foremasts rigged square and the aftermast rigged fore-and-aft

Beam – the breadth of a ship.

Before the mast – traditionally sailors lived forward of the main mast while officers berthed aft. Sailing before the mast was sailing as an able or ordinary seaman.

Best bib and tucker – slang, one's best clothes

Binnacle - a stand or enclosure of wood or nonmagnetic metal for supporting and housing a compass

Body and soul lashings - lashings of twine around the waist, pant legs and wrists to prevent the wind from blowing open or up a sailor's oilskins

Bogie stove – also bogy and bogey, a small cabin stove.

Bolt-rope – a line sewn into the edges of a sail.

Bowsprit - a large spar projecting forward from the stem of a ship.

Brace, Braces - on a square-rigged ship, lines used to rotate the yards around the mast, to allow the ship to sail at different angles to the wind.

Brig – as two masted ship, square-rigged on both masts.

Brassbounder – a ship's apprentice, from the row or rows of brass buttons on an apprentice's dress jacket.

Bulwark - plating along the sides of a ship above her gunwale that provides some protection to the crew from being washed overboard by boarding seas.

Bunt - the middle part of the sail. When furling the sail, the last task is to "roll the bunt," which is hauling the furled bunt on the top of the yard and tying it with gaskets.

Buntlines – small lines used to haul up the bottom of the sail prior to furling. There are usually four to eight buntlines across the foot of the sail. When a sail is to be furled, the buntlines and the clewlines are hauled, gather up the sail. When the sail is supported by the buntlines and clewlines, the sail is said to be hanging in its gear.

Burgoo – a porridge of coarse oatmeal and water

Capstan – a vertical windlass used for raising yards, anchors and any other heavy object aboard ship.

Clew – the lower corners of a square sail or the lower aft corner of a fore and aft sail.

Clewlines – lines used to haul up the lower corners of a sail prior to furling. See also, buntlines.

Clipper ship - a very fast sailing ship of the mid 19th century that had three or more masts and a square rig. The clipper ship era began the 1830s and ended around 1870.

Close-hauled – when a ship is sailing as close to the wind as it can. A square-rigged ship could usually sail no closer than five points to the wind.

Compass Points – the compass is divided into 32 points. Each point is 11.25 degrees.

Course – In navigation, the course is a direction that the ship is sailing, often also called a compass course. In sails, a course is the lowest square sail on a mast. The main course is often called the main sail and the fore course is often referred to as the fore sail.

Coxcombing – a variety of different styles of decorate knot work using hitches and whipping. French Whipping is a common style of coxcombing.

Cringle - an eye through which to pass a rope, a small hole anywhere a sail, rimmed with stranded cordage. Similar to a grommet.

Cro'jack – the mizzen course. See **Course**

Crosstrees - two horizontal struts at the upper ends of the topmasts used to anchor the shrouds from the topgallant mast.

Davits – frames used to store ships boats which can be quickly swung over the side to allow the boats to be lowered.

Deal planks – A softwood plank, often fir or pine

Dogwatch - a work shift, between 1600 and 2000 (4pm and 8pm). This period is split into two, with the first dog watch from 1600 to 1800 (4pm to 6pm) and the second dog watch from 1800 to 2000 (6pm to 8pm). Each of these watches is half the length of a standard watch. Effect of the two half watches is to shift the watch schedule daily so that the sailors do not stand the same watch every day. See **Watches.**

Doldrums - region of the ocean near the equator, characterized by calms, light winds, or squalls

Donkey's breakfast – a thin sailor's mattress typically filled with straw

Downhaul – A line used to pull down a sail or yard

Fife rail - a rail at the base of a mast of a sailing vessel, fitted with pins for belaying running rigging. See **pin rail.**

Figurehead - a carved wooden decoration, often of person, at the prow of a ship. While figureheads are often carvings of women, they can also be of men as well as animals or mythological creatures.

Flying jib - a sail outside the jib on an extension of the jibboom

Fo'c'sle house, or fo'c'sle – the accommodation space for sailors. At one time in merchant ships, sailors were berthed in the raised forward part of the ship referred to as the fo'c'sle. Later when the accommodations were moved to a cabin on the main deck the deck house continued to be referred to as the fo'c'sle.

Footropes – a rope <u>of</u> cable secured below a yard to a provide a place for a sailor to stand while tending sail.

Fore-reaching – a form of heaving-to in which the ship continues to slowly sail forward on a close reach rather than losing ground and drifting backward.

Foremast – the forward-most mast

Foresail – the fore course, the lowest square sail on the foremast

Forestay – stay supporting the foremast

Freeboard – the amount of ship's hull above the water, the distance from the waterline to the deck edge.

Freeing port – in a steel bulwark, a heavy hinged flap that allows water on deck to flow overboard

French leave – departing without permission, explanation or leave

Furious Fifties – the name given to strong westerly winds found in the Southern Hemisphere, generally between the latitudes of 50 and 60 degrees

Futtock shrouds - shrouds running from the outer edges of a top downwards and inwards to a point on the mast or lower shrouds, and carry the load of the shrouds that rise from the edge of the top. See **shroud**.

Gaff rig is a sailing rig (configuration of sails, mast and stays) in which the sail is four-cornered, fore-and-aft rigged, controlled at its peak and, usually, its entire head by a spar called the gaff.

Gammoning band - The lashing or iron band by which the bowsprit of a vessel is secured to the stem to opposite the lifting action of the forestays.

Gantline - a line rove through a block for hoisting rigging, spars, provisions or other items

Gaskets - gaskets are lengths of rope or fabric used to hold a stowed sail in place, on yachts commonly called sail ties.

Gunwale – also gunnel, the upper deck edge of a ship or boat.

Half-deck – the cabin where the apprentices are lodged. The location of the half-deck can vary between ships, from the cabin to the tween deck to a separate cabin on deck. The half-deck refers not to a specific location but to its function as home to the apprentices.

Halyards – a line used to raise a sail or a yard. Originally from "haul yard."

Hatch – an opening in the deck of a ship. The main deck hatches are the main access for loading and discharging ship's cargo.

Hatch coaming - A raised frame around a hatch; it forms a support for the hatch cover.

Hatch cover - planks usually held together by metal strapping which form a rectangular panel. These were supported over a hatch by hatch beams. The hatch covers were then made watertight by stretching a tarpaulin across the hatch which was held tight by wedges.

Hatch wedges – wedges used to secure the hatch tarpaulin

Hawser - a thick cable or rope used in mooring or towing a ship.

Heave to, hove to – in extreme weather conditions, to heave to allows the ship to keep a controlled angle to the wind and seas by balancing effects the reduced sail and and a lashed helm, to wait out the storm. The ships drifts backwards slowly generally under control without the need for active sail-handling.

Jackstay - an iron rod, wooden bar, or wire rope along a yard to which the sails are fastened.

Jib - a triangular staysail that sets ahead of the foremast

Jib-boom - a spar used to extend the length of a bowsprit on sailing ships.

Jibe also gybe - a sailing maneuver in which the course changes so that the wind crosses the stern.

Larboard – the left side of the ship. Later know as the port side.

Latitude - a measure of the north-south position on the Earth's surface. Lines of latitude, or parallels, run east–west as circles parallel to the equator. Latitude ranges from 0° at the Equator to 90° at the poles.

Lazarette – a below deck storage area in the stern of the ship

Leeward – the direction away from the wind

Lee rail - The deck edge on the side of the ship away from the direction from which the wind is blowing. The **weather rail** is the on the other side of the ship.

Limey – slang for a British sailor or ship. Also called lime juicers. From the British policy of issuing lime or lemon juice to sailors to prevent scurvy on long passages.

Liverpool deck – on some of the later windjammers, an accommodations cabin/deck amidships which spanned the entire beam of the ship.

Liverpool pantiles – slang for hard bread said to resemble roofing tile in shape, consistency and flavor.

Local Apparent Noon – the moment when the sun is observed to be at its highest point in its travel across the sky. By measuring the altitude (the angular distance from the horizon) and noting the time difference between Local Apparent Noon and Greenwich time, a ship's officer can determine the ship's latitude and longitude. See **Sun Sight** and **Sextant**.

Longitude – a measurement of the east-west position on the Earth's surface, an angular measurement, usually expressed in degrees. Points with the same longitude lie in lines running from the North Pole to the South Pole. By convention, one of these, the Prime Meridian, which passes through the Royal Observatory, Greenwich, England, establishes the position of zero degrees longitude. The longitude of other places is measured as an angle east or west from the Prime Meridian, ranging from 0° at the Prime Meridian to +180° eastward and –180° westward.

Lying a-hull – similar to being hove to except that no effort is made to maintain control of the ship's hull in relation to the wind and sea. Sails are furled and the ship is allowed to drift, generally sideways to the seas.

Main mast – the largest mast on a sailing ship. The middle mast on a three masted ship.

Main sail – the main course, the lowest square sail set on the main mast

Mainstay – stay supporting the main mast leading forward on the centerline of the ship

Marline - a small, usually tarred, line of two strands twisted loosely left-handed that is used especially for seizing and as a covering for wire rope

Marlinspike - A marlinspike is a polished iron or steel spike tapered to a rounded or flattened point, usually 6 to 12 inches long, used in ropework for unlaying rope for splicing, for untying knots, opening or closing shackles and a variety of related tasks.

Marlinspike sailor – a sailor who become proficient at knot tying, splicing, ropework, sewing, and use of a marlinspike

Meridian or line of longitude - half of an imaginary great circle on the Earth's surface terminated by the North Pole and the South Pole, connecting points of equal longitude.

Mizzen – the aftermost mast and smallest mast, the third mast on a three masted ship.

Mooring lines – lines or hawsers used to hold the ship fast against a dock

Monkey rigged – Sailors were expected to provide their own work gear, including boots, foul weather gear and spare clothes for the voyage. Sailors who arrived without necessary gear were said to be "monkey rigged."

Official Log Book – the official record of the voyage, listing crew signing on and off. A record is also kept of discipline, injuries, births or deaths that occur on the vessel, as well musters and drills.

Ordinary, ordinary seaman – a less experienced sailor not rated Able. Not trusted for tasks such as steering without supervision.

Outhaul – a line used to haul or stretch a sail on a yard or boom

Pannikin - a small metal pan or cup

Peak Halyard – a line that raises the end of a gaff

Peggy - a sailor assigned to menial tasks

Pierhead jumpers – the last sailors brought aboard a ship before she sails, often purchased from boarding house masters or crimps

Pin rail - a strong wooden rail or bar containing holes for pins to which the running rigging is belayed fastened on sailing vessels usually along the ship's rail.

Point of sail - a sailing vessel's course in relation to the wind direction. When the wind is astern the ship is on a "run." When the the wind is coming across the side, the ship is on a "reach." When the wind is more from aft it is a "broad reach." When the wind is on the beam, it is a "beam reach" and when the wind is forward of the beam, it is a close reach. When a ship is sailing as course as close to the wind as possible it is "beating" or "going to weather."

Poop deck – the raised afterdeck. The helm is aft on the poop deck.

Ratlines - small lines secured horizontally to the shrouds of a ship every 15 or 16 inches forming rungs, allowing sailors to climb aloft.

Reach – a point of sail in which the wind is blowing across the side of the ship. When the wind is more from aft it is a "broad reach." When the wind is on the beam, it is a "beam reach" and when the wind is forward of the beam, it is a close reach.

Reef – to reduce the size of a sail by tying in ropes or gaskets in cringles in the reef-bands which are parallel to the top of the sail.

Roaring Forties - the name given to strong westerly winds found in the Southern Hemisphere, generally between the latitudes of 40 and 50 degrees

Robands - small plaited lines used to tie the square sails to the yards

Rogue wave - a large and spontaneous ocean surface wave that occurs well out to sea, and is a threat even to large ships. Rogue waves have been known to reach over 100 feet in height.

Rolling hitch - (or Magnus hitch) is a knot used to attach a rope to a rod, pole, or other rope.

Rolling the bunt – when furling a sail, rolling the middle section of the sail up on the yard to be secured with gaskets.

Royals, Royal sails – the traditionally, the highest sails on any mast. The sails in order from the lowest to the highest – course, topsail (usually upper and lower topsail), topgallant sail (often upper and lower t'gallant sails) and the royals. Some ships set skysails above royals.

Run – the point of sail in which the wind is directly behind the ship.

Running rigging – rigging used in the raising, lowering and trimming of sails and other gear aboard ship. Running rigging is intended to move, whereas standing rigging is not.

Sailor's palm – a tool of leather and metal which fits on a sailor's hand so that he can use his palm to push a heavy sewing needle through tough material such as rope, leather and canvas.

Salt horse – sailor slang for salted beef

Scupper - opening in the side of a ship at deck level to allow water to run off

Serving and parceling – to protect rigging again chafe, the wrapping of canvas (parceling) over the rigging followed by tightly wound marline (serving). The rigging is them usually tarred over.

Sextant - an instrument used to measure the angle between any two visible objects. When used to navigate at sea, the sextant is used primarily to determine the angle between a celestial object and the horizon.

Shanty – a sailor's working song used when handing sail, pumping or using the capstan.

Shantyman – a sailor who leads the singing of the shanty

Sheet – a line used to control a sail, secured to the sail clew

Ship-rigged – a vessel with at least three masts square-rigged on all masts.

Shroud – standing rigging supporting the mast from side to side

Slop chest - store of clothing and personal goods carried on merchant ships for issue to the crew usually as a charge against their wages

Sou'wester - a waterproof hat having a very broad rim behind, favored by seamen

Spanker - a gaff rigged fore-and-aft sail set from and aft of the after most mast.

Square sail – a sail, usually four sided secured to a yard rigged square or perpendicular to the mast

Standing rigging – the fixed rigging that supports the masts, yards and spars of a sailing ship. Standing rigging includes stays and shrouds and unlike running rigging is not intended to move.

Starboard – the right side of a ship, nautical term for the right

Stays – standing rigging used to support the masts along the centerline of the ship. Each mast has backstays and forestays.

Staysail – a fore and aft sail set on a stay, either between the masts or between the bowspriat and the foremast

Sun sight – the most common sight taken in celestial navigation. A ship's officer with a sextant can determine the ship's latitude by measuring the sun's altitude (height above the horizon) at Local Apparent Noon. With an accurate chronometer, the officer can also determine latitude observing the time of Local Apparent Noon as compared to the time in Greenwich, England.

Square-rigged – A ship or a mast with sails set on yards rigged square, or perpendicular to the centerline of the ship.

T'gallant fo'c'sle – the space beneath the raise deck on the bow of the ship. The space could be used for stores and gear or as an accommodations space for the crew.

T'gans'ls , t'gallant, top gallant sails – the sails set above the topsails. In many windjammers the t'gallant sails were split, like the topsails, into upper and lower t'gallant yards and sails to make sail handling easier.

Tack - a maneuver by which a sailing vessel changes course by turnong the bow across the wind. **Tack** can also be the the side the wind is blowing from. A starboard tack is when the wind **is**

blowing across the starboard side of the vessel. As a part of a sail, the **tack** is the corner of a sail on the lower leading edge usually secured to a gooseneck.

Throat Halyard – a line that raises the end of a gaff nearer to the mast, as opposed to the peak halyard which raises the end further from the mast.

Tiller – a spar acting attached to a rudder post of a boat or ship that provides leverage for the helmsman to turn the rudder. The helmsman can push or the tiller directly, or it may also be moved remotely using relieving tackle or a ship's wheel.

Top - a platform on each mast at the upper end of the lower mast section whose main purpose is to anchor the shrouds of the topmast that extends above it. The top is larger and lower on the masts but performs the same function as the cross trees.

Top-hamper – slang for the sails, masts and rigging of a ship. Can also refer to only the light upper sails and rigging.

Topping lift – a line used to support the yards when the yard is lowered or the sail is furled. Depending on the rigging of the ship the lifts can also be used to adjust the angle of the yards when under sail.

Topsail – the sail above the course. A large and powerful sail, after 1850s most topsails were split into upper and lower topsails to make sail-handing easier. Windjammers tended to have upper and lower topsails.

Turk's head – an ornamental knot that resembles a small turban

Vang – A line used to swing a boom or yard.

Watches - regular periods of work duty aboard a ship. The watches kept on sailing ships usually consisted of 5 four-hour periods and 2 two-hour periods. On many merchant ships the watches were divided into the captain's and the mate's watch or starboard and port watches. The captain did not stand a watch so the Second Mate stood the watch in his stead. By tradition, the captain's watch stood the first watch on the sailing of the ship from its home port, while the mate's atch took the first watch on sailing on the return voyage.

Weather rail – The deck edge on the side of the ship in the direction from which the wind is blowing. The lee rail is the on the other side of the ship.

Wet dock - A wet dock is a dock in which the water is impounded either by dock gates or by a lock, allowing ships to remain afloat at low tide in places with high tidal ranges. The level of water in the dock is maintained despite the raising and lowering of the tide. This makes transfer of cargo easier. It works like a lock which controls the water level and allows passage of ships.

Wharfinger - an owner or manager of a wharf

Windward – the direction from which the wind is blowing

Windbound – ship that is becalmed, incapable of moving due to lack of wind

Windjammer - a large square rigged sailing ship common in the later portion of the 19th and early 20th century, often built of steel or iron, designed for maximum cargo capacity.

Worming – wrapping a thin line in a cable's strands before serving and parcelling

Yard – a spar rigged horizontally, perpendicular or "square" to a ship's mast, used to set a square sail.

Yard Arm – the extreme outer end of the a yard.

Go Down to the Sea in Books with Old Salt Press

HELL AROUND THE HORN

BY RICK SPILMAN

Hell Around the Horn is a nautical thriller set in the last days of the great age of sail. In 1905, a young ship's captain and his family set sail on the windjammer, *Lady Rebecca*, from Cardiff, Wales with a cargo of coal bound for Chile, by way of Cape Horn. Before they reach the Southern Ocean, the cargo catches fire, the mate threatens mutiny and one of the crew may be going mad, yet the greatest challenge will prove to be surviving the vicious westerly winds and mountainous seas of the worst Cape Horn winter in memory. Based on an actual voyage, *Hell Around the Horn* is a story of survival and the human spirit against overwhelming odds.

ISBN 978-0988236011

GO DOWN TO THE SEA IN BOOKS WITH OLD SALT PRESS

THE SHANTYMAN
by Rick Spilman

Chosen as one of Kirkus Reviews' Best Indie Books for 2015

He can save the ship and the crew, but can he save himself?

In 1870, on the clipper ship *Alahambra* in Sydney, the new crew comes aboard more or less sober, except for the last man, who is hoisted aboard in a cargo sling, paralytic drunk. The drunken sailor, Jack Barlow, will prove to be an able shantyman. On a ship with a dying captain and a murderous mate, Barlow will literally keep the crew pulling together. As he struggles with a tragic past, a troubled present and an uncertain future, Barlow will guide the Alahambra through Southern Ocean ice and the horror of an Atlantic hurricane. His one goal is bringing the ship and crew safely back to New York, where he hopes to start anew.

Based on a true story, *The Shantyman* is a gripping tale of survival against all odds at sea and ashore, and the challenge of facing a past that can never be wholly left behind.
ISBN978-0-9941152-2-5

GO DOWN TO THE SEA IN BOOKS WITH OLD SALT PRESS

HONOUR BOUND
by Alaric Bond

Honour Bound is the 10th book in The Fighting Sail Series by Alaric Bond. Satisfied that he has forged HMS Kestrel into a formidable weapon, Commander King is keen to take her to sea once more. But the war is not progressing well for Britain, and his hopes of remaining in Malta are shattered as Kestrel is moved closer to the action.

And so begins a story that covers two seas and one ocean, as well as a cross-country trek through enemy territory, a closer look at the French prison system and a reunion with several familiar faces.

Containing breathtaking sea battles, tense personal drama and an insight into the social etiquette of both Britain and France, *Honour Bound* is a story brim-filled with action and historical detail.

ISBN 978-1943404155

GO DOWN TO THE SEA IN BOOKS WITH
OLD SALT PRESS

THE MONEY SHIP

by Joan Druett

Money ships were wrecks of treasure-galleons belched up from the bottom of the sea after tremendous storms, yielding doubloons and all kinds of precious treasure ... gold bars and bullion, chests of brilliant gems.

Oriental adventurer Captain Rochester spun an entrancing tale to Jerusha, seafaring daughter of Captain Michael Gardiner — a story of a money ship, hidden in the turquoise waters of the South China Sea, which was nothing less than the lost trove of the pirate Hochman. As Jerusha was to find, though, the clues that pointed the way to fabled riches were strange indeed — a haunted islet on an estuary in Borneo, an obelisk with a carving of a rampant dragon, a legend of kings and native priests at war, and of magically triggered tempests that swept warriors upriver. And even if the clues were solved, the route to riches was tortuous, involving treachery, adultery, murder, labyrinthine Malayan politics ... and, ultimately, Jerusha's own arranged marriage.

ISBN 978-0994124647

GO DOWN TO THE SEA IN BOOKS WITH OLD SALT PRESS

BRITANNIA'S GAMBLE

by Antione Vanner

Naval adventure in the Victorian Era

It's 1884. A fanatical Islamist revolt is sweeping all before it in the vast wastes of the Sudan and establishing a rule of persecution and terror. Only the city of Khartoum holds out, its defence masterminded by a British national hero, General Charles Gordon. His position is weakening by the day and a relief force, crawling up the Nile from Egypt, may not reach him in time to avert disaster. But there is one other way of reaching Gordon... A boyhood memory leaves the ambitious Royal Navy officer Nicholas Dawlish no option but to attempt it. The obstacles are daunting – barren mountains and parched deserts, tribal rivalries and merciless enemies – and this even before reaching the river that is key to the mission. Dawlish knows that every mile will be contested and that the siege at Khartoum is quickly moving towards its bloody climax. Outnumbered and isolated, with only ingenuity, courage and fierce allies to sustain them, with safety in Egypt far beyond the Nile's raging cataracts, Dawlish and his mixed force face brutal conflict on land and water as the Sudan descends into ever-worsening savagery. And for Dawlish himself, one unexpected and tragic event will change his life forever...
ISBN 978-1943404186

GO DOWN TO THE SEA IN BOOKS WITH OLD SALT PRESS

BLACKWELL'S HOMECOMING

BY V.E. ULETT

Volume III of the *Blackwell's Adventures* series

In a multigenerational saga of love, war and betrayal, Captain Blackwell and Mercedes continue their voyage in Volume III of *Blackwell's Adventures*. The Blackwell family's eventful journey from England to Hawaii, by way of the new and tempestuous nations of Brazil and Chile, provides an intimate portrait of family conflicts and loyalties in the late Georgian Age. *Blackwell's Homecoming* is an evocation of the dangers and rewards of desire.
ISBN 978-0-9882360-7-3

Made in the USA
Las Vegas, NV
20 December 2021